TWISTED

Books by Jo Gibson

OBSESSED

TWISTED

AFRAID

And writing as Joanne Fluke

Hannah Swensen Mysteries

CHOCOLATE CHIP COOKIE MURDER
STRAWBERRY SHORTCAKE MURDER
BLUEBERRY MUFFIN MURDER
LEMON MERINGUE PIE MURDER
FUDGE CUPCAKE MURDER
SUGAR COOKIE MURDER
PEACH COBBLER MURDER
CHERRY CHEESECAKE MURDER
KEY LIME PIE MURDER
CANDY CANE MURDER
CARROT CAKE MURDER
CREAM PUFF MURDER
PLUM PUDDING MURDER
APPLE TURNOVER MURDER
DEVIL'S FOOD CAKE MURDER
GINGERBREAD COOKIE MURDER
CINNAMON ROLL MURDER
RED VELVET CUPCAKE MURDER
BLACKBERRY PIE MURDER
JOANNE FLUKE'S LAKE EDEN COOKBOOK

Suspense Novels

VIDEO KILL
WINTER CHILL
DEAD GIVEAWAY
THE OTHER CHILD

Published by Kensington Publishing Corporation

TWISTED

JO GIBSON

KENSINGTON PUBLISHING CORP.
www.kensingtonbooks.com

KTEEN BOOKS are published by

Kensington Publishing Corp.
119 West 40th Street
New York, NY 10018

All Kensington titles, imprints, and distributed lines are available at special quantity discounts for bulk purchases for sales promotion, premiums, fund-raising, and educational or institutional use.

Special book excerpts or customized printings can also be created to fit specific needs. For details, write or phone the office of the Kensington Special Sales Manager: Kensington Publishing Corp., 119 West 40th Street, New York, NY 10018. Attn. Special Sales Department. Phone: 1-800-221-2647.

Kensington and the K logo Reg. U.S. Pat. & TM Off.
KTeen is a trademark of Kensington Publishing Corp.

ISBN-13: 978-1-61773-240-9
ISBN-10: 1-61773-240-0
First Kensington Trade Paperback Printing: July 2014

eISBN-13: 978-1-61773-241-6
eISBN-10: 1-61773-241-9
First Kensington Electronic Edition: July 2014

10 9 8 7 6 5 4 3 2 1

Printed in the United States of America

Contents

My Bloody Valentine

This one's for you, Heidi.

*With a ton of thanks to John Scognamiglio,
my editor*

Prologue

It was the first week of February at Hamilton High, and everybody was going stir-crazy. Winter had arrived in full force, and the streets of Clearwater were piled high with snow. Another winter storm had hit, and icy snow was blowing against the cafeteria windows so hard, the panes were rattling and bowing in slightly with each new gust of wind.

Amy Hunter pushed back her long brown hair and sighed as she surveyed the dishes of food that lined the steam table in the student lunchroom. There were lots of choices today, but there wasn't one single thing that she wanted for lunch.

"What's the matter, Amy?" Colleen Daniels, Amy's best friend since grade school, frowned slightly. "It doesn't look *that* awful."

Amy sighed again. "I know. The mac and cheese actually looks edible, but I can't face the thought of eating it. I guess I'm really not hungry."

Colleen slipped on the glasses perched on top of her head. She never wore them unless she absolutely had to because one of the guys had told her that she looked much better without them. And then she stared hard at Amy.

Amy began to get a very uncomfortable feeling in the pit of her stomach. Colleen had decided that she wanted to be a biologist, and the way she was staring made Amy feel like a bug under a microscope. "What is it, Colleen? You're staring at me."

"Sorry." Colleen took off her glasses and shrugged. "It's not like you, that's all. You're always hungry at lunch. Are you sick?"

"No. I'm fine."

"Are you depressed because Brett went out with Tanya again?"

"Shh!" Amy looked around, but no one was within hearing distance. She didn't want anyone else to know that she had a giant-sized crush on Brett Stevens, the star player on Hamilton High's basketball team. "I'm not depressed. I'm just . . . not hungry, that's all."

Suddenly Colleen began to smile and her whole face lit up. "I got it. I know exactly what's wrong with you. You're in love . . . right?"

"I don't think so." Amy shrugged. "At least, I'm not any more in love than I was last week."

"Well, what is it, then?" Colleen plopped some mac and cheese on her plate and picked up a bowl of salad.

"I don't know. Maybe it's just winter."

Colleen looked thoughtful. "Okay. I'll buy that. Winter's a real drag and we're all sick of it. Have some hot chicken soup and you'll feel better. That's what my grandma always says."

Amy nodded and ladled some soup into her bowl even though she doubted it would help. The soup was a bilious shade of yellow, the noodles looked like fat white worms, and there was absolutely no trace of chicken visible.

"Come on." Colleen picked up a buttered roll and tossed it on Amy's plate. She added a dish of butterscotch pudding and a generous helping of lasagne. "Let's go. Michele and Gail are saving a place for us."

"But, Colleen . . . I can't eat all this!" Amy stared down at her tray in dismay.

"Don't worry about it. If you can't finish it, somebody will."

Amy nodded. She knew exactly which "somebody" Colleen

was referring to. Her mother called Colleen "the human disposal," and she always made plenty of food whenever Colleen came over for dinner. Colleen had a huge appetite, and she never gained any weight. If Amy hadn't been best friends with Colleen, she might have hated her. Although Amy wasn't a bit overweight, she had to watch every calorie while Colleen could eat huge bowls of ice cream with all sorts of gooey and delicious toppings and never even stretch out the seams in her size five jeans.

The girls were waiting at their usual table, and Michele Porter, a pretty cheerleader who looked like a pixie with her short black hair, stared at Amy's tray as she plunked it down on the table. "Are you going to eat all that?"

Amy shook her head. "I don't think so. I'm going to give it to Mrs. Chambers so she can send it to the starving children in Europe."

Michele cracked up, but Gail Baxter looked puzzled. Of course, looking puzzled was nothing new for Gail. She'd spent years perfecting her dumb blonde act. Gail had short, curly blond hair, bright blue eyes, and a perfect figure. She was also a straight A student, but she was convinced that her high test scores would scare the boys off. Gail went into her ditzy blonde act whenever a boy was around, and she'd sworn to kill anyone who even mentioned that she was going to Harvard when she graduated.

"Mrs. Chambers ships food to Europe?" Gail's eyes widened. "I didn't know that!"

Jessica Ford, a slightly overweight redhead, came up just in time to hear Amy's comment. She cracked up, too, and turned to explain it to Gail. "You couldn't know because you weren't here for second grade, but Mrs. Chambers used to lay a guilt trip on us if we didn't finish our lunch. She'd say, *'Eat your lunch, girls. There are starving children in Europe.'* So we'd eat our lunch, even if we didn't like it. Except for Amy."

"That's right." Colleen started to laugh. "Amy absolutely hates broccoli. And one day we had this beef and broccoli casserole that was really gross. When Mrs. Chambers reminded us that there were starving children in Europe, Amy handed her the tray and asked her to send it to them."

Gail laughed. "Smart move, Amy. Never give way to manufactured guilt. It's dehumanizing, and it turns you into a victim. It's a well-proven fact that actions which are motivated purely by guilt eventually increase the level of human suffering. Hegel said it best in the nineteenth century when he was discussing the issue in—"

"Careful, Gail. Your IQ is showing." Amy grinned as she interrupted her. "And here comes the basketball team."

Gail glanced toward the door and immediately put on her ditzy blonde look. The basketball team was trooping into the lunchroom, wearing eye-popping, bright green blazers. "Okay. I'll tell you later, if you're interested."

All the girls watched as the basketball team filled their trays from the steam table. Kevin Thomas, the student coach, stood to the side, checking their names off on a clipboard. Amy felt a little sorry for Kevin. He'd been on the team last year, but he'd been in a car accident during the summer, and they were still doing orthoscopic surgery on his knee. At least Kevin had survived. His twin sister, Karen, who'd been driving the car, had been killed.

Brett was at the head of the line, and Amy sighed as she watched him fill his tray. He was tall with dark hair and sexy blue eyes, and he looked a little like a young Elvis Presley. Brett was a lifeguard at the lake in the summer, and even though this was the middle of the winter, he still had a great tan.

Neal Carpenter was right behind Brett, and he was at least three inches taller. Neal was skinny, with short sandy hair and incredibly long arms and legs. When he was off the court, he was a total klutz, always tripping over his own feet. But when someone passed him a basketball, he was as graceful as a white-tailed deer running over a snow-covered field.

Amy watched as the rest of the team filled their trays. They were all friends of hers. Clearwater wasn't a large town, and she knew everyone in her class. Most of them had been around since grade school. With the exception of Brett, who'd moved to Clearwater two years ago, and Tanya, who'd rolled in from California last year, Amy knew all of their parents and they knew hers. Perhaps that was why she was so fascinated by Brett. She'd never seen him fall off his tricycle, or get braces on his teeth. He'd come here as a handsome sophomore with a past in another town. That made him exciting and mysterious. And he even looked good in his awful bright green blazer.

There was a big game coming up tomorrow night, and Coach Harvey was really into psychology this year. For three days preceding an important game, the team wore bright green blazers to set them apart from the other students. They sat at a large table in the rear of the lunchroom, and they ate together. This was supposed to promote unity, but it didn't really work unless Coach Harvey was there.

"Here comes Miss Popularity." Colleen nudged Amy. "And look at her sweater . . . it's the same color as the team blazers."

Amy glanced toward the door of the lunchroom. Tanya Ellison was standing just inside the door, waiting to be noticed by the basketball team. And they would notice her; Amy was sure of that. Tanya's sweater was incredibly tight.

"I can't believe it!" Michele sighed. "She actually looks good in that awful kelly green!"

Gail nodded. "True, but it's too bad she's so poor. Maybe we should take up a collection."

"What are you talking about?" Jessica stared at Gail in amazement. "Tanya's father owns a whole chain of movie theaters. He's the richest guy in town!"

"Maybe, but his daughter's wearing hand-me-downs."

"Hand-me-downs?" Amy was puzzled. "I don't get it."

Gail laughed. "Look at the size of her sweater. It used to belong to a much smaller girl."

The other girls cracked up while Amy did her best to maintain her composure. Her parents had always told her that it wasn't nice to laugh at someone else's expense. But her friends' laughter was infectious, and Amy just couldn't keep a straight face. Gail's joke was funny, and what she'd said was perfectly true. Tanya's sweater really was too tight.

Colleen reached over Amy's dish of butterscotch pudding to shake Gail's hand. "Thanks, Gail. You managed to make Amy laugh. She's been acting like it's the end of the world all day."

"What's the matter, Amy?" Michele looked concerned.

"Nothing that summer couldn't fix. I'm just sick of the cold and the gray skies, and winter. We don't even have a holiday until Easter, and that's almost three months away!"

"There's Presidents' Day," Jessica spoke up. "We get a long weekend for that."

Amy shook her head. "Presidents' Day doesn't count. It's just a made-up holiday, and nobody ever celebrates. What are they going to do? Have the band play 'Yankee Doodle' and march down a snowbank?"

Michele cracked up. "At least you haven't lost your sense of humor. And you're forgetting about one of the best holidays of the year. Valentine's Day is coming up."

"That doesn't count, either." Amy sighed. "It's fine if you've got a boyfriend. Then you get flowers, or jewelry, or an incredibly romantic Valentine card. But I don't have a boyfriend, and Valentine's Day means nothing to me."

Colleen reached out to help herself to Amy's buttered roll. "Cheer up, Amy. I personally guarantee that you'll get at least one card. I'll tell Danny to send you one."

"Thanks a lot! If I get a card from your brother, my parents'll lock me in my room until I graduate."

"Hey . . . Danny's not that bad." Colleen began to frown. "His hair's growing out, and the dye'll be gone pretty soon. And he's getting good grades."

Amy thought fast. Colleen was very sensitive about her bad-boy brother. "I'm sorry, Colleen. Danny's okay, and I like him a lot. But you know my parents . . . they think any guy who rides a motorcycle is depraved."

Colleen didn't look convinced, but she nodded. And then she

turned to Michele and started to talk about a new routine the cheerleaders were practicing. Amy looked down at her chicken soup, and winced. Her big mouth had almost gotten her in trouble with her best friend. Colleen didn't like to be reminded that her brother, Danny, was the worst nightmare of every Clearwater girl's mother. They assumed that Danny was a juvenile delinquent because he'd dropped out of school in his junior year to go on the road with his punk-rock band. The band had done all right for the first year, but then they'd lost their drummer and gone belly-up. And now Danny was back at Hamilton High, two years older than anyone else, finishing out his Senior year.

"Maybe we should do something special for Valentine's Day this year." Jessica looked thoughtful. "I miss the parties we used to have when we were kids. Everybody got Valentine cards back then."

Amy nodded. "Right. When I was in third grade, I got one that had a fir tree on the front. And the back said, *'I pine for you.'*"

"I bet you've still got it!" Colleen grinned. "I kept the one I got from Pete Brooks."

"What did it say?" Michele looked interested. She'd gone out with Pete just last week.

"It was shaped like a lamp and it said, *'To my Valentine. You light up my life.'*"

Jessica nodded. "Very nice. Remember those little heart candies with the words stamped on them?"

"Of course." Gail smiled. "You could never read what they said because the printing was so smeared."

"And the pink ones tasted like Pepto Bismol!" Michele made a face. "I never could stand those. I liked the yellow ones, though. I think they were supposed to be banana. Why are you smiling like that, Amy?"

Amy waited until all the girls were quiet, and then she dropped her bombshell. "We all liked Valentine's Day when we were kids in elementary school. Why don't we do it all over again?"

"Do what?" Colleen was puzzled. "Have a third grade party?"

"No. But we could have a dance."

"That won't work." Gail shook her head. "Valentine's Day is in the middle of the week. We can't have a dance on a school night."

"Then we'll do it on Saturday night. That's even better because everyone can come. We could even make it a Sadie Hawkins dance."

"What's that?" Gail looked interested.

"My grandmother told me about it. It's a dance where the girls ask the boys."

"Great idea!" Gail nodded. "It's perfectly in synch with women's rights, and it's about time Hamilton High entered the twentieth century. We sit at home by the phone and wait for the boys to call us, and this is supposed to be the age of the woman."

Michele grinned. "That sounds good to me. Maybe we could decorate the gym with red and white streamers, and sell tickets and refreshments and everything."

"Hold the phone." Amy frowned. "I hate to bring this up since the whole thing was my idea, but we have a minor problem. We have to get Mr. Dorman's permission to use the school gym."

Gail shrugged. "No problem. We've got a student council meeting this afternoon, and Colleen and I will talk him into it. We'll tell him that any profit we make can go to the library fund."

"That should work." Colleen nodded. "The library fund is Mr. Dorman's pet project. He's always complaining that we don't have enough library books."

Jessica pulled out her notebook and began to write out a list. "Let's see . . . we'll need streamers, and party favors, and tickets. And if there's enough money, we can even hire a live band."

"We could be starting a school tradition." Amy began to smile again. "Hamilton High's Valentine's Day Dance could wind up being even bigger than the prom!"

Tanya passed their table, just in time to hear the tail end of Amy's comment. She stopped in her tracks and turned to stare at Amy. "What could be bigger than the prom?"

Amy managed to put a friendly smile on her face, even though she didn't like Tanya. As president of the senior class, she had an obligation to be friendly. "We thought it would be a good idea to hold a Valentine's Day Dance."

"I'll help." Tanya pulled out a chair and sat down without being invited. "We'll need to hold a contest for the King and Queen of Hearts. That's the way they did it at my old school in California."

As the other girls began to discuss how they should vote for the King and Queen, Amy sat there, silently. She didn't like the idea of a King and Queen of Hearts. It was simply a popularity contest, and someone always ended up with hurt feelings. She wanted to object, but if she did, Tanya would think it was because she was afraid of losing.

"What's the matter, Amy?" Colleen noticed Amy's silence, and nudged her.

Amy shrugged. And then it hit her, the perfect objection. "I don't see how we can have a contest for the Queen and King of Hearts. The dance has to be a fund-raiser, and a contest won't bring in any money for the book fund. I'm sorry, Tanya, but it just won't work."

"Maybe it will." Tanya looked thoughtful. "Hold on a second. I just thought of a way to turn the contest into a real money-maker."

Amy watched as Tanya stood up and waved at the team table. "Brett? Come over here a second, will you? We need your advice."

Brett looked pleased as he walked over to their table. It was clear he liked the idea of being asked for advice. "What is it, Tanya?"

"We're planning a Valentine's Day Dance, and we want to have a contest for the King and Queen of Hearts; but it's got to be a fund-raiser. Do you think your father could print up some Valentine cards that we could sell for a profit?"

Brett shrugged. "Sure. Just work up a design and I'll find out how much it'll cost."

"Good!" Tanya returned to her seat, leaned back and smiled at him. "Let's keep it simple. How about a red heart on the front with two H's in fancy lettering for Hamilton High?"

"That's easy. My dad can do that, no problem."

Tanya looked smug. "I knew we could count on you, Brett. We'll sell the cards for votes. One vote for every card sold. The girls'll vote for king, and the boys'll vote for queen. And we'll post the totals on the school bulletin board every day. If somebody's favorite candidate is running behind, they'll buy more cards."

"Brilliant!" Brett began to grin. "The team can help. We'll sell the cards in the cafeteria. That'll give us something to do during lunch."

"Do you think Coach Harvey will let you do it?" Colleen looked worried.

"Sure. It'll get him in good with Mr. Dorman. He'll be all for it."

Tanya took charge again. "Okay. The team sells the cards, and the girls who have a free period after lunch can count the votes. Then we can post the standings before sixth period."

Just then, the bell rang for the end of lunch break, and Tanya pushed back her chair. "Come on, Brett. You can walk me to history class, and we'll discuss the layout of those Valentine cards."

Amy frowned as Tanya took Brett's arm and they walked off together. Tanya had a class after lunch, and so did Jessica, and Michele. And Gail and Colleen had student council business to do. She was the only girl who had fifth period free, and Tanya knew it. And Tanya had just stuck her with the task of totalling up the card sales and counting the votes!

One

Of course he'd heard about the Valentine's Day Dance. Everyone was talking about it in the halls, and even during class. The dance, itself, sounded like a pretty good idea. Winter was a drag, and it would give them something to do. Although he didn't really enjoy dances, he might go just to relieve the awful boredom.

The contest for the King and Queen of Hearts was another matter. He was all for fund-raising, but this contest could cause a lot of trouble in the halls of Hamilton High. Everyone knew who the king would be. The queen was a toss-up, though, and any one of the girls could win. It all depended on how much money a guy was willing to spend on his favorite girl.

That made him think of Karen, and he clenched his hands into fists to keep them from shaking. Karen might have been queen if she were still alive. She'd been the head cheerleader, the editor of the school paper, and the president of the student council. Karen had always been very popular, until the girls had decided to gang up on her.

He swallowed hard, past the lump in his throat. He really missed Karen, and it was hard not to think about her. He knew he had to accept what had happened, but he still half-expected to see Karen in the halls at school, opening her locker to take out her books, or cheerleading at one of the games, or sitting at a table in the lunchroom, surrounded by a crowd of friends.

He took a deep breath and steadied himself. He had to hang on to reality. Karen was dead, and there was an empty place in his heart that no one else could fill. There would never be another girl like Karen, and he had blown it. If he'd known what was going to happen, he would have saved her somehow. But she was gone, and he hadn't even had the chance to tell her how much he loved her.

There was a frown on his face as his thoughts turned to the King and Queen of Hearts. Karen would have loved the contest, and he would have made sure that she won. Karen would have been the one to sit on the throne with a silver crown on her lovely black hair. The other girls weren't worthy enough to be queen.

But Karen was dead, and it made him furious to think that one of the other girls would be queen, especially after the way they'd treated her. They'd gossiped about her, and criticized her for things she hadn't done. Karen had told him all about it, and it still made him smolder with anger.

Karen had caught the flu last summer, and Tanya, the new girl in town, had seemed very glad to see her when she'd recovered enough to join their usual table at the Hungry Burger. Since Tanya had seemed interested, Karen had told her all about how she'd been unable to eat anything except saltine crackers and dry toast. And then Karen had left the table to order a Coke, and Tanya had seized the opportunity to start the vicious gossip that Karen had overheard.

Wasn't it odd that Karen Thomas had caught the flu when no one else in Clearwater was sick? What if it wasn't the flu? What if Karen had another, more serious problem?

The other girls had been shocked. What was Tanya implying? Did she think that Karen was pregnant!? Tanya had laughed. It was possible, wasn't it? After all, there could be a reason why Karen was so popular with the boys.

Amy had tried to stop the gossip, but no one had listened to Amy's advice about how much harm gossip could do. The rumors had flown, thick and fast, and soon Karen had been the subject of every whispered conversation. It had been too much for Karen to bear. The girls she'd thought were her friends, had been spreading rumors about her, behind her back.

He clenched his fists, and took a deep breath to keep from exploding. He knew that Karen's fatal car accident had been the girls' fault. Oh, they hadn't killed her directly, and there was no way to prove that they were to blame. But he knew, in his heart, that they'd killed her just as surely as if one of them had stabbed her, or shot her, or pushed her over a cliff. Their cruel gossip had distracted Karen so much, she hadn't been concentrating on her driving. And that was why she'd spun out on the old gravel road to the lake, and plunged down the embankment to her death.

Karen had died instantly. Her neck had snapped. But Karen's tormentors were still alive, giggling in the halls, gossiping in the cafeteria, and planning their stupid king and queen contest.

He began to smile then, as he thought of a perfect way to do one last favor for Karen. She would want him to make certain that the Queen of Hearts was worthy of the honor.

It was time to live up to the private nickname Karen had given him. She'd called him "Cat," and cats were cunning and clever animals.

He'd devise a test, and if the girl failed, he'd make sure that she wouldn't be elected. Cat would eliminate her from the contest in the same way that they'd eliminated Karen from his life.

Permanently.

After all, there was no way that they could elect a dead girl as Valentine's Day Queen.

Two

It was another typical winter day. The mercury in the thermometer was stuck firmly on the zero mark, and the skies were a dull gray that reminded Amy of the battleship pictures in her American history book. At least the wind wasn't blowing. That was a plus. But the local weatherman had warned that gusty winds and snow flurries could arrive before the end of the day.

Amy glanced in the mirror and forced a smile. She'd dressed in her most colorful blouse this morning, a bright yellow background printed with red and pink and orange flowers with bright green leaves. The blouse reminded her of the hot summer days she wished were here, and it went very well with her favorite dark brown slacks and matching blazer. Amy was trying her best to be cheerful this morning, but it just wasn't working. She was just as depressed as she'd been yesterday.

It took only a moment to brush her hair. Amy pulled it back and fastened it with the hammered gold barrette that Colleen had given her for her last birthday. She'd have to do it all over again when she got to school. The hood of her parka messed up any hairstyle she fashioned at home; but she had a mirror in her locker, and it was easy to redo. She gave one final glance in the mirror, and nodded. She wasn't beautiful, but she looked her best. Then she slipped into a pair of brown loafers and hurried down the stairs to the kitchen.

"How's my favorite flower child?" Amy's father looked up from his newspaper. "That blouse is a real eye-popper."

"Thanks, Dad . . . I think." Amy grinned at him. There was no way she wanted her mother to know how depressed she was. Then she'd ask a lot of questions and worry herself sick.

Amy's mom was what Amy called a "P.M.W." That stood for "Professional Mother and Wife." Dorothy Hunter had given up her career as a court recorder when she was pregnant with Amy, and she'd devoted herself to making a perfect home for her daughter and husband. Amy's mom was always reading articles in women's magazines about warning signs. She was constantly on the alert for the six danger signs of teenage drug addiction, and the five warning signals of anorexia, and the nine probable indicators of potential teenage suicide. Dorothy Hunter would never believe that the weather was responsible for her daughter's depression, even though it was perfectly true.

Amy's mother smiled as she set a bowl of hot cereal in front of Amy. "I think you look very nice, honey."

"Thanks, Mom." Amy stared down at her cereal, and sighed. She hated oatmeal, but her mother insisted that it was a good breakfast, even though Amy had shown her several studies claiming that oatmeal had no more nutritional value than Pop Tarts.

Amy's dad pushed back his chair. "I have to run. We've got a big meeting this morning, down at the plant. Do you want a ride to school, Amy?"

"Definitely." Amy grinned and took several mouthfuls of her oatmeal, just enough so that her mother wouldn't feel hurt. She swallowed, hating the taste which always seemed slimy to her, and then she pushed back her chair.

"That's all you're going to eat?" Amy's mother looked very worried.

"I had enough, Mom. It's a big bowl, and I'm not really that hungry." Amy thought fast as she noticed her mother's concern. "We're having beef stew for lunch at school, and it's my favorite. But thanks for making my breakfast. It was delicious."

"You're welcome, honey." Amy's mother looked pleased. "Do you want me to pick you up after school?"

"No, thanks." Amy carried her bowl to the counter and washed it out before her mother could see that she hadn't eaten very much. "I'll catch a ride with one of the kids. And don't worry, Mom . . . I'll come straight home. I have to finish my homework before the basketball game tonight."

Amy watched while her dad kissed her mom good-bye. It was a ritual they went through every morning, and Amy thought it was sweet. Her father never left the house without giving her mother a hug and a kiss.

"Come on, flower child . . . let's go." Amy's dad picked up his briefcase and his keys and motioned to her. "You'd better put on full survival gear. It's cold out there."

Amy nodded and took her parka out of the closet. She slipped it on, stuffed her shoes in her tote bag, and pulled on her bulky warm boots. Then she picked up her book bag and turned to smile at her parents. "I'm ready, Dad. Bye, Mom. See you after school."

Amy's dad waited until they pulled out of the driveway, and then he turned to grin at her. "Dunkin' Donuts?"

"Yes!" Amy grinned back. "I'll run in if you park in front. What do you want?"

"A cinnamon bun that's full of carbohydrates and cholesterol."

Amy nodded. "I noticed Mom was reading a health magazine the other day. She's got you on a diet again . . . right?"

"Right. She gave me one piece of whole grain toast, no butter. And a two-egg-white omelette with chopped broccoli."

"She must have heard that broccoli was a cancer preventative." Amy grinned at him.

"I guess so. I used to like broccoli, but we've been having it every day for the past week. Make sure that cinnamon bun's dripping with gooey frosting, Amy. I wouldn't want to go to work feeling deprived."

Amy laughed and hopped out when her dad pulled up to the

Dunkin' Donuts shop. The inside of the shop was steamy, and it smelled incredibly good.

"Hi, Amy." Mrs. Beeseman, who was working behind the counter, gave Amy a smile. "Has your mother got your dad on another one of those health-food diets?"

Amy nodded. "Broccoli, egg whites, and dry whole grain toast. He wants the usual, Mrs. Beeseman, and so do I."

Mrs. Beeseman flipped open a small pink cardboard box and put a cinnamon bun and a maple bar inside. Then she took the money Amy handed her, and gave back her change. "See you tomorrow morning?"

"Probably." Amy nodded. "Mom's diets usually last for at least two weeks."

It was only a few blocks to the school, but Amy and her dad had finished their goodies by the time they pulled up in front. Amy gathered up her book bag and her shoes, and gave her dad a kiss on the cheek. "Thanks for the ride, Dad. And thanks for the carbohydrates and cholesterol."

"Anytime, kiddo. And don't tell your mom. See you tonight."

Amy waved good-bye as her dad drove away, and then she walked up the sidewalk. Even though her dad had dropped her off right in front of the school, she was shivering as she pushed open the heavy double doors at Hamilton High and stepped into the semiwarmth of the entryway. She stamped the snow off her boots on the rubber grid that was provided especially for that purpose, and opened the inner door that led into the school, itself. The moment she stepped inside, Amy took her shoes from her tote bag, removed her boots, and slipped on her shoes. Then she headed up the stairway to her locker, carrying her boots with one hand. Boots weren't allowed on the wooden floors of Hamilton High hallways. Students were required to carry them up to their lockers, and leave them there until it was time to go home.

"Hey, Amy." Colleen, who had the locker next to Amy, greeted her with a smile. "How about this weather? It's supposed to warm up to above zero today."

Amy nodded. "I heard that. But then it'll be warm enough to snow again. You just can't win in the winter."

"You're a regular prophet of doom. Lighten up, Amy. Aren't you glad that Mr. Dorman gave us permission to hold the Valentine's Day Dance?"

"Yes. Of course I am. But I probably won't have a date."

"Come on, Amy." Colleen's frown deepened. "I just can't take all this doom and gloom first thing in the morning. Isn't there anything that'll make you happy?"

Amy began to grin. "Sure. If Tanya Ellison slipped on the ice and sprained her ankle, it would definitely cheer me up."

"I get it." Colleen began to grin, too. "Then she wouldn't be able to go to the dance, and you'd ask Brett. Is that right?"

Amy nodded. "That's the general idea. Of course I don't wish her any permanent injury . . . that wouldn't be nice. I'll settle for a little sprain that'll keep her out of action for—oh, my God!"

"What?" Colleen looked puzzled. Amy's face had gone pasty white.

"It's . . . it's Tanya!"

Colleen swiveled around to see. And then she gasped, too. Tanya was standing at her locker, and she was leaning on two crutches.

"Oh-oh!" Amy looked very guilty. "You don't suppose?"

Colleen shook her head. "No way. Things don't happen just because you want them to."

"I know. But, Colleen . . . I said it, and then it happened!"

"Wrong." Colleen looked very serious. "It happened before you said it. Tanya must have sprained her ankle last night. She's already got the crutches."

"That's true, but I still feel guilty. I was wishing that something would happen so she couldn't go to the dance."

"Hi, girls. What's up?"

Amy turned around to find Brett standing directly behind her, carrying a large box. How much had he heard? Amy did her best to maintain her composure; but her cheeks began to feel hot, and she knew she was blushing.

"Hi, Brett." Colleen spoke up when she realized that Amy

was practically speechless. "Amy and I were talking about poor Tanya. Do you know what happened?"

"Poor Tanya?" Brett looked thoroughly mystified.

Amy took a deep breath and managed to find her voice. "Yes. We just noticed that she was on crutches."

"Oh, the crutches!" Brett started to grin. "Tanya borrowed them from the hospital. Her first-aid class is having a drill this morning, and she's playing the part of an accident victim."

"You mean she didn't sprain her ankle?" Colleen tried not to look disappointed.

"No. Tanya's fine. But I'll tell her that you guys were concerned about her. That's really nice." Brett lifted the lid off the box and handed Amy an envelope. "Here, Amy. This is for you. Take a look when you've got a minute, and let me know what you think."

"Sure, Brett. Thanks." Amy waited until Brett was out of sight, and then she turned to Colleen. "I don't know whether I'm relieved or disappointed."

"Me, neither. What did Brett give you?"

"I don't know." Amy looked down at the envelope. "It feels like a card."

"Open it and see."

Amy hesitated. "But what if it's something personal?"

"Come on, Amy. We're best friends. Whatever it is, you're going to tell me, anyway."

"True." Amy nodded, and opened the envelope. And then she gasped as she drew out a Valentine's Day card. "It's a Valentine. And it says, 'Be Mine' on the front. I can't believe it! I got a Valentine from Brett!"

Colleen stared at the card for a moment, and then she shook her head. "I really hate to burst your bubble, Amy, but that card has a red heart with H. H. in the center for Hamilton High. Don't you remember what we were talking about in the lunchroom, yesterday?"

"Oh." Amy's smile of pleasure faded quickly. "I get it. These are the cards that Brett and his dad printed up for us to sell?"

"I think so, but I could be wrong. Why don't you open it and see if he wrote anything inside."

Amy opened the card, and sighed as she saw the blank space inside. "You're right, Colleen. This is just a sample. I should have known that Brett wouldn't give me a Valentine."

"But he *did* give you a Valentine." Colleen made an effort to raise Amy's spirits. "I don't have one, and I bet no one else does, either. He singled you out, Amy. He wanted your approval and that's a very good start."

Amy didn't look convinced. "Maybe. But he'll never take me to the dance."

"How do you know? You haven't asked him. Why don't you beat Tanya to it?"

Amy shook her head. "She's probably already asked him."

"Maybe. But maybe not. I think you should try to get to him first. The worst he can say is no."

"Yes, but . . ." Amy stopped and looked thoughtful. Colleen really did have a point. Tanya always left things to the last minute, and it was possible she hadn't asked Brett to the dance yet.

"Well?" Colleen began to grin. She knew Amy was wavering. "Are you going to do it?"

"I'm not sure. I'll think about it, okay?"

"There's nothing to think about. If you want him to take you to the dance, you have to ask him. It's that simple."

Amy took a deep breath for courage and nodded. "Okay. I'll ask him. It's like you said, Colleen. The worst he can do is say no."

It turned out that Amy was in luck. She didn't have to count the ballots alone. Mr. Dorman had decided that at least three class members should be present while the votes were tallied, and he'd excused Gail and Colleen from their student council duties so that they could help Amy. He'd also given them permission to use the faculty lounge, which was deserted during fifth period.

"What a dump!" Colleen glanced around her in dismay. The long table in the center of the room was littered with coffee cups, and empty lunch trays. "There's no place to spread out our ballots on the table. I guess we'll have to clear these dishes and wipe it off."

"And that's exactly why Mr. Dorman let us use it!" Amy started to laugh. "You girls have been taken, big-time. Mr. Dorman knew we'd have to clean up the lounge to use the table."

Gail nodded. "Amy's right. The cooks usually clean it right before they go home. I guess Mr. Dorman figured he'd free them up for bigger and better things."

"Like thinking up new ways to poison us?" Amy started to laugh.

"Exactly." Colleen laughed, too. "Come on, you two. We might as well make the best of it. At least the teachers have cold drinks in the refrigerator, and we can help ourselves."

In less than ten minutes the table was clean, the dishes were stacked neatly in the rubber tubs the kitchen had provided, and the girls were enjoying their favorite soft drinks from the teachers' refrigerator. They'd developed a system for counting the votes. Gail would unfold the votes and read them aloud. Then she'd hand them to Colleen, who would verify them. Amy would do the actual count by making a tally mark on the lists Mr. Dorman had given her, one for the Senior boys, and one for the Senior girls.

Their first task had been to separate the votes. That wasn't difficult because the names were written on hearts cut out of construction paper. There were red hearts for the Valentine Queen, and green hearts for the Valentine King.

They'd counted the green votes first, and Brett had taken a decisive lead for Valentine's Day King. He'd chalked up thirty votes out of the fifty-two that had been cast. Now they were counting the votes for Valentine's Day Queen, and there were many more of them. It was pretty obvious that the boys had purchased more cards than the girls.

Gail unfolded another red heart, and frowned as she read the name inside. "Here we go again. It's another vote for Tanya."

"That figures." Colleen sighed as she verified the vote. "Chalk up another one for Tanya. How many does that make, Amy?"

"Fifteen. Out of twenty. You've got one, Gail's got one, Jessica's got one, and Michele's got two."

"Here's one for you, Amy." Gail unfolded another red heart.

"For me?" Amy looked astounded. "Who'd vote for me?"

Colleen grabbed the heart-shaped ballot out of Gail's hand. "Let me see. I know everybody's handwriting."

"Yes?" Amy held her breath. She hoped the vote had been cast by Brett.

"I don't know. It's printed. And that means it could be anybody. Maybe you've got a secret admirer, Amy."

"Oh, sure." Amy sighed. "It's probably from your brother and you made him do it."

Colleen shook her head. "No, it's not. Danny had to go to the dentist at eleven this morning, and he's not back yet. He missed lunch and that's when they sold the cards."

"Are you sure it's not from Danny?"

"I'm positive. Somebody else must have voted for you."

Amy began to grin as she turned back to her tally sheet and put a check mark by her own name. Even though the skies outside were still gray, it made the whole day seem much brighter. Someone had actually cast a vote for her! Maybe Colleen was right and she did have a secret admirer. She just wished she knew who he was.

Three

Cat scowled as he studied the bulletin board. They'd posted the totals during fifth period, but this was the first chance he'd had to look.

The bulletin board had been decorated since he'd seen it this morning, and it was a total mess. Cat remembered the old joke Mr. Dorman had told them, that the camel was a horse that had been designed by a committee. Even though it was a joke and Cat knew it, he decided that the same committee had decorated the bulletin board.

The bulletin board was covered with red construction paper. That, in itself, was just fine. But someone had cut Cupids out of glossy pink paper and stuck them up in a random design with ribbons of blue lace running between them. Silver hearts formed a frame in the center of the board, and there was a shiny, gold bow on top of the center heart. White clouds made of cotton balls dotted the red background, and four big purple hearts, made of garish, metallic paper, were attached to the corners. The only part that was the least bit tasteful was the white piece of paper that was thumbtacked to the center of the frame. It was the list of votes for Valentine's Day King and Queen, and it was typed very neatly.

Cat read the list with interest. Brett Stevens had the lead for Valentine's Day King, just as he'd predicted. But Tanya Ellison had the most votes for Valentine's Day Queen, and that just wouldn't do.

"Hi." Amy walked up to him and smiled. "The bulletin board looks nice, doesn't it?"

Cat smiled back, searching for something positive to say. There wasn't much. "It's really . . . uh . . . colorful. Who counted the votes?"

"I did, along with Colleen and Gail. Mr. Dorman wanted three of us, so there wouldn't be any mistakes."

Cat nodded. "Good idea. Is he going to let you sell the cards every lunch hour?"

"That's the plan. Mr. Dorman's really happy. This is only our first day, and we made eighty-three dollars for the library book fund."

Cat nodded again. He was glad the money was going to a worthy cause, even though he didn't approve of the contest. "I see your name is up there."

"Yeah, at the bottom!" Amy laughed. "It was nice, getting a vote."

"Would you like to be Valentine's Day Queen?"

"Don't be silly." Amy gave a little laugh. "I don't even stand a chance. Just look at Tanya's total. Thirty-seven votes!"

"Do you think she'll win?"

Amy shrugged. "I'd be really surprised if she didn't. The boys all like her, and she got almost ninety percent of the votes today. See you later. I've got to get home and do my homework before the game. We're going to take the Bonnerville Tigers to the cleaners tonight, aren't we?"

"That's the plan." Cat waved as Amy turned to go. "See you at the game."

Cat smiled as he watched Amy walk away. He'd decided that it would look strange if he didn't buy a Valentine card, and he'd cast his vote for Amy. Now he was glad. She'd seemed really happy that she'd gotten a vote and Amy had been a true friend to Karen.

Amy had seemed certain that Tanya would win, and Cat was afraid that she was right. Tanya was very popular, and Brett had lots of money to spend on votes for her. Since Brett was going with Tanya, he wouldn't vote for anyone else. And Tanya would win, hands down.

As he turned away from the bulletin board, Cat thought about Karen. He could feel her presence with him now, and he could almost see her staring down at the bulletin board with a dismayed expression on her lovely face. But Karen had never been a vindictive person. She'd always believed in giving everyone a second chance. That was exactly what she'd want him to do with Tanya. He'd warn Tanya to shape up, and put her to the test.

If Tanya failed, he'd just have to eliminate her from the contest.

The gymnasium smelled like popcorn, sweat, and floor polish, but no one seemed to mind. The game was far too exciting to care about the strange combination of scents that were associated with basketball in the winter.

Amy sat with Colleen in the first row of seats, right behind the bench that had been set up for the cheerleaders. Gail, Jessica, Michele, and Tanya had left after doing their routine at halftime. Now they were in the girls' locker room, waiting for Hamilton High's band to start the school song. Right after the trumpet fanfare, they would run onto the floor, green and white pom-poms waving, to lead the students as they sang.

The band started to play the Bonnerville Tiger's school song, and Amy rose to her feet. "Come on, Colleen. We're supposed to stand."

"Why?" Colleen complained as she pushed herself to her feet. "They don't stand up for our school song."

"That doesn't matter. Mr. Dorman says it's a sign of respect."

"Then, why don't they respect us?"

"I don't know."

"I do." Colleen began to grin. "Because they're going to lose and they know it!"

Amy glanced over at the scoreboard to see if she'd missed something. Just as she'd thought, the game was tied at forty-seven, forty-seven. Colleen had sounded very confident, but Brett had two fouls. Two more and he was out, and without Brett, their chances of winning went down the tube.

"But the score's tied." Amy moved closer so that Colleen could hear her. The band was playing the Bonnerville song very loudly, perhaps to make up for the fact that the clarinets didn't seem to know the music. "And the Bonnerville Tigers are really on tonight. They've only missed one free-throw. How can you be sure that we're going to win?"

"Danny told me. He's sitting right behind us."

Amy glanced behind her. Colleen's brother, Danny, was sitting four rows back, his arm draped casually around Megan Stillwell, who'd dropped out of school last year. Megan was working at Tom-Tom's Truckstop out on the highway, a horrible greasy spoon with the motto, *Tom-Tom's—You Can't Beat Our Food.*

A sigh escaped Amy's lips. Megan wasn't very bright. She'd flunked out of school. But she had a perfect figure, and she was so pretty, she could have been a model with her gorgeous shoulder-length auburn hair and deep, sea green eyes. Megan knew how to show off her figure. She was wearing a low-cut black sweater and gold hoop earrings that glistened in the lights overhead.

Danny had cut his hair again. It was very short now, and he looked a lot like Keanu Reeves had in *Speed.* He was even wearing a clean white shirt, unbuttoned at the neck and with the sleeves rolled up. He looked incredibly sexy.

Megan didn't seem to notice that she was staring, but Danny did. He caught Amy's eye, and winked. Before Amy could stop herself, she winked back. Then she blushed and turned away quickly, before Danny could see how he had affected her.

As the band finished the Bonnerville song, the Hamilton High crowd began to cheer. It was almost time for their team to take the floor. Amy cheered, too, being careful not to lift her arms too high. She was wearing a cotton forest green sweater that had been much longer before she'd washed it.

"Did you hear what I said?" Colleen had to shout over the

noise of the crowd. "Danny says the Tigers are definitely going to lose."

Amy nodded. "I heard you. But what does Danny know about basketball?"

"Nothing, but he's dating their coach's daughter. And she told him that the Tigers always fall apart in the second half."

"Let's hope she's right." Amy started to cheer again as the band played their trumpet fanfare, and the Hamilton High Chargers ran onto the floor. The cheerleaders were right behind them, and they led the crowd as they all started to sing the school song. Amy had always thought that the school song was insipid. It was about dear old Hamilton High and how it would live in their hearts forever. But she'd never expressed that opinion verbally. Mr. Dorman had written the lyrics when he was a first-year teacher, and now that he was the principal, all the students and faculty pretended to love it.

When the school song was over, Amy and Colleen sat back down in their seats and watched while the cheerleaders did a new cheer that they'd rehearsed at the pep rally that afternoon. Naturally, it featured Tanya, who did a series of back flips at the end.

"I hope Tanya's wearing her pants." Colleen grinned.

"What do you mean?" Amy looked shocked. "Of course she's wearing her pants . . . isn't she?"

"Just watch."

Colleen was still grinning as Tanya prepared to go into her series of back flips. The cheerleaders were wearing new outfits, long-sleeved white turtlenecks under short green satin jumpers, with flared skirts that were lined with white satin. The new outfits hadn't been ready at the pep rally this afternoon, but they'd been delivered in time for the game.

As Amy watched, Gail, Jessica, and Michele stretched out into splits, one leg forward and the other leg back, clearing the floor for Tanya. Tanya did a little jump, bouncing off the small trampoline that was at the edge of the floor, and started to do her series of back flips.

The moment Amy saw Tanya's green satin pants, she started

to laugh. There was a message sewn across the rear in white satin ribbon. "Oh-my-God! Her pants say 'BEAT TIGERS!' "

"I know." Colleen nodded. "Gail told me she had them made especially for this cheer. All the other girls have to wear plain green, but Tanya gets to wear a bulletin board. Gail says she's going to change the message for each game."

Amy began to laugh so hard, tears came to her eyes. "I wonder what she's going to do next week."

"Next week?" Colleen looked puzzled.

"We're playing the Farmington Mountain Lions. Do you think there'll be room for BEAT MOUNTAIN LIONS?"

"Sure. She's already working her way up to it." Colleen gave a mean little smile. "Danny told me he saw her pigging out last night at the Hungry Burger. She ordered giant fries and two double-doubles with bacon and cheese. And she washed it all down with a chocolate shake."

Amy raised her eyebrows. "If Tanya keeps eating like that, there'll be room on her pants for BEAT MOUNTAIN LIONS, and the time and temperature, and the latest stock market quote! Did Danny say if she was with Brett?"

"She wasn't with anyone. When Danny asked, she told him that Brett was tied up with his parents all night. His whole family went to a party at his grandmother's house."

Amy nodded. And then she began to smile. Brett had gone to a family party, and he hadn't taken Tanya along. Perhaps their relationship wasn't quite as tight as everyone thought. That was bad news for Tanya, but it was very good news for Amy!

Four

As soon as the cheer was over, Tanya came over to sit on the bench while Jessica, Michele, and Gail hurried back to the girls' locker room to get their sports bags.

"How do you like our new outfits?" Tanya turned around to talk to Amy and Colleen.

"Very nice." Amy put on a smile. It wasn't in her nature to be unfriendly, even though she really didn't like Tanya. "That color looks very good on you, Tanya."

"That's why I picked it." Tanya looked smug. "Daddy told me I could order anything I wanted."

Amy nodded. She'd already guessed that Tanya had chosen the cheerleader outfits. They made the other girls look less attractive. The extremely short skirt emphasized Jessica's heavy thighs, the bright green washed out Gail's pale coloring, and the turtleneck flopped around Michele's neck. The only cheerleader who looked really good in her new outfit was Tanya.

"Why did your father tell you to pick out the outfits?" Colleen looked puzzled.

"Because he paid for them." Tanya smiled. "They cost a fortune, but Daddy said he wanted me to have the best."

Colleen nodded. "I see. Did he pick up the bill for your pants, too?"

"Of course. And the crowd loved it! Did you hear all the stomping and whistling when I did my back flips?"

"We heard." Amy tried to think of something nice to say, but absolutely nothing occurred to her. She was saved from an embarrassing silence when the other girls came rushing back.

"Here's your bag, Tanya." Michele handed Tanya her expensive leather sports bag. "Why don't you show Amy and Colleen the cards you found in your locker? Maybe they can figure out who sent them."

"I think they already know." Tanya frowned as she pulled three red envelopes from her gym bag. "Somebody thinks these dumb little poems are really cute. You write poetry, don't you, Amy?"

Amy nodded. "Sometimes. But I haven't written anything in a long time."

"These are signed by somebody named Cat." Tanya was frowning as she stared at Amy.

"Cat?" Amy was thoroughly puzzled. "Who's that?"

"Isn't your middle name Katherine?"

"One of them is, but . . ."

"And isn't Cat a nickname for Katherine?"

"I guess so." Amy shrugged. "But I never use my middle name, and nobody's ever called me Cat."

"Just listen and see if you recognize this poem." Tanya was still frowning as she opened the envelope and pulled out the Valentine card inside. "It says, '*Roses are red, violets are blue. A queen should be kind, faithful and true.*'"

Amy smiled. "That's kind of cute. But I didn't write it, Tanya."

"I didn't expect you to admit it. And I suppose you didn't write this one, either." Tanya opened the second envelope. "This one says, '*Roses are red, violets are blue. Pass my test and the queen could be you.*'"

"Look, Tanya." Amy was beginning to get exasperated. "I didn't write those poems, and I didn't send you any cards!"

"Are you sure?"

"Of course I'm sure!" Amy sighed. "My poetry is all blank verse."

"What's that?" Tanya looked confused.

"That's poetry that doesn't rhyme." Colleen answered the question. "And Amy's poetry is very good, not at all like the stuff you just read."

"Well . . . okay." Tanya opened the third card and handed it to Amy. "Here. You read this one. I just found it at halftime."

Amy opened the envelope and took out the card. The message was printed, and she shivered as she scanned it quickly. The third poem was chilling.

"Read it, Amy," Colleen urged.

Amy swallowed hard. And then she read the poem. "It says, *'Violets are blue, roses are red. An unworthy queen is better off dead.'* And it's signed by Cat, just like the others."

"That's scary!" Gail shivered.

"It sure is!" Michele nodded. "Aren't you nervous, Tanya?"

"Of course not." Tanya gave a little laugh, and then she stared straight at Amy. "These are probably from a girl who's jealous because I'm so popular. Maybe this girl even wishes she could be pretty enough to date Brett. Right, Amy?"

Before Amy had time to reply, the warning buzzer sounded, and the cheerleaders left the bench to do one last cheer before the start of the second half. Amy sighed in pure frustration. She'd denied sending the cards, but it was clear that Tanya still thought she was Cat.

Amy was standing at the concession line, when someone tapped her on the shoulder. She whirled around and found herself face-to-face with Danny.

"Hey . . . Amy." Danny gave her a lazy grin. "Can I buy you a beer?"

"Sure. I'll have whatever they've got on tap which is probably root beer." Amy grinned up at him. She knew Danny was joking. No alcoholic beverages were sold on the school grounds.

"So what are you really having? I'll get it."

"Just a Diet Coke." Amy smiled at him. "All this cheering is making me thirsty.' "

"A *Diet* Coke?" Danny raised his eyebrows as he moved up

to join her in line. "You don't have to be on a diet, Amy. You look perfect to me."

"That's because I drink Diet Coke." Amy laughed, but she felt a blush rise to her cheeks. She'd never been comfortable accepting compliments.

"Good game, huh?"

"Only if we end up winning." Amy glanced at the scoreboard where the score was still tied. "I thought you were the one who said that the Tigers always fall apart in the second half."

Danny shrugged. "That's what I was told."

"By the coach's daughter?"

"Right." Danny looked slightly embarrassed. "That'll teach me never to believe a woman. She was probably saying what she thought I wanted to hear. I guess all women do that, huh?"

Amy shook her head. "This one doesn't."

"Really?" Danny was still grinning. "Let's try it and see. What do you think of my date?"

Amy drew a deep breath. She'd practically promised to be honest. "I think she's gorgeous. And you're handsome. You make a very attractive couple."

"Okay." Danny grinned. "Do you think I should get involved with her?"

"No way. Megan's pretty and she's probably a lot of fun, but she's not smart enough for you."

"You think I'm smart?"

Amy nodded. "Absolutely. You're one of the brightest guys I know. I think you'd be bored with Megan in less than a month. Then you'd break up, and both of you would wind up getting hurt."

"Come on, Amy . . . how bright can a guy be if he drops out of school to start a rock band?"

Amy raised her eyebrows. "You've got a point, but that doesn't mean you're not bright. It just means you did a stupid thing a couple of years ago. Now you're working to correct your mistake, and that shows some real intelligence."

"So you think I'm smart, and you said I was handsome. Are you coming on to me, Amy?"

Amy's cheeks began to feel hot, and she knew she was blushing. Was she coming on to Danny? She had to be honest. "I . . . I really don't know if I am or not, but I don't think so. I think I just like you."

"And you like me because I'm Colleen's brother?"

"That's part of it." Amy nodded. "But I also like you, because you're you."

Danny began to grin again, and he slipped his arm around Amy's shoulders. "Amy, Amy, Amy. You're going to get in trouble being so honest. Some guy might just take advantage of you."

Amy nodded. "I know. But you wouldn't, would you?"

"Well . . ." Danny smiled his lazy smile, the one that was rumored to make girls feel faint. But then he shook his head. "No, Amy. I'd do my absolute best not to take advantage of you."

Amy smiled back at him, not quite sure whether she was disappointed in his answer, or not. Danny was a very handsome guy, and he was terribly sexy. His arm felt very good around her shoulders, and she had the surprising urge to nestle her head against his chest to feel the crisp, starched material of his shirt on her heated cheeks. But she didn't. That wouldn't have been appropriate. And Amy was always very careful to behave appropriately.

"One Diet Coke, a big orange, and a ginger ale." Danny gave his order, and then he turned to Amy. "Does Colleen want something, too?"

"No. She got a giant Slurpy about ten minutes ago." Amy watched as Danny pulled out his billfold and put a ten-dollar bill on the counter. "Are you sure I can't pay you back?"

"You can get the next one." Danny handed Amy her drink. "Are you two girls going down to the Hungry Burger after the game?"

"I guess so. How about you?"

"I'll be there about ten-thirty. I have to drop Megan off at Tom-Tom's first. She's working all night. Will you save me a place next to you?"

Amy nodded, and turned to go. She knew she was blushing

again. She was sure the phrase *Save me a place next to you* didn't constitute a date, but it was the best offer she'd gotten all year!

"By the way, Amy . . ." Danny stopped Amy with a hand on her arm. "I traded in my Harley for a car. Do you think that means I'm trying to be respectable?"

"No. It's winter, and I think it means you're trying to be *warm!*"

Amy grinned as she walked back into the gym. Danny was fun and she enjoyed talking to him. She was glad that he was Colleen's brother, because she could see him more often that way. Of course, it wouldn't be right to tell Danny that. Then he really *would* think that she was trying to pick up on him!

"What took you so long?" Colleen looked curious as Amy came back to her seat. "And why are you blushing like that?"

Amy sat down, and took a big gulp of her Diet Coke. There was no way she'd tell Colleen that her blush was a reaction to the things Danny had said. "I'm not blushing, Colleen. I'm just hot. It's very warm in here."

The referee blew his whistle, and to Amy's relief, Colleen turned her attention back to the game. "Oh, look! They're sending Brett in!"

"It's about time!" Amy watched as Brett ran out on the floor. "Let's just hope he can win the game for us."

For the next two minutes, Amy sat on the edge of her seat as the score went back and forth. The Hamilton High Chargers would make a basket and pull ahead by two points, and then the Bonnerville Tigers would shoot to even the score. The score was tied, and there were only twenty-three seconds left on the clock, when the referee blew his whistle.

"Oh-oh! I think it's a foul against Brett!" Amy turned to Colleen in alarm as the referee pointed to Brett. Brett raised his arm and both girls winced. It was a personal foul, and the Tigers had two shots at the free-throw line.

"It's okay." Colleen tried to stay calm. "They won't make it. Just watch."

The first free throw bounced against the rim, but it toppled in. Amy groaned, along with all the other Hamilton High students. Now the Tigers were up by one point.

"They can't make it two in a row." Amy tried to sound confident, but she clasped her hands tightly together as the ball arced up in the air. She held her breath as it hit the rim again, but this time it didn't bounce in. "Thank God! Now all we have to do is . . . oh, no!"

Amy gasped as the Tigers recovered the rebound, and the ball flew through the air again, clearing the net with a swish. Now the Tigers were ahead by three points. It would take two baskets to catch up, and there were only fifteen seconds left on the clock. Without really realizing she was doing it, Amy jumped to her feet with the rest of the crowd, and joined in the cheer that was bouncing off the walls of the gym.

"Go Chargers, go! Go Chargers, go! Go Chargers, go Chargers, go Chargers, go!"

The cheer seemed to lend new energy to the team. Neal Carpenter dribbled down the court and passed the ball to Brett. Brett looked very determined, but there was little he could do since the Tigers were double-guarding him. But Brett was a team player, and he knew he didn't dare risk a shot when there was no opening. He passed the ball to Neal, and Neal took an off-balance shot. But somehow the ball rimmed the basket, and toppled in.

"Do it again! Do it again! Do it again!"

The crowd roared, and Amy glanced at the clock. Only ten seconds left, and the Tigers had the ball. Naturally, they tried to stall to run out the clock, but somehow, Neal managed to steal the ball.

"Oh, my God!" Amy jumped up and down as Neal passed the ball to Brett. There was only one second left, and Brett was almost a full court away from their basket. One more step and Brett released the ball, just as the buzzer for the end of the game sounded. And then there was complete silence as hundreds of pairs of eyes watched the ball fly through the air.

Amy was frozen in place, her mouth open and her hands

clasped together as the ball approached the basket. It looked good. Very good. It hit the rim, hesitated there for a split second, and then it dropped down, through the net.

"Oh, my God!" Amy reached out to hug Colleen, and they both jumped up and down. "I can't believe it! We won!"

The crowd couldn't seem to believe it either, and it was a full second before everyone started to scream and whistle and stomp their feet on the bleachers. The cheerleaders rushed out to do a final cheer, but the crowd was too excited to pay any attention.

After the excitement died down, and the team went off to the showers, Colleen turned to Amy. "You're going to do it tonight, aren't you?"

"Do what?"

"Ask Brett to the dance. Tanya always goes home after the game to change her clothes and do her hair. Brett'll come down to the Hungry Burger with the team, and it'll be at least half an hour before Tanya shows."

Amy swallowed hard. She'd rather wait a few days, to work up her nerve, but she wasn't about to admit that to Colleen. "Maybe Brett won't come in with the team. He could be driving Tanya home."

"No. Tanya drove her own car. I saw it in the lot. This is your big chance to get Brett alone. Don't blow it, Amy."

"Right." Amy nodded, and got up to follow Colleen out of the gym. She'd promised to ask Brett and she would. But she wasn't quite sure how to do it. She didn't have any trouble talking to Brett at school. They were always kidding back and forth and comparing notes on their assignments. Why was it so easy to talk to a guy about everything else except what you really wanted to ask him?

Five

Tanya swore as she slipped on a rut in the parking lot and icy slush soaked into her tennis shoes. It hadn't been snowing when she'd left for the game, and she'd left her boots at home. Now she'd have to drive home with wet shoes, and the heater in her little red Miata wasn't working right. Her father would pay to have it fixed. Daddy always came through with money. But that meant her Miata would be in the garage for several days, and there was no way Tanya wanted to be stuck in this hick little town without her car.

Winter was a royal pain. Tanya unlocked the driver's door and reached inside to pull out her scraper, a foot-long wooden pole, slightly thinner than a broom handle, with a wedge-shaped piece of plastic at one end and a brush at the other. The name stamped on the handle had worn partially off with use, but Tanya could still read it. It said, *Ice Begone, Compliments of Ford's Hardware, serving the Clearwater community since 1932.* Jessica's father owned a hardware store, and he'd let her give them out as Christmas presents this year.

Tanya thought about Jessica as she brushed the snow from her windshield. Jessica's grandfather had built the hardware store, and he'd raised his family in a two-bedroom apartment on the second floor. When he'd died, Jessica's father had taken over the store, and that's where Jessica had lived all her life. Jessica helped out in the store on weekends and during the summer, and her father had promised that the business would be hers, someday. It seemed like a fate worse than death to Tanya. Jessica would be staying in Clearwater, running the family hardware store, and living in the second-floor apartment for the rest of her life.

"Why didn't we stay in California?" Tanya grumbled as she brushed the snow from her car. Her hands felt like they were frozen, and she rubbed them together to warm them before she tackled the ice on her windshield. She should have worn her fur-lined gloves; but it hadn't been this cold when she'd left the condo, and she'd left them behind with her boots.

It took some muscle, but Tanya finally managed to scrape all the ice from her windshield. At least she wouldn't have to scrape her windows again tonight. When she got to the underground condo garage, the rest of the ice would melt while she was getting dressed. And Brett would be very sweet about scraping her windshield for her when she left the Hungry Burger to go home.

She pulled her jacket down carefully before she slid behind the wheel, but the seat was still icy cold. Tanya shivered as she started the engine, and waited for it to warm. There was no heat, but at least the tape deck was working.

Tanya slipped a jazz tape into the deck and smiled. She loved jazz, but no one else in Clearwater was sophisticated enough to enjoy it. Brett liked Country Western, and that's all they listened to when they were together. Tanya hated it, but she pretended to like it when she was with him.

Brett was on her mind as Tanya put the car in gear and pulled out of the parking lot. He wasn't the man of her dreams; but he was the best there was in Clearwater, and that meant he'd just have to do, for now. When spring came and the roads were clear, she'd drive up to Madison and check out the college guys. They were bound to be more interesting, especially since the university attracted students from all over the country. Guys from New York or California would be much more cosmopolitan, and she wouldn't have to listen to conversations about cows, or corn, or cheese making. In the meantime there was Brett, and it was a status symbol to date the best jock at Hamilton High.

As she turned down Elm Street, Tanya glanced at her watch in the light from the dash. It was already nine forty-five, and she'd promised to meet Brett at the Hungry Burger in less than an hour. She had to hurry, or she'd be late.

Tanya pumped her brakes cautiously when she came to the stop sign on Fourth Avenue. The first time she'd driven on the icy winter streets, she'd locked her brakes and gone into a skid, almost hitting a parked car. Since that frightening moment, Brett had given her some winter driving lessons, and she'd learned to be very careful when she drove around corners or stopped for stop signs.

It was only after she rounded the corner that she saw it, a car with its hood raised, stalled at the side of the street. Brett had told her about the unwritten law for motorists in the winter. If you saw someone stalled by the side of the road, you were supposed to stop and offer assistance. People had been known to freeze to death in stalled cars in the winter. But that happened out on the highway, not in town. This driver only had to walk for a couple of blocks to get help.

There was a frown on Tanya's face as she approached the stalled car, and recognized it. Should she stop, or not? It would be a major inconvenience, and she'd waste a lot of time. It would make her so late, she wouldn't have time to do her hair, and she wanted to look her best tonight.

Tanya averted her eyes and stared straight ahead as she passed the car. She felt slightly guilty, but it just couldn't be helped. She was on a tight time schedule, and this was a busy street. Someone else would drive by and stop.

It was almost ten by the time Tanya pulled into the underground condo garage. She parked in her spot and rang for the elevator, tapping her foot impatiently while she waited for it to arrive. It didn't take long, and moments later, Tanya was inside her family's fourth-floor condo.

She headed straight for her room, shedding her clothes and hopping in the shower immediately. Her parents weren't home, so she didn't bother to shut the door. They'd gone to a party at the condo recreation room, and they wouldn't be home until late.

It didn't take long for Tanya to shower and dress in her favorite outfit, a white knit dress that hugged her figure and made her look like a queen. She was sitting at her dressing table, styling her hair, when she thought she heard someone walking down the hallway, outside the condo door. But that was impossible. Everyone who lived in the building was supposed to be at the party. She must be imagining things.

When she was finished with her hair, Tanya added just a touch more blush to her cheeks, and smiled at her reflection in the mirror. She looked totally gorgeous, just the way the future Valentine's Day Queen of Hamilton High was supposed to look.

Tanya walked out to the foyer and opened the door to the closet. She had two winter coats, but both of them were parkas. Too bad she didn't have anything dressier. Queens were supposed to wear furs, weren't they?

The moment Tanya thought of it, she started to smile. Her mother had an ermine jacket that would look incredible with her white knit dress. Of course, she really shouldn't wear it without permission, but she couldn't ask since her mother wasn't here. Should she? Or shouldn't she? Tanya wavered for a brief moment, and then she pulled the coat from its padded hanger, and slipped it over her shoulders. The soft fur felt luxurious against her neck, and she smiled as she glanced in the mirror on the back of the closet door. The coat was perfect. Absolutely perfect. She looked every inch a queen.

A glance at the grandfather clock standing in the entryway, and Tanya grabbed her purse and car keys. If she didn't hurry, she'd be late. She was in such a rush as she opened the door and stepped out into the hall, she almost tripped over a giftwrapped package that someone had left in front of the door.

Tanya began to grin as she picked up the package. It was wrapped in glossy pink paper and topped with a bow printed with pink and white hearts. She hadn't been imagining those footsteps in the hallway. Brett had been here, and he'd left her this present.

She ripped off the bow, slit the paper with the edge of one long pink fingernail, and lifted the lid of the small white jeweler's box. And when she saw what was inside, she gasped with pure pleasure.

It was a pendant, a lovely gold heart on a thin gold chain. Except half of the heart was missing, and there was a jagged edge where it should be. The pendant was like a jigsaw puzzle with only two pieces, and Brett had the other half of the heart. If they put them together, they'd fit perfectly to make a whole heart.

Tanya smiled happily. Brett was probably down at the Hungry Burger right now, wearing the other half of the heart. She slipped the chain around her neck, stuffed the box and the paper in the potted plant that stood outside her parents' door, and headed for the elevator to go down to the condo garage. After she pressed the button to summon the elevator, she glanced at the ornately framed mirror on the wall. The pendant looked absolutely gorgeous around her neck.

After a long moment of waiting, Tanya pressed the button again. The elevator was very slow tonight. She waited another few moments and then she began to frown. Someone must have stopped the elevator on one of the other floors. If she wanted to get down to the Hungry Burger on time, she'd have to use the stairs.

Tanya's face was a study in irritation as she headed for the stairwell. Her parents' condo was on the fourth floor, and she was wearing high-heeled boots.

When she pulled open the door to the stairwell, Tanya's frown deepened to an angry scowl. The light was burned out. Usually the maintenance man was very prompt about replacing burned-out light bulbs, but he must have missed this one.

As she stared into the dark stairwell, Tanya hesitated. She really didn't want to go into that dark, closed space. But Brett was down at the Hungry Burger, and it wasn't wise to leave him alone for too long. There were other girls who would love to date him, and they wouldn't hesitate to take advantage of Tanya's absence.

Tanya took a deep breath and started down the stairs, gripping the rail tightly. It gave her an uneasy feeling to walk down into the darkness. Her knees were shaking and her steps were unsteady and she moved deeper and deeper into the darkness until she reached the third-floor landing.

"That wasn't so bad." Tanya spoke aloud, just to reassure herself, and then she started down the second set of steps. She'd almost reached the next landing when she heard the sound of heavy breathing. Someone was in the stairwell with her! And that someone was right behind her!

Every bad horror movie Tanya had ever seen on late-night television flashed through her mind. She whirled around, her face a study in terror; and then her eyes adjusted to the darkness, and she recognized who was behind her. "Oh, my God! Why didn't you say something? You scared me half to death!"

Tanya's knees sagged and she felt almost giddy with relief. But that relief didn't last for more than an instant. He was wearing a half-heart pendant, the same as hers. Was this some kind of joke? But before she had time to ask him about it, strong arms reached out to push her down the stairs, her neck snapping in the fall.

Six

It was the Monday after Tanya's death, a gray winter day with snow clouds so thick, there was no real proof that the sun existed. Of course, everyone had heard about Tanya's terrible accident. It had been the only topic of conversation in the halls and in the classrooms, before and after class.

When Tanya hadn't come home on Friday night, her parents had checked the condo garage and found her car in its parking spot. They'd assumed that Brett had picked her up, and they'd called his house to check. But Brett had told them that he hadn't seen Tanya all evening. That had led to a full-scale search, and the sheriff's deputies had found her lifeless body in the condo stairwell.

"I still can't believe it!" Colleen leaned over to whisper to Amy.

"I know. It's so awful," Amy whispered back. They were sitting in their fourth-period Biology class, and Mr. Humphrey was giving an incredibly boring lecture about the pituitary or the pancreas; Amy was never quite sure which was which. He had his back to the class, drawing a diagram on the blackboard, and almost everyone in the class was whispering back and forth, discussing Tanya's accident.

Before Mr. Humphrey could complete his drawing, the bell rang for lunch. Amy and Colleen sat politely until he'd finished his sentence, given the homework assignment, and dismissed the class. Mr. Humphrey had sent over half of his class to detention when they'd bolted from their seats on the first day of school, and now no one moved a muscle until he had formally dismissed them.

It was a somber group around the lunch table when Amy and Colleen joined Jessica, Gail, and Michele. Even though no one had really liked Tanya that much, they certainly hadn't wanted her to die.

"Okay." Michele put down her fork, and frowned. "Who wants to go to the funeral? It's tomorrow afternoon."

Amy looked at Colleen, who nodded. "We'll go with you."

"Good. I don't think I could take it alone. How about you, Jessica?"

"I'll go. I think we should all be there. It might make her parents feel better if her classmates show up."

"Gail?" Michele turned to Gail. "Don't you want to go?"

Gail looked very uncomfortable as she nodded. "Of course. But I've already made other arrangements. I'll see you there."

"Are you going with your father?" Amy asked the obvious question.

"Uh . . . no. My father's working. I'm going with . . . uh . . . Brett."

"But Brett was going steady with Tanya." Amy frowned slightly. "Won't it look a little strange if he shows up at her funeral with you?"

"Not really. It's not a date, or anything like that. He said he didn't want to go alone, and I offered to go with him. Besides, Brett might have thought he was going steady with Tanya, but she wasn't going steady with him."

"What do you mean?" Michele's eyes widened. "I thought they were a couple. Everyone did. They were going to the Valentine's Day Dance together, weren't they?"

"Brett said Tanya hadn't asked him yet. Everyone just assumed they were going together."

Colleen nudged Amy, and Amy sighed. Colleen was still mad at her because she hadn't asked Brett to the dance. But the time just hadn't seemed right on Friday night. Brett had been very upset when Tanya hadn't shown up at the Hungry Burger, and he'd left early, before Amy'd had a chance to even talk to him.

"Hold it a second." Colleen slipped her glasses off the top of her head, a signal that she was going to get to the heart of the matter. "You said that Brett might have thought he was going steady with Tanya, but she wasn't going steady with him. What's that supposed to mean?"

Now Gail looked even more uncomfortable, and Amy could tell she wished she hadn't opened her mouth. "Look . . . I probably shouldn't have said anything, but Brett was there when the sheriff's deputies found Tanya. And he said she was wearing one of those little gold hearts around her neck."

"What little gold hearts?"

All four girls asked the question in unison, and Gail explained, "I'm sure you've seen them in jewelry stores. They're hearts cut in half, like a jigsaw puzzle. The guy wears one half, and the girl wears the other. It's very romantic, and it's supposed to mean that you're not complete unless you're with the one you love."

"And Brett didn't give Tanya the heart?" Colleen pursued the topic.

"No. It was from someone else. The deputies found the wrapping and the box stuffed in a potted plant by Tanya's door."

"Does Brett know who gave it to her?" Michele was curious.

"He hasn't got a clue. He had no idea that Tanya was dating someone else."

"Poor Brett!" Amy sighed. "Does he think that's why Tanya didn't ask him to the dance?"

"What else is he supposed to think? After all, she was wearing another guy's heart."

The cafeteria door opened, and the basketball team trooped in. They were wearing their green blazers, and every team member had a black ribbon pinned to his sleeve.

"Are they wearing those ribbons for Tanya?" Jessica turned to Gail.

"Yes. Brett told me it was Kevin's idea. They're wearing black ribbons because Tanya was their head cheerleader."

Amy nodded. "It's a nice tribute. My great-grandfather wore a black band around his sleeve for a whole year after my great-grandmother died."

"I hope they're not going to wear them for *that* long." Gail shivered slightly. "I think this whole mourning thing is creepy. It'd be different if Tanya had been a nice person, but she wasn't. And poor Brett is taking this very hard."

Amy winced as she stared at Brett. He really did look awful. His face was gray, and it was clear that he hadn't slept well for several nights. "I wish there was something we could do to help him."

"He told me that there's only one thing that'll make him feel better." Gail lowered her voice so she wouldn't be overheard. "Brett wants to punch out the guy who gave Tanya that heart, but he doesn't know how to find him."

Amy thought for a minute, and then she nodded. "I think our best bet is to watch everyone who comes to the funeral. If Tanya's other boyfriend loved her enough to give her that heart, I'm sure he'll show up to pay his last respects."

"But how are we going to recognize him?" Jessica frowned slightly. "Do you think he'll wear his half of the heart?"

"Maybe. We'll just have to keep our eyes open."

"So what should we do if we spot him?" Michele looked excited. She loved intrigue.

"I'm not really sure. But we have to be careful that Brett doesn't realize who he is right then. It'd be awful if there was a fight at Tanya's funeral."

Gail started to giggle. "A fight at Tanya's funeral? That might turn a dull event into something interesting."

"Gail!" Amy looked shocked. "Just think about how Tanya's parents would feel!"

Gail shrugged. "Okay, okay. It was just fun to imagine, that's all. I didn't really wish it would actually happen."

"Okay. Let's work out a game plan." Amy turned to Gail. "If any of us spot Tanya's other boyfriend, we'll let you know right away. Your job is to hang on to Brett and keep him occupied. Whatever you do, don't let him go."

"I wasn't planning to let him go."

Gail gave a smug little smile, and Amy glanced at Colleen. Colleen was frowning, and so were the rest of the girls. They'd never seen this side of Gail before, and they didn't like it.

"Brett?" Gail waved at Brett as he headed for the team table. "Come over here for a second, will you?"

Brett set down his tray and walked to their table. "Hi, Gail. What's up?"

"Not much." Gail reached out to take his hand. "I just wanted to find out . . . are you okay?"

Brett nodded, and then he smiled at her. "I'm all right. Thanks, Gail. Catch you later, okay?"

Brett gave Gail's hand a squeeze, and then he went on to the team table. Amy followed him with her eyes, and then she noticed that the boxes of Valentine cards were sitting in the middle of the team table.

"They're going on with the contest?" Amy was surprised. No one had told her, and she was the class president. But Gail nodded, and leaned forward to tell them the latest.

"Mr. Dorman talked to Tanya's parents. He asked them if they wanted to have an empty chair for the Valentine's Day Queen, in honor of Tanya. She was way ahead in the contest, you know. But Tanya's father said he thought Tanya would have wanted the contest to go on, because it would give another girl a chance for a wonderful evening."

"Tanya's father sounds nice." Amy was pleased. It was a good way to handle an unfortunate situation.

"Of course, the whole thing's ridiculous." Gail gave a little laugh. "We all knew Tanya, and she wouldn't have wanted the contest to go on without her. Tanya never cared about anyone else's happiness."

Amy frowned. "But, Gail . . . you don't know that for sure. And it's not fair to say mean things about Tanya when she's not here to defend herself."

"Why not? Tanya was a stuck-up snob. We all know that. She held her nose so high in the air, she would have drowned if it rained. Why deny the truth, now that she's dead?"

"I didn't mean that we should deny the truth. But . . . it just seems wrong to criticize her now, that's all."

There was an uncomfortable silence, and then Gail shrugged. "Okay, if that's the way you want it. Are you and Colleen going to count the votes next period?"

"I guess so." Amy looked puzzled. "Why wouldn't we?"

"No reason. I just wanted you to know that I can't be there. Besides, I know how it's going to turn out, anyway."

The rest of the lunch period was filled with small talk about Friday night's basketball game and their hard-won victory. When the bell rang, Brett brought the box with the votes and the money they'd collected to Amy and Colleen. And then he took Gail's arm and walked her to the lunchroom door.

"Are you thinking what I'm thinking?" Colleen stood up and grabbed the vote box.

"I think so." Amy picked up their lunch trays and sighed. Now that Tanya was dead, it certainly looked as though Gail was moving in on Brett. Perhaps she should have taken Colleen's advice and asked Brett to the dance on Friday night, while she'd still had a chance.

Amy and Colleen had just cleaned off the teachers' table, when there was a knock at the faculty lounge door. Amy went to open it, and her eyes widened as she saw who was standing outside. "Kevin. What are *you* doing here?"

"Mr. Dorman sent me to take Gail's place . . . if you girls don't mind, that is."

"Why should we mind?" Amy gestured toward the table. "We'll be through much faster with three people working. Grab a Coke from the teachers' refrigerator, Kevin. It's a bonus we get for clearing the dishes off their lunch table."

Kevin opened the door to the teachers' refrigerator, and smiled as he surveyed the contents. "Hey . . . who said teachers aren't well paid? They've got Snapple in here!"

"Help yourself." Colleen grinned at him. "Mr. Dorman said we could. And then come over and join us."

Kevin carried his Snapple over to the table and sat down. "Okay. I'm ready. Which ones do we count first?"

"The green ones." Colleen pushed the vote box over to Kevin. "You can separate them as we go. Just pull out a heart and read the name inside."

Amy reached out to touch Kevin's arm. "Hold it a second, Kevin. Before we get started, I just want to tell you that I think the team ribbons for Tanya are very nice."

"You do?" Kevin looked shocked. "I thought you didn't like Tanya."

Amy struggled for words. It was difficult to explain how she'd felt about Tanya. "I guess that's true, in a way. I didn't really like her. But she was in some of my classes, and I feel bad about what happened to her. And since she was the head cheerleader, I think the team ought to do something to show their respect."

"That's what I thought. Thanks, Amy." Kevin picked a green heart out of the box. "Shall we start? This one's for Brett."

Colleen took the heart from Kevin and nodded. "Right. Chalk up one vote for Brett."

"And this one's for . . . Brett again." Kevin handed the heart to Colleen, who verified it.

Five minutes later, they were preparing to count the last vote for king. There had been a few lone votes for other guys, but Brett had received ninety percent of today's vote.

"I wonder if we should bother to open this one." Kevin grinned as he held up the last green heart. "I think I already know how this is going to turn out."

Amy nodded. "Me, too. And that's what Gail said when she told us she wouldn't be here. She knew Brett would get the most votes for king."

"Was she talking about king . . . or queen?" Kevin raised his eyebrows.

"King. At least I think she meant king. How could she know who'd get the most votes for queen?"

"Because Brett's voting for her now. And he told me that they're going to the Valentine's Day Dance together."

"Oh. I see." Amy tried not to show how disappointed she was. She'd known that Gail was moving in on Brett, but she hadn't expected it to happen quite so fast. "Shall we count the votes for queen now?"

One by one, the red hearts were unfolded and counted, and Gail's total grew steadily. She had received nineteen votes out of the first twenty.

"You were right, Kevin." Colleen glanced at Amy's tally sheet. "It looks like Gail is going to get most of the votes today."

Kevin nodded. "Most . . . but not all. Here's one for you, Amy."

"For me?" Amy's face mirrored her surprise. "I know we're not really supposed to do this, but do you recognize the writing?"

"It's printed."

Kevin handed the heart to Colleen, who nodded. "It's just like last Friday, Amy. I think it's the same printing, but it's hard to tell."

"I wish I could figure out who was voting for me." Amy looked wistful.

"Why?" Kevin stared at Amy. "What possible difference does it make?"

"Because I'd really like to have a date for the Valentine's Day Dance. And the person I was planning to ask is already going with someone else. If I knew who was voting for me, I'd ask him instead."

Seven

It was one-thirty in the afternoon, and Tanya's funeral started at two. Mr. Dorman had excused the whole Senior class at lunchtime, so that they could go home and dress for the funeral. Since school was over at three, and the funeral would last for at least an hour, they weren't expected to come back to school until the following morning.

Amy shivered a little as she walked down the street toward the Porter Fine Furniture Store, where she was to meet Jessica, Michele, and Colleen. She'd borrowed her mother's trench coat, which wasn't very warm, but her bright pink flowered parka had seemed inappropriate for such a somber occasion.

"Amy! Wait up!"

Amy turned and began to smile. Colleen had never been very athletic, but she was running as fast as she could, her long black dress coat flapping behind her like the tail of some gigantic crow.

"I'm glad I caught you!" Colleen was panting as she arrived at Amy's side. "Your mom said you'd just left, and there's been a change of plans. Danny's taking us."

"Danny's going to Tanya's funeral?"

Colleen nodded proudly. "I talked him into it."

"You're kidding!" Amy was totally surprised. "When I asked Danny if he was going, he told me that he hates funerals. And he swore that he was never going to another one . . . except for his own."

"I know. He always says that. I must have heard it a million times by now. Come on. We're all meeting at the Hungry Burger. We'll leave from there."

Amy nodded, and started to walk again, in step with Colleen. The Hungry Burger was only a block and a half away, so they didn't have far to go. "Tell me, Colleen. How did you get Danny to change his mind?"

"I explained that since Tanya had been his classmate, it was his duty to attend her funeral."

"An appeal to his social obligations . . . that's good." Amy nodded. "What else?"

"I said it might seem like an insult to Tanya's parents if he was the only member of the Senior class who didn't show up."

"Application of peer pressure, and a concern for the emotional well-being of others . . . that's good, too. What else?"

"I told him that we really wanted to go, but it was too far to walk and he was our only hope."

"An appeal to his vanity by admitting that he was the only person who had the power to rescue us. Very good, Colleen. What else?"

Colleen frowned. "What makes you think there was anything else?"

"I know Danny. He wouldn't have bought any of those other arguments. There was something else, wasn't there? Something you're not telling me?"

"Well . . . yes." Colleen nodded. "But it's really not worth mentioning."

"I think you'd better tell me."

"Oh . . . all right." Colleen sighed deeply. "I promised him that we'd do his laundry and iron his shirts for the next four weeks."

"Dearly beloved, we are gathered here together to say our earthly good-byes to Tanya Rachael Ellison, beloved daughter of Virginia and Spencer Ellison."

The minister intoned the familiar words, and Amy shuddered. She could understand why Danny hated funerals. They were sad and depressing, and the funeral service reminded Amy that death was inevitable.

"Are you okay?"

Danny leaned close to whisper in Amy's ear, and she nodded. The other girls were sitting near the front of the church, but Amy had waited for Danny to find a parking spot, and when he'd returned to the church on foot, they'd taken a pew in the rear. Amy felt a tap on her arm, and she turned to see that Danny was holding out his handkerchief.

"Thanks, but I'm not crying." Amy leaned over to whisper in his ear.

Danny reached out with the white linen square and gently blotted her cheeks. When he pulled his handkerchief away, Amy was amazed to see that it was wet with tears.

"But . . . I didn't know I was crying." Amy was embarrassed.

"It's okay." Danny reached out to squeeze her hand. "I've got tears in my eyes, too . . . and I hardly knew Tanya. That's the reason I don't like funerals."

Amy nodded. Danny was still holding her hand, and she didn't even think of pulling away. It felt warm, and friendly, and very comforting. He held her hand through the rest of the service, and he didn't let it go until the minister had spoken his final words and the formal church service had ended.

The pallbearers, dressed in somber black suits, walked to the front of the church and surrounded Tanya's casket. The organ was playing softly, and Amy leaned close to Danny again to speak softly in his ear. "Did Colleen tell you that we're trying to spot Tanya's mystery boyfriend?"

"She told me. That's why I picked a spot in the back of the church. I've been here before, and the ushers always let the people in the front go out first. We'll be able to see their faces when they pass us."

"Good thinking." Amy nodded, and then she reacted to the rest of what Danny had said. "You've been in this church before?"

Danny nodded. "Yeah. I dated the former minister's daughter. She used to drag me to service every Sunday to hear her father preach. I think she was trying to reform me, but it didn't work."

"I see." Amy nodded and stifled a grin. Everyone should have known that Danny couldn't be reformed. She glanced at the front of the church again, and she realized that the pallbearers were lifting Tanya's casket. "What are they doing?"

"They're carrying the casket out to the hearse. Then they'll drive it to the cemetery."

Amy nodded. She watched as the pallbearers picked up the casket and carried it slowly down the middle aisle of the church. When the casket passed their pew, Amy shuddered. She was glad that they'd closed it and she couldn't see Tanya, but she had an almost overwhelming urge to jump to her feet and open the casket so that Tanya could breathe.

"Easy, Amy." Danny slipped his arm around her shoulders. "Tanya's not in there. It's just her body."

"I know, but . . ." Amy stopped in mid-sentence. She was very embarrassed about her irrational reaction to the closed casket.

"You wanted to lift the lid, so she could breathe?"

Amy nodded. It seemed almost as if Danny had read her mind. "That's exactly how I felt. But how did you know?"

"I felt the same way, the first time I went to a funeral. Maybe we'd better not go to the cemetery."

Amy thought about it for a second, and then she shook her head. "No. We have to go. It's expected."

"Okay." Danny nodded. "The ushers are up in front now. We'd better watch."

Amy blinked back a fresh rush of tears as Tanya's parents stood up. Mrs. Ellison was weeping softly, and Tanya's father looked pale and strained. They started down the center aisle, and Amy was faced with another quandary. She wanted to acknowledge them somehow, but was it appropriate to smile at a funeral?

"What can I do?" Amy poked Danny.

"Nod as they pass you. Just let them know that you're here

and you care. A smile wouldn't really be wrong, but it wouldn't be exactly right, either."

Amy nodded as the Ellisons passed her. And then she turned to look at Danny. He'd done it again. He'd read her mind about whether she should smile or not.

Brett and Gail were ushered out next, and Amy frowned as they passed her. Brett's eyes were red, and she could tell he'd been crying, but Gail looked perfectly composed. Her arm was tucked through Brett's, and she looked stunning in a light blue wool dress with tiny diamond earrings. Amy wasn't sure if she was imagining it or not, but Gail's eyes appeared to sparkle, and she seemed almost happy as she walked down the aisle with Brett. It reminded Amy of the weddings she'd seen, and how radiant the bride had been as she'd walked down the aisle with her new husband. After they'd passed, Danny leaned close and whispered, "Gail looks like she's practicing for her wedding."

Amy didn't say anything. She just chalked another point up for Danny. He'd read her mind again.

Although Amy and Danny watched every guy who was ushered down the aisle, there was no one who looked like he could have been Tanya's mystery boyfriend. It was the same at the graveside: They knew most of the mourners, and there weren't any likely candidates.

Amy was shivering by the time they'd all piled into Danny's parents' station wagon again. The wind had begun to blow, and she'd nearly frozen, waiting for the minister to finish his prayers. "Maybe I was so cold, I didn't notice, but I didn't see any mystery boyfriends."

"Me, neither." Danny reached out to pat Amy's shoulder. "Cheer up, Amy. At least there wasn't a fight."

Michele laughed from the backseat, where she was riding with Colleen and Jessica. "There wouldn't have been one anyway. Gail was hanging on to Brett's arm so hard, he couldn't even move."

"You didn't see them in the car." Colleen spoke up. "I don't think Brett's heater works."

"Why not?" Michele sounded curious.

"Because they were huddling so close together, you couldn't have pried them apart with a crowbar."

Amy winced. She really wanted to say something about how they shouldn't gossip, but she wasn't quite sure how to do it. She'd just opened her mouth to speak up, when Danny cleared his throat.

"Now girls . . ." Danny sounded stern. "You know it's not nice to gossip. If you gossip about somebody else, they might just gossip about you."

Jessica giggled. "They can go ahead and do it. My life's an open book. It's blank, but it's open."

That cracked everyone up, Amy included. But all the while she was laughing and releasing the tension from the funeral, she was wondering why Danny always seemed to read her mind and anticipate exactly what she wanted to say.

Eight

It was Wednesday afternoon, and Amy, Colleen, and Kevin had just finished counting the votes. Amy had typed them up neatly, and as she walked down the hall to post them on the bulletin board, the loudspeaker crackled into life.

"Attention all students . . ." Amy recognized Mr. Dorman's deep voice. "The National Weather Service has determined that road conditions are hazardous, and the scheduled basketball game with the Farmington Mountain Lions has been postponed. I repeat, there will be no basketball game tonight. That is all."

Amy sighed as she reached the bulletin board and tacked up the latest contest results. There was clearly a new leader for Valentine's Day Queen. Gail had a total of eighty-five votes, and Jessica, her closest competitor, had only twenty-three.

"Hey, Amy . . . are you going down to the Hungry Burger tonight?" Danny grinned as he approached the bulletin board from the opposite direction.

"I guess so. We always do when there's no game. How about you?"

"I'll be there. How's the horse race coming?"

"Danny!" Amy laughed. "It's not a horse race and you know it!"

Danny grinned. "Too bad it isn't. I'd bet Gail to win."

"I don't think you could find anybody to take your bet.

Brett's been spending a lot of money buying her votes, and she's way ahead of everyone else."

Danny glanced at the list, and nodded. "You're right. It's pretty one-sided. But the rest of you are getting some votes."

"Not enough to win. Jessica's the closest with twenty-three, and Michele's got nineteen. And then there's Colleen with twelve."

Danny raised his eyebrows. "Twelve? Are you sure?"

"I'm positive. We count the votes twice to make sure they're right."

"And she really got twelve?" Danny began to grin. "That's great! Maybe I can stop spending my money on her."

Amy was curious. "How much did you spend?"

"Five bucks. I didn't want her to be the only girl without any votes. Do you have any idea who's been voting for her?"

"Not really. I didn't recognize the handwriting."

Danny shrugged. "Oh, well. Whoever it is, I owe him one. I was getting tired of spending my hard-earned cash on this dumb contest."

"Danny?" Amy turned to look up at him. "Can I ask you a personal question?"

"Sure, Amy. What is it?"

Amy began to blush. She hated to ask, but she really wanted to know. "I've got a total of five votes. Are you . . . uh . . . spending your money to buy me votes, so I won't be embarrassed?"

Danny shook his head. "Not me. Don't get me wrong, Amy. I would have written in your name, but I noticed that you were getting votes on your own."

"Thanks . . . I think." Amy laughed, and then she turned serious. "I wonder who's voting for me."

"I don't know. Can't you tell by his writing?"

Amy shook her head. "No. He always prints. Do you think you could ask around, without being too obvious about it?"

"Sure. But why do you want to know?"

"Well . . ." Amy hesitated. She was terribly embarrassed. "If I tell you, will you promise not to say anything to anyone else?"

Danny nodded. "I promise. Now tell me."

"I don't have a date for the dance. I was going to ask Brett, but he's going with Gail, and I don't know who else to ask. If I can find out who's voting for me, I'm going to ask him."

"That sounds like a risky proposition. It could be someone you don't like."

Amy shook her head. "I don't think so. If he's voting for me, I'll probably like him."

"He might be short, with zits and sweaty palms."

"So?" Amy shrugged. "It's like my grandmother used to say: *Handsome is as handsome does.* And it was very handsome of him to vote for me. Besides, it's only for one night, and I really want a date for the dance."

"He could be incredibly stupid. After all, he's . . ."

"Voting for me!" Amy laughed as she finished the rest of his sentence. "Thanks a lot, Danny. After all that's happened, I needed a laugh. But will you try to find out for me soon? It's really important."

Danny nodded, and started down the hallway. But before he got very far away, he turned back to grin at her. "If I can't find out, and you really want a date, you can always ask me. I'm not taken."

"Right." Amy grinned back. "I'll definitely keep that in mind."

As Danny disappeared around the corner, Amy's grin faded, and she looked very thoughtful. It was a well-known fact that Danny never attended any of the Senior class dances. He'd told Colleen that it was because he was older, and it would bore him to tears to sip ginger ale from a paper cup, and dance around the gym with a girl who was still in high school. When Danny had said that she could ask him to the dance, he'd certainly been kidding . . . hadn't he?

Cat frowned as he rummaged in his locker for a missing library book. He'd cleaned out his locker at Christmas break, but it was a mess again. There were piles of papers on the floor, and his books were no longer arranged in alphabetical order by author as they'd been at the start of the year. Now that Karen was dead, a little thing like an organized locker just didn't seem to matter anymore.

He managed to locate the library book, mashed in the corner, under an old pair of sneakers. He pulled it out, dusted it off on the sleeve of his jacket, and frowned. There was only one section of his locker that was still neat and clean, and he'd hidden it from prying eyes. He glanced around, checking to make sure the halls were deserted, and then he removed the large three-ring binder that blocked the top shelf.

"Karen." Cat sighed as he stared at her photograph. It was an eight-by-ten print that the school photographer had taken last year. He'd framed it, and now it was propped up on the top shelf of his locker, surrounded by a circle of the pretty white, vanilla-scented candles she'd loved so much.

Something glittered in the center of the ring, and Cat smiled as he fingered the thin gold chain holding the half-heart pendant. Perhaps his locker wasn't the best place to keep it.

Cat picked it up, and wondered if he should wear it around his neck. No, that would be much too dangerous. If anyone spotted it, they might guess that he'd killed Tanya.

"You understand about the heart, don't you, Karen?"

Cat smiled as he said the words. Karen had always loved puzzles, and the half heart was a puzzle that no one else would be able to solve. It was a symbol for the way that Tanya had broken Karen's heart by gossiping about her. When Cat had finished taking Karen's revenge, he intended to bury the half-heart pendants with her. But Karen's revenge was far from over, and he had to find a safe place to store the charm.

His backpack was sitting on top of his locker, and Cat grinned as he remembered the pocket inside. It was intended for pens and pencils, but it was a perfect hiding place for the pendant. He opened the backpack, unzipped the pocket, and slipped the other half of Tanya's pendant inside. He'd carry it with him to remind himself that his work was far from finished.

"They posted the results of the contest, Karen. Now that Tanya's dead, Gail's in the lead with eighty-five points, and everyone's sure she's going to win. Is Gail the right girl for queen?"

Cat listened, but of course the photograph didn't speak. Karen's smile was frozen in time, forever young and forever beautiful. As he studied her lovely image, a cold draft seemed to emanate from the depths of the locker, and he shivered with anticipation.

"Is that you, Karen? Are you with me?"

Cat shut his eyes, and tried to be perfectly receptive. He felt that Karen was with him, but she still hadn't spoken to him. Perhaps she never would. They hadn't seemed to feel the need to speak when Karen was alive. They'd sat close together, perfectly silent, their minds on the same wavelength. On most occasions, he'd known exactly what Karen had been thinking.

"Karen . . . you've got to let me know. Was Gail one of the girls who hurt you?"

Cat frowned as he tried to remember everything Karen had told him on the night she'd cried in his arms. He was almost sure she hadn't mentioned Gail by name, but perhaps Karen hadn't known exactly who her enemies had been.

"This is very important, Karen. Do you want me to test Gail to see if she's worthy to be the Valentine's Day Queen?"

Cat listened intently, but there was nothing to hear. There was silence, broken only by distant and indistinct murmuring from the classroom down at the end of the hall.

"Please, Karen. I've got to know what you want." Cat's voice was shaking with intensity. "If you can't speak to me, try to give me a sign."

As Cat stood there, trembling, another icy draft swirled around his feet. And then a door slammed across the hall with a bang that made him jump. Cat hurried to the closed door, and peered through the glass pane at the empty classroom inside. No one had been near the door to slam it.

It must have been a sign from Karen.

"Yes, my darling Karen . . . I understand."

Cat walked back across the hall, and took down Karen's photograph. He smiled at her lovely image, gently touched his lips to hers, and replaced it on the shelf. Then he put the three-ring binder back in place and closed and locked his locker. He was smiling as he headed back to the library with the missing book. Karen had broken through the barrier between the dead and the living to give him a sign. That meant she was pleased with what he was doing to keep her memory alive in his heart.

Several students nodded to him as he walked back into the library. He was well-liked at school. He saw Amy, sitting at a table in the back of the room, and he was almost tempted to join her. Amy was a nice person, not like the others, but he walked past with a smile. He had work to do, and he had to be alone.

Cat sat down at a small table in the front, which was so close to the librarian that most students avoided it. Then he opened his notebook and began to plan out the rest of his day. He had to devise a test for Gail, a fair test that would tell him what sort of person she really was.

If she passed, he would let her be queen.

But if she failed, he would arrange another accident that would take her out of the contest.

For good.

Amy and Colleen pushed open the glass door to the Hungry Burger, and a blast of noise assaulted their ears. It was the after-school hangout for the whole Senior class, and every booth was taken.

"Oh-oh." Amy began to frown. "I guess we should have gotten here earlier."

Colleen nodded. And then she smiled as someone in the back of the crowded room began to wave frantically. "It's okay. Jessica and Michele have that big booth in the back, and they saved a place for us."

Amy was smiling as she followed Colleen through the crowd, but her smile changed to a frown the moment she saw who else was sharing the booth. Kevin was there, and that was fine, but Gail and Brett were huddled together in the farthest corner.

"Amy . . . come on." Colleen grabbed her hand and pulled her forward as Amy hesitated. "Don't let them know that they bother you. That way you win, and they lose."

"Huh?" Amy was clearly puzzled. "You're not making any sense, Colleen. Where did you hear a dumb thing like that!?"

Colleen shrugged. "My mother. She's just as bad as yours, in a way. Mine has crazy sayings, and yours has crazy diets."

"That's true." Amy sighed. "I don't know how much longer my dad's going to put up with this one. She started him on tofu and bottled water this morning. It's supposed to clean all the poisons out of his system, or something like that."

Danny came up just in time to hear Amy's comment. "I really feel for your father. Have you ever tried tofu? It tastes like milk Jell-O."

"That's exactly what Dad said. He dumped it in the ivy plant while Mom wasn't looking."

"It'll probably die of lack of nutrition." Colleen started to frown. "Why doesn't your dad put his foot down and tell her he wants a real breakfast?"

"He loves her, and he understands that she's just concerned about his health. And he knows it's only a matter of time before she switches him to a new diet."

Danny nodded. "I guess you have to compromise if you want a marriage to work. But in the meantime, what does your dad do for food?"

"We stop at Dunkin' Donuts every morning. Mrs. Beeseman always has a hot cinnamon bun ready for Dad. He never eats lunch, so that's okay, but then he has to come home to whatever Mom decides is a healthy dinner."

Danny looked thoughtful. "Why don't you print up a fake fad diet?"

"A what?"

"A fad diet, just like the ones your mother follows. Make a list of all your father's favorite foods and write down some great-sounding reasons why he should eat them. Your mom'll never know the difference."

Amy began to smile. "That's really a good idea . . . and it might just work. But how do I get Mom to fall for it?"

"Send it to her through the mail. Make up some catchy title like the Fit and Trim Nutritional Guide."

"I could do that. But what do I use for a return address? I can't give my own."

Danny thought for a moment, and then he grinned. "Call yourself the Y.M.A. Nutritional Council. That stands for your name spelled backward, and it sounds legitimate. And make up a fake post office box in New York City."

"But isn't that cheating?"

"I guess it is, in a way." Colleen shrugged. "But we learned about well-balanced diets in Home Economics class, and we probably know more about nutrition than the people who make up those other diet sheets."

"You're right, and I'll do it." Amy grinned at them. "You guys are terrific . . . you know that?"

"Of course we do." Danny nodded, and then he put his arm around her shoulders. "Come on, Amy. Let's go sit down."

Amy was smiling as she approached the booth. Danny's arm felt good around her shoulders, and the sight of Brett and Gail, cuddling in the corner, didn't bother her nearly as much as it had before.

Nine

Jessica looked up as Colleen, Amy, and Danny slid into the booth. "Hi, guys. We've got a problem, and we were waiting for you."

Amy nodded. Michele looked very upset, and so did Kevin, and Neal. Even Brett had lost his usual smile, and Gail seemed ready to burst into tears. "What is it, Jessica?"

"Remember those crazy Valentine cards that Tanya got the night of her accident? Well, Gail got two of them today."

Gail shivered visibly. "The first one was there when I got to school this morning. And I found the second one right after school. Somebody dropped them through the vent in my locker."

Gail's voice was shaking, and Amy felt a stab of sympathy. Even though Gail hadn't been very friendly lately, Amy felt sorry for her now. It was clear that she was truly frightened.

"I'd like to see those Valentine cards." Amy took charge.

"Here." Gail pushed two red envelopes across the table. "They're from the same person . . . I just know it. And he's really weird!"

Amy opened the first envelope. The message was printed, just as it had been on Tanya's cards. She took a deep breath, and read it aloud: " 'Roses are red, lilies are white. A queen should always do everything right.' And it's signed, 'Cat.' "

"Nice sentiment." Danny turned to Gail in surprise. "Why are you so upset about that?"

Gail motioned to Amy. "Read the other one. Then you'll understand."

" 'Roses are red, violets are blue. Pass my test and the queen could be you.' " Amy's voice shook slightly. "That's exactly the same message that Tanya got!"

Colleen shrugged. "But that's not so bad. Tanya's third card was the scary one. And you didn't get one like that."

"I didn't get it . . . yet." Gail still looked very worried. "But what if I do?"

Amy reached out to pat Gail's shoulder. "Don't borrow trouble. It's like Colleen's mother always says . . . if you don't let it bother you, then you win and he loses."

"That's the silliest thing I've ever heard!" Gail began to frown. "Besides, it *does* bother me. Tanya got the cards, and look what happened to her! She's dead!"

Now Brett began to frown. "But, Gail . . . Tanya's death was an accident. How could the cards have anything to do with it?"

"What if it *wasn't* an accident? You remember what was in the third card, don't you?"

Amy nodded. "I'll never forget it. It said, *'Violets are blue, roses are red. An unworthy queen is better off dead.'* "

"Exactly!" Gail shivered. "The third card was a threat. And I think the person who sent the cards pushed Tanya down those stairs!"

There was silence for a moment, and then Danny spoke up. "Come on, Gail. You're just jumpy, that's all. Tanya was wearing high-heeled boots, and she tripped."

"But Tanya was a dancer, and she was used to wearing high heels. I know they said she lost her balance, but I don't believe it! I think the weirdo who sent these cards was with Tanya that night. He gave her the half-heart pendant, and then he shoved her down the stairs."

"But . . . why would he do something like that?" Danny was puzzled.

"Because Tanya didn't pass his test . . . whatever that was. And he decided that she shouldn't be queen. That's why."

There was another long silence, and Amy shivered slightly. Gail had voiced the questions that had been in her mind ever since she'd heard about Tanya's accident.

Brett put his arm around Gail and hugged her. "I'm afraid you've got a point. The cards, the pendant, Tanya's accident . . . if you add it all up, it does seem suspicious."

"Exactly!" Gail smiled briefly at Brett, but then she looked worried again. "We've got to find out who's sending these cards! He could be Tanya's killer!"

Now it was Danny's turn to look worried. "I agree with you, Gail. I think we should try to find out, but let's not jump to conclusions. The person who sent the cards could be nothing more than a practical joker. He might not be the same person who gave Tanya the pendant. And even if you do suspect foul play, the sheriff already wrote Tanya's death off as an accident."

"Danny's right." Amy nodded. "Whoever this person is, he's innocent until proven guilty. We have to remember that."

"And there's no way we can find out who sent the cards, anyway." Neal shook his head. "He just signs himself *Cat,* and we can't tell by his handwriting because he printed."

"Printed?" Danny turned to Amy in surprise. "Didn't you say those votes you got for queen were printed?"

Amy blushed. "That's true. My votes were printed. And I . . . I kept the one I got today. Hold on while I find it. It's in my purse."

Brett groaned. "I know what that means. Whenever a girl says she's got something in her purse, it takes hours to find it."

"Wrong." Amy reached into her purse and pulled out a red construction paper heart. "I have a very efficient filing system."

Neal nodded. "Sure. You filed it under *P* for *purse.* It was just blind luck that you found it."

"No . . . honestly." Amy began to blush. "I really *do* have a filing system. I put the special things in this little zippered pocket, and I stuff the things I want to save for a long time in the deep pocket in the center. The pocket with snaps on the outside of my purse is for the things I need every day, like my comb, and my lunch card, and my money, and my keys, and . . ."

"And we thought we had it hard with our car keys and our wallets!" Danny started to laugh. "How many pounds does your purse weigh?"

"It's not *that* heavy!" Amy grinned, in spite of herself.

"Oh, no? Then why does your left shoulder dip down two inches lower than your right?"

"Hold it, you two!" Brett held up his hands. "Let's take a look at Amy's vote."

Amy nodded, and unfolded it. And then she pushed it across the table to Brett, along with Gail's Valentine cards. "Can you tell if they're from the same person?"

Brett stared at the samples of printing for a moment, and then he nodded. "It's the same person. I'm willing to bet on it. Look at the way he crosses his letters, especially the capital *A.*"

"Brett's right." Danny compared the two samples. "They're crossed diagonally. Most people cross them with a straight line."

"Here's something else." Brett pointed to the note. "This card is printed in block letters, and so is Amy's name on the vote. If we could get a sample of everyone's printing, I think we could identify the writer."

"But how?" Kevin was curious. "Lots of people print in block letters, don't they?"

"See how the letters are slanted slightly to the left? That's something distinctive to look for. And he gives some of his letters a loop, just like he's writing instead of printing."

"You're really good at this!" Amy smiled at Brett.

"Thanks." Brett smiled back. "It's because I work in my dad's print shop, and part of my job is comparing different styles and typefaces. If we could get a sample of everyone's printing, I think I could identify this guy."

"Are you sure?" Danny frowned slightly.

"Yeah. I really think I could do it."

"Okay. You're on." Danny reached across the table to shake Brett's hand. "I'll provide the samples for you."

Amy turned to Danny in surprise. "That's a great idea, but how are you going to do that?"

"Just leave it to me." Danny squeezed her hand under the table. "I'll have them for you by lunchtime tomorrow."

Cat was frowning as he went up to the counter and got in line to order another Coke. It would be tragic if they solved the puzzle before he'd finished Karen's revenge. He'd just have to think of some way to throw them off the track.

He thought about Karen as he waited for the girl in front of him to place her order. What would they do if Karen were here, right now, at the Hungry Burger? Would they invite her to join them at the back booth, and accept her as a friend? Or would they be very polite to her face, but gossip about her behind her back, as they'd done in the last few weeks of her life?

The week before Karen had died, she'd asked him to take her to the Hungry Burger. But when they'd joined the crowd at the big booth in the back, all the conversation had stopped, and there had been an uncomfortable silence before it had started again. Karen had known that they'd been talking about her, and it had hurt her deeply.

He put a smile on his face as he realized that several of his classmates were staring at him. He had to pretend to be just part of the gang. It was the only way they'd take him into their confidence. He was a wolf among sheep, and he had to keep up his disguise. They might panic if they knew what his real intentions were.

Cat turned to look at Amy, and his smile changed to something warm and genuine. Everyone had heard her say that Cat should be innocent until proven guilty. Of course he was guilty, but that was beside the point. Amy had spoken up to protect his rights.

And then there was the matter of the vote. Cat had been terribly flattered when Amy had pulled the construction paper heart out of her purse. It had meant so much to her that she'd kept it. He almost wished he could tell her that he was the one who'd voted for her, but now he could never declare himself. They'd compared his printing, and they'd realized that he was the one who'd sent the cards to Tanya and Gail. It didn't really matter in the grand scheme of things, but it was still a minor inconvenience. He'd have to change his style of printing so that no one could recognize it.

His gaze turned to Gail, and he frowned again. She was shallow and silly; but he had promised Karen that he'd test her, and he would fulfill his promise. The test would take place tomorrow, during the school day. She'd be less suspicious then.

If Gail passed his test, he would let her be queen. That was only fair.

But if she failed, he would eliminate her, just as he'd eliminated Tanya.

Ten

The next day at lunch, everyone was talking about the Valentine give-away that WROQ was sponsoring. There would be a drawing at the Hamilton High Valentine's Day Dance, and twenty students would win WROQ caps and T-shirts. The grand prize was a stack of top-ten CDs, and Danny was passing around a sign-up sheet.

The usual crowd was gathered around the team table when Danny approached with the sheet. He handed it to Amy with a flourish, and sat down next to her. "You guys can start in on this one. After school is over, I'm going to get the one I posted by the front entrance."

"I don't believe it!" Amy glanced down at the list of neatly printed names. Danny had gotten a sample of everyone's printing, just as he'd promised he would. "Is the contest a fake?"

"Of course not. Crazy Mark Hannah's going to do the drawing himself."

"Crazy Mark Hannah, the Top Banana, the guy with a peel?" Brett was impressed. "He's WROQ's top DJ!"

Danny nodded. "I said I'd write some theme music for one of his shows, and he promised to help me out with the drawing."

"And you got everyone here to sign up?" Amy smiled when Danny nodded. "That was absolutely brilliant, Danny!"

"The instructions I wrote at the top say to print your full

name and address. I figured that would give us enough letters to work with."

"Perfect." Brett nodded. "But how about the people who aren't here today?"

"We'll catch them tomorrow. Mr. Dorman says I can pass the list around in homeroom. Anybody who misses out today can sign up tomorrow."

Kevin looked worried. "But how about us? We can sign up, can't we?"

"Sure. Knock yourself out." Danny pushed a blank sign-up sheet across the table. "It's a legitimate contest. We're just going to examine the names before we drop them in the fishbowl, that's all."

Kevin nodded, and printed his name and address. Then he passed the paper to Gail, who did the same. It took only a few minutes for the paper to circulate around the table, and it came to rest in front of Danny.

"You'd better sign it, too." Amy nudged him. "It won't look right if you don't."

Danny grinned at her. "Do you think I'm Cat?"

"Of course not. But someone else might, and you can prove you aren't by signing up."

"Okay." Danny nodded, and printed his name and address. Then he shoved the paper to Amy. "How about you?"

Amy put down her name. And then she handed it to Brett and pushed back her chair. "I'm going to get some water. Does anyone else want anything?"

"I'd like some water, too." Danny nodded. "Do you need some help?"

"No. I'll get it." Amy hurried to the counter and got two paper cups full of water. It was lukewarm, and she walked to the ice machine, which was close to the team table. She was just about to push the button for ice, when she heard Gail's voice.

"What do you think, Brett?" Gail sounded worried, and Amy peered around the ice machine to see what was the matter. "Is one of us Cat?"

Brett examined the list, and shook his head. "No. As far as I'm concerned, everyone at this table is in the clear."

"Are you sure? Tanya said she thought that Amy wrote those poems."

Brett frowned slightly, and then he glanced at Amy's name again. "No way, Gail! Amy's printing is completely different. And there's no way she could have voted for herself in the queen contest. The boys have to vote for girls, and the girls have to vote for boys. That's the rule."

"Well . . . maybe." Gail didn't look convinced. "But Amy counted the votes. She could have slipped in a couple for herself. Anybody can cut a heart out of red construction paper. And she did have one in her purse."

Amy was so shocked, her mouth dropped open. She couldn't believe that Gail suspected her of being Cat.

"You're crazy, Gail!" Colleen looked just as shocked as Amy was. "Amy would never do something like that! What possible motive could she have?"

"Jealousy. You know that Amy was always jealous of Tanya. Tanya was pretty, and popular, and she was dating Brett." Gail turned to give Brett a smile. "Unpopular girls like Amy always dream of dating the best-looking guy, and being queen of the dance."

Danny shook his head. "Hold on, Gail. You're going wacko if you think Amy had anything to do with those Valentine cards. And she'd never vote for herself for queen. She's the most totally honest person I know."

"And how about the half-heart pendant?" Colleen sounded outraged. "And your theory that the person who gave Tanya the necklace pushed her down the stairs? How can you possibly think that Amy would do something like that?!"

Gail looked as if she wished she hadn't brought up the subject. "Look . . . I didn't say that Amy killed Tanya. But I still think she might have sent those cards. She knew she could never win the contest for queen, so she struck out at the girl who was leading the contest."

"Listen to me, Gail." Brett turned to her, and Amy noticed that he wasn't smiling. "What you're saying is . . . well . . . it's just impossible! I haven't known Amy as long as you have, but I know she didn't send those cards."

Kevin nodded. "That's right. Amy would never do something like that. You're accusing the wrong person."

"And you're accusing her behind her back." Colleen spoke up. "That's not fair."

"I think the stress is getting to you, Gail." Michele sighed deeply. "You might not realize it, but you've changed completely since this contest started. Now all you think about is being queen. It's like you've turned into another person."

Jessica nodded. "You used to be our friend, and we want you back the way you were. This contest is making you crazy. Maybe you should think about taking your name out of the running."

Gail gave a mean little laugh. "Oh, sure. That's what you'd like, isn't it, Jessica? You've got the most votes after me. If I pulled out, you'd be queen!"

There was an uneasy silence at the table. And then Brett stood up. "Come on, Gail. Get your coat. We're going out for a walk."

"But it's snowing outside, and I'll ruin my hair." Gail turned to scowl at him. "That's the dumbest idea I've ever heard! Do you have any idea how cold it is out there?"

Brett nodded, and pulled her to her feet. "It's twenty degrees above zero."

"But that's below freezing!" Gail shivered. "Give me one good reason why I should go for a walk with you!"

"Because you need it. It might help you chill out before you lose *all* your friends."

Gail was fuming as she walked down the hall to her locker. School was over for the day, and the afternoon had been a disaster. Brett had been impossible when they'd gone on their walk. He'd talked about the value of friendship, and how she'd let this contest for queen go to her head. He'd lectured her the whole time they were outside, and Gail had been on the verge of telling him that she didn't want to go to the dance with him after all, when the bell had rung and they'd been forced to come inside.

Even though she'd been free during fifth period, Gail hadn't helped to count the votes. There was no way she wanted to spend a whole hour with Colleen and Amy. She'd gone to the library instead, but that had been a mistake. Everyone there had wanted something from her.

Gail had promised Jessica and Neal that she'd study with them, but she'd pleaded a headache. And when Kevin had come in, halfway through the period, to ask to borrow her history notes, she'd lied and told him she'd left them at home.

Sixth period had been just as bad. She'd refused to help her Chemistry partner because she just hadn't felt like being charitable to a bonehead who couldn't remember the formulas for idiotically simple compounds like sodium chloride and hydrogen peroxide. And when the girl at the next table had asked if she knew how to figure out atomic weight, Gail had lied and said that she didn't have a clue.

Naturally, Gail had blown her part of the oral report in seventh-period English class. The other students on her panel had been depending on her to bring up their grades, but that was just tough. It was a dog-eat-dog world, and she didn't see why she should knock herself out when she already had an *A* in the class. And after the final bell had rung, she'd sat at her desk for a full five minutes so she wouldn't have to run into Brett in the hall, and risk another boring lecture.

Gail stashed her books in her locker, and sighed. There was an emergency cheerleader practice after school today. Now that Tanya was dead, they had to work out some three-person cheers before the next game. But Gail just didn't feel like going. Jessica and Michele couldn't learn their steps without her coaching, but it wasn't her fault that they were so stupid.

As she passed the bulletin board, Gail's spirits brightened a bit. She was still in the lead for queen, and there was no doubt in her mind that she'd win . . . unless Brett decided not to vote for her anymore. Perhaps she should wait to tell him what a self-righteous pig he was, and be nice to him until the contest was over.

Gail hurried down the stairs and ran down the hall toward the boys' locker room. She was willing to eat crow, as long as she could be queen. Brett was standing in the hall, next to Neal, and she put on her most charming smile.

"Brett? Could I please talk to you for a minute?" Gail motioned to him, and Brett followed her down the hallway. When they were out of earshot, she managed to work up a teary-eyed look. "I'm sorry I was so awful today. I guess you guys were right, and the contest is really getting to me."

Brett nodded, but he didn't smile. Gail let a tear run down her cheek, and wiped it away with the back of her hand. Thank goodness she could cry on demand. Boys always caved in when girls cried. It was a fact of life.

"I've been thinking about what you said, and maybe I *should* withdraw from the contest. I want you to know that . . . that my friends are more important to me than being Valentine's Day Queen."

Brett nodded again, and he seemed to thaw a bit, because he reached out to wipe the tear from her cheek. "Think about it carefully, Gail. Would you really pull out of the contest to save a few friendships?"

"Of course I would!" Gail let another tear spill down her cheek. "I'll do it first thing tomorrow morning. And I'll tell Mr. Dorman to split up my votes and give them to the other girls. The only reason I really wanted to win was . . . well . . . it's my dad. When my mom was alive, she always talked about the time she was the Homecoming Queen at Hamilton High. Dad was captain of the football team, so he was Homecoming King, and that's the night he proposed to her. He's been really depressed ever since she died, and I thought it might make him happy to see me crowned as Valentine's Day Queen."

Brett looked a little uncertain. "Gosh, Gail . . . I didn't know your mom was dead. I'm really sorry. When did it happen?"

"Four years ago. She was there one day, and . . . gone the next." Gail made her lower lip quiver. Actually, her mother was alive and living in Sacramento with the guy she'd run off with, but since her dad never talked about it, no one else knew.

"I didn't know they had Homecoming Queens back when your mother was in school." Brett sounded curious. "How long ago was it?"

"Uh . . . I'm not really sure." Gail struggled to think of something. "But Mom got married right out of high school, and I was born two years later, so I guess it was over twenty years ago."

Brett smiled at her. "What was your mom's name?"

"Elizabeth. She used to joke around about having the same name as the English queens." Gail smiled back, but her mind was racing. She knew she'd better not say any more about her mother. The best way to keep from being caught when you were lying was to keep everything simple so you could remember what you'd said. "The things you said on our walk made me stop and think. Now I realize that I had a totally selfish reason for wanting to be queen, and I really don't deserve the honor after the horrible way I acted today!"

"Well . . . I guess that's true. But anyone can make a mistake. And if you're really sorry, maybe you could apologize to the other girls."

"Oh, I will!" Gail managed to look totally sincere. She'd get through the required apologies somehow. "But I still think I'd better withdraw from the contest . . . don't you?"

Brett began to frown. "Well . . . maybe not. I can see why you want to make your dad happy, and that's really not a selfish reason. But how about the stress? Can you handle it?"

"I . . . I think so. And you can tell me if you think I'm acting crazy again. I'm just so upset about those cards, especially after what happened to Tanya. And I can't help thinking that the same thing might happen to me!"

"Don't worry, Gail. I'll protect you." Brett slipped his arm around her shoulders and gave her a light kiss on the forehead. "We'll stick this out together and make your dad happy. I'll even call him personally and invite him to come to the dance to see your coronation."

"Oh, that would be wonderful! Dad would just love it! I know he would!" Gail thought fast. Her father traveled a lot on business, and if she was lucky, he'd be out of town. Of course, if Brett called him today, Dad would stay home for the dance. And then he might just blow her whole sad story about Mom being the Homecoming Queen.

Brett looked anxious as he noticed Gail's worried expression. "What's the matter, Gail?"

"I was just thinking . . . please don't call my dad right away. I don't want you to ask him until the very last day of the contest."

"But, Gail . . . if I don't ask him right away, he could make other plans."

Gail nodded. "I know. But think about how he'd feel if he thought I was going to win, and I didn't."

"That's impossible." Brett hugged her a little tighter. "I'll make sure you win, Gail. You can count on me."

"I know you will. But I just don't want to tempt fate, that's all. You never know what'll happen for sure, until the last vote is counted. And I certainly don't want to risk disappointing my dad. I'm all he has left, now that Mom is gone."

"I understand. And I guess you're right." Brett smiled down at her. "You're a really good daughter, Gail. I think it's wonderful that you're so concerned about your dad's feelings."

Gail nodded. It certainly wouldn't do to tell Brett that her dad didn't care what she did as long as the house was clean. "Well . . . I might not be the best daughter in the world, but I try to be. We have to . . . uh . . . stick together as a family. You know what I mean?"

"Sure I do. I've got to run, Gail. The guys are waiting for me. You're going to cheerleader practice, aren't you?"

"Uh . . . sure I am!"

"Then I'll see you after we're through, down at the Hungry Burger. And don't forget to apologize to Jessica and Michele. The sooner you do it, the easier it'll be, and it'll make you feel a whole lot better."

"Right." Gail nodded and smiled, but she felt more like frowning. Now she'd have to go to cheerleader practice. And she'd have to apologize to Jessica and Michele. She'd have to be nice to Brett and all her other classmates until the contest was over. The whole thing left a bitter taste in Gail's mouth, but she would do it. It was worth almost anything to be Valentine's Day Queen.

Eleven

Brett frowned as he paged through the copies of Hamilton High's yearbooks. Something about Gail's sudden transformation had made him suspicious, and he'd come up to the library to do some research to find out if she had been telling the truth.

He'd added up the numbers and figured out which yearbooks he should check. And when he hadn't found Gail's parents' names, he'd gone back to check five years earlier and five years later. The football teams were all pictured in the yearbooks, but Gail's father, Howard Baxter, hadn't been in any of the pictures. And although Brett didn't know Mrs. Baxter's maiden name, he hadn't been able to find any girl named Elizabeth who had been crowned as Homecoming Queen.

Brett closed the last yearbook and placed it back on the library shelf. Now he knew the truth. Gail wanted to be the Valentine's Day Queen so badly, she'd lied to him. And that made him furious!

What should he do? Brett sat at the table and drummed his fingers impatiently on its wooden surface. He had to do something. That card Gail had received from Cat had said it all. A queen should be kind, faithful and true, and Gail didn't deserve to be queen.

* * *

The halls were silent and deserted when Cat prepared to slip the third Valentine card through the vent in Gail's locker. He knew she'd have to come back to get her coat, and she'd see it then. Naturally, she'd go running down to the Hungry Burger, but she would never get there. Cat's plan was foolproof. He'd worked it all out very carefully, and Gail would never see any of her friends again.

Some instinct stopped him, and Cat hesitated, the card in his hand. He was sure that Gail had apologized to Michele and Jessica, and it was possible that one or both of the girls would come up to Gail's locker with her. If Gail found the third card in their presence, she would never start out for the Hungry Burger alone.

Cat gazed down the empty corridor. Of course he couldn't see Karen, but he knew that she was there. She had stopped him from dropping the card in Gail's locker. "You've got to tell me, Karen. Where shall I put the card?"

No answer came from the silent halls, or the empty classrooms. But a cold breeze swirled around Cat's feet, and suddenly he knew exactly what to do.

"I'll do it, Karen. I'll do it right now." Cat was smiling as he put on his parka and boots. "She won't be queen, I promise you that."

For a brief moment, when Gail was spinning the dial on her combination lock, she wished she'd asked Jessica and Michele to come upstairs with her to get her coat. They were friends again, now that she'd apologized, and she didn't want to be all alone in the hallway if there was another Valentine card from Cat. But when she pulled open the door to her locker and peeked inside, Gail gave a deep sigh of relief. There was nothing on the floor. No distinctive red envelope had been slipped through the vent of her locker today.

Even though she knew she was being silly, Gail jumped as she heard a soft noise behind her. It was a sort of muffled click, and it sounded as if someone had closed a door to one of the classrooms. Perhaps one of the teachers was working late.

As she walked down the hallway, carrying her boots, Gail peeked into the classrooms. They were all deserted. The sound she'd heard must have been caused by the cold draft she'd felt seeping down the corridor. Even though the school was well insulated and heated in the winter, the cold air still seeped under the doors and around the windows on very cold days like this.

It was snowing when Gail pushed open the outside door, and she was glad she'd remembered her boots. The snow had stopped during seventh period, but it was falling again now. As she went down the steps to the sidewalk, Gail noticed a set of boot prints in the snow. Someone had just left the school. It couldn't have been Michele and Jessica because there was only one set of footprints.

Gail giggled as something funny occurred to her, something she could never tell anyone else. It was mean, but it was funny, and she laughed as she hurried down the walkway to the parking lot. Jessica and Michele had been incredibly clumsy in cheerleader practice. If the boot prints had belonged to them, each pair would have had two left feet!

It didn't take long to reach her car. Gail had come to school early this morning and chosen a covered spot very close to the building, and her windshield was free of ice. She stuck her key in the lock, and then she frowned. Her car was unlocked, and she distinctly remembered locking it this morning.

Gail stepped back, and wondered if she should open the door. Someone had been in her car. She was sure of it. Or was she? Perhaps she'd only thought she'd locked it. The locks on her old Plymouth Valiant never worked well in the winter.

An icy wind blew around the corner, and Gail made up her mind. She'd open the door, peek inside, and check to see if anything was missing. If it was, she'd walk back to the telephone at the school entrance and call the police.

Gail used her mitten to open the door. She'd seen enough cop movies on television, and if there were prints, she didn't want to smudge them. But when she looked inside, everything seemed to be untouched. Her library books were piled in the passenger seat, exactly where she had left them. And her extra parka was folded very neatly in the backseat.

Convinced that she'd been imagining things, Gail slid into the driver's seat. She started the car, made sure it was idling properly, and stared out at the snowy parking lot, waiting for it to warm up enough to drive. No sense turning on the heater yet. If the car wasn't warm enough, it would just blow cold, frigid air out of the vents.

While she was waiting, Gail turned on the radio. WROQ was playing a soft, dreamy song, and she smiled as she thought of how she'd look dancing with Brett. He was tall and handsome, and she was tiny, blond and pretty. They'd look like Prince Charming and Cinderella at the Valentine's Day Dance. There would be photographs of them together. They always took pictures at the big dances for the school yearbook. And since the Valentine's Day Dance was a new tradition, they might just send out a photographer from the paper.

She would wear a beautiful white dress, like a bride. White was one of her very best colors. Of course, she hadn't saved enough money for a new dress, but she knew where her dad hid his stash. He'd never suspect her of taking it. He'd just think he'd blown it at some bar. And if he asked where she'd gotten the money for her dress, she'd lie and tell him that she'd earned it babysitting.

The car was warm now, and Gail flicked on the heater. She took off her mittens, tossed them on the passenger seat, and then saw it, the small gift-wrapped package that had been placed on the cracked vinyl seat cushion. It was beautifully wrapped in pink foil paper, tied with a silver bow. And under the package was a red envelope addressed to her.

Gail laughed out loud, she was so pleased. Brett must have come out here after basketball practice and left this gift in her car. It was almost enough to make her reconsider dumping him after the dance was over, but not quite. Brett wasn't right for her. She needed someone older, with much more money. There was no way she wanted to settle down and stay in Clearwater forever!

There was a smile on Gail's face as she opened the package. But her smile faded fast as she caught sight of the contents. Nestled inside, on a cushion of red velvet, was a half-heart necklace, just like the one that Tanya had received. The necklace was pretty, and normally Gail would have been delighted, but not now, not after what had happened to Tanya. If this was Brett's idea of a joke, he was sick!

Gail was so angry, her hands were shaking as she tore open the card. Maybe Brett thought this whole thing was funny, but she didn't! She was already planning out what she'd say when she confronted him at the Hungry Burger, when she caught sight of what was inside the envelope, and let out a gasp of fright.

It was another Valentine card from Cat! And the poem inside was identical to the one that he'd sent Tanya! It said, *Violets are blue, roses are red. An unworthy queen is better off dead.*

Gail didn't stop to think. She just ripped the card in half and threw it out the window. Then she put her car in gear and screeched out of the parking lot, swerving on the ice as she reached out to push the locks down on the doors. Cat had been here, right here in her car! And it was clear that he intended to kill her!

Gail's first instinct was to drive straight home, but she quickly reconsidered. Her father wasn't there, and she would be all alone. She needed people around her, people who could protect her from Cat.

She stopped at the stop sign on Fourth and Oak, just as the song on the radio ended, and Crazy Mark Hannah came on to announce another. "WROQ presents their daily Oldie but Goodie. Here's one you haven't heard in awhile, 'Moonshadow' by Cat Stevens."

As the familiar song started to play, Gail's eyes widened. And then she began to shake so violently, she could barely grip the wheel. Cat Stevens. Brett's last name was Stevens. Was it just a strange coincidence, or could Brett be Cat?

Suddenly it all clicked in place. Brett had told her how upset he was when Tanya hadn't asked him to the dance. What if he'd suspected that Tanya had found a new boyfriend? And what if he'd been so jealous that he'd killed her?!

Gail shook her head. No, that couldn't be true. She'd received the same threats from Cat, and Brett had no reason to be upset with her. Unless . . .

A frightened whimper formed deep in her throat, and Gail swallowed hard to hold it in. She would not give way to terror. And then she whispered the answer to her own question. "Brett found out I was lying!"

Brett hated liars. He'd said that once, when they were all gathered around the lunch table. Gail could remember his exact words . . . now, when it was too late.

They had been talking about Jerry Connors and the stolen car the police had found parked in the alley behind his parents' garage. Jerry had sworn that he hadn't known the car was there. And he'd claimed he had nothing to do with the theft, right up until the moment the police had found his fingerprints all over the steering wheel.

"I don't understand why he didn't tell the truth." Brett had sounded angry as he'd gazed around the table. *"They gave him plenty of chances to confess, and they would have gone easy on him if he'd just admitted he'd made a mistake. But Jerry lied, and liars always get in trouble. If a person's done something wrong, he should be brave enough to admit it. Lying is the coward's way out!"*

They had all nodded. But then Amy had spoken up. Amy was always the one to ask the philosophical questions. *"Which do you think is worse, Brett? Lying about stealing something. Or the stealing, itself?"*

"Lying. At least that's the way I look at it. I hate it when a person lies to me. It means they don't trust me enough to tell me the truth."

But how had Brett found out that she'd lied? Gail mentally reviewed what she'd told him. She'd said her mother was dead, and all her friends knew never to mention her mother. She was safe on that count. But then she'd said that her mother had been Homecoming Queen. And she'd given her mother's first name. And she'd also claimed that her father had been the captain of the football team.

Gail shuddered. Brett had probably gone up to the library to look at the old school yearbooks. And when he hadn't found a picture of her father or her mother, he'd known that she had lied to him.

But would he threaten her for a little white lie like that? Gail's mind spun in terrified circles. Everyone knew that Cat was crazy. His little poems were the work of a certified lunatic. And if Brett was Cat, he was definitely crazy enough to kill her.

A car honked behind her, and Gail almost jumped out of her skin. As she swiveled around to see who it was, she half-expected to see Brett glaring at her. But it wasn't Brett. It was only a red-haired lady with two small children in the backseat.

The lady rolled down her window and shouted something that Gail couldn't hear. Since she was no threat, Gail rolled her window down, too.

"What's the matter?" The lady looked concerned. "Are you in trouble?"

Gail almost said yes, until she realized that the lady was referring to car trouble. After all, she'd been parked at the stop sign for the past five minutes. "No. I . . . I'm okay."

Gail pulled away from the stop sign and drove down the street, even though she wasn't quite sure where to go, or what to do. Someone had threatened to kill her, and she was almost sure she knew who it was. What should a person do in a situation like that?

The police. The minute Gail thought of it, she turned on Fifth Street and headed toward the highway. The sheriff's department had handled everything when Tanya had died, and they would protect her from Cat.

The highway had just been plowed, and Gail increased her speed. The sheriff's station was only five miles away, and she felt a little better now that she'd decided on a course of action. She'd tell the sheriff everything, and he would arrest Brett. When Cat was locked behind bars, she would be safe.

No one seemed to be on the highway today. It was only four forty-five, and the few cars that made up the rush hour in Clearwater wouldn't appear on the highway until after the local businesses closed at five.

Gail reached out and flicked on her headlights. Nights came early in the winter. On the shortest day of the year, December twenty-first, the sun had set at four-seventeen. The days were a little longer now, but it still got dark before five.

The twin beams of her headlights made the world seem smaller. The road looked like an endless tunnel, with the banks of snow the snowplow had left at the sides of the road forming sheer white walls to define the space. The snowbanks were high, almost eight feet, and Gail knew that she had to drive carefully. If she went into a skid and slipped off the highway, she'd crash into a solid wall of snow.

As the darkness closed in, and the dusky sky turned as black as ink, Gail began to tremble again. She knew she was safe in the enclosed cocoon of her car, but now that the night was here, all sorts of horrible thoughts flashed through her mind. What if Brett guessed where she was going and came after her? If he didn't turn on his lights, she'd never know he was behind her until he rammed her with his car. Brett's Cadillac was much bigger than her Valiant. He could bump her right off the road. And then, when she was stuck in a ditch and helpless, he could . . .

Gail bit back a scream as she heard a thumping noise at the rear of her car. But then she realized that she'd just taken a curve very fast, and her bowling ball was in her trunk. As she'd swerved around the curve, it had rolled from side to side, bumping against the spare tire.

Without even thinking, Gail stepped down on her accelerator. The faster she got to the sheriff's station, the better. But then she heard another noise, one that made her wrinkle her forehead in concern. The engine in her Valiant was knocking!

Gail groaned, and said a little prayer. If her car broke down, and Brett came along behind her, she was dead meat. Somehow she had to get to the sheriff's station before that happened!

The Homestead Hill Grocery was right ahead of her, at the bottom of the hill, and Gail drew a sigh of relief as she passed it. Only two miles to go and she'd be there. All she had to do was drive up Homestead Hill, and then it was all downhill to the sheriff's station.

The Valiant began to knock harder as it struggled up the incline. Homestead Hill was a long, slow, gentle slope rising steadily for at least half a mile. But the last few hundred feet were steep, and Gail held her breath as the Valiant chugged steadily upward, finally cresting the top of the hill. She'd made it! Now all she had to do was floor it, and if the Valiant died on her, it would still coast all the way to the sheriff's station. It was a straight line from here to there, with the exception of one sharply sloped curve.

Gail stomped on the gas, and the Valiant faltered. Maybe flooring it wasn't such a good idea, after all. She pressed the gas pedal down very slowly, by increments, and that seemed to work just fine.

The lights on the dash flickered on and off, but that didn't disturb Gail. The Valiant had a short somewhere, and the dash lights had flickered ever since her father had given it to her. That was one of the reasons her father had handed Gail the keys to the Valiant, and bought a new car for himself. No one seemed to be able to fix it, and her father did a lot of night driving. He'd told her that the flickering lights were much too distracting.

Gail had solved the problem. Since the dash lights acted like a strobe, and they went on and off at regular intervals, she'd turned them down to the lowest setting and learned to blink in time with the flickers. This would have looked a little silly if anyone else had been in the car; but Gail seldom drove at night, and when she did, she was alone.

There was no doubt that she was picking up speed. Gail gave the Valiant a little more gas and wondered how fast she was going. There was only one way to tell, so she blinked several times and caught sight of the needle. Sixty miles an hour and she was going downhill. She didn't have to be a rocket scientist to know that sixty miles an hour was much too fast.

Since the roads were icy, Gail was very careful as she touched her brakes. New cars had anti-lock brakes, but the Valiant was ten years old. If her brakes locked up, she'd be in big trouble.

Gail gave a sigh of relief when she stepped on the pedal and her brakes didn't lock. But as the seconds ticked by, she realized that her car wasn't slowing. Gail stepped on her brake pedal again, but the Valiant didn't respond. What was the matter with her brakes?

She blinked and managed to catch a glimpse of the speedometer again. And she gasped as she realized that the needle was hovering at sixty-five. She was picking up too much speed, and Deadman's Curve, the site of several fatal accidents, was only a quarter of a mile away!

Gail didn't stop to worry about whether her brakes would lock or not. She just stomped on the pedal and pushed it all the way down to the floor, hanging on to the wheel as tightly as she could.

But absolutely nothing happened! The Valiant didn't swerve, or shudder, or skid. It just kept on going, faster and faster, racing toward Deadman's Curve.

Gail didn't scream. There wasn't time. She just fought the wheel, and prayed that she could steer her way around the curve. But when she caught another glimpse of the speedometer, she knew that her effort would be in vain. The Valiant had hurtled down the icy slope, and the needle on the speedometer was stuck at eighty!

That was when Gail screamed. It was a scream of terror and pure frustration. She was going to die, and she knew exactly who had sabotaged her brakes. It was Cat. He'd struck again, and there was no way she could tell anyone who'd done it. It was too late, much too late, and she was going to die!

The half-heart necklace. Gail reached down and found the box. She grabbed the necklace with one hand and slipped it over her neck. It was too late for her, but at least it would give the sheriff a clue.

And then the Valiant barreled into the curve, and Gail saw the guard rails flickering past her with a speed so fast they looked like toothpicks. She'd almost made it, almost managed to steer her way out of the curve, when the Valiant hit an icy patch and she hurtled into eternal darkness.

Twelve

Amy and Danny were sitting in a booth at the Hungry Burger, waiting for Colleen to join them. School had been awful. Everyone had walked around in shock, unable to believe that Gail was dead. Mr. Dorman had called for an assembly before first period, and he'd given them the sad news. Of course, most of them had heard it already. When Gail hadn't shown up to meet Brett after cheerleading practice, he'd gone out looking for her. He'd found her wrecked car, out on the highway, and driven straight to the sheriff's station to report it.

Bad news traveled fast, and Brett had called Neal to tell him. Neal had called Jessica, and Jessica had lost no time in calling Michele. The moment Michele had heard, she'd called Colleen and Amy, and within the hour, the news of Gail's fatal car accident was all over town. Amy's grandmother had told her an old saying, and it seemed to be true in Clearwater. Bad news could travel halfway around the world before good news had time to put on its shoes.

Amy took a sip of her chocolate milk shake. Chocolate milk shakes usually made her feel good, but today the therapy didn't seem to be working. All she could think about was how Gail's brakes had failed, resulting in her death. She looked up at Danny, and blinked back a tear. "Where do you think she was going?"

"I'm not sure." Danny knew immediately who she was talking about. He always did. "My guess is the sheriff's station. It's the only building out there, except for a couple of farms."

"But why would she go there?"

Danny shook his head. "I don't know for sure. But one of the deputies stopped by Ernie's garage while I was there, and he said Gail was wearing one of those half-heart necklaces, just like Tanya."

"Oh, my God!" Amy shivered. "Do they know who gave it to her?"

Danny shook his head. "Do you know if she ever got that third card from Cat?"

"I don't know whether she did or not. But Jessica and Michele left the school before Gail did. And when Gail went up to her locker to get her coat, it could have been there, waiting for her. That's where she found the first two."

"But how about the necklace? The box was too big to fit through the vent in her locker."

"You're right. I didn't think of that." Amy frowned, her mind whirling. And then she nodded as she thought of a possible explanation. "I know what might have happened. Cat could have stuck it in her car."

"That makes sense. And it would explain what Gail was doing out on the highway. She might have figured out who Cat was, and gone straight to the sheriff to tell him."

"But she never made it. Cat killed her first. We know that, but we can't prove it. I wish Gail could have left us some sort of clue."

"She did." Danny looked very serious. "Gail was wearing the half-heart necklace. I think she knew that she was going to die, and she put on the necklace to let us know that Cat was responsible."

Amy's eyes welled up with tears. "Poor Gail! It must have been awful, trapped in her car, knowing she was going to die."

"Yeah." Danny gave Amy another hug. "Come on, Amy. Crying's not going to do any good. Let's concentrate on proving our case against Cat. The first thing we need is motive. Why did Cat kill Gail?"

"Because she was going to be Valentine's Day Queen. It's the same reason he killed Tanya."

"Okay. I'll buy that. But why didn't he want them to be queen?"

Amy looked at Danny in surprise. "He told us why. Remember the Valentine cards? Cat thought the queen should be kind, faithful and true. And Tanya and Gail didn't pass his test, so he killed them because they were unworthy."

"We know that, but the sheriff doesn't buy it. Brett said he told him about the Valentine cards, but the sheriff thinks they were just a prank . . . especially since no one can prove that Tanya and Gail were murdered. The sheriff has listed both of their deaths as accidental."

"So what do we do?" Amy looked worried.

"I'm not sure. What do you think we should do?"

"I think we should cancel the contest before someone else is killed."

Danny nodded. "That makes good sense to me. But it'll be pretty rough on Jessica. She's in the lead, now that Tanya and Gail are dead."

"I know. She's already planning out what to wear to her coronation. I don't think I'd better even suggest it."

"Why not?"

Amy sighed. "Because Jessica will say it's just sour grapes on my part."

"Sour grapes?" Danny stared down at her with a puzzled expression. "What does that mean?"

"It means they'll assume that the only reason I want to cancel the contest is because I couldn't win."

"But you could! You're pretty, and popular, and you stand just as much of a chance as any other girl."

"Right." Amy couldn't help sounding sarcastic. "I'm so popular, I don't even have a date for the dance. And the guy I was going to ask, the mysterious person who voted for me, turns out to be Cat!"

"Okay. He was a bad choice. But you can get a date for the dance. I told you before . . . ask me."

Amy frowned slightly. She knew Danny was only being kind. "Thanks, but I don't accept charity. And the only reason you'd agree to be my date is because I'm your sister's best friend."

"Think again, Amy. I'd never take a girl I didn't like to a dance. Life's too short to be stuck with a loser all night."

"You'd go with me if I asked you?"

Danny nodded. "Sure. Are you asking?"

"Uh . . . yes. I mean . . . I guess so." Amy's cheeks began to burn, and she knew her face was turning red. "But I don't want you to do me any favors!"

"Okay. I won't. But you have to do one for me."

Amy groaned. "Oh-oh. Colleen and I are already doing your laundry. What else do you want?"

"I want something much more personal, something only you can do."

Danny was grinning the grin everyone said was sexy, and Amy knew he had something definite in mind. She blushed even harder, and looked down at the table.

"Don't you want to know what it is?"

Danny's voice was low and intimate, teasing and sexy at the same time. It made Amy look up to find that he was staring at her intently.

"Oh . . . well . . ." Amy's voice faltered. She found it very difficult to meet Danny's eyes, but she did. And then she took a deep breath and blurted out the question. "All right, Danny. What is it?"

"I want you to wear something sexy. You have a very good figure and you should show it off. Black silk would be nice, or something in bright red satin. Just make sure it has a low neck. I don't want to blow my reputation by going out with someone who's dressed up like Little Bo Peep."

Amy knew her face was beet-red. She'd never looked like Little Bo Peep in her life! "Sorry, Danny . . . I'm fresh out of black silk dresses. And I don't have any bright red satin, either."

"No problem." Danny was still grinning his sexy grin. "I'll buy you a dress, the next time I get out to the mall. What size do you wear?"

"I . . . I . . . that's none of your business!"

Danny leaned forward to stare at her. His gaze started at the top of her head and traveled all the way down to the tips of her toes. "Okay. You should wear about an eleven. Or maybe a nine, if it has a full skirt. Am I right?"

Amy's mouth dropped open. Danny was right! But she was too embarrassed to reply.

"That's one of the cute things about you, Amy. You're really shy, and I know it's not an act. I'll ask Colleen all your sizes. I know you two don't have any secrets from each other." Danny slipped his arm around Amy's shoulders again, and gave her a little squeeze. "You'll wear the dress I pick out for you, won't you?"

Amy wished she could sink through the floor. If Danny picked out her dress, it was bound to be something spectacular, something so revealing she'd curl up and die rather than wear it in public. But if she didn't wear it, his feelings would be hurt. Amy wasn't at all sure why she was worried about that, but she knew she didn't want to hurt Danny's feelings.

She simply had to think of a good excuse so she wouldn't have to accept the dress!

"Look, Danny." Amy latched on to an excuse and ran with it. "My parents would never let me accept a dress from you. It's too personal. And much too expensive. A gift like that just wouldn't be . . . uh . . . appropriate."

Danny nodded. "You're right. I should have thought of that. Your birthday's in March, isn't it?"

"Uh . . . yes." Amy was surprised that Danny had remembered her birthday.

"I'll talk to Colleen, and we'll both go in on your present this year. Your parents will let you accept an early birthday gift from both of us, won't they?"

"Well . . . uh . . . yes, I think they will. But you really shouldn't . . ."

"It's settled, then." Danny gave her a little hug. "I'll look forward to seeing you in that dress, Amy."

Before Amy could say another word, Colleen came through

the front door of the Hungry Burger. She headed straight for their booth and slid in on the other side.

"Hi, guys." Colleen was breathless. "You'll never guess what just happened to me!"

"What happened?" Amy was extremely grateful for the interruption. Her conversation with Danny had been so personal, she was embarrassed.

"Jessica and Michele want me to take Gail's place! The cheers don't look good with only two cheerleaders, so I'm going to join them at the game tonight!"

"They must be desperate." Danny grinned at his sister. "You're not really the cheerleader type."

"I'm not *that* bad! Besides, it's just until they can hold try-outs for some new girls."

Amy nodded. "Congratulations, Colleen. I think you'll make a great cheerleader. Are you going to the try-outs when they hold them?"

Colleen shrugged. "I don't know. I guess it all depends on whether I make a fool of myself at the game tonight. You'll watch and tell me if I look okay, won't you, Amy?"

"Of course." Amy smiled at her. And then she gave a little sigh. "I'm going to miss talking to you at the game, though. It'll be the first time I've ever gone to a game alone."

Danny shook his head. "You won't be alone. And I guarantee you won't miss Colleen. You'll have me to talk to, and I'm much more interesting."

"Says who?" Colleen glared at him.

"Says me." Danny slid out of the booth and stood up. And then he reached down to ruffle Amy's hair. "I have to run. I'll drop Colleen off at the school at six-thirty, and I'll pick you up at seven, okay?"

"Uh . . . sure. I'll be ready."

Amy stared after him as he made his way through the crowd and went out the front door. Danny really was handsome, now that he'd cut all the green dye from his hair.

"I don't believe it!"

Amy turned to see that Colleen was grinning at her. "You don't believe what?"

"I don't believe my brother! He asked you for a date, and you said yes."

"I did?" Amy began to blush. "But it's not exactly a date, Colleen. Danny's just giving me a ride to the game. He gives us rides all the time. You know that."

Colleen shook her head. "I know he does, but it's more than that. He's dropping me off, and *then* he's picking you up. And he's sitting with you at the game. That's a date, Amy. Maybe you didn't realize it, but you just made a date with Danny."

"Oh, I don't think so." Amy knew she was starting to blush, so she looked down at the table. "He's just being nice because he knew I didn't want to sit alone. It's just friendship, Colleen. That's all."

"Sure. I'm going to order a burger. Do you want me to get something for you?"

"No, thanks. I don't want to spoil my appetite. Mom's making french fries and hamburgers for dinner. And we're having hot fudge sundaes for dessert."

"You're kidding!" Colleen looked surprised. "What happened to her tofu diet?"

"She threw out the tofu the minute she read the new diet sheet that came in the mail. We're having barbecued chicken and potato salad tomorrow night, and pot roast on Sunday. Dad's really happy about Mom's new diet."

"This new diet . . ." Colleen started to grin. "Is it from Y.M.A.?"

"Of course. Mom's really impressed by the way it contains something from every food group. And she loves the way we rave about her cooking. It's turning out exactly the way Danny said it would when he helped me make up the diet sheet."

"Danny helped you?" Colleen's grin widened. "You're spending a lot of time with my brother, aren't you?"

"Well . . . yes. I guess I am."

"But you still say you're just friends?"

"Of course." Amy nodded quickly. "Danny's not at all serious about me. He's still dating Megan."

"No, he's not. They broke up, almost a week ago. You're the only girl he's seeing now."

Amy started to blush again. She certainly wasn't going to tell Colleen that she'd invited Danny to the Valentine's Day Dance. Colleen would assume it was a real date, when it was just two friends going somewhere together. "That doesn't mean anything, Colleen. He's just between girls, that's all."

"Hmm." Colleen lifted her eyebrows. "Maybe you're right. You're really not his type at all."

Amy felt an uncharacteristic stab of jealousy. "What's *that* supposed to mean?"

"You're much too innocent to date Danny. And you're much too nice."

"Oh." Amy wasn't sure if she should feel complimented or not. "Thanks . . . I think."

"You're welcome. I'm starving. All that exercise at cheerleading practice made me hungry. Are you sure I can't get you something to eat?"

"I'm positive."

"Okay. Save my place." Colleen took one step toward the counter, but then she turned back, a thoughtful expression on her face. "Look, Amy . . . I love my brother, but you're my best friend. And I think you should watch out around Danny. He's older, and he's got lots of experience with girls."

"But Colleen . . . it's not like that. I told you, we're just friends."

"That's what they all say, at first. But I've watched Danny start up with a lot of girls, starting with the Hansen twins when he was in Junior High, right up through Megan Stillwell last week. The only one he was ever halfway serious about was Karen Thomas."

"Danny dated Karen?" Amy was surprised. She hadn't heard about that. "When?"

"It was right after he came home last spring. Karen's parents didn't like it, but she went out with him anyway. And then she died, and it was all over."

"That's sad." Amy sighed.

"I know, but that's not the point. Believe me, Amy . . . I've seen my brother in action, and I know Danny's definitely getting ready to make a move on you."

Amy waited until Colleen had left, and then she began to frown. Was Colleen right? Was Danny getting ready to make a move on her? She really didn't think so, but if he was, exactly how would she deal with that?!

Thirteen

By the end of the game, Amy was convinced that Colleen was wrong. Danny was friendly and nice, but he hadn't said anything that made her think he was about to make a move on her. When Hamilton High won, they'd jumped to their feet and he'd hugged her; but everyone was hugging everyone else, and Amy was sure that it really didn't mean anything at all.

"Hey, Amy!" Michele ran up to them as they were leaving the gym. "I'm having a post-game party at the store, and you're both invited. My folks are gone for the weekend."

"You're having a party at the store?" Amy looked surprised. Michele's family ran a furniture store.

"There's more room at the store, and it'll be fun. I hooked up one of the sound systems my dad sells, and there's plenty of couches and chairs. The party starts in thirty minutes, so be there."

Danny turned to Amy as Michele raced off to invite more people. "How about it, Amy? Are you up for a party?"

"Well . . . I guess so. But I thought you weren't interested in teenage parties."

"Normally, I'm not. But I've never been to a party in a furniture store. It'll be a first." Danny slipped his arm around Amy's shoulders and grinned down at her. "I'm big on firsts. You know . . . first date, first kiss, first love, things like that. How about you? Are you big on firsts?"

"Oh . . . well . . . that depends on which firsts you're talking about." Amy wondered if Colleen had told Danny that she'd never gone on a date, never been kissed, and never really been in love. She didn't want to say anything that might show Danny how naive she was, so she changed the subject to a much safer first. "How about your first bicycle? Do you remember that?"

Danny laughed as he pushed open the door, and they stepped out into the cold. "Of course. It was a shiny red Huffy, with training wheels. The first thing I did was take them off. I didn't want the other kids to think I was a sissy."

"But training wheels help while you're learning to ride." Amy frowned slightly. "How did you learn to ride without them?"

"Very painfully. I skinned up my knees for the first week, but I finally caught on. Colleen probably told you. I never do things the easy way."

Amy nodded. "Like coming back to finish school when you're two years older than everyone else. That can't be easy for you."

"You're right." Danny nodded. "But it's something I have to do. I thought it would be so great to be out in the real world . . . but it wasn't."

Danny unlocked his car and opened the door so that Amy could get in. She waited until he'd slid in behind the wheel, and then she turned to him. "Was it scary, out there all alone?"

"Not at first." Danny started the engine to let it warm up. "I was too dumb to be scared. I didn't get scared until I realized that I didn't know how to do a lot of things that most people take for granted."

"Like what?" Amy was curious.

"Like figuring out the bills and paying them every month. I went straight from living at home to renting my own apartment. I'd never been on my own before, and I had no idea how to live on a budget. I made enough money, but I spent it as fast as I got it. And then I got into big trouble at the end of the month."

"Tell me about it." Amy leaned back against the seat and smiled up at him.

"Okay." Danny slipped his arm around her shoulders and pulled her close. "When I signed my contract, the money seemed like a fortune. I'd never made that much before, so I went right out and rented this really great apartment. I didn't realize that I'd only get part of my salary."

"Only part? I don't understand."

"Taxes." Danny shrugged. "That's the difference between gross and net. It gave me my gross salary on the contract; but when I got my first paycheck, they took out all the taxes, and the total was a lot smaller than I thought it would be."

"But it was still enough, wasn't it?"

"It would have been if I hadn't gone overboard. But everything I bought had to be the best that money could buy. I got the best sound system, the best television, the best furniture, the best clothes, the best motorcycle, you name it. And the food . . . I was so stupid, you wouldn't believe it!"

"I'd believe it." Amy giggled, and snuggled a little closer. The car was beginning to warm, and it was cozy, sitting close to Danny in the darkened parking lot. "Why was food expensive?"

"Because I didn't know how to cook. I went out to the best restaurants, and that adds up. It finally got to the point where I couldn't afford it anymore."

Amy nodded. "So what did you do?"

"I bought a cookbook, and I followed the recipes."

"That makes sense."

"Not really."

Danny was grinning as he pulled away from her, put the car in gear and drove out of the parking lot, but Amy was a bit disappointed. She had liked the way he'd held her close, and she hadn't wanted it to end quite yet. She felt her hopes rise as they pulled up in front of Porter's Fine Furniture. The store was dark, and there were no other cars on the street. Perhaps Danny would hold her close again while they waited for the others to arrive.

"We must be the first ones here." Danny parked directly in front of the store, and let the car idle.

Amy nodded. "I guess we'll just have to wait until Michele shows up. Tell me more about the cookbook, Danny. Why didn't it make sense?"

"I bought the wrong one. I picked up a copy of Julia Child's *Mastering the Art of French Cooking*. I'd seen her on television, and everything she did looked so easy."

"Oh-oh!" Amy started to laugh. "What happened?"

Danny grinned and pulled her over next to him again. "Well . . . I learned to make *Soupe Catalane Aux Poivrons.*"

"Wonderful. What's that?"

"It's Catalonian pepper and leek soup, very good, but it takes forever to cook. And then I tried *Ris De Veau A La Financiere.*"

Amy nodded and snuggled up to Danny's side. "I'm impressed, but I don't know what that is, either."

"Braised sweetbreads garnished with truffles, mushrooms, and olives. That was very expensive, and once I found out what sweetbreads were, I never made it again."

Amy frowned slightly. Should she admit that she didn't know what sweetbreads were? Danny would probably think she was an idiot, but it was best to be honest. "Sorry, Danny . . . I don't know anything about sweetbreads. What are they?"

"Maybe I shouldn't tell you." Danny looked down at her in a way that made Amy's knees weak. "It might make you sick."

"Of course it won't! Julia Child is a world-famous chef. If she makes it, it's got to be good."

"You're sure?"

"I'm positive." Amy gave an emphatic nod. "So tell me, Danny . . . what are sweetbreads?"

"They're the pancreas and thymus glands from a calf."

"Oh, gross!" Amy shuddered. "That's not funny, Danny!"

"I know. And it really wasn't funny when I spent the whole day cooking a gourmet meal that I couldn't eat!"

"You mean, it's really true?" Amy pulled back to stare at Danny. "You're not just putting me on?"

"It's true. When Renee asked me what we were having for dinner, I told her. And that was when she mentioned what sweetbreads were. She thought it was wonderful that I was so cosmopolitan."

Amy's eyes widened. Who was Renee? She wished she had the nerve to ask, but it was really none of her business. "What did the sweetbreads taste like?"

"I don't know. I just pushed them around on my plate and filled up on the bread. And the next morning, I called Colleen and asked her to send me some of Mom's recipes for real meat and potatoes."

Amy couldn't stand it any longer. She simply had to ask. "Uh . . . Danny? Who's Renee?"

"My agent's ex-wife. We lived together for a while. Renee was an actress, very beautiful, and very expensive. That's one of the ways I blew all my money. She wasn't satisfied with dinner at McDonald's. She wanted to go to trendy places, where she could be seen."

"Oh." Amy nodded. And she wished that she hadn't asked. There was no reason for her to feel jealous, but she did. Danny had lived with a beautiful actress. "Do you . . . uh . . . still see her?"

Danny shook his head. "We only lasted for a couple of months. Renee had a thing about singers, and I was the newest guy in town. She moved on when a newer guy came on the scene."

"That's . . . that's awful!" Amy stared up at Danny in shock. "You must have been terribly hurt."

"I was, at first. But then I realized that it's the sort of thing you should expect when you're involved with the rock world. The hours are insane, the groupies steal everything of yours that isn't nailed down, the performances drain every ounce of your energy, and it's impossible to have any kind of normal life. That's one of the reasons I got out. I could have stayed and started another band. I had plenty of backing. But I had enough sense to realize that it wasn't the life for me. I'd rather be here, at Hamilton High, with you and Colleen. You care about me as a person."

There was a long silence. Amy wasn't quite sure what to say. But then Danny reached out and tipped up her chin so she had to meet his eyes.

"You do care about me, don't you, Amy?"

Amy nodded. Danny's eyes were so intense, it was hard for her to speak. "I . . . I . . . of course I do! You know that."

"But how much do you care?" Danny began to grin as he closed the gap between them. "Do you care this much?"

Amy trembled as Danny came closer and closer. Now he was so close, he was almost brushing her lips with his. Amy's mind spun in crazy circles. Was he going to kiss her? Should she pull away? Or should she wrap her arms around his neck, and let him do what she'd been wanting for what seemed like forever? But just as she felt the first feather-light brush of his lips, there was a honk behind them, and Amy pulled back, startled.

"Saved by the honk." Danny chuckled as he turned around to see who it was. "You must have a guardian angel, Amy."

"I . . . I . . . yes. I guess I must." Amy scraped a place clear on the window to look out. Michele and Colleen were parked behind them and as she watched, two more cars pulled up.

"Looks like we have company." Danny shrugged, and turned off the ignition. "We'd better go, or we'll be the subject of a lot of gossip at school tomorrow."

"You're right." Amy sighed, and began to button up her coat. She wasn't quite sure whether she was glad or disappointed to see her friends arrive.

"Should we continue this discussion later?" Danny reached out to touch her cheek with the tip of his finger. "Or would you rather forget it ever happened?"

Amy drew in her breath sharply. Shakespeare had been wrong. To be, or not to be, wasn't the question. It was to kiss, or not to kiss. And even though it was far from appropriate, Amy wanted Danny to kiss her with every fiber of her being.

"Well . . . ?" Danny was still grinning his sexy grin. "What's the answer, Amy?"

Amy let her breath out in a shuddering sigh as she made up her mind. "I'd like to continue . . . please."

Fourteen

It was the strangest party that Amy had ever attended. The Porter Fine Furniture store was arranged in a series of cubicles resembling rooms, each one displaying a grouping of furniture. The walls of the rooms were less than five feet high, so Michele's father could see when shoppers had stopped to linger over a particular selection.

Michele had planned her party carefully. She'd used the dining room groupings for food, and the living room groupings for drinks and entertainment. She'd even allocated one bedroom cubicle, the one with the largest king-sized bed, as a place to put coats and boots. It was an enormous party. Michele had invited almost everyone she knew from Hamilton High. Friends and acquaintances were wandering from one cubicle to another, stopping to eat, or listen to music, or relax on over-stuffed lounge chairs and couches. Porter's Fine Furniture store was a perfect place for a party. It gave the illusion of a mansion with countless interconnected rooms, and there was always a corner for privacy.

Amy and Danny started in the Mediterranean dining room, helping themselves to the big bowl of chips and dip on the polished mahogany wood table. Then they worked their way to the Danish Modern living room for cold drinks which were set out on the teakwood bar. They ended up in a cubicle that resembled a family room, with a conversation pit that featured a U-shaped leather couch, and two leather swivel recliners arranged around a low circular table. Neal and Jessica were seated on one side of the couch, Michele and Colleen were in the middle, and Brett and Kevin were lounging in the recliners.

"Hey . . . how's it going, guys?" Brett looked up as they walked in. "Great party, huh?"

Amy nodded. It *was* a good party. There was dancing in the large living room with the fake fireplace, and Michele had put tapes of movies on all the large-screen television sets. But everyone here in the family room looked very subdued.

"What's the matter?" Danny asked the question that was on Amy's mind. "You all look worried about something."

Kevin nodded. "We are. When Jessica went up to her locker, after the game, she found a Valentine card from Cat."

"Oh, no!" Amy turned to Jessica with alarm. "What did it say?"

"The usual. Except the rhyme was different this time. Maybe he's getting bored, writing the same thing all the time."

Amy sat down on the other side of the couch and reached for the red envelope that Jessica pushed to her across the low table. She opened it and started to frown as she scanned the message inside.

"What does it say?" Danny sat down next to her and slipped his arm around her shoulders.

"It says, 'Roses *are red, and crowns are gold. A Valentine queen has values to uphold.*' And it's signed, '*Cat.*'"

Danny leaned over her shoulder to examine the card. "It looks like Cat's printing."

"I think so, too, but we'd better check. I saved the vote I got today." Amy reached in her purse and pulled out the red heart she'd saved after they'd counted the votes. "Here it is."

Brett got up to look at the card. And then he examined Amy's vote. "It's the same as the last time. It's definitely Cat's printing."

"But who *is* he?" Jessica's voice held a desperate note. "We've got to find out!"

Amy nodded. And then she cleared her throat. What she was about to say would be about as popular as a pack of dogs in a sausage factory, but she knew she had to suggest it. "I think we should consider canceling the queen contest. It's just too dangerous."

"You want to cancel the contest?" Jessica looked as if Amy had just slapped her in the face. "But that's not fair!"

"I know it's not. But we all care about you, Jessica. And you're in the lead. Cat's already sent you one card. What if he sends you more?"

"Amy's got a point." Michele nodded. "Maybe Cat didn't have anything to do with what happened to Tanya and Gail, but you're still taking a terrible chance."

Jessica shrugged. "Maybe I am, but it'll be worth it if I get to be queen. Besides . . . I don't think Cat is dangerous. He just sends those cards as a sick practical joke, that's all. What happened to Tanya and Gail is just a coincidence."

"A *coincidence?*" Amy was shocked. "How can you possibly believe that? Tanya and Gail were both in the lead for queen, they both got Valentine cards from Cat, and they're both dead. There's got to be a connection."

"Not necessarily. Tanya died because she tripped on the stairs, and Gail was in a car accident. It's awful, but these things happen."

"How about the half-heart necklaces they were both wearing?" Danny spoke up to defend Amy's position. "That has to mean something."

"Maybe. But I've got that worked out. If someone sends me a half-heart necklace, I'll just throw it in the trash."

"But how about the threats Cat makes?" Amy took up the argument again. "He says you have to pass his test to be queen, and then he warns you that an unworthy queen is better off dead. Doesn't that worry you at all?"

Jessica laughed and hugged Neal. "It did, but I'm not worried now. Neal's promised to be my personal bodyguard. He's going to stick to me like glue, until the night of my coronation."

"That should work." Kevin nodded. "Neal's big enough to take on anyone that bothers you. But what about when he goes to basketball practice? He can't be with you then."

"I'll have him drop me off at the hardware store, and Dad'll protect me. Or I'll stay at home with Mom. There's really nothing to worry about as long as I'm with someone all the time."

"Will you promise me that you'll never go anywhere alone?" Amy was still concerned.

"Sure. I'll even take my mother to the bathroom with me if it makes you feel any better. I think it's sweet that you're so concerned about me, Amy . . . but I really think you're going off the deep end over this whole thing. I'll live to be the Valentine's Day Queen. You can bet on it!"

Michele raised her eyebrows, and laughed. "I'd watch my back if I were you. Don't forget that I'm in second place. If something happens to you, I'll be next in line for queen."

"Michele!" Amy was shocked.

"Relax, Amy." Michele leaned over to give Jessica a hug. "Jessica's been my best friend since the first grade. She knows I was only kidding, don't you, Jessica?"

"Of course I know."

Jessica nodded, but Amy noticed that she wasn't smiling. And the moment that Michele stopped hugging her, Jessica moved closer to Neal. Amy wished that she'd voiced her objections to the queen contest more strenuously when Tanya had first suggested it. All this competition wasn't good, and it was ruining friendships that had been in existence for years.

Danny's arm tightened around her shoulders, and Amy looked up to find him watching Jessica and Michele. Danny had noticed how Jessica had moved away from Michele, and Amy was sure it had bothered him as much as it had bothered her.

"Let's go get some food." Danny stood up and held out his hand to Amy. "Does anybody want anything?"

Michele nodded. "You could bring us back a pizza. They're all on the table in the Colonial dining room."

"Anything else?" Amy got to her feet.

There were several other requests, and Amy and Danny agreed to bring back all the food they could carry. After they'd left the family room area, Danny led Amy into one of the deserted living room cubicles and pulled her down on a couch. "Amy? I have to ask you something."

"Yes?" Amy frowned slightly. Danny looked very serious.

"All the rest of the girls want to win the contest. How about you? Don't you want to be queen?"

Amy looked up at him, and shook her head. And then she gave a relieved smile. "No way, Danny. And don't you dare vote for me! I'm really glad that I'm not even in the running."

The party was still going strong when Amy and Danny left. It was eleven-thirty, and Amy had a midnight curfew. They parked in front of her house with fifteen minutes to spare, and Amy hesitated, her hand on the door. Would Danny remember what she'd said earlier, about continuing their conversation?

"Oh, no you don't!" Danny reached out to grab her hand. "Don't forget the promise you made."

"What promise?"

Amy tried to sound as if she didn't know what he was talking about, but it didn't work very well. Danny just laughed and pulled her close.

"Hey . . . you know exactly what I'm talking about, don't you?"

Amy nodded. She had to be truthful. "Yes. I do. But you made a promise, too, that night at the game."

"I did?" Danny sounded surprised. "What did I promise?"

"I asked you if you'd ever take advantage of me, and you said you wouldn't."

Danny sighed. "That's because I didn't know I'd feel this way about you. Are you going to hold me to it?"

"Yes."

"And you think that if I kissed you, I'd be taking advantage of you?"

Amy thought for a minute, and then she shook her head. "No. Not as long as I wanted you to."

Danny started to grin his sexy grin. "And do you want me to kiss you?"

"I . . . uh . . ." Amy stopped. Thank goodness it was dark! She knew she was blushing, because her cheeks felt as if they were on fire.

"Well?"

Danny was still smiling his sexy grin, and Amy began to shiver in excitement. "Yes . . . I do want you to kiss me. I'm not sure if it's a good idea, but I thought it over and I . . ."

Amy's voice trailed off as Danny reached out to tip up her chin with his hand. Her mouth was still open, and she clamped it shut as his face came closer and closer. She'd never been this close to anyone before, and it was a little frightening to know that she was alone in a car with someone who could make her tremble all over.

"If you keep your eyes open, they'll probably cross."

There was laughter in his voice, and Amy winced as she quickly shut her eyes. Would he know that she'd never been kissed before?

And then she waited, and waited, holding her breath for the moment his lips would touch hers.

"Sweet."

Amy felt the word, even more than she heard it. It was a puff of air against her lips, and she had the insane urge to giggle. Of course, giggling wasn't appropriate . . . but, then, neither was sitting here, holding her breath, waiting for Danny to kiss her.

And then Danny's lips brushed hers, very lightly. And Amy felt a current of pleasure ripple through her, from her toes all the way up to the hair on her head. She sighed, and did something without thinking, something she never would have done if she'd stopped to consider it carefully. She reached up with her arms and placed them around his neck, pulling him even closer. And then she sighed again, and moved her mouth against his.

The kiss went on for what seemed like forever, lips pressed together, warm and soft, with a firmness that was surprising. Amy sighed again, and let her fingers touch Danny's shoulders, moving up to feel the short hair at the base of his neck. Although her eyes were closed, she thought she could see him staring at her in the darkness. But it was only an illusion because his image was replaced with swirling spots of bright red, and electric blue, and deeply gorgeous purple.

"Wow!" Amy breathed the word against his lips and snuggled a little closer. Kissing Danny was wonderful, much better than she'd thought it would be. But then it was over, and she opened her eyes to find him smiling at her. So she said the first thing that came to her mind.

"Thank you, Danny." Amy felt limp, as if she'd been swimming in the river all day and now she was stretched out on the sand, basking in the warmth of the sun. "I'm glad you kissed me."

Danny chuckled, and then he laughed, a deep, rolling sound that made Amy feel good. "You're amazing, Amy. You haven't learned any of the tricks. Most girls would have played the game a little, teased and flirted, things like that . . . and then they would have acted shocked when I kissed them. But you just say whatever's on your mind."

"I know." Amy sighed. "That's always been my worst fault."

"It's not a fault. It's wonderful. So tell me . . . how did you like your first kiss?"

"You . . . you knew!" Amy's cheeks turned hot with embarrassment. Colleen must have told him that she'd never been kissed.

Danny laughed. And then he said something that let her know he'd read her mind again. "No, Colleen didn't tell me."

"Then . . . how did you know? Was I terribly bad at kissing?"

Danny chuckled again. "You're not bad at all. As a matter of fact, I'd say you're a natural. But when you thanked me, I figured that it was your first kiss."

"Oh. I see." Amy nodded. "Is that why you stopped? Because it was my first kiss?"

Danny nodded. "That's part of it. And the other part is that I promised I wouldn't take advantage of you."

"But you weren't! I . . . I liked it." Amy felt terribly disappointed. "If I'd been older and more experienced, would you have kept on kissing me?"

"Well . . . yeah. I guess so. But that kiss would have been different."

"How?" Amy couldn't help being curious.

"Well . . . uh . . ." Danny stopped, and frowned. "Look, Amy. It's something I can't really explain."

"Then show me."

Danny shook his head. "No, Amy. I can't do that."

"Why not? Just pretend that I'm Renee, and kiss me the way you'd kiss her."

Danny laughed, and reached out to tousle her hair. "I really don't think that's a very good idea."

"Well, I do!" Amy faced him squarely. "Come on, Danny. How am I supposed to learn how to kiss when no one will teach me?"

Danny started to laugh. "Asking a question like that could get you into a lot of trouble. It's a good thing you're with me, and not some other guy."

"That's just it. I *am* with you, and I know I can trust you. That's why I'm asking you to show me."

"You're sure that's what you want?"

Danny was grinning his sexy grin, and Amy's breath caught in her throat. But she really wanted to know, so she nodded. "Yes. I'm positive."

"You really know what you're asking?"

"Of course." Amy nodded, and moved over to cuddle up against him. That felt so wonderful she reached out to wrap her arms around his neck. Then she smiled up at him, and sighed. "Go ahead, Danny. I'm ready."

Danny groaned, deep in his throat. And then he bent down to kiss her lightly. "Open your lips, Amy."

"But . . . why?" Amy stared up at him.

"Just do it. You want me to kiss you like I kissed Renee, don't you?"

Amy nodded, and parted her lips. And then she gasped as Danny gathered her close in his arms and took possession of her mouth. His warm tongue slid over her lips, and darted between them, tasting the heat of her mouth.

"Oooh!" Amy gasped, and her mind floated free. Danny's tongue was darting into her mouth, licking and tasting, making delicious shivers run through her whole trembling body. She couldn't think, or analyze what she was feeling. She could only feel, and gasp with wonderful pleasure.

"Enough?" Danny pulled back to touch her nose with the tip of his finger.

"Nooo." Amy didn't wait for him to ask again. She just pulled his face down to hers and started the kiss again. It was different this time, and it lasted even longer. And when Amy pulled away, she was breathless.

"Oooh, Danny! That was wonderful! I felt hot and cold at the same time, and my toes started to tingle!"

Danny threw back his head and laughed. "That's definitely a first. I've never had that effect on a girl before."

"That's because I'm not just any girl. Let's do it again and see what happens."

Danny raised his eyebrows. "You're really asking for trouble, Amy, and it's getting late. Don't you think you'd better . . ."

"No." Amy reached out for him again, before he could raise any more objections. "Once more, Danny . . . please? Then I'll go in, I promise."

Danny laughed, but Amy noticed that this time he reached for her. His lips came down on hers, and she sighed as the kiss deepened. Again, she didn't think. She just reacted to the thrilling sensations flowing through her. Every inch of her body felt graceful, and she seemed to be floating on a sea of pure pleasure, riding the waves and cresting their peaks for an eternity.

Her tongue swept out to merge with his, thrusting and licking and tasting. And her fingers wound through his hair and stroked the sides of his head. She felt suddenly beautiful and brilliant and very, very desirable. And then it was over, and he was holding her in his arms and smiling at her.

"How was it, Amy?" Danny brushed back her hair with his hand in an incredibly tender gesture.

"Ooh . . . it was wonderful! And the music . . . it was incredible!"

"Music?"

"Yes. I'm not exactly sure, but it was like classical, and folk, and jazz, and blues, and the best of rock, all rolled up into one. It was the most fabulous music I've ever heard!"

"Amy?" Danny's voice was shaking slightly. "Will you promise me something?"

"Oh, yes! What is it?"

"Remember when I promised not to take advantage of you?"

"Yes, Danny." Amy breathed the words. She'd never felt so happy and content in her life. "I remember."

"I'd like a promise from you, too."

"Yes, Danny." Amy smiled up at him. "What is it?"

"I want you to promise not to take advantage of me!"

Fifteen

Jessica was smiling as she turned off the alarm clock and got out of bed on Monday morning. Normally, she hated to go to school on Mondays, but this Monday was different. After two whole days of being chaperoned by Neal and her parents, Jessica was looking forward to a day at school, a day when she didn't have to worry about what was lurking around the next corner. Despite what she'd told Amy, Jessica was worried about what had happened to Tanya and Gail. She didn't think that Tanya and Gail had actually been murdered; but they had been the victims of very bad luck, and she didn't want to take any chances.

For one brief moment, on Sunday night, Jessica had almost caved in under the pressure. She'd actually picked up the phone to call Amy to tell her that she agreed, and the contest should be canceled.

Since Neal had gone home, and there had been nothing to do, Jessica had spent her time writing letters. She'd written one to her grandmother that was long overdue, one to her favorite aunt in Idaho, and a third to a boy she'd met when the Hamilton High cheerleaders had gone to a convention at the University.

Since Neal didn't know about the college boy she'd met, Jessica had walked down the inside stairs to leave the letters in the mailbox that was attached to the brick wall outside, next to the plate glass window that displayed the newest items her father had ordered for the hardware store. The mailbox was only a step from the door, so she'd felt safe going outside alone. But when Jessica had pulled open the latch to drop her letters inside, there had been an envelope in the box.

Jessica had pulled out the envelope without really looking at it, and carried it back inside. She'd assumed that the postman had come back after the regular Saturday delivery with a letter he'd found in the bottom of his bag. But when she'd glanced at the letter in the light, she'd wished she'd left it in the box.

The envelope was red, and it was addressed to her, but it hadn't come through the regular mail. There had been no stamp or cancellation, and someone had just dropped it in the hardware store mailbox. Jessica had stared down at the envelope for a long moment, and then she'd carried it upstairs to her room, to open it in privacy. She'd known exactly who it was from. All Cat's Valentines came in red envelopes.

There had been a poem inside, just as she'd known there would be. It hadn't been exactly the same as the ones that Tanya and Gail had received, but it had carried a similar message.

Roses are red, their leaves are green. You'll pass my test if you want to be queen.

Jessica had shuddered, and stared down at the poem for a long moment. And then she'd hurried to the phone on her dresser. But before she'd dialed Amy's number, she'd reconsidered. She'd meant what she'd told Amy, and she still didn't think that Cat was dangerous. He was just a sick freak, and there was no way she'd let him spoil the fun she'd have being crowned as Valentine's Day Queen.

"Creep! Here's what I think of you!" Jessica had torn the card into as many pieces as she could and dropped them in her wastebasket. And she'd spent the whole night tossing and turning, wondering whether she'd done the right thing.

After a shower, and several minutes in front of her makeup table, Jessica had felt much better. She'd managed to hide the dark circles under her eyes, and a little blush had worked wonders to make her look fresh and rested. Now, no one would be able to tell she'd been worried all night, and Amy wouldn't dare to suggest that they cancel the contest.

Jessica dressed in her favorite outfit, a navy blue turtle-necked sweater with a matching pleated skirt, just like the ones they'd worn in the fifties. Jessica loved the fifties styles, and she had several pleated skirts, a couple of old-fashioned sweater sets, and a real poodle skirt. She knew the fifties styles looked good on her. Girls hadn't been so thin then, and if she'd gone to Hamilton High in the fifties, she would have been just the right size. Now she was considered too heavy, because girls these days were all skin and bones.

A glance in the mirror, and Jessica was satisfied. Her hair was perfect, as it always was. She was very lucky that she'd inherited her mother's naturally curly red hair. All she had to do was keep it cut short so it wouldn't get bushy, and run a brush through it in the morning.

Her mother was standing at the stove, frying something that smelled wonderful, and she turned to smile. "Good morning, honey. Are you hungry?"

"I am now." Jessica grinned as she realized that her mother was making French toast. Her mother's French toast was fried in butter, and it was delicious, drenched in homemade apricot syrup. "I can only have one piece, though. I want to be able to fit into my new dress."

But French toast was seductive, and Jessica ended up eating two pieces, despite her resolve. When she was finished, she left her plate on the table. Her mother would clean up. She always did. And then she started to gather up her books.

"Jessica?"

"Yes, Mom." Jessica hid a frown. She knew exactly what her mother was going to ask, and she didn't really want to do it.

"Would you mind the store while your father eats breakfast?"

"Uh . . . sure, Mom," Jessica agreed, reluctantly.

Jessica's mother seemed to sense her reluctance, because she sighed deeply. "You do have time, don't you, honey? Neal doesn't usually come early."

"Neal's never early." Jessica gave a bitter little laugh. "He picks me up so late, we always have to run to get to our first class on time."

Jessica was frowning as she went down the inside stairs and pushed open the door to the hardware store. She hated to watch the store in the morning. There were never any customers, and time dragged by. The only thing that made it tolerable at all was that she could see everything that was happening on the street outside.

"Good morning, Dad." Jessica decided to be polite. She was going to hit her dad up for money later this week, and she didn't want to get on his bad side. She even forced a smile as she hurried down the gardening aisle, which was normally filled with wheelbarrows, rakes, and gardening tools. In the winter, the items from the gardening aisle were stored in the back, and it had been restocked with shovels, bags of salt that were used to remove ice from sidewalks, and snow blowers. "Mom sent me down to watch the store while you have breakfast."

"Thanks, honey. Just buzz me if Neal comes before I get back."

"No problem." Jessica shrugged. "It's like I told Mom. Neal's never early."

"Troubles in paradise?" Jessica's father looked concerned.

"Oh, no . . . nothing like that." Jessica reassured him. Her mother and father really liked Neal. "We're never actually late for school. We just have to hurry, that's all."

Jessica's father nodded. "That's a small fault, honey. You could do a lot worse than Neal Carpenter. Your mother and I think he's a fine boy."

"Neal's just fine. I like him a lot." Jessica did her best to sound enthusiastic. There was no way she wanted to get into a discussion about how bored she was with Neal. Then her father would try to convince her that Neal was the greatest thing since disposable flashlights, and she really couldn't cope with that this morning. "You'd better hurry, Dad. Your French toast will get cold."

Jessica was thoughtful as she watched her father head for the stairs. He'd looked a little tired this morning, and she knew she hadn't been pulling her share of the load in the store. She'd been too busy with cheerleading and parties and hanging out with the gang at the Hungry Burger. But this was her Senior year and she was entitled to have some fun, before those days were gone forever. Life wasn't all work, even though her mother and father seemed to think it was.

There was a frown on Jessica's face as she stared out through the plate glass window. She knew her mother and father wanted her to take over the store someday, and she'd wanted it, too, until the Valentine's Day Queen contest had changed her whole outlook. Things were different now, and Jessica had a big decision to make.

Jessica had always assumed she'd stay in Clearwater, and marry Neal. He was nice, and she liked him a lot. But Neal had bored her to tears this weekend, and there were other guys out there she'd never get a chance to meet if she buried herself behind the hoes, and the rakes, and the bags of fertilizer forever. Once she got to be Valentine's Day Queen, everyone would look at her in a new light. It would prove that she was prettier, and smarter, and more popular than the other girls. She might have a chance for bigger things, things she'd never even considered before, like moving somewhere else and starting an exciting career that had nothing to do with hardware.

A guilty sigh escaped Jessica's lips. Her parents would be terribly disappointed if she left home. They'd been counting on her to carry on the family tradition. She was the fourth generation of Fords, and they wanted Ford Hardware to go on forever. But this was her life, and she had the right to live it the way she chose.

What would her parents do if she left? Jessica's frown deepened as she considered the problem. She really didn't want to leave them in the lurch, but they could always hire one of the locals to help them out in the store. It would still be Ford Hardware, even if they hired someone else to run it. But who would they hire?

Jessica began to smile as she thought of a perfect solution.

Neal was fascinated by the hardware business. He was always asking her questions about what they stocked, and why. And her parents seemed to like Neal a lot. Perhaps they could hire him to help out when she moved away and left him behind.

She caught a movement out of the corner of her eye, and Jessica glanced up at the plate glass window. Kevin Thomas and Bob Pelski had stopped by the window on their way past, to wave at her. Jessica waved back, even though she didn't like Kevin or Bob that much. Kevin and Bob were losers. They'd end up staying in Clearwater forever, just like most of her classmates at Hamilton High.

A shiny red truck pulled up to the curb across the street, and Jessica watched as Wade Parker got out and swaggered up the sidewalk in his cowboy boots. Wade had been the hottest prospect at Hamilton High four years ago, when Jessica had been a Freshman. He'd been captain of the football team, the highest scorer on the basketball team, and the most popular boy in the Senior class. Wade's father owned a huge turkey farm on the outskirts of town, and Wade had always had plenty of money to spend. At the beginning of Wade's Senior year, his father had bought him a brand-new red Chevy pickup with mag wheels, a full stereo system, and white leather upholstery. It had been the envy of every other guy in school, and the girls had gone crazy, trying to get him to take them for a ride.

Jessica hadn't been immune to Wade's charms. She remembered staring at him in the halls with awe, wishing that he would notice her. But, of course, he hadn't. There had been no reason for Wade Parker to notice a pudgy Freshman girl with curly red hair and a yearning look in her eyes.

Wade Parker had been voted most likely to succeed in the high school yearbook, and everyone had expected him to do something great. But Wade hadn't been chosen for an athletic scholarship, and none of the professional teams had drafted him. Regular college was out, since Wade had failed to keep up his grades, and he'd ended up settling down in a house by one of his father's turkey farms, and marrying Laurie Swensen, Hamilton High's head cheerleader.

Jessica watched as Wade pulled open the door to Millie's cafe and walked in. He'd been going to Millie's for breakfast every morning since Laurie had left him. The rumor around town was that she'd found him at the Starlight Motel on highway eight, with one of her best friends. It was probably true. Wade wasn't the type to settle down for long.

There was a new dent in Wade's truck, a watermelon-sized depression right in the back, on the tailgate. He had a reputation for drinking and driving, and he'd probably had another accident while he'd been driving home after a night at one of his favorite bars. It was a wonder that Wade hadn't lost his license; but so far his accidents had been solo spinouts, and he hadn't been required to report them to the police.

"What happened to you, Wade?" Jessica asked the question aloud, but she already knew the answer. If Wade had left, he might have had a chance. But he'd stayed in Clearwater, the place where people died at the age of twenty and didn't get buried until fifty years later.

Someone honked outside the window, and Jessica looked up. Neal was here. He'd pulled up, right in front of the store, but he wasn't going to bother to come in for her. He never did.

Jessica pressed the buzzer. She'd done her duty, minding the store, and now her mother or her father could take over. Actually, she'd done her duty for years and years, ever since her father had taught her to make change. Over the years, she'd spent long days sitting behind the counter, waiting on customers and being bored out of her skin.

"It's definitely time for a change," Jessica muttered to herself as she shrugged into her coat and picked up her books. There was no way she'd settle down in Clearwater like a dutiful daughter, and wind up like Wade Parker. She'd start making plans today, and right after she graduated, she'd leave Clearwater and all of its boring residents in her dust!

Sixteen

Cat put on a smile as he approached the bulletin board. Amy was just getting ready to post the results of today's vote, and she turned as she heard his footsteps.

"Hi." Amy smiled at him. "Are you holding your breath, waiting to see today's results?"

"Not really. I think I can guess who's in the lead. It's Jessica, right?"

Amy nodded, and tacked up the sheet of typing paper. "She really cashed in today. Another twenty-two votes, and that puts her almost forty votes ahead of Michele."

"Hey . . . you got another one." Cat pointed to Amy's name on the list.

Amy frowned slightly as she nodded. "I know. I think it was from Cat again. I'm beginning to recognize his printing."

"Did you save it?"

"It's right in here." Amy patted her purse. "That's just in case Jessica gets another one of his Valentines."

"Do you think she will?"

"I don't know. I hope not. She's only had one, so far."

"One?" Cat was surprised. "Are you sure?"

"That's what she said. And I can't think of any reason why she'd lie about it."

"No . . . I can't think of any reason she'd lie, either. Unless . . . no." Cat laughed and shook his head. "That's really ridiculous."

"What's ridiculous?" Amy looked curious.

"Well . . . maybe she wouldn't want you to know if she got another card. After all, you're the one who suggested canceling the Valentine's Day Queen contest."

Amy's eyes widened. "You might be right! But don't you think she'd be too scared to keep something like that to herself?"

"She didn't act very scared when she got the first card. And she said she doesn't think Cat is dangerous. She thinks he's just a . . ." Cat stopped. He really didn't want to recall what Jessica had called him. "I don't remember exactly what she called him."

Amy sighed. "A weird practical joker. But I'm really afraid she's wrong. I think Cat is deadly serious. What do you think?"

"I think he is, too." Cat nodded. At least Amy seemed to have some respect for him. "Why do *you* think he's sending those cards?"

"Well . . . it could be that he objects to the contest. It does seem to bring out the worst in everyone. Maybe I shouldn't say this, but . . . no. I'd better not."

"Go ahead." Cat encouraged her. "You can tell *me.*"

Amy took a moment to think it over, and then she nodded. "Okay, but you've got to realize that I'm not trying to be critical. I know I can't win the contest, so I'm not jealous or anything like that."

"Okay." Cat nodded. "Go on."

"And I want you to promise never to repeat this. It could turn into gossip, and I wouldn't want that."

Cat nodded again. "Go ahead, Amy. Tell me."

"I watched Tanya, when she was in the lead for queen. And because she had the most votes, she seemed to think that she was better than anyone else."

"How could you tell?" Cat laughed. "Tanya always seemed to have a very high opinion of herself."

"Well . . . maybe. But that's not what I meant. Tanya changed when she was in the lead. Maybe I'm not doing a good job of explaining it, but I know she did."

Cat nodded. "I think I understand. You're trying to say that by virtue of being in the lead for queen, she stopped being grateful, and began to think she deserved it."

"Exactly!"

Amy's face lit up in a smile, and Cat felt ten feet tall. She really looked beautiful when she smiled. And then she turned serious again.

"It's like my dad always says, *'Power tends to corrupt, and absolute power corrupts absolutely.'* "

"Lord Acton." Cat nodded. "I believe he was referring to the English royalty."

"You're probably right. But the queen contest is our own little taste of royalty, right here at Hamilton High."

"You've got a point." Cat smiled at her. "We've even got the crowns and the coronation. How about Gail? Do you think she became corrupted by the contest?"

Amy sighed, and then she nodded. "In a way. Colleen and I were Gail's friends before the contest started. But after she took the lead, she seemed to feel that she didn't have to be nice to us anymore. It was like she couldn't be bothered with anyone on our level."

"How about Jessica?" Cat tried not to appear too anxious. He really wanted Amy's opinion of Jessica. "Is the same sort of thing beginning to happen to her?"

Amy frowned slightly, and then she shook her head. "Not yet. At least, I don't think it is. Michele would know. She's Jessica's best friend."

"Are you going to ask her?"

Amy looked shocked. "Of course not! If I did that, Michele would start looking for signs of trouble, and when you start looking for trouble, you usually find it."

"That's very true." Cat laughed, and picked up his book bag. It was time to move on. He had to find Jessica, and see if she could pass his test. "See you later, Amy. And thanks for the insights about Hamilton High's royalty. You know, I really think you'd be the best choice for queen."

Amy smiled again. "Thanks . . . I think. But please don't vote for me. I think it's a lot safer at the bottom of the heap."

Cat was grinning as he walked away. He wished he could tell Amy that she didn't have anything to worry about. Cat approved of her, and he wouldn't send her any threatening Valentines if she were in the lead for queen.

Jessica was in a horrible mood as she walked down the hall to her sixth-period classroom. Her mother had called, right after fifth period, and asked her to come straight home from school to take care of the store. When Jessica had objected, her mother had told her that it was an emergency. One of Dad's friends had been taken to the hospital, and they wanted to go to visit him.

"Hey, Jessica! Wait up!" Michele ran down the hall to catch up with her. "Are you going down to the Hungry Burger after school?"

Jessica frowned. The whole gang would be there, and she would be stuck behind the hardware store counter again. "No. I can't go. I have to work at the store."

"But Neal can't go with you. He's got basketball practice." Michele looked worried.

"I know that. Neal's got basketball practice every day after school."

"But, Jessica . . . you're not going to be there alone, are you?"

Jessica laughed. Michele was beginning to wear on her nerves with all of her paranoid fears about Cat. "I won't be alone. With any luck, I'll have a customer or two."

"I'd better go with you." Michele looked determined. "You won't have customers all the time. And when you're free, we can study for the big history test."

Jessica almost groaned out loud. There was nothing worse than studying with Michele. Michele wanted to go over every section at least ten times, and it took her forever to memorize dates and events. Rather than risk a horribly boring study session, Jessica shook her head.

"I can't study, Michele. I won't have time. I promised my dad I'd start checking the inventory."

Michele sighed. "Okay. I'll just have to study later. I'll help you with the inventory, instead. I can count boxes and things like that."

"I'm not sure that's a good idea." Jessica hedged for time. She knew she had to think of some way to get rid of Michele. She wanted to be alone, all alone, for just a little while. She'd had someone hovering at her side for three solid days, and she was getting sick of it!

"Why not?"

Jessica sighed. Michele was unbelievably stubborn. She just didn't want to take the hint. There was only one way she could get Michele to leave her alone. She'd have to make her mad.

"Look, Michele. I just don't want you around, okay?"

Michele started to frown. "But . . . why?"

"I'm tired of you. It's that simple. You've been hanging around me all day, and I'm sick of it!"

Michele blinked back the tears that were beginning to form in her eyes, and then she shook her head. "I know you don't mean that, Jessica. You're just under a lot of stress, that's all. I understand. But I won't let you go down to the store alone. A friend wouldn't do that to another friend."

"Maybe I don't want you to be my friend. Maybe it's time for me to get a new friend. And maybe that's why I don't want you around. Did you ever think of that?"

Michele blinked a little faster, but a tear rolled down her cheek anyway. "You don't really mean that, do you?"

"Yes! And it just so happens I've got a new friend, so you don't have to worry about me being all alone. Why don't you just get lost, Michele. Go find something else to do and stop bothering me!"

Michele took one look at Jessica's face, and then she burst into tears. "But . . . I'm only trying to help you."

"Well, stop trying! I don't know why you're so concerned about me, anyway. You said it all the other night at your party.

If Cat really is a killer, and he kills me, you'll be next in line for Valentine's Day Queen!"

"But, Jessica! I was just joking! You know I was!"

Jessica shrugged. "Maybe you were, and maybe you weren't. But that doesn't really matter. The only reason you got any votes at all is because the boys feel sorry for you."

"Jessica! How could you?!" Michele's mouth dropped open. And then she turned on her heel and ran down the hall.

Jessica watched her go with a smile of satisfaction on her face. Thank goodness she'd gotten rid of Michele. And the fact that they weren't friends any longer was no big loss. Michele wasn't the right friend for her anyway. She would have had to cut her loose when she left Clearwater, and this whole staged fight had saved her a lot of trouble.

As Jessica walked down the hall, she passed a group of students getting books from their lockers. She nodded to them very regally, and held her head high. After all, she was their Valentine's Day Queen.

What Jessica failed to notice was that one particular pair of eyes was staring at her with unusual intensity. Cat had heard every word she'd said to Michele. He'd seen the tears roll down Michele's cheeks, and he'd watched Jessica smile as her former friend had run away, down the hall. There was no reason to give Jessica his test. She had just flunked a test of her own making, and now she could never be Hamilton High's Valentine's Day Queen.

Seventeen

After forty-five boring minutes of sitting behind the counter in the hardware store, waiting for a customer to come in the door, Jessica was regretting her hasty decision to cut Michele loose. There had been no customers, and it was a little eerie, being alone for the first time in several days. What if Michele had been right? What if Cat really did plan to kill her? She was all alone and this would be a perfect opportunity for him.

There was a loud thump that seemed to come from the storeroom, and Jessica jumped up from her stool. She was halfway to the door before she heard an accompanying meow, and she laughed out loud. It was only the store cat patrolling the area. Her father kept a big yellow tomcat in the back storage area to catch the field mice that always seemed to come in during the fall and winter.

"Hey, Bruiser . . . did you catch your supper?"

Jessica grinned as the cat meowed again. Bruiser was a real character. If you asked him a question, he meowed. She'd held long conversations with Bruiser on the days she'd worked at the store, and one day she'd worked him up to twenty-three meows before he'd grown bored and stalked off to the back storage area to look for mice.

Jessica looked up as she heard a car engine. It was Brett's

mother, and she was making a U-turn at the corner. Jessica hoped she was coming to the hardware store to buy something.

It would he nice to have a customer. But Brett's mother parked across the street, instead, in front of Millie's Cafe. Jessica watched her walk in, and then come out several minutes later, carrying a square bakery box. Jessica didn't have to look inside the box to know what was in it. It was one of Millie's pies, and Brett had mentioned that his mother always picked up a cherry pie on Monday night for dessert.

Although Clearwater had a population of over five thousand, it was a small town at heart. And everyone in town was interested in everyone else's business. Since the Stevens family had only lived here for a little over a year, Mrs. Stevens didn't know how things were done in Clearwater. She had no idea that most of the Clearwater women thought that buying a pie, instead of making it yourself, was the height of laziness.

Seeing Brett's mother made Jessica think of Brett. He really was handsome, and he was going off to college after he graduated. Brett would be a success, Jessica was sure of it. He wasn't anything like Neal, who'd told her he'd be content to settle down in Clearwater and stay close to his friends and family.

Perhaps she should try to date Brett. Jessica began to smile at the thought. She'd be with him at the coronation because he was bound to win the contest for Valentine's Day King. They would dance the coronation dance together, and sit side by side on the thrones for the ceremony. She hadn't actually asked Neal to the dance yet, although everyone assumed they were going together. Perhaps she should tell Neal to find another date, and ask Brett to take her to the dance. But would that be fair to Neal?

Jessica sighed and shook her head. Of course it wouldn't be fair. She'd gone out with Neal for over a year, and he expected her to go to the Valentine's Day dance with him. Telling him to find another date wouldn't be fair at all. But life wasn't fair, and Neal would get over it, sooner or later. She had to consider her own happiness.

The more she thought about it, the better it sounded. Neal would understand that since she was going to be the queen, she had an obligation to date the king. She could even suggest that he take someone unpopular to the dance, someone who wouldn't otherwise have a date . . . like Amy, or Colleen.

Someone else was pulling into the parking spot that Brett's mother had vacated. Jessica peered out through the window and recognized Mr. Waller as he got out of his old green Honda. Mr. Waller was a widower, and he always ate his evening meal at Millie's Cafe. Mr. Waller was carrying several packages, and Jessica started to grin. The rumor around town was that Mr. Waller was sweet on Millie, and since he was the town mailman, he always hand-delivered her packages, instead of leaving a little notice in her mailbox.

"The mail!" Jessica jumped up the moment she thought of it and hurried toward the front door. Her parents had been in a hurry when they'd left, and they'd probably forgotten to bring in the mail. There might be a letter for her. Or if she was lucky, there would be a notice from the Riverside Mall, twenty miles from Clearwater, telling her that the new shoes she'd ordered for the dance had arrived.

There was a big stack of mail in the box, and Jessica carried it inside. She spread it out on the counter and let out a whoop of pleasure as she saw the postcard notice from Ivert's Footwear. Her shoes were here, and she could hardly wait to drive out to the mall to get them.

Jessica went through the rest of the mail, sorting it into piles on the counter. There was a hunting and fishing magazine for her father, a letter from her grandmother in Arizona, a book of recipes her mother had ordered, several bills, and a whole stack of ads. But when Jessica saw the envelope that had been hidden at the very bottom of the pile, she gasped in fright.

It was a red envelope with no stamp and no postmark, but her name was printed on the front. Was it another Valentine from Cat? She wished she'd paid more attention when Brett was discussing his printing.

Jessica's fingers trembled as she picked up the envelope. She had the urge to toss it in the big wastebasket under the counter, but perhaps it wasn't from Cat. It could be a Valentine from someone else. Most Valentines came in red envelopes.

Slowly and carefully, almost as if she were dealing with a rattlesnake that was ready to strike, Jessica loosened the glue on the flap. Then she drew out the card inside, and shivered. It said, *Violets are blue, roses are red. An unworthy queen is better off dead.*

"No!" Jessica stuck the card back in the envelope and resealed it quickly with the glue stick that her father kept on the counter. She still didn't think that Cat was a killer, but a card just like this had brought bad luck before. It was almost like the curses that the ancient witches had put on people, and she had to get rid of it quickly.

Jessica picked up the envelope and hurried back out the front door. She stuck it back in the mailbox and closed the lid with a bang. Perhaps she could break the curse if she put it back where she'd found it, and no one knew that she'd read it.

She felt a little better as she went back inside and took her place at the counter again. She didn't actually believe in curses, but it never hurt to play it safe.

Jessica reached for the phone to call Michele and ask her to come down to the store to keep her company. But then she remembered that Michele was no longer her friend, and she hung up before it could ring. There was always Neal.

Basketball practice was over by now, and he would be at home.

But he wasn't, and Jessica sighed as she hung up the phone. Where was Neal? He was supposed to be her bodyguard, and she was here all alone.

It was getting dark inside the store, and Jessica got up to turn on the bright overhead lights they used at night. The daytime lights had to be shut off first. The old wiring was overloaded, and the fuses would blow if both sets of lights were on at once.

Jessica flicked the switch behind the counter and frowned as the daytime lights went off. It was really getting dark fast.

The switch that controlled the overhead lights was on the wall by the storage room door, and Jessica shivered slightly and headed for the tool aisle. It was even darker back here, and the blades of the hatchets and axes gleamed in the reflected light from passing cars on the street. They looked sharper and more menacing than they ever had in the daylight. Every time a car passed on the street outside, and its red taillights were deflected on their shiny metal surfaces, it looked almost as if they were covered with blood.

Jessica walked a little faster, but she was careful not to stumble. The tool aisle was crowded. They'd just received a new shipment, and there were still boxes of things to be shelved.

It was getting very dark now, and Jessica wished she'd thought to turn on the lights earlier. As the rush-hour traffic increased on the street, the headlights from the almost steady stream of cars swept the interior of the store, making the shadows of the tools and implements sway and move in crazy and frightening patterns.

She took a deep breath and told herself that no one had ever been hurt by a shadow; but her heart beat faster, and her legs began to shake. The moving shadows made the big scythe seem to swing from side to side, as if it were ready to drop from its overhead hanger. And the dark shadow of the hedge clippers resembled a huge pair of scissors with wickedly sharp blades. Even the shadow of something familiar and ordinary, like a garden rake, seemed to turn into a lethal weapon with its elongated, sharp points.

Just then the bell on the front door tinkled, and someone came into the store. Jessica whirled to look, but it was too dark to see who it was.

"Mr. Ford? Jessica? Is anybody here?"

A voice called out in the gathering darkness, and Jessica gave a huge sigh of relief as she recognized it. "I'm here. Stay right there and I'll turn on the lights."

"Do you need some help?"

"No. I know where they are. I just have to get there."

There was a moment of silence, and then Jessica heard him chuckle. "This is a hardware store, isn't it?"

Jessica winced as she stubbed her toe on the edge of a wheelbarrow, and her voice was much sharper than usual. "Of course it is. You know that."

"Doesn't Ford Hardware carry flashlights?"

"Very funny!" Jessica gave an exasperated sigh. He was right. She should have thought to grab a flashlight while it was still light enough to see. But he didn't have to remind her of that.

"Do you want me to find one for you? There's a display right here, by the front door."

"No, thanks." Jessica began to frown. His voice had sounded closer, but perhaps that was just her imagination. She hoped he wasn't trying to come back here. He'd probably trip and hurt himself, and then he might try to collect on her father's insurance. "Stay right there. I can manage just fine on my own."

A few more moments of groping in the darkness, and she'd made it to the back wall. The wall switch was right in front of her, and Jessica was about to flick it on when she heard the sound of breathing behind her. She'd told him not to come back here, but he hadn't listened to her.

"I told you not to come back here!" Jessica turned toward him with a frown. It was so dark that she couldn't see his face, but she knew he was there. She could hear him breathing. "It's too dark to see. What if you'd tripped over something?"

He laughed, and Jessica gasped as he grabbed her hand, pulling it away from the light switch. It was a laugh she'd never heard him use before, scary and menacing.

"Don't you know, Jessica? A Cat can see in the dark."

"But you're not a . . ." Jessica couldn't finish the sentence. Her vocal cords were suddenly paralyzed with fear. He was Cat! She was alone with Cat! And Cat had threatened to kill her!

"I've got a little present for you. It's something you really deserve. Hold still while I put it around your neck."

Jessica struggled, trying desperately to pull away, but he was much stronger than she was. And then she felt something cold on her neck, and she reached up to grab it. It felt like a chain, a thin gold chain, and she screamed as she realized that it was a half-heart necklace, just like Tanya and Gail had been wearing.

"Wait! Please! You made a mistake! You can't—"

But Jessica never finished her thought. There wasn't even time to scream before something sharp and pointed smashed into her head, knocking her into a sea of perpetual darkness.

Eighteen

They were all gathered around a table in the lunchroom when Danny and Amy came in. Michele and Colleen looked very sad, and Neal's eyes were red, as if he'd been crying. He sat between Brett and Kevin, and Amy was glad that he had friends to comfort him. Neal had been the one to find Jessica in the back of the store, and he'd have to live with the memory of that grisly sight forever.

Amy went straight to Neal and hugged him. It must have been awful, finding Jessica dead. Danny patted him on the back, and then they sat down in the two vacant chairs. Everyone knew the details, and there was no need to talk about that. Jessica had been reaching for the light switch when she'd stumbled and fallen, striking her head on a sharply pointed shovel.

When Neal had left basketball practice, he'd gone down to the Hungry Burger, where he'd planned to meet Jessica. Michele had been there, and she'd told him that Jessica was working in the store. Neal had been angry, at first. Why hadn't Michele gone with Jessica? There was supposed to be someone with her every minute. But Michele had explained about the fight they'd had, and how Jessica had told her to get lost.

Neal had decided to patch things up between the two girls, and he'd called the hardware store to talk some sense into Jessica. But Jessica hadn't answered, even though he'd let the phone ring over ten times. That was when he'd driven down to the store, and found it dark with the front door open.

There had been a flashlight display by the front door, and Neal had grabbed one. He'd walked through the store, calling Jessica's name, getting more and more worried with each step. And then he'd found her, and when he'd realized that she was dead, he'd called the authorities.

The sheriff had promised that there would be a full investigation. There always was when someone died all alone. But he'd told Neal and Jessica's parents that it looked like an accident to him.

Amy didn't agree. There was the half-heart necklace that Neal had found around Jessica's neck, the same type of necklace that Tanya and Gail had been wearing. And even though Jessica had admitted to receiving only one Valentine from Cat, Jessica's mother had found the pieces of another Valentine in her wastebasket. If there had been two Valentines, there could have been a third, one that Cat might have taken with him, after he'd murdered Jessica.

They all sat in silence for a moment, and then Danny nudged Amy. "You'd better tell them what you decided, Amy."

"Yes." Amy sighed deeply. As president of the Senior class, she had an obligation to be frank. "Let's look at the facts. You all know about the Valentines from Cat and the half-heart necklaces. Maybe the sheriff thinks that's just coincidence, but three girls who were in line for the throne have died. There's something going on, and we've got to stop it. I'm going to Mr. Dorman's office, right after lunch, and I'm going to ask him to cancel the contest."

Michele began to frown. "That's not really fair, Amy. I'm next in line. If you cancel the contest, I'll lose my chance to be queen."

"But you'll be alive." Danny reminded her. "Think about it, Michele."

"I *have* thought about it. I know you and Amy think that Cat murdered Tanya and Gail, and Jessica. I did, too . . . until I went to see Madame Zane. Madame Zane knows everything about the past and the future."

"You went to a fortune-teller?" Amy was surprised.

"That's right. But Madame Zane's not just a fortune-teller. She's also a psychic, and she told me exactly how they died."

Amy glanced at Colleen, and she could tell that her friend was trying very hard not to laugh. And then she turned to look at Danny, who wasn't quite as polite as his sister.

"You've got to be kidding!" Danny shook his head in disbelief. "Do you really believe in stuff like that?"

Michele glared at Danny. "Madame Zane is entirely legitimate. She's not like those fake fortune-tellers you see at the county fair. She uses channeling to actually communicate with the dead."

"Channeling?" Neal didn't look quite as dubious as everyone else. "What's that?"

"It's sort of like an interpreter. You see, it's impossible to speak directly with the dead. Madame Zane got in touch with White Feather. She's an Indian princess who died over two hundred years ago. And White Feather carried my questions to Tanya, and Gail, and Jessica."

"Wait a second . . ." Brett held up his hand. "If it's impossible to speak directly with the dead, how did Madame Zane speak to White Feather?"

"That's different. Madame Zane can communicate with White Feather because she's accepted the fact that she's passed over to the other side."

Colleen nodded, and Amy could tell she was trying very hard not to giggle. "Go on, Michele. Tell us what happened."

"It's very simple. Madame Zane went into a trance, and she asked White Feather my questions. Then White Feather interpreted them for Tanya, and Gail, and Jessica."

Neal started to grin for the first time that day. "Hey, Michele . . . that sounds just like the United Nations."

"That's true, in a way." Michele nodded. "But the interpreters at the United Nations work instantaneously, and this took a long time."

"How long?" Kevin asked the question that was on all their minds.

"Almost an hour. But finally, White Feather contacted Madame Zane again. She gave her the answers, and then Madame Zane told me."

Danny snorted. "Let me guess. Madame Zane gets paid by the minute?"

"Of course not!" Michele looked very offended. "I told you she was legitimate. There's a minimum charge for every session, but that's entirely reasonable. Channeling is extremely exhausting work."

Danny looked like he wanted to laugh, and Amy gave him a warning glance. And then she turned to Michele. "Which questions did you ask?"

"I asked them if they'd been murdered, and they said no. And then I asked if Cat had anything to do with their accidents, and they said yes."

"Did Madame Zane tell you what that meant?" Kevin leaned forward.

"Yes. Tanya said that the Valentines got her so nervous, she tripped while she was running down the stairs. And Gail said that she was so busy thinking about Cat's messages, she took the curve too fast."

"How about Jessica?" Neal looked anxious. "Did she say anything?"

"Yes. She said the same thing happened to her. She was stressed out because of Cat's Valentines, and she stumbled when she went to turn on the store lights. And then she apologized for fighting with me, and she promised that she'd always be my best friend, throughout eternity."

Colleen nodded. "Okay. Let me get this straight. You're saying that all three of them were so nervous about Cat that they got careless?"

"Exactly!" Michele looked around the table and smiled. "That's all there was to it. They just stressed out."

Amy frowned slightly. "You didn't ask about the half-heart necklaces?"

"No . . . I forgot. But I'm going back to see Madame Zane tomorrow. I can find out then."

"That's it?" Neal looked disappointed. "That's all you asked them?"

"Well . . . there was one other thing that I asked Jessica, but it's personal. And it doesn't have anything to do with her death. It . . . uh . . . it has to do with the contest."

"Then you'd better tell us." Amy's voice was firm. "Come on, Michele . . . what was it?"

Michele started to blush, and she looked very uncomfortable. "I told her that you wanted to cancel the contest, and she said not to let you do it, that the school book fund needed more money. And then she told me that since she couldn't be here, she really wanted me to be the Valentine's Day Queen."

"Oh, brother!" Danny muttered under his breath, and Amy poked him again. But Michele heard him, and she gave him a glance that was full of venom.

"Sorry, Michele." Danny sighed deeply. "I really didn't mean to make fun of you, but I just can't swallow this whole psychic thing. Don't you realize that Madame Zane was conning you? She made up the whole thing out of thin air, so that she could get money from you."

"No, she didn't! I know Madame Zane's not a fake. She's told me things in the past."

"Like what?" Amy was curious.

"Like the time I was afraid I'd flunk my chemistry test. Madame Zane told me that if I'd go to a tutor every night after school, I'd pass. And I did!"

"Yes, but—" Amy stopped abruptly as Danny poked her. And then she sighed deeply. Danny was right. It was a waste of breath to argue with Michele.

"That's the real reason I don't want you to cancel the contest." Michele looked at Amy with tears in her eyes. "Jessica really wanted it to go on."

Amy nodded. There was no use trying to convince Michele

that Madame Zane was a fake. She'd already made up her mind. "Look, Michele. I'm just worried about you. If we go on with the contest, you could be in danger. Cat's Valentines made the other girls so nervous, they died."

"But they won't make me nervous." Michele shook her head. "Jessica warned me, and so did Tanya and Gail. I'm prepared."

Danny squeezed Amy's hand, and Amy squeezed back. She knew exactly what he meant. Michele's mind was made up, and nothing she could say would change it.

"Okay. I guess it's your decision." Amy nodded. "But you will be careful, won't you, Michele?"

"Of course I will. And thank you, Amy. This means so much to me!"

Michele gave Amy a radiant smile, but Amy couldn't smile back. She was convinced that Michele was wrong, and the other girls had been murdered.

She couldn't help feeling that someone very evil and sinister was about to strike again.

It was close to eight o'clock when the doorbell rang, and Amy got up to answer it. A delivery man from the mall was outside, and he handed her a dress box.

"Amy Hunter?"

"Yes." Amy nodded. "But I didn't order anything from the mall."

The delivery man shrugged. "It's got your name and address on the slip. If you didn't order it, it's probably a gift."

Amy was puzzled as she carried the box inside. The delivery man was right. Her name and address were written on the slip, but the sender's name was blank. But then she remembered Danny's promise, and she grinned. Danny had gone to the mall and picked out her dress. She could hardly wait to see it!

"Who was that, dear?" Amy's mother called out from the kitchen. She was baking brownies, one of the healthy foods on the diet sheet that Amy and Danny had fabricated.

"Oh . . . nothing." Amy hid the box behind her back. "It was just someone for me, that's all."

Amy ran up the stairs to her room, carrying the dress box. She was so excited, she could hardly wait to see what was inside. Would it be black and slinky? Or red with a plunging neckline?

But Amy's face fell as she took the lid off the box and saw what was inside. It was a simple light blue silk dress with a moderate neckline, long sleeves, and a full, sweeping skirt. The dress was beautiful, but it wasn't at all what she'd expected.

Amy shrugged, and got out of her clothes to try on the dress. It looked lovely, but it was exactly the sort of party dress that her mother would have chosen for her. What had happened to the sexy outfit that Danny had promised to send?

Just then the phone rang, and Amy picked up the line in her room. "Hello?"

"Amy." It was Danny's voice. "Do you like the blue dress?"

Amy grinned. "Thank you, Danny. I love it. And so will my mother and father! But I thought you said you were going to send me a sexy dress."

"I did. Look under the tissue paper, and you'll find it. It should fit. I took a lot of time describing you to the saleslady."

"You mean you didn't ask Colleen my size?" Amy's eyes widened.

"No. She wasn't home when I left for the mall. Try it on, and then read the note. That'll explain everything."

"Okay." Amy had a big smile on her face when she hung up the phone. Danny had sent her two dresses! She lifted the tissue paper in the box, and gasped as she drew out the second dress.

No wonder she hadn't noticed that there was another dress in the box! It was made of thin black silk, and there wasn't very much of it. It was just a thin wisp of material, glimmering in the light, and Amy's hands trembled as she tried it on.

Amy stared at herself in the mirror in utter disbelief. Danny had sent her a cocktail dress, and she looked smart and sophisticated, and very, very sexy.

The dress had a Grecian top that crisscrossed over the front to form a very low neckline, held in place by a thin strap at the back of her neck. Amy giggled as she turned and caught sight of her back. Her hair covered the strap at the back of her neck, and it looked like she was completely topless! Leave it to Danny to pick out a dress like this!

The skirt floated down to just above the knee, and it was surprisingly modest. But when Amy turned, she noticed that the material flared out, providing a very provocative glimpse of her legs.

Amy laughed. And then she blushed as she imagined Danny in the dress store, describing her figure to the saleslady. He'd been absolutely right to send her two dresses. There was no way she could wear a dress like this to the Valentine's Day Dance. Her parents would never let her out of the house!

There was a note in the bottom of the box, and Amy unfolded it carefully. And then she blushed even more as she read it.

> *Amy—I didn't change my mind. I still don't want you to look like Little Bo Peep. But I want you to promise to wear the blue dress to the dance. I know it'll look great on you.*
>
> *Keep the black dress in a safe place, and put it on whenever you want to know exactly how I feel about you. It'll be our secret. But don't wear it for me unless you want me to forget that promise I made.*

Amy's blush grew even hotter as she slipped out of the black dress and folded it carefully in a piece of tissue paper. She placed it high on her closet shelf, and sighed happily. Danny was wonderful, and she knew exactly what he meant. When he'd given her the dress, he was telling her that he thought she was desirable and sexy. And by warning her not to wear it to the dance, he was telling her that he didn't want the other guys to think of her that way.

There was a third message in Danny's note, a message that came through loud and clear. Danny had promised he wouldn't take advantage of her. But if she ever changed her mind and wanted him to, all she had to do was wear the sexy black dress.

Nineteen

Michele laughed as she drove down the street toward the Hungry Burger. Madame Zane had been a stroke of genius, and she was proud of herself for thinking of it. There was no such person, but she was the only one who knew that. And Amy had agreed to go on with the contest.

She'd convinced them all that she wasn't worried about Cat, and they had believed her. Of course that wasn't true. But Michele had a plan to keep herself safe, and being crowned as Valentine's Day Queen was worth a little risk.

All the other girls had changed when they'd realized that they were in the lead for queen. Tanya had become even more obnoxious, Gail had ignored everyone else and made a fool of herself over Brett, and Jessica had forgotten who her friends really were. If Cat had killed them, as Amy seemed to think, Michele could understand why he'd done it. He'd even warned them to behave themselves in the silly little rhymes on his Valentine cards, but they'd all been too dumb to listen.

Michele was determined to do everything right. She remembered every one of Cat's warnings, and she wouldn't make the same mistakes the other girls had made. It would take some effort, but she was sure she could convince Cat that she was the best choice for queen. All she had to do was act sweet and kind for the next five days, and Cat would approve of her. Michele knew she could do it. She was the best actress in the Senior class.

What should she do first? Michele sighed as she pulled up to the curb in front of the Hungry Burger and got out of her car. Treating all her friends to a platter of fries would be good. She had the money. Her mother kept the grocery money in a teapot on the counter, and Michele had snitched five dollars. Her mother would never miss it, since she usually asked Michele to do the shopping.

Michele didn't bother to lock her car. It was so old, no one would steal it anyway. And then she headed into the Hungry Burger with her head held high. She'd make the rounds today, and be friendly to everyone there, even if she couldn't stand them. A queen was supposed to treat all her subjects equally.

The Hungry Burger was almost deserted, and it didn't take her long to say hello to everyone who was there. When she had fulfilled that duty, Michele headed back to their usual booth, the big round one in the back. She ordered a Coke and told the waitress to put on a platter of fries when everyone else came in. And then she sat there, planning out all the little lies she'd tell to make everyone think she was wonderful.

"What do you think we should do, Karen?" Cat turned toward the empty passenger seat as he asked the question. He was the only one who could see that she was riding next to him. "She lied to me. I checked, and no one's ever heard of Madame Zane."

The motor purred, the heater hissed out warm air, and the cold wind whistled through the vent that didn't quite close all the way. The tires made a swishing sound on the snowy highway, but Cat heard his dead love's voice perfectly.

There was a long moment while Cat listened, blocking out all sounds except the sweet cadence of her voice. And then he nodded. "All right. I'll warn her, and then I'll give her a chance to tell the truth. Her car should be in front of the Hungry Burger. She skipped out of school early."

Cat's hands were trembling slightly as he parked and opened

the glove box. There was a red envelope inside, the Valentine card he'd prepared for Michele. "What if she lies to me again, Karen? What do you want me to do?"

There was another long silence, a silence so long that his breath began to cloud the windshield. And then Cat smiled, and picked up the envelope. "I love you, too, my darling Karen. And you're absolutely right. A queen should never lie to her subjects. If Michele keeps on lying, I'll kill her for you."

Michele waved and smiled as she got into her car, but the moment her face was hidden behind the frosty windshield, she frowned deeply. Running for queen was a lot of work! Being nice wasn't all it was cracked up to be, and she'd had to bite her tongue constantly to keep from saying the wrong thing.

"Oh, well . . . it'll be worth it." Michele started her car, and put on her smile again as she got out to scrape her windshield. Then she climbed back inside and drove toward home, maintaining what she hoped was a friendly expression all the way.

She didn't see the red envelope on the passenger seat until she'd pulled into the garage. Perhaps that was a blessing. She probably would have plowed straight into a snowbank if she'd noticed it while she was driving.

Michele picked up the envelope and carried it into the house. And when she was inside, she opened it. There was a poem inside, signed with Cat's name, and her eyes widened as she read the rhyme he'd written.

Roses are red, violets are blue. Let this serve as a warning to you. Not one step toward the throne will you take, unless you admit that Madame Zane is a fake.

She didn't stop to think. Michele just hurried to the fireplace and turned on the gas. She struck a match and lit the logs. And then she tossed the envelope into the flames. She'd enlarged on her Madame Zane story around the table at the Hungry Burger. She'd told everyone that Madame Zane had advised her to burn any Valentines that she might receive from Cat, so that the flames could cleanse their negative energy and render it powerless.

Michele began to feel better as the flames licked through Cat's message and turned it into ashes. She almost believed her own lie. It sounded good enough to be true, but she still had to take some precautions.

What, exactly, did Cat's rhyme mean? The news of her encounter with the psychic had spread like wildfire, and everyone at school had heard her story about Madame Zane. She'd just spent an hour at the Hungry Burger, telling more lies about the wise old psychic, and it would be terribly embarrassing to have to admit that she'd made up the whole thing.

But she didn't have to admit it! Michele began to smile. All she had to do was admit that she might be wrong about Madame Zane. From this moment on, whenever anyone asked her about it, she'd say that she was having doubts about whether the messages she'd received through the psychic were true. That should take care of the problem. And if Cat was really crazy, and he sent her a second warning Valentine, she'd make a public announcement that she was dropping out of the contest for personal reasons. That was bound to satisfy him, and then she'd be safe.

Just then the telephone rang, and Michele raced to answer it. It was a good thing her mother had ordered a long phone cord, because she received six calls from her friends while she was putting the chicken in the oven and peeling the potatoes. Most of the calls were about Madame Zane. Everyone wanted to know more about her sessions with the psychic.

Michele was very careful about what she said. She made sure that every single caller knew that she was having second thoughts about Madame Zane's abilities. And she admitted that her desire to hear from her dear, dead friends again might very well have clouded her judgment. There was really no way to tell whether Madame Zane had been in touch with Tanya, and Gail, and Jessica. That was why she wasn't going back for any more sessions. It was expensive, and as Michele's friends had pointed out, Madame Zane might be nothing more than a very good actress.

When she'd finished setting the table, Michele glanced at the clock. It was almost six, and it was time to walk the dog. She always walked Happy, their old collie, before her parents came home. When they'd bought Happy, over twelve years ago, she had promised to faithfully walk him every morning and night. Of course, she had been only six years old, and she hadn't realized that walking Happy would turn into such a chore. Thank goodness it was almost over! There was no way Happy could last much longer.

"Happy! Come here, boy!" Michele whistled, but Happy didn't come. That wasn't unusual. Happy was going slightly deaf, and he was already blind in one eye. She went looking for him and found him in his favorite spot, curled up next to her father's recliner in the living room. She woke him up, dangled the leash, and watched as he got slowly to his feet.

"Come on, Happy. Time to go out."

Happy plodded along at her side as Michele got her coat and mittens, put on her boots, and snapped on his leash. Then she opened the door and led him outside.

It was a cold night, and Michele shivered as she walked down the sidewalk. She took the same path she always did, around the corner and down the alley, to the burned-out house on the corner. Happy liked to nose around the debris, and that was where she snapped off the leash and let him wander for a few minutes.

The burned-out house had belonged to a family who'd gone bankrupt. Everyone thought they'd started the fire so that they could collect on the insurance, but no one had been able to prove it. The family had moved away, and the house was still sitting there, waiting for someone to buy the land, tear it down, and rebuild. Michele's mother worked for a real estate company, and she had the listing on the property. She'd told Michele that she didn't expect any offers until spring, when demolition and construction could start.

"Here you go." Michele snapped off Happy's leash and walked to her usual spot, next to two existing walls that protected her from the cold wind. She rubbed her hands together and stomped her feet to keep warm. Happy was taking his own sweet time, but she had to wait until he was ready to go home. There was no way she wanted to clean up a mess on the rug!

There was a sound above her, and Michele looked up. She could see the stars through the burned-out rafters, but nothing was moving. And then Happy growled, deep in his throat, and stared up at the rafters, too. That made Michele a little nervous. Happy didn't growl very often.

"What is it, boy?" Michele called out. "Is there a cat up there?"

Happy moved surprisingly fast as he plodded through the snow to her feet. He growled up at the rafters again, and Michele laughed and shook her head. Happy had been quite a cat chaser in his day. He'd been a car chaser, too, but those days were gone forever. Now it was all he could do to walk around the block.

There was another sound from the rafters, and Happy did something he'd never done before. He nipped at her sleeve and pulled. Michele pulled back and swatted him across the nose. "Bad dog! No, no!"

But Happy lunged for her sleeve again, and Michele began to get a little nervous. Happy was a collie, just like Lassie, and she'd watched every one of the old Lassie movies on television, when she was a little girl. Lassie had always pulled little Timmy away from danger. Was Happy trying to protect her from something?

And then she heard it again, a noise that sounded like footsteps over her head. They were to heavy for a squirrel or a cat. Happy was right! Someone was up on the rafters!

But before she could turn and run, there was a crack like a gunshot as a heavy beam fell, smashing her into oblivion.

Twenty

The next day at school was horrible. No one could believe that Michele was dead. When her dog had come home, dragging his leash, Michele's parents had gone out to look for her. They'd found her at the burned-out house, crushed by one of the heavy rafters that had fallen under the heavy weight of the winter snow.

Even the sheriff had admitted that something strange was happening in Clearwater. Four girls had died, and Clearwater had never had so many accidents in such a short space of time. But there was no proof that Michele's death was suspicious, even though she'd been wearing a half-heart necklace just like the ones that Tanya, and Gail, and Jessica had worn. The sheriff believed that if Michele had received a Valentine threat from Cat, she would have mentioned it to one of her friends who'd called just minutes before her death.

To make matters even worse, Colleen was gone. Danny had explained it to Amy this morning, when Colleen hadn't shown up for school.

Colleen had been terrified when she'd heard that Michele was dead, especially since Michele's death had put her in the lead for queen. She'd been so upset, her parents had asked Danny to drive her to their grandmother's house in Madison, over sixty miles away. There hadn't been time for a phone call, but Colleen had left a message for Amy, begging her to drop out of the contest. Now that Colleen was gone, Amy might take over the lead.

Amy was sorry her friend was gone, but Colleen had promised to come back, right after the dance. And she wasn't very worried about the contest because she was sure that some other girl would take over the lead. There was no way she'd get enough votes to be queen, since Cat was the only one who'd ever voted for her.

Now it was sixth period, and it was time to count the votes that had been cast at lunch. Amy and Kevin walked down the hallway, accompanied by Brett, who was taking Colleen's place.

"I really don't see how we can go on with the contest." Amy pushed open the door to the faculty lounge. "Four queen candidates have died already. And Colleen was so scared, she left town!"

Kevin nodded. "What you're saying is true. But how about the book fund? Mr. Dorman told me that if we keep on for just a few more days, we'll have enough money for a complete science section."

It didn't take long to clear off the table and put the teachers' dishes away. When they were through, Brett turned to Amy. "How about you, Amy? If you end up in the lead for queen, will you drop out, like Colleen did?"

"I . . . I really don't know." Amy sighed deeply. "I know that the library really needs a new science section, but I'm not sure I'd be willing to risk it. I guess I'm just hoping that someone else will take over the lead, and I won't have to make a decision like that."

"Okay. Are we ready?" Kevin set the box on the table. "It's really heavy today. I think the book fund made a lot of money."

Amy took out her lists of names and sat down at the table.

"I'm ready. If we finish fast enough, I might have time to go to the library to review my notes for the big History test."

"I'll join you." Brett nodded quickly. "It's going to be a tough test. I really hate essay questions."

Amy gave a wry little grin. "Me, too. Multiple choice are

much easier, and so are true and false. If you don't know the answer, you can usually make an intelligent guess. But you can't guess on an essay question. Either you know it cold, or you don't."

"But you studied, didn't you?" Kevin turned to Amy.

"Of course. I've been studying all week. But there's a lot of material to cover, and it's hard to remember it all. How about you? Have you been hitting the books?"

"Every night." Kevin looked a little sad. "But it used to be a lot easier, when I had someone to study with."

Both Amy and Brett were silent for a moment. They knew who that someone was. Kevin had always studied with his twin sister, Karen. And ever since Karen had died in the auto accident last year, Kevin had been studying alone.

"Why don't you do the review with us?" Amy suggested. "We could really use the help."

Brett nodded. "Good idea. The more the merrier, and maybe your notes are better than ours."

Kevin began to smile. "Hey . . . thanks for inviting me. It never hurts to review everything one more time."

"When are they going to post the results of the test?" Brett turned to Amy. "You found out, didn't you?"

As Amy nodded, she felt her stomach churn. She'd studied last night, but she still felt unprepared, and this test was very important. It counted for fifty percent of their final grade. "They're going to post them tomorrow night."

"Hold on a second." Kevin looked confused. "Tomorrow's Friday. If they're posting the results tomorrow night, how are we going to see them before Monday morning?"

Amy laughed. "That's exactly what I asked Mr. Dorman. And I talked him into giving me a key, so I can come in and copy down the results. The scores will be posted by initials, right inside his office door."

"That's great!" Kevin looked very relieved. "I don't think I could have waited until Monday. The suspense would have killed me."

Brett nodded, and reached into the box to pull out a vote. He handed it to Kevin, and Kevin unfolded it.

"It's for you, Amy. And it looks like Cat's printing. He's still voting for you."

Amy sighed. "Lucky me. Next?"

"This one's for you, too." Kevin unfolded another heart. "And it looks like the same printing."

Brett took the second vote and compared it to the first. "That's right. It's a second vote from Cat."

"That's strange." Amy began to frown. "Cat's never voted for me twice in the same day. I wonder why he did that?"

As Kevin continued to read the votes, and the marks by her name began to grow into double digits, Amy's hands started to shake. It was almost like Cat was deliberately trying to put her into the lead!

"Here's the last one." Kevin unfolded the vote, and read it. "It's for you again, Amy."

"But . . . I don't want to be queen!" Amy couldn't keep her voice from trembling. "I never wanted to be queen!"

Brett slipped his arm around Amy's shoulders, and gave her a little hug. "Maybe you didn't want to be queen, but it's pretty obvious that you're Cat's choice. You're in the lead, Amy."

"But, why does he want me to be queen? So he can send me threatening Valentines?" Amy shivered.

"Maybe not." Kevin looked thoughtful. "I think Cat likes you, and he thinks you'll make a good queen. And I bet he won't send you any threatening Valentines."

Amy turned to Kevin with fear in her eyes. "But, why did he choose me? I'm no better than any of the other girls. And look what happened to them! I'm going to tell Mr. Dorman to take my name off the list of candidates."

"Don't do that, Amy." Brett looked worried. "Kevin could be right. Cat must like you, or he wouldn't have voted for you. Just try it for a couple of days, and see if you get any Valentines. We really need more science books."

Amy was shocked, and it showed on her face as she turned to

stare at Brett. "Do you really think that science books are more important than my safety?"

"Of course not! If I thought you were in any danger, I'd run right down to Mr. Dorman's office and take your name off the list myself! But I really think that Cat is trying to tell us something by casting all these votes for you. And Kevin does, too. Right, Kevin?"

Kevin nodded. "That's what it looks like to me. You're the only person that Cat has ever voted for."

Amy sighed. It was true that Cat had never voted for anyone else. But she didn't like the idea that someone like Cat had hand-picked her for queen.

"Will you stay in the contest, at least until tomorrow?"

Brett looked anxious, and Amy shook her head. "I don't know. I just don't like it."

"Come on, Amy." Kevin smiled at her. "We'll all take turns guarding you, if it makes you feel better. And you won't be sorry you stayed in the contest when you see all the new books the library fund can buy."

Amy thought about it for a moment, and then she nodded. "All right. I'll stay in until tomorrow. But if I get just one threatening Valentine from Cat, I'm out of the running for good!"

Cat smiled as he passed the bulletin board and saw Amy's name at the top of the list. He'd spent a lot of money putting her there, and now he had to make sure she didn't get so nervous, she'd withdraw from the contest.

"What do you think, Karen? Would she make a good queen?" Cat whispered the words. He didn't want to take even a remote chance that he'd be overheard.

But Karen didn't answer, and Cat began to get very nervous. Amy was his choice. Wasn't she Karen's choice, too?

"I don't have to test her, do I, Karen? I mean . . . she's perfect! And I know she never gossiped about you."

And then he heard Karen's sweet voice floating in the stillness, and he smiled as she reassured him that Amy would make a perfect queen. Karen agreed that Amy was kind, and sweet, and good, and she told him that Amy had never once gossiped about her.

As Karen went on speaking, Cat began to frown. It seemed that Karen had plans for Amy . . . big plans. She was Karen's choice for much more than queen.

"Are you sure, Karen?" Cat shivered as a cold draft seeped around his ankles and snaked its way down the hall. "What if Amy doesn't want to go?"

Cat listened for a moment, and then he put his hands over his ears. What Karen had told him to do was so dreadful, he wanted to block out the sound of her voice. But blocking his ears did no good. Karen's voice was still loud and clear. Her words resounded up and down the hall with so much force, that he could hear them right through the hands that were clamped tightly over his ears.

"THEN TAKE HER AND BRING HER TO ME. IF YOU LOVE ME, YOU'LL DO IT. I WANT AMY HUNTER WITH ME, FOREVER!"

Twenty-one

Amy felt good about her History test. She'd managed to answer all ten of the essay questions, and when she'd read them over, the answers had sounded clear and concise . . . to her. Of course, her opinion wasn't the one that counted. Essay tests were subjective, and it was all up to her teacher.

When the bell rang for dismissal, Amy went to her locker. She spun the dial and opened the lock, but then she hesitated, her hand on the door. She almost hated to open her locker for fear there'd be a red envelope from Cat inside. But when she jerked open the door and there was no envelope, Amy breathed a big sigh of relief. Perhaps Brett and Kevin had been right. If she was Cat's choice for Valentine's Day Queen, he'd have no reason to send her any frightening Valentine messages.

Amy slipped on her coat and boots, picked up her books, and headed for the stairway with a crowd of students. Brett and Kevin had reminded her that there was safety in numbers, and she wanted plenty of people around her. She went down the steps, carefully avoiding the side with the open rail, and hurried to the flagpole, where Danny had said he'd meet her.

"Hi, Danny." Amy smiled as she found him leaning against the flagpole. But Danny didn't smile back. He just grabbed her arm and pulled her over to a secluded spot where they could talk.

"You're staying in the contest!?" Danny was clearly shocked. "You've got to be crazy, Amy! My sister was so freaked about being in the lead, she had to leave town!"

"I know, Danny. But I'm taking it one day at a time. If I get a Valentine from Cat, I'm withdrawing my name right away."

"That might be too late." Danny looked very worried. "Cat could kill you without sending a Valentine. That's what he did with Michele."

"Maybe not. Michele could have gotten a Valentine that she didn't tell us about. Don't forget that she really wanted to be queen."

"And you don't?"

"No." Amy shook her head. "I've never wanted it. You know that. Besides, Brett and Kevin are going to protect me. They promised me they'd have someone with me every minute."

Danny's eyes narrowed. "Brett, huh? It seems to me that you used to want to date him."

"I did. But I don't want to date him now."

"Oh, yeah?" Danny raised his eyebrows. "Why's that?"

"Because that was before I got to know you. And now that I know you, I don't want to go out with anybody else."

Danny stared at her for a moment, and then he threw back his head and laughed. "Look, Amy. You're not supposed to say things like that to a guy. Girls are supposed to keep guys guessing whether they like them or not."

"Oh." Amy nodded sagely. "Do you like it when a girl keeps you guessing?"

"No. I hate it. If a girl keeps me guessing, I never know where I stand."

"But you know where you stand with me, don't you?"

Danny nodded. "Sure. You just told me."

"Good." Amy started to grin. "Then you don't have to worry about it. And that means I did you a big favor by telling you."

Danny looked down at her for a second, and then he laughed again. "I can't quite figure out whether you're hopelessly dumb when it comes to guys, or incredibly smart."

"But you like me the way I am?"

Danny slipped his arm around her shoulders and gave her a hug. "Let's go find Brett and Kevin so they can work out their schedule with me. There's no way I want them hanging around you every minute."

"Okay." Amy moved closer, and matched her steps with his. "But you still didn't tell me if you like me the way I am."

Danny hugged her a little tighter. And then he smiled. "Yes, Amy. You're perfect, just the way you are."

It had been a very stressful day. Amy was stretched out on her bed, listening to music and trying to relax, when there was a knock on her door. A second later, she heard her mother's voice.

"Amy? Could I talk to you for a minute?"

"Sure. Just a second." Amy switched off her stereo, stashed the tape that Danny had given her under her pillow, and went to open the door. Her mother hated rock music, and Danny's band had played punk rock. "Come in, Mom."

"You must be growing up. Your room's not messy anymore." Amy's mother walked over to the bed, and sat down. "I just wanted to talk to you about the Valentine's Day Dance."

Amy's heart pounded hard in her chest. Her mother looked very worried. Had she heard that Danny was Amy's date for the dance? She'd been meaning to tell her parents that she was going to the dance with Danny, but the time just hadn't seemed right.

"What is it, Mom?" Amy tried not to show how nervous she was.

"I ran into Colleen's mother today, and she mentioned that Colleen and Danny had chipped in to buy you an early birthday present . . . a dress for the Valentine's Day dance?"

Amy nodded. "That's right, Mom. They did."

"She also said that Colleen was busy, so *Danny* picked it out at the mall."

Amy couldn't help it. She started to laugh. No wonder why her mother was so worried! And then something wonderful happened. Her mother began to laugh, too.

It felt so good to laugh with her mother, Amy sat down on the bed and hugged her. It was something they hadn't done in a long time, and it felt wonderful.

When her mother had recovered somewhat, she turned to Amy with tears of laughter in her eyes. "I just kept thinking . . . what could a boy with *green* hair possibly know about . . ."

"Style, and taste, and refinement?" Amy finished the sentence for her mother, and they both cracked up again. "But Mom . . . Danny doesn't have green hair in the back anymore. Now it's . . . it's . . ."

"Red?"

Amy's mom giggled like a teenager as Amy shook her head. "No, Mom. It's not red. It's . . ."

"Purple!" Amy's mother cracked up again.

"No, Mom." Amy was laughing so hard, her sides hurt. "And it's not yellow, or blue, or pink, either. Danny cut the green part all the way off with a razor. And now it's so short he's practically . . ."

"Bald?!" Amy's mother clutched at her sides. "Oh, Amy! He's not bald, is he?"

"No, not exactly. It's just a really close buzz cut. When you look at him from the back, he looks like he's in the Marines."

"Oh, dear!" Amy's mother reached for a tissue and wiped her eyes. "I guess that's better than green hair. And it's bound to grow back. Now . . . how about the dress? How awful is it?"

Amy giggled. "It's not awful at all, Mom. If you can stay for a minute, I'll try it on for you."

"I've got all the time in the world. My fudge is setting up, and all I have to do is cut it when it's ready." Amy's mother leaned back against the pillows and laughed. "Take your time, honey. And while you're changing, I'll be thinking about shawls, and stoles, and ways we can cover it up."

Amy was grinning as she hurried to her large walk-in closet. Her dad had converted it to a dressing room with a mirror and vanity when she'd reached high school. She took the blue dress from the rack and put it on. And then she took a few moments to sweep her hair up into a passable French twist, secured with the gold barrette Colleen had given her.

"Okay, Mom. Here I come." Amy came out of the dressing room and struck a model's pose. "What do you think?"

Amy's mother sat up and blinked. And then she started to smile. "Why, Amy! There's no way Danny could have picked out this dress by himself. The saleslady must have helped him, because it's just beautiful!"

"I knew you'd like it." Amy grinned a secret grin. Her mother had everything backward, and perhaps that was good. Danny had told her he'd picked out the blue dress by himself. The saleslady had helped him with the other dress, the sexy black dress that her mother would never see!

School was over, and they were all sitting in the back booth at the Hungry Burger. There was much more room in the booth now, and Amy felt sad as she glanced around her. Colleen was missing, and so were Tanya, and Gail, and Jessica, and Michele. Now there were only Brett, Kevin, Danny, Neal, and Suzie Douglas, Neal's new Chemistry partner.

Suzie smiled at Amy. She was a shy girl who'd just transferred to Hamilton High from Bonnerville, and she seemed very nice. "Neal told me about all the awful things that've happened. Cat hasn't sent you any Valentines, has he, Amy?"

"No. Not yet." Amy shook her head. Every time she'd opened her locker in school today, she'd expected to see a red envelope. But there had been no message from Cat. He'd voted for her again at lunchtime, but he hadn't sent her any of his frightening poems.

"It's almost five-fifteen." Brett glanced at the big clock on the wall behind the counter. "I wish they'd hurry with those test results. Waiting is making me nervous."

Danny nodded. "I know exactly what you mean. When I had the band, I used to get the jitters every time they played my intro. I'd stand there in the wings and shake until it was time to run out on the stage."

"I heard about your band." Suzie smiled at him. "My best friend at Bonnerville went to one of your concerts, and she said one of your songs was really incredible."

Danny grinned. "That's always good to hear. Which song was it?"

"I can't remember the name, but it was about a guy who thought he was up on a ledge, watching his life go by."

"Oh, *that* one! It was called—" Danny stopped and frowned. "Let's just forget it, okay?"

"But, why?" Amy was curious. "Is it really X-rated, or something like that?"

"No. It's just an ordinary title. But I'd rather not talk about it, considering what's been happening around here."

Suzie started to laugh. "I remember it now! And I can understand why you don't want to mention it. But you wrote that a long time ago, right?"

"That's right." Danny nodded, and then he turned to Amy. "What time are those results supposed to go up, anyway?"

"Between five and five-thirty. I told Mr. Dorman I'd be there at a quarter to six, so I'll leave here in ten minutes."

"It doesn't make sense to copy down the whole list." Brett tore a page from his notebook. "Let's just put down our initials and Amy can pick out our scores."

Amy nodded as Brett passed the list around the table. That made perfect sense. If some students didn't care enough to come to the Hungry Burger to get their test results, they could wait until Monday morning to see them.

"Do you want another Coke, Amy?" Danny slid out of the booth and stood up.

"Sure. I'd love one." Amy smiled at him. He still looked a little upset, and as he walked up to the counter to order, she tried to figure out why. He'd given her several tapes of his music, and she hadn't thought there was anything unusual about the titles of his songs. She frowned slightly as she tried to remember every song on the tapes.

"Nobody Home" was her favorite. And then there was "Do It Right," and "Far Corner," and "Lovin' Around," and "Space Inside." If you flipped the tape over, it had "River Boy," and "Just Leave," and "Cat Walk," and . . .

Amy's knees started to tremble, and she tried to keep the

shock from showing on her face. "Cat Walk." That was the song about the guy on a ledge. And Danny had told her that he'd been writing about his life. Was it possible that Danny was . . . ?

Amy did her best to push the traitorous thought from her mind. No. Absolutely not. And she certainly wouldn't mention the title of his song to anyone else! She knew that Danny had nothing to do with the Valentine threats, or the accidental deaths that weren't really accidental. Danny wasn't Cat. He couldn't be!

"What's the matter, Amy?"

Kevin looked concerned, and Amy forced a smile. "Nothing that getting those test results won't cure."

"It was awful, wasn't it?" Suzie sighed deeply. "I'm just glad my score doesn't count. History class at Bonnerville was a lot easier."

Amy nodded, but her eyes followed Danny as he headed back toward their booth. And then she thought of something that made her feel much better. There was no way that Danny could be Cat. His printing was different. She'd seen it the day they'd all printed their names for the WROQ drawing. They'd drawn no conclusions as to Cat's identity from that test. Of course, he'd been sitting right next to her when Brett had analyzed Cat's printing. And he could have changed it, so it wouldn't be recognized.

"Amy?" Danny set the glass in front of her, and Amy jumped. "What's wrong? You look freaked."

Amy nodded quickly, and then she used the same excuse she'd used with Kevin. "I am freaked. I'm really worried about my test score."

"Only a couple minutes more, and you'll know." Danny slipped his arm around her shoulders. And then he looked up as the waitress called his name.

"There's a telephone call for you, Danny. I think it's your sister. She says she really needs to talk to you."

"Go ahead." Amy put on a smile. "One of the other guys can take me up to the school."

"I'll do it." Kevin volunteered. "Come on, Amy. I'm just as worried about my test score as you are."

Danny nodded, and got up from the booth. "Okay. Watch out for her, Kevin."

"I will." Kevin looked very serious. "You don't have to worry about Amy. I'll keep her right with me, forever."

"You don't have to go quite that far." Danny laughed. "But don't let her out of your sight."

Amy was laughing, along with everyone else, as she went out the door. But when she climbed into Kevin's car, she noticed that he wasn't even smiling. He must be really worried about her safety.

Amy reached out to touch his hand. "Don't worry, Kevin. I trust you."

"I know you do." Kevin nodded and put the car in gear. They rode in silence for several minutes, until they pulled up in front of the school. That was when Kevin turned to smile at her. "You make such a perfect queen, Amy. You're the only girl in the Senior class who's kind, and faithful, and true."

Twenty-two

Amy couldn't help being a little nervous as she walked up the sidewalk toward the school with Kevin at her side. Kevin had used an unusual combination of words to describe her, and that made Amy very uneasy. Although she hadn't received any Valentines from Cat, she remembered the poems that the other girls had found in their lockers. And one of them had been, *Roses are red, violets are blue. A queen should be kind, faithful, and true.*

"Do you have the key?"

Kevin turned to look at her. His eyes were so intense that Amy almost said she'd left it at the Hungry Burger. But before she could stuff her key ring back in her pocket to hide it, Kevin reached out and took it from her hand.

"Here. I'll open the door for you, Amy."

"Thank you, Kevin." Amy did her best to sound perfectly normal. She was sure that she was just nervous about her test score, and that was the reason why she was so jumpy. Kevin's choice of words had to be accidental. After all, he'd been at the table when they'd read the poems that Cat had written on the Valentines. And the intense look in his eyes could be easily explained by the fact that they were going to look at their test scores. She was nervous about hers, and so was Kevin.

The school was eerie at night. The bright banks of fluorescent lights in the hall were partially turned off at night to save on electricity, and only the ones at the ends of the halls were on. That made the tall shapes of the lockers that lined the halls seem to loom up, out of the darkness, as Amy and Kevin walked past.

As they climbed the stairs to Mr. Dorman's office, Amy shivered. Their footsteps sounded very loud in the silent and deserted halls.

When they reached the principal's office, Amy turned to Kevin. "I know it sounds silly, but I promised Mr. Dorman I wouldn't let anyone else into his office. You don't mind waiting out here, do you, Kevin?"

"No. I don't mind waiting for you, Amy." Kevin's voice was very tense. "We've waited for you for a long time."

What did *that* mean? Amy's hands were shaking as she unlocked the door and stepped inside, closing it tightly behind her. Kevin was acting very strange tonight. And then she remembered what he'd said to Danny when they'd left the Hungry Burger. *You don't have to worry about Amy. I'll keep her right with me, forever.*

Amy's knees were shaking as she turned back to look out through the pane of glass in the door. Kevin wasn't watching her. He was staring down the hall, and his lips were moving. He seemed to be talking to someone, but there was no one else here!

Was he praying? Amy frowned. It seemed useless to pray for a good grade now. It was too late. The results were already posted, and a low grade couldn't miraculously change into a higher one. Perhaps Kevin was religious and he believed in miracles. Religion didn't necessarily have to make sense.

Amy shivered as she watched Kevin in the dim light filtering down the hall. He looked very strange . . . but it was more than strange.

Kevin looked totally insane.

That was when Amy caught sight of the grade sheet that was posted by the door. One set of initials seemed to pop out at her, almost as if they were highlighted in red.

Kevin A. Thomas.

K.A.T. Kevin was Cat! Amy didn't stop to think. She just flipped the lock on the door as quietly as she could, locking herself in, and Kevin out. Her heart was pounding in her chest as she hurried to the secretary's desk. She had to call for help!

But there was no dial tone when she lifted the receiver, only a faint trace of static on a closed line. Mr. Dorman had switched off the phones when he'd left for the day, and anyone who wanted to use the line had to punch in a code to get a dial tone.

Amy put the receiver back in its cradle. The phone was useless to anyone who didn't know the code. She couldn't call for help, but she had to do something!

That was when she heard the sound of glass breaking, and she whirled to see Kevin's arm reaching through the shards of glass to unlock the door. Amy was so frightened, she said the first thing that came to her mind.

"Kevin . . . I know you're Cat. But why did you do it? I just don't understand!"

Kevin unlocked the door and came into the room, stepping carefully over the broken pieces of glass. "Careful, Amy. There's a mess here, and I don't want you to cut yourself."

Amy could feel the room starting to spin around her. Kevin was totally insane. He was more concerned about the glass on the floor than he was about killing Tanya, and Gail, and Jessica, and Michele. "Why, Kevin? Why did you kill them?"

"I had no choice, Amy. Don't you see? I had to make sure they didn't win the contest. They weren't worthy enough to be queen."

Amy drew a deep breath for courage. It was too late to run and there was nowhere to go. "But . . . what did they do?"

"They were cruel to Karen. They gossiped and they said things that weren't true. You tried to stop them but it didn't work."

"You killed them because they gossiped?" Amy tried to make some sense out of what Kevin was saying.

"That's part of it, but it's not the only reason. I told you, Amy. They weren't worthy. I gave them a second chance, but they couldn't pass my test. You're the only one who's worthy enough to be queen."

Amy took another big breath, but black spots still swirled in front of her eyes. She remembered that night at the Hungry Burger, last summer, when Tanya had been gossiping about Kevin's sister, Karen. She'd tried to stop it, but the other girls hadn't listened. And now they were dead.

"You do understand, don't you, Amy?"

Kevin was staring at her and Amy shuddered. His eyes were cold and dead, just like the girls he'd killed. Somehow, she had to get him to take her back down to the Hungry Burger, where someone could call the police.

"I'm trying to understand, Kevin. I really am. And I want you to tell me all about it on the way back down to the Hungry Burger."

"The Hungry Burger?" Kevin frowned slightly.

"That's right. Everybody's waiting to find out how they did on the History test. You wouldn't want to disappoint your friends, would you? You know how important our grades are."

Kevin laughed. It was a laugh totally without humor, and when Amy heard it, she knew that it was impossible to reason with him.

"Our grades aren't important, Amy. You see, we won't be here to take our finals and graduate. We're going on a journey together, a trip to a place where we'll never have to worry about anything again."

Amy began to shake so hard, she could barely speak. "What do you mean?"

"Amy, my perfect Queen of Hearts. You were Karen's friend and I know how much you miss her. Don't you see what an honor this will be? We're going to see her."

"But, Kevin . . ." Amy fought to keep from screaming. "Karen is dead."

Kevin smiled a terrible smile. "Yes, Amy. I know."

"Then how can we possibly go to see her?"

Kevin tipped her head up, and looked into her eyes. Amy's

knees buckled as she realized exactly what he meant. And then she did something she'd never done before in her entire life. She fainted, dead away.

Colleen sounded much more relaxed, and Danny was glad. She'd asked about the queen contest, and he'd told her that Amy was in the lead, but they were all taking turns guarding her. And then she'd asked about the big History test, so he'd explained how they'd all written down their initials so Amy could go to the school to get their grades.

"You mean you put down your initials?" Colleen sounded amused. "Dumb move, big brother."

Danny was puzzled. "Why's that?"

"Think about it. Matthew Underwood Daniels. M.U.D. Your name is mud!"

Danny laughed, even though he didn't think it was that funny. "I wouldn't talk, Colleen Olivia Daniels. Your initials spell cod."

"True." Colleen giggled. "How about Brett? Do you know his middle name?"

"It's Lawrence. That makes him B. L. S."

"I think that stands for bliss." Colleen sighed deeply. "How about Neal?"

Danny did his best to remember the names on the sheet. "I think it's Ian. That's N.I.C."

"That fits. Neal's nice."

"How about Amy?" Danny tried to keep from seeming too eager.

There was a silence, and then Colleen laughed. "I don't think I'd better tell you. Amy'll kill me if anyone finds out her middle name."

"Come on, sis. I already know her initials. They're A.G.H. What's her middle name?"

Colleen laughed again. "Well, actually she has two middle names, and one is Katherine, but you'll never guess the other, so don't even try."

"Gladys?"

"No way. It's much worse than that."

Danny tried several other names, including Gail, Glenda, and Gloria. But each time Colleen told him that he was wrong.

"Come on, Colleen." Danny sighed deeply. "I'm going to find out. I'll just sneak a look at her driver's license. Why don't you just save me the trouble and tell me?"

There was a long silence, and then Colleen laughed. "Okay, but you can't ever tell her that I snitched on her. Is it a deal?"

"Sure. What is it?"

"Gwendolyn."

"Gwendolyn?" Danny grinned as he repeated it. "That's not so awful."

"Amy thinks it is. She absolutely despises it. But it's not as bad as Kevin's middle name."

"What's that?"

Colleen laughed so hard, she could barely tell him. "It's Archibald!"

"No! You're putting me on, Colleen."

"It's the truth, honest. Mom was in the hospital having me when Kevin's mother was there with the twins, and she saw the little name cards the nurses put on their cribs. Kevin Archibald Thomas, and Karen Amelia Thomas. Mom thought it was cute, because Mrs. Thomas raised Persians and Siamese, and the babies' initials spelled—"

"Kat!" Danny's voice shook as he gasped out the word. "Oh, my God! Kevin is Cat! And Amy's with him right now!"

Danny didn't bother to hang up the phone. He just dropped it. It swung back and forth on its cord, making high-pitched, tinny sounds, as he raced back to the booth for his car keys.

"Hey, Danny. Take a look at these." Neal held up several half-heart necklaces. "Brett used one of Kevin's pens to write down everyone's initials. And when he put it back in Kevin's backpack, he found these!"

"Amy's in danger!" Danny's voice was shaking as he grabbed his keys. "Kevin is Cat!"

Brett didn't waste any time. He slid out of the booth and

grabbed his coat. "I'll go with you. You need somebody to back you up."

"And I'll be there, just as soon as I call the sheriff." Neal got up and raced for the phone. "I'll tell him to meet us at the school right away."

Danny was in the lead as they raced for his car. He knew it would take the sheriff awhile to get to the school, but there was no way he could wait. The girl he loved was in danger, and it was up to him to save her.

At first Amy thought she was dreaming. There were glimmering lights behind her eyelids, and she almost opened her eyes. But then she remembered what had happened in Mr. Dorman's office with Kevin, and she kept her eyes closed, stalling for time. She didn't think that Kevin would kill her when she was unconscious, and she needed to think of some way to divert him.

Kevin was whispering, very near to her ear, and Amy tried not to shiver as she made out his words. But what she heard was so alarming, she almost gasped out loud. He was talking to his dead sister, Karen, telling her that they would soon be together. And he was promising to bring Amy with him, so that Karen would have a friend.

The whispering stopped, and Amy heard Kevin's footsteps receding. They got softer the farther away he walked, and she risked opening her eyes just a fraction of an inch so that she could peek out.

What she saw frightened Amy so dreadfully, she could barely keep from screaming in terror. She was in the faculty lounge, stretched out on the floor, with a circle of candles arranged all around her. It reminded her of the old horror movies she'd seen on late-night television. She was the living sacrifice, surrounded by a ring of flickering lights, waiting for her executioner to appear. And the instrument of her death was inside the circle of candles, a knife with a sharp, wickedly gleaming blade.

Amy felt faint as she saw the other item that Kevin had placed inside the ring of flames. It was Karen's picture, inside a silver frame. Amy stared at it for a moment, and then she began to understand. It was clear that Kevin was insane with grief for his dead twin sister, and he was taking revenge against the girls who had gossiped about Karen. Kevin had wanted Karen to be queen, and he'd killed any girl he'd thought was unworthy of the honor.

But now he was preparing to kill her, just like he'd killed Tanya, and Gail, and Jessica, and Michele. And she was Kevin's choice for queen. He'd even told her that he thought she'd be perfect, and that didn't make sense at all!

Amy shivered. Perhaps it did make sense to Kevin. Kevin was insane, and crazy people weren't rational. It would be useless to appeal to Kevin's sense of reason. He thought he was talking to his dead sister, and there was no way she could convince him that he wasn't.

There was only one thing in her favor. When she didn't come back with the test scores, Danny, and Brett, and Neal would come to the school to look for her. But that might be too late! She had to think of something fast, something that would stall Kevin long enough for them to break into the school to save her.

As Amy stared at Karen's picture, several memories came back. Karen had always smiled at her in the hall, and once they'd even studied together. Amy had thought that Karen Thomas was very nice. If Karen were still alive, she'd be horrified at what her twin brother was planning.

But Karen was still alive, in her brother's mind. And perhaps Amy could convince Kevin that Karen was alive in her mind, too. It was worth a try. Time was running out, and it was her only chance.

Amy took a deep breath, and shut her eyes. And then she began to speak in a very soft, slow voice, trying to make Kevin believe that she was in a trance.

"Yes, Karen. I can hear you. It's wonderful to hear your voice again. I've missed you so much this year."

There was the sound of a sharply indrawn breath behind her, but Amy stayed very still, with her eyes closed. It was extremely important that Kevin think she was still unconscious.

"Of course I'll help you, Karen. What do you want me to do?"

The footsteps approached her quickly now, and Amy made her body relax. A ghost of a smile flickered across her face, and she sighed deeply.

"Yes, I know that Kevin misses you, too. And I'll tell him that you love him. Is there anything else?"

She could hear Kevin breathing behind her, and it sounded like he was gasping for air. Amy moaned softly, and spoke again.

"Of course I'll help to keep your memory alive. Just tell me how to do it."

Kevin was so close to her now, Amy could feel his breath on her face. She wanted to open her eyes and scream, but she moaned again, instead.

"Yes, Karen. I promise I'll write a piece about you for the school yearbook. I'll do it this weekend and turn it in on Monday morning. Is there anything else I can do?"

Amy heard a sound in front of the school. A car was pulling up near the entrance. Danny and the boys were here to save her, but they didn't have a key. They'd have to break into the school, and that would take time.

Something warm and wet splashed against her cheek, and Amy almost jumped. And then she realized that Kevin was crying, and she moaned again, to cover the sound of the glass that was breaking down the hall. Danny and the guys were inside. It was almost over, but she had to keep Kevin occupied and let them know where she was.

"No, Karen. You don't have to worry about Kevin. He's our friend and we'll take care of him. We all like Kevin very much."

Another tear splashed against her face, and Amy didn't even wiggle. But then she had a thought that made her blood run cold. Kevin had a knife, and Danny and the boys were coming to save her. Would Kevin use the knife on them?!

Amy knew she was playing with fire. It would be very risky to mention the knife, but somehow she had to convince Kevin to get rid of it.

"You're afraid that Kevin will cut himself with the knife? Yes, Karen. I'll tell him to toss it out the window."

"Nooo!" Kevin's voice was very loud, and he wailed like a frightened child. "I want to go with you, Karen! I don't want to stay here all by myself!"

Amy's eyes flew open as Kevin reached for the knife. She rolled quickly, snatching it up, and leaping to her feet. Then she whirled and ran toward the faculty rest rooms, where there was a door she could lock.

But Kevin had a speed born of desperation, and he covered the distance between them in the space of a heartbeat. He lunged at Amy, and she screamed, struggling to keep the knife away from him. Before she could scream a second time, Kevin's hands clamped around her neck, squeezing hard, trying to get her to drop the knife.

Amy felt her knees grow weak as she struggled for air. Black spots were whirling in front of her eyes, and her grip on the knife began to slip. She knew she couldn't let go. Danny was coming, and Kevin would kill him. But after another few agonizing seconds, she just couldn't hang on any longer.

There was a clatter as the knife fell to the floor. And then the door crashed in. That was when things started to happen very fast.

Danny barreled into Kevin, sending him flying, and Brett raced to Amy to help her to her feet. And then Amy was in Danny's arms while Brett stood guard over Kevin. Danny was holding her tightly, stroking her hair and telling her that everything was going to be all right. But it wasn't. Not for Kevin.

There was the sound of footsteps racing down the hall, and Neal and the sheriff appeared in the doorway, followed by two deputies. Brett glanced at them for just an instant, but that was enough time for Kevin to do what he'd meant to do all along.

Kevin grabbed the knife with both hands and pointed it at his chest. And then he fell forward to the floor, driving it in to the hilt. He looked at Amy as he fell, and Amy heard the last words he whispered.

"I'm coming, Karen. Wait for me. I'm coming to be with you forever!"

Epilogue

Amy slept late on Saturday morning. After the sheriff had taken her statement, he'd driven her home and told her parents what had happened at the school. He'd praised Amy's quick thinking and called her a heroine, but Amy didn't feel like one. She just felt sad that so many of her friends had died.

After Amy's parents had gotten over their shock, they'd hugged Amy, and told her how proud they were of her. And then they'd asked her if there was anything they could do to help her.

Amy had been able to think of only one thing that might help. She'd said she just wanted her life to get back to normal. So she'd watched a television program with her parents and gone up to bed, trying to convince herself that it was just an ordinary night.

It must have worked, because when Amy got up in the morning, she felt like her old self. She dressed, and hurried downstairs to help her mother with breakfast. It was Saturday morning, and the Valentine's Day Dance was tonight. This was her very last chance to tell her mother that she'd asked Danny to be her date.

"That smells wonderful, Mom!" Amy smiled as she approached the stove, where her mother was standing. "What are you making?"

"Apple pancakes. They used to be your dad's favorites."

"But, Mom . . ." Amy was so surprised, she spoke without thinking. "I didn't put apple pancakes on my diet sheet. I mean . . . the diet sheet that came in the mail from . . ."

Amy stopped, and began to blush. There was no way to talk herself out of this one. She'd have to confess that she'd written the diet sheet. "You know, don't you, Mom?"

"I know." Amy's mother laughed. "You weren't very subtle, Amy. You listed all of your father's favorite foods, but you didn't put down one single thing that he didn't like."

"Are you mad at me, Mom?" Amy felt terrible.

"No, honey. I was driving both of you crazy with my silly diet sheets, wasn't I?"

Amy nodded. "Uh . . . yes, in a way. But I shouldn't have tried to fool you. That wasn't right."

"That's true." Amy's mother slipped her arm around Amy's shoulders and gave her a hug. "But that diet sheet of yours was actually very good. You managed to get in all the basic food groups, and you did a nice job balancing the saturated and unsaturated fats. Did someone help you with it?"

Amy nodded. "Danny did. And Colleen went over it with us. She had a book on nutrition. But I'm sorry, Mom. I shouldn't have been so sneaky. I should have come to you and talked about the problem. It's just . . . I really didn't think you'd listen to me."

"I hope you know that you can come to me and talk about your problems now." Amy's mother hugged her again. "I'm on your side, honey. I've always been on your side. And if we have a problem, we should try to work it out."

Amy nodded again. And then she took a deep breath and blurted out the biggest problem in her life.

"Mom? I've got something to tell you, and I hope you won't be upset. I didn't mention it before, because I . . . I just couldn't! I know how all the mothers in Clearwater feel about Danny. They think he's awful because he dropped out of school to start his band, and they don't want their daughters to date him. But Danny's back in school now. And he's on the honor roll. And he's . . . he's really nice, Mom. And that's why I . . . I asked him to be my date for the Valentine's Day Dance. I can go with him, can't I, Mom?"

Amy's mother smiled. "Yes, you can. Your dad and I were very impressed with Danny when he came to ask us if he could take you to the dance."

"Danny came here?" Amy was so shocked, her mouth fell open. "But . . . when?"

"Almost a week ago. But I asked him not to tell you that he'd asked us for permission to date you. I wanted you to come to me, and you did."

"Oh, Mom!" Amy threw her arms around her mother's neck and hugged her. "I've been really stupid, haven't I?"

Amy's mother hugged her back. And then she smiled. "Not really. It's all a part of growing up, Amy. It's hard for kids to re-alize that their parents have gone through the very same things."

"The very same things?" Amy blinked. "You're kidding, aren't you, Mom? I mean . . . you dated Dad in school. You told me that you went steady with him when you were a Senior. And Dad was . . . he was Dad. He was never the bad boy in town!"

"Oh, no?" Amy's mother smiled. It was a smile that was full of secrets, and Amy's eyes widened with surprise. "Let's go out to the mall for lunch, next Saturday . . . just the two of us. I think you're old enough to hear some very interesting stories about the things we did when we were in high school."

It was midafternoon when the doorbell rang. Amy opened it, and grinned as she saw Colleen.

"I'm back." Colleen hugged Amy. "Danny told me what hap-pened when he came to pick me up this morning. You're a hero, Amy!"

Amy laughed. It was wonderful to see Colleen again. "It's heroine, and I'm not, really. I was scared to death."

"Are you going to the dance?" Colleen sounded wistful.

"Yes, and so are you. Your date's picking you up at seven."

"My date?" Colleen was shocked. "But, Amy . . . I don't have a date!"

"You do now. Danny and I worked it out. And put on your best dress because you're going to be the Valentine's Day Queen."

"I am?" Colleen looked very confused. "But, Amy . . . I thought *you* were supposed to be the queen."

"Not anymore. I talked to Mr. Dorman this morning, and I convinced him that the votes I got from Cat shouldn't count. And that means you won!"

"Oh, Amy! Thank you!" Colleen hugged her again. "But who's my date?"

Amy just smiled a secret smile. "You'll find out, when he picks you up tonight."

Everything had worked out perfectly. Colleen had been thrilled when Brett had come to pick her up for the dance, and she'd been even more delighted when Danny had told her that the whole thing had been Brett's idea. Colleen had always wanted to date Brett, but since Amy had been interested in him first, she hadn't wanted to jeopardize their friendship.

When Amy and Danny arrived at the dance together, Colleen's eyes had nearly popped out of her head. But once she'd gotten over the shock, she'd been delighted. She'd confessed that she'd always wanted Amy to date her brother. Since they were best friends already, it was absolutely perfect.

The Valentine's Day Dance had been incredibly wonderful. Danny and Amy danced every dance together, and they'd applauded wildly when Colleen had been crowned queen, and Brett had taken the throne as king.

Now the dance was over, and Danny pulled up in front of Amy's house. He turned to her with a smile, and Amy noticed that he kept the engine running. "Do you have to go in right away?"

"Not really." Amy glanced at her watch in the light from the dashboard, and smiled a secret smile. "I still have almost fifteen minutes before we get blinded by the porch light."

Danny pulled Amy into his arms and kissed her. It was a sweet kiss, full of promises. But promises weren't quite enough for Amy, and she turned the kiss into something wild, and wet, and so perfectly wonderful that both of them were gasping when it ended.

"I guess I'd better behave myself." Danny's voice was strained. "You didn't wear the black dress tonight."

"I know. Are you terribly disappointed?" Amy's voice was low and breathless.

Danny took a moment to think about it, and then he chuckled. "No. Not really. Tonight was perfect, just the way it was. But you will wear it someday, won't you, Amy?"

"Well . . ." It was Amy's turn to hesitate, and the silence grew between them until neither one of them could stand it any longer. And then Amy snuggled very close and reached out to touch his lips with the tip of her finger. "I'm not sure exactly when, but I'll wear it. Believe me, Danny . . . that's one thing you can positively count on."

séance

Prologue

Kelly Bridges frowned at her reflection in the mirror. Girls in love weren't supposed to look like death warmed over, with dark circles under their eyes, and hands that trembled as they held the phone. Tears weren't supposed to gather in their eyes, and run down their cheeks. They weren't supposed to feel like throwing something against the wall so hard it would break, or screaming in pure frustration. Love was wonderful. That's what everyone said. But everything would have been much easier if Kelly Bridges hadn't been in love with Tommy Jackson.

"Okay, Tommy. I'll meet you in an hour. And I love you, too." Kelly sighed deeply as she hung up the phone. She wiped her eyes with a tissue and turned to the mirror to study her reflection, again. She had light brown hair that curled slightly at the tips, dark blue eyes that were almost violet in color, and a slim figure that she maintained by strict dieting. She would have been beautiful if she'd been smiling, but Kelly had absolutely nothing to smile about.

Tears began to gather in her eyes again, and she blinked them back. She was so miserably depressed, she'd had to force herself to get out of bed this morning. It didn't matter that Tommy was back in town, after his summer construction job. It made no difference that she'd been accepted by the college of her choice, the same college that had offered Tommy a full athletic scholarship.

It wasn't important that Tommy had just made the last payment on her engagement ring. Her life was a complete and total mess.

The plans they'd made had been wonderful. Kelly sighed, and a wistful smile flickered across her face. Tommy had asked her mother if he could give her an engagement ring on Halloween, when they would celebrate her eighteenth birthday. The wedding was scheduled for June, right after their high school graduation, and they'd planned to spend the summer getting settled in a small apartment close to the university campus where they'd both enroll as freshmen in the fall.

Kelly swallowed hard, past the lump in her throat. Tommy still had his dreams, but hers had turned to ashes. There would be no college for her, no golden autumn days watching Tommy play football, no group study sessions in their cramped living room, no socializing with the other students over spaghetti dinners. Now, the whole scenario had changed, and she had been written out of the picture.

What would happen to Tommy? Kelly shivered a little, picturing him all alone on campus. But Tommy was a popular guy and he wouldn't be alone for long. He'd get an apartment with a couple of roommates from the football team, or maybe he'd live in a frat house, and date the sorority girls. Tommy would start a new life, a life without her. And before his first year of college had passed, he'd forget that he'd ever loved a girl by the name of Kelly Bridges.

Before she could start to feel any more sorry for herself, Kelly picked up the keys to the ancient Dodge that Tommy had helped her repair, and headed for the door. She'd asked Tommy to meet her at Jerry's Roadhouse, a decrepit place out on the highway, where they wouldn't be likely to run into anyone they knew. Kelly just hoped that the back room at Jerry's was as dark as she remembered. When she told Tommy her awful secret, she didn't want to have to see the expression of painful disbelief on his face.

The August night was dark, and the warm breeze from the open window caressed Kelly's face as she drove down the highway. It was a perfect, romantic evening with brilliant stars glittering overhead. The air was heavy with the scent of blooming flowers, deep red clover, yellow buttercups, and white and purple lilacs.

Kelly shivered and rolled up the window. It was too late to smell the perfume in the air, to breathe in the scent of bright tomorrows filled with promise. Her fate was signed, sealed, and delivered. There would be no future joy for her.

A tear rolled down her cheek, and she wiped it away with the back of her hand. Where was her courage? She'd always been strong, and she needed all the strength at her disposal to face Tommy. She could break down later, after Tommy had left her life forever. Then she could afford the luxury of tears to mourn all the bright and loving moments they would have shared together.

But what if it wasn't true? Shouldn't she wait to tell Tommy until she'd gone to a doctor to confirm her suspicions? Kelly hesitated, the car slowing to a snail's pace on the gravel road. Perhaps she'd been too hasty to jump to a conclusion. It was possible her symptoms were misleading, even psychosomatic. They could be caused by nothing more serious than simple stress.

Kelly frowned slightly as she stopped the car and tried to think. She knew she'd been under a lot of stress lately. She was nervous about her performance on the SATs and it would be another two weeks before she got her scores. Things weren't exactly a picnic at home, either. She knew her younger sister was sneaking out of the house at night, and she was still trying to decide whether it was her duty to tell her mother. Then there was her mother's new boyfriend. Kelly didn't like him, but it wasn't really her place to object. And the wedding was turning out to be a real problem. Her mother wanted a huge affair with all the relatives, but that would be horribly expensive. Tommy's parents had offered to share some of the cost, but Kelly didn't really want a lavish wedding. She preferred to have a simple ceremony, and save the extra money for their college expenses.

Work had been a strain, too. Kelly had a summer job with Foothill Appliances and she was on a straight commission, no salary. She was on the verge of making a very big sale, enough to pay for the wedding and most of their college expenses, but none of that mattered now, not if what she feared was true.

A car horn honked, and Kelly looked up to see Sheriff Newsome waving at her. He rolled down his window and shouted a question. Did she have car trouble?

"No, I'm fine." Kelly made herself smile past the tears that had gathered in her eyes. "I was just looking for something in my purse."

When the sheriff drove off, Kelly put her car in gear and got on the road again. If she didn't hurry, she'd be late for her meeting with Tommy. Not that it would really matter . . . nothing really mattered anymore.

She was just cresting Appleton's hill when she saw the lights blinking in the distance. The arms on the crossing gate were closing, and Kelly could hear a train whistle in the distance. The eight o'clock freight train was coming, and it always took at least five minutes to clear the crossing. She would be late, but there wasn't a thing she could do about it. The arms on the gate were already closed.

Kelly pressed down gingerly on the brake pedal. The brakes had a tendency to grab and pull to one side, something Tommy had promised to fix for her just as soon as he had a spare afternoon. But even though Kelly had braked, the car didn't slow.

She frowned and pressed down a little harder, but the car kept right on gaining speed. What was wrong? The brakes had always been a little finicky, but they'd never failed before! Kelly pulled the handle of the emergency brake, but that didn't work either, and she felt herself beginning to panic. She had to think of some way to stop before she reached the crossing, and it was at the bottom of the hill!

"Okay. Here goes!" Kelly gripped the wheel tightly and tromped down hard on the brakes. The car would skid, but she was prepared. But nothing happened! The car kept right on hurtling forward, even though the brake pedal was jammed all the way to the floor.

There wasn't time to think, only to react, and Kelly jerked the wheel to the right. The ditch wasn't that steep and it was bound to slow the car and stop it.

There was a horrible jolt as one wheel hit the edge of the ditch. The car tipped steeply, but it kept right on going, scraping and shuddering its way down the hill. Kelly fought the wheel, trying to steer over to the other side of the road, but it was no use. The old Dodge was riding on the lip of the ditch, heading straight down to the crossing.

And then she heard it, the blast of the train whistle, much louder this time. The eight o'clock train was rounding the bend, hurtling down the track full speed ahead. The engineer was totally oblivious of the horrible wreck that was only a few heartbeats away.

Someone must have seen her, because there was a metallic squeal so loud it seemed to rip the fabric of the night apart. It was the distinctive sound of metal scraping metal, and sparks began to fly beneath the train. They had engaged the brakes. They were trying to stop. But could they stop in time?

For a moment, Kelly thought they'd make it. The train seemed to slow, but perhaps that was because her old Dodge was moving so fast. And then she was on the tracks, feeling desperately for the door handle. But there was no time. The bright light was upon her, crushing the life from her body and plunging her into the endless darkness.

One

Jennifer Larkin, Jen to her friends, was prepared to make an entrance. She was dressed in her best school outfit, a soft blue skirt that was tight enough to hug her slim hips, with a matching jacket-type vest. Her blouse was navy blue silk with a wide collar and she was wearing small gold earrings, and a shiny gold clasp in her hair.

As she approached the door to room 206, Jennifer reached up to touch her hair. It had always been a problem, and there didn't seem to be a solution. Most of Jennifer's hair was light brown, but it had traces of blond, chestnut, and even deep red. It was almost as if fate were somehow making up for the fact that she was an only child by giving her strands of hair from every ancestor on both sides of the family.

Hair color wasn't the only problem. Texture was also a factor. Jennifer's hair fell to just below the middle of her back, and it was as thick and straight as a board. It couldn't be curled. She had tried.

Right after last Christmas, Jennifer had spent her holiday money on an expensive haircut and perm. She'd been delighted with her new look, but it hadn't been more than a week before all her curls were gone. Jennifer's hair had a mind of its own. It wanted to be multicolored, thick and straight, and there wasn't a thing she could do about it. Jennifer had settled for buying barrettes and clasps to hold it back, and given up on fancy hairstyles.

Her eyes were her best feature. Jennifer knew that. They were as blue as a summer's sky, fringed with long, dark lashes. And the rest of her face wasn't bad, either. Her lips were generous, her cheekbones were high, her nose was straight and not too large, and her skin was smooth. Jennifer knew that she was a long way from beautiful, but she certainly wasn't ugly. She looked nice, maybe even pretty, but Tommy Jackson had never so much as looked at her with interest.

Jennifer took a deep breath, and hesitated with her hand on the door. What if someone asked her why she was so dressed up? What would she say? She couldn't admit that she'd worn her best outfit for Tommy. What excuse could she make that would sound reasonable?

Another question popped into Jennifer's mind and she started to frown. What if no one said anything about how she was dressed? Wouldn't that be even worse? It would mean that her friends didn't care enough about her to notice what she wore.

Jennifer sighed and tried to push the worries out of her mind. She'd always been overly worried about things. Even as a small child, Jennifer had imagined the worst that could happen in any situation. That was why her father had called her "Mousie," and she was very grateful that none of her friends knew about the nickname. She'd done her best to get over her fears, but every once in a while, all of her doubts and worries came back to haunt her. She took a deep breath and concentrated on thinking positive thoughts. Today was the day that Tommy would notice her. He'd take one look at her and say, "Hey, Jen. You really look good today."

She pushed open the door and walked into the classroom, her lips curving up in the smile she'd practiced in front of her mirror. Tommy and his twin brother, Tim, were sitting in the front row.

"Hey, Jen." Tim grinned at her. "You really look good today."

Jennifer could feel herself blushing. It was the right comment, but it had come from the wrong twin. "Thanks, Tim. Hi, Tommy."

"Hi, Jen." Tommy looked up and gave her a little wave. He

was always polite and friendly. And then he turned around and went back to his conversation with Tim.

Jennifer thought about interrupting. She knew Tim wouldn't mind. But they seemed to be talking about something serious, so she walked back to her assigned seat. Her knees were shaking a bit as she sat down. Had Tommy even noticed her new outfit? Probably not. But Tim had, and it was a real pity she wasn't in love with *him*. At least she'd have a chance with him.

"Jen . . . did you write down our math assignment?" Susie Romano slid over next to her.

"Sure, Susie . . . here." Jennifer opened her notebook and handed it over for Susie to copy. She liked Susie, a plump, dark-haired girl who just happened to be the biggest gossip at Foothill High. Susie didn't mean to gossip, but she worked weekends at her parents' deli. Everyone who came in had a story to tell about someone else, and Susie was a very good listener.

"Thanks, Jen." Susie handed back the notebook and waved at Ronnie Hughes as he came in the door. "I have to go talk to Ronnie. Mrs. Kramer came in for sliced turkey breast last night, and she said his second cousin, Mary Ellen, was moving to New York."

Jennifer watched as Susie hurried over to intercept Ronnie. Susie had been trying to pick up on Ronnie for ages, but Ronnie didn't seem to realize that she was interested. Ronnie was tall and thin, more at home on a catwalk than on the ground, and totally fascinated by stage lighting. His parents owned the Foothill Bakery, and Susie had threatened to pop out of a cake, dressed up like a light bulb, if Ronnie didn't ask her out soon.

"Hi, everybody!" Cheryl Maloney came into the room, wearing a tight yellow sweater. She was a transfer student from Los Angeles and she'd appeared in a crowd scene on *General Hospital*. She'd even brought the clip to drama class so everyone could watch it.

Tommy grinned at Cheryl. "Hi, Cheryl. Come here a second, will you?"

Jennifer felt a stab of jealousy as Cheryl sat down next to Tommy. He hadn't smiled at her like that. Of course, she didn't have long blond hair like Cheryl, and she wasn't wearing a tight yellow sweater.

"Hey, Jen . . . nice outfit!" Brian Garvey gave her a wave as he came in. Brian was the computer expert of the senior class, a short, dark-haired guy who looked like a nerd, but wasn't. Brian had done all their special effects and sound mixing for the past three years. He loved anything technical and was always coming up with complicated simulations that looked very real on the stage.

Right behind Brian was Melanie Carpenter, a tall, thin redhead who was totally gorgeous. Melanie had done some modeling and she wanted to be an actress, but she wasn't a bit stuck-up about it. She was definitely the best actress in the senior class. She'd had the lead in the last three plays and they'd sold out for every performance.

Just as Jennifer was about to ask Melanie what she was doing for her oral history report, Dale Prescott walked in. He sat down next to Melanie, flipped open his briefcase, and handed her some papers. Dale's father, Dalton Prescott, was a state senator, and he was already grooming Dale for a political career. Melanie's dad was the mayor of Foothill, and Dale had just come from one of his youth advisory meetings. There was no way Jennifer wanted to get stuck discussing politics with Melanie and Dale. She just wasn't in the mood for a debate about the November election, or a rundown of what the city council had done lately.

Since there was no one to talk to, Jennifer stayed in her seat and stared at the back of Tommy's head. Love was strange. Tim was sitting right next to Tommy, and even though he was every bit as handsome, he didn't make Jennifer's heart flutter and her knees turn weak.

The Jackson twins were different. There was no doubt about that. They were fraternal twins, not identical, and no one could tell they were twins unless they noticed their eyes.

Jennifer sighed as she thought of Tommy's green eyes, so deep and dark they reminded her of tropical foliage in an exotic rain forest. Of course, she'd never actually seen a rain forest, but that didn't matter. Tommy's eyes were the color a rain forest should be.

Since Tim had to wear glasses, Jennifer had never really noticed that his eyes were the same deep shade of green. She'd discovered it quite by accident a few weeks ago, when Tim had taken off his glasses at the library to clean them.

Tommy was taller, well over six feet, with broader shoulders and sun-streaked hair. Tim was two inches shorter, with darker hair and the strong, lightly muscled body of a swimmer. Body build was one reason the twins excelled in different sports. Tommy was the captain of Foothill High's football squad, and Tim was on the track and swim teams.

Their personalities were also very different. Tommy was aggressive and full of self-confidence, while Tim was shy. Tommy got by in school by cramming for tests. He seemed perfectly content to be in the top half of the class while Tim studied every night to maintain his straight-A average.

There was another major difference, one that really bothered Jennifer. Tim was her friend and she spent time with him almost every day, but Tommy didn't even seem to know that she existed.

After she'd arranged her books and flipped open her notebook, Jennifer sat there, four seats away, and gazed at the back of Tommy's head. More than six weeks had passed since Kelly's funeral, and he still looked terribly sad. It made Jennifer want to move up to the empty seat behind him, and reach out to give him a hug. Poor Tommy. She knew she could comfort him, if he'd only—

"Knock it off, Jen. You're drooling over him again."

Jennifer's cheeks turned beet-red, and she whirled around with a guilty look on her face. Had someone guessed how she felt about Tommy? But it was only Alexia Sussman, Jennifer's best friend, and Lexie knew all about it. "Not so loud, Lexie. Someone could have—"

"They didn't." Lexie interrupted, something she did quite often. "Relax, Jen. No one was close enough to hear. And

Tommy's so busy talking to Tim, he's not paying any attention to us."

"I know." Jennifer sighed deeply. "He said hello to me, but I don't think he even noticed my new outfit."

"Take it from me, Jen. Guys never notice details like that. It's just not in their nature. But that doesn't mean Tommy didn't think you looked good."

"I hope you're right."

"I am." Lexie sounded very confident. She'd grown up with three older brothers, and she considered herself an expert on guys.

As Lexie unzipped her backpack and took out her books, Jennifer thought about Lexie. They'd been best friends since first grade, the year that the Sussman family had moved to Foothill. Lexie looked a little like a pixie, with black naturally curly hair, and she was short, only five feet four. Since Jennifer was almost four inches taller, she sometimes felt like a giant when she walked down the hall next to her friend.

Lexie straightened her stack of books and leaned forward to stare at Jennifer intently. She was always very serious when she tried to play matchmaker, and she'd been pushing Jennifer to get things going, ever since the day Jennifer had finally admitted she thought she was in love with Tommy.

"I take it you didn't talk to him yet?"

"No. Not yet." Jennifer shook her head. "But I will, I promise."

"When?"

"Soon." Jennifer couldn't help blushing slightly. Lexie didn't seem to realize how difficult it was to talk to the boy you were crazy about.

"Well, you'd better hurry. How are you ever going to get Tommy to ask you out, if he doesn't even know that you like him?"

Jennifer shrugged. They'd had this conversation before. "I'm just not ready, Lexie. I have to plan out exactly what I'm going to say."

"How hard can that be? Just catch him alone and ask him if he'd like to go to a movie with you. The worst he can do is say no."

"I know that." Jennifer looked worried. "But what if he does? If Tommy turned me down, I'd be really embarrassed. I just don't think I could handle it."

Lexie was silent for a moment and then she sighed. "I don't know what to do with you, Jen. You're really lacking in the chutzpah department."

"Chutzpah? What's that?"

"It's a Yiddish word. I can't translate it exactly, but it's a combination of nerve, self-confidence, and effrontery. You know what effrontery is, don't you?"

"It's guts." Jennifer grinned. "I'm not a total dunce, Lexie. And *chutzpah* means guts?"

"Well . . . not entirely, but it's close. Do you want me to give you an example?"

Jennifer nodded. Lexie had spent two weeks with her great-grandparents this summer, and she'd learned a lot of Yiddish words.

"Chutzpah is a guy who murders his parents and then tries to collect welfare because he's an orphan."

Jennifer laughed out loud. Lexie had a way with words and she was a walking, talking unabridged dictionary. Lexie claimed it was hereditary. Her father owned the *Foothill Gazette* and her mother was a freelance editor for a book company who sent her manuscripts from New York. It wasn't surprising that Lexie was going to Smith to get her degree in journalism.

"So what are you going to do about Tommy?" Lexie leaned close so they wouldn't be overheard. "If you don't make a move soon, some other girl will get to him first."

"I know. That's why I asked Mr. Bensen to make Tim my chemistry partner. I've been going over there almost every day, but so far Tommy hasn't seemed very interested."

Lexie sighed. "That's because you made a strategic mistake. Tommy probably thinks you're interested in Tim, and you know how close they are. You've got to make it clear that the only reason you're hanging around with Tim is to get close to Tommy."

"But that's not true." Jennifer started to frown. "Tim's my friend and I like him a lot."

"More than Tommy?"

Jennifer's frown deepened. "Well . . . no. At least I don't think I do. But I don't want Tommy to think that I'm using Tim to get close to him. And I don't want Tim to think it, either."

"Why not?" Lexie raised her eyebrows. "Isn't that exactly what you're doing?"

Jennifer opened her mouth to protest. That wasn't what she was doing at all! But just then Miss Voelker came into the room, followed by their student teacher, Mr. Peterson.

Everyone adored Mr. Peterson. The first day of school, when Miss Voelker had introduced him, they'd all just sat there and stared. And then the whispers had started, gathering in volume until someone, Jennifer didn't remember exactly who it had been, asked the question, "Are you Pete?"

Mr. Peterson had laughed and they'd known for sure. He was Pete, the totally off-the-wall guy who'd starred in the Central Motors used-car commercials. They were on every Saturday, right in the middle of the *Night Owl Movie*, and Pete had done some incredibly funny things.

In the first commercial, he'd driven through the front door of a church to scoop up the bride in a used Ford Bronco. He'd also taken four couples to the prom in an old black hearse, and herded cattle in a beat-up Cadillac convertible with steer horns wired to the front bumper. Pete had dressed up like Santa and driven around with five decorated Christmas trees in the shovel of a battered snowplow, and he'd pulled up to the drive-in window of a bank on a tractor-lawn mower. Pete was a drama major who'd put himself through college by doing television commercials, and everyone was glad he was their student teacher.

Jennifer noticed that Pete looked unhappy, and so did Miss Voelker. Everyone in class seemed to realize that there was something wrong, because there was silence as Miss Voelker walked to the front of the room and sat down at her desk.

"I've got some bad news." Miss Voelker sounded very upset. "Pete? Why don't you tell them?"

Pete walked to the front of the room. "I'm sorry, guys . . . but we're going to have to cancel the fall play this year. We just found out that the new theater wing won't be finished until after Christmas."

There were predictable groans from the class. They'd all been looking forward to performing in the new theater. Jennifer raised her hand. "Isn't there another theater that we could use?"

"We tried to find one," Pete answered her. "Miss Voelker and I called every decent-sized auditorium in town, and they're booked up solid until Christmas. We even tried the other schools in the area, but they have their own fall plays."

Jennifer sighed. "That's awful news! I feel really bad about disappointing the kids."

"The kids?"

Pete looked puzzled and Miss Voelker explained. "We always open on Halloween night with an early show for the children. They love being the first ones to see the fall play. The curtain goes down around eight at night, and that leaves them plenty of time to go trick-or-treating."

"This is going to be a bad year for the kids," Dale spoke up. "They won't have a play and trick-or-treating's not allowed this year."

"No trick-or-treating?" Jennifer turned to Dale in surprise. "Why not?"

"The city council voted to ban it. It's just too dangerous. Most kids get so excited on Halloween, they forget about watching for cars. The mayor was hoping that we could do something, and I said we'd let the kids come to the play in costume and give out prizes for the best outfits. It was supposed to be like a party so the kids wouldn't miss trick-or-treating, and now that's out, too. Maybe we should just cancel Halloween this year."

"We can't do that!" Jennifer looked shocked. "Kids love Halloween. Next to Christmas, it's their favorite holiday. We just have to do something."

"I agree with Jennifer," Miss Voelker said. "But what can we do?"

There was total silence and Jennifer began to blush as everyone stared at her expectantly. "How about skits? We could write them and act them out. They could be about ghosts and witches and monsters and murder . . . anything that's scary and spooky. You could even grade us, Miss Voelker, and they could be part of our class work."

"That's a good idea," Miss Voelker said. "But where would we perform these skits?"

"Anywhere. We could do them in the park, or on the playground, or even in the library."

"Wait a second . . ." Pete looked thoughtful. "Why don't we do a haunted house? It'd be a great setting for the skits, and Brian could rig some special effects."

"Sure." Brian looked eager. "I could do a hand coming up from a grave, and ghosts moaning and groaning, doors opening and closing by themselves, all sorts of stuff like that."

Dale started to grin. "Why don't we use my uncle's lodge up at Saddle Peak? It's closed until ski season, and I'm almost sure he'd let us have it for a week."

"Saddlepeak Lodge?" Miss Voelker was clearly impressed. "But, Dale . . . it's huge!"

"I know. There'd be plenty of room if we wanted to bus the kids in and let them stay overnight. And there's a full, restaurant-sized kitchen. I'll call my uncle right now and make sure we can use it."

After Dale had left, Miss Voelker opened her notebook and started to make a list. "We'll need chaperones if we plan to keep the children overnight. I'm sure I can get some of the parents and teachers to help us. The children can bring their sleeping bags and spend the night in the lobby by the big rock fireplace."

Susie raised her hand. "My parents'll send up some food from the deli. If we do something simple like hot dogs and potato salad, it'll be easy."

"I'll bring cookies," Ronnie offered. "We always give them out as treats at the bakery. Since nobody's going trick-or-treating this year, we'll just pack them up and take them to the lodge. After the entertainment is over, we can read ghost stories and have cookies and hot chocolate."

"Let's plan out the entertainment." Pete walked to the blackboard. "Does anyone have any suggestions?"

Everyone did, and they kept Pete busy writing on the blackboard. They decided they'd work in groups and each group would have fifteen minutes to do their skit. Brian and Ronnie would coordinate the lights, the sound, and the special effects, and every group would be in charge of their own props and costumes. The kids would "stumble" on the skits as they were escorted through the haunted lodge by Pete, who would act as their narrator.

"It's all set." Dale came back into the room with a smile on his face. "My uncle thinks it's a great idea, and he's going to pick up the tab for the food and the transportation. We can use the lodge for two full weeks and we can decorate it any way we want, just as long as we clean it up when we're through."

Everyone started to cheer, but Dale held up his hands for silence. "I saved the best news for last. My uncle says that if our haunted lodge is a success, he'll let us hold it every year. The kids are going to have the time of their lives, and we're going to start a new Halloween tradition!"

Two

Jennifer knew she'd never been so terrified in her life. Her knees were weak, her stomach was in knots, and her teeth were chattering so loudly she was surprised that her friends in the lobby couldn't hear them. This wasn't about being timid, which she knew she was. This was flat-out fear, much worse than anything she'd ever experienced before. She was going to die. Right here. Right now. She was frozen in place, paralyzed by fright, and death was staring her straight in the face.

Somehow, Jennifer managed to force her clenched jaw to open. But before she could scream for someone to help her, a familiar voice called out. "Hey, Jen. I'll do that."

Jennifer felt a hand on her shoulder, and suddenly she could move. She backed down the ladder and turned around to give Tim a grateful smile.

"Hand me the cobwebs, Jen. I'll hang them if you steady the ladder for me."

Jennifer didn't quite trust her voice so she handed Tim the basket of cobwebs. She wasn't shaking quite so much now, and the floor felt wonderfully solid beneath her feet. She'd only been on the third rung of the ladder, but she still felt dizzy and her head was spinning. Thank goodness Tim hadn't noticed how frightened she'd been!

Her fear of heights was one shameful secret that Jennifer hadn't shared with anyone. She knew her friends would think she was a coward, and she'd decided not to tell them. Her fear had a fancy name: acrophobia. And there was a treatment called aversion therapy, but it sounded so scary when Jennifer had read about it, she knew she'd never be able to do it. It really didn't matter, anyway. She didn't want to work as a house painter or a window washer on a high-rise building. She planned to be an elementary school teacher, and if she was very careful not to get near any ledges or ladders, no one would ever guess that she had a problem.

Jennifer sighed as she watched Tim climb the ladder. She was very lucky that he was here. They'd all driven up to Saddlepeak Lodge right after school on Thursday afternoon. The supplies they'd ordered had come in the mail, and they had two weeks to decorate the haunted lodge. Pete had given everyone a job to do, and he'd put her in charge of hanging the fake cobwebs on the grand staircase that led to the second floor.

The bottom part had been easy. Jennifer had draped the cobwebs carefully over the rail. But when Pete had come to look at the work she'd done, he'd asked her to hang a few up higher, from the rafters at the top of the stairwell. Of course, Jennifer had been too embarrassed to tell him that she was afraid of heights, so she'd tried her best to do it. And she would have failed miserably if Tim hadn't come along to bail her out.

Jennifer bit her lip nervously as Tim stood on the top step of the ladder and draped a lacy cobweb from the rafter. Tim didn't seem to mind heights at all. He even looked down, something she couldn't have done in a million years, and then he did the unthinkable. As Jennifer watched, Tim let go of the ladder and waved at her!

Jennifer gasped and gripped the sides of the ladder tightly to keep from screaming. Tim was going to fall! She just knew it! Since she couldn't bear to watch what was about to happen, she shut her eyes and prayed. Tim just had to get down safely! If he didn't, it would be her fault!

The seconds ticked by and the waiting was an agony. Jennifer held her breath and kept her eyes shut. And then, miraculously, she heard a voice very close to her ear.

"Jen? You can let go of the ladder now."

Jennifer's eyes flew open and she took a deep gulp of air. Tim was down! And he was safe! Jennifer was so thankful, she threw her arms around him and gave him a big, shaky hug.

"Hey . . ." Tim started to grin. "Maybe I ought to take up climbing ladders as a career. You've never hugged me before."

Jennifer could feel her cheeks turning hot. Thank goodness everyone else was working in the lobby! "I'm sorry, Tim. I was sure you were going to fall. And then, when I saw you were safe, I was so glad I just . . . well . . . I just hugged you, that's all."

"Don't apologize. I liked it. But you didn't have to worry. I'm used to heights."

"You . . . you are?" Jennifer hoped she didn't look as surprised as she felt. How could anyone get used to heights?

"Sure. Tommy and I worked for my cousin all last summer."

Jennifer gave a sheepish grin. She'd completely forgotten that Tim and Tommy's cousin owned a roofing company.

"What do you think?" Tim stood back and looked up at the rafters. "Are those cobwebs straight?"

Jennifer pretended to look up, but she didn't. Just the thought of how high Tim had climbed made her knees feel weak. "They're perfect, Tim. Thanks for helping me. Did Pete tell you what we're supposed to do next?"

"He said we could work on our skit until Ronnie gets here with the rest of the decorations."

Jennifer sat down on the stairs. They were having real trouble with their skit. They'd tried a ghost story, but it hadn't seemed scary enough, and now they were looking for something new. Time was running out. They only had two weeks until Halloween and they had to settle on an idea soon.

"How about an escaped lunatic?" Tim sat down next to her.

"Maybe . . ." Jennifer frowned slightly. "But Melanie's doing something about a crazy actress."

"A witch?"

"Lexie's a witch. And Brian's a vampire, so you can forget about that. Most of the good stuff's already taken."

"Okay. How about murder? We could do a psychotic serial killer."

"That sounds too much like Susie and Dale's skit. What's Tommy doing?"

"Something with Cheryl. I'm not exactly sure what it is, but she does a lot of screaming. They've been practicing in the living room."

Jennifer frowned slightly. "Your living room?"

"Right. Every time Mom and Dad go out, Cheryl comes over to practice her bloodcurdling screams. That's why I've been spending so much time at the library. Cheryl's really loud."

Jennifer took a deep breath. She didn't want to ask, but she needed to know. "Are Tommy and Cheryl dating?"

"Not really. I think it'll be a while before Tommy starts dating again. He's still too upset over Kelly."

"That's what I thought. He looks so sad. Sometimes I wish there was something I could do."

"You like Tommy, don't you?"

Tim turned around on the step so he was facing her, and Jennifer tried her best not to blush. "Tommy's a friend. I've known both of you since kindergarten."

"Then you'd help him if you could . . . wouldn't you?"

"Of course. But what can I do?"

"Ever since the night that Kelly died, Tommy's been having nightmares. My room's right next to his, and I hear him sometimes, calling Kelly's name in his sleep."

"That's so sad!" Jennifer blinked back the tears that came to her eyes.

"I know. If I tell you something in confidence, you won't repeat it, will you, Jen?"

Jennifer didn't hesitate. She just shook her head. "No, Tim. I promise I won't repeat it to anyone."

"I asked Tommy why he was so upset. And he told me that he can't help thinking about Kelly's state of mind the night she died."

"You mean . . . the suicide?" Jennifer winced a little as she said the words. She'd heard the rumors, but she didn't like to repeat them.

"Tommy really needs to know whether Kelly committed suicide or not. It's driving him crazy, Jen. He's going over everything they said to each other, everything they did, trying to figure out if he's to blame."

"But that's . . . that's crazy!" Jennifer frowned deeply. "Kelly loved Tommy. I know she did!"

"Tommy knows that, but he thinks there was something wrong. The night she died, Kelly called Tommy and asked him to meet her at Jerry's Roadhouse, out on the highway."

"But . . . why?" Jennifer's frown deepened. "Jerry's Roadhouse is a dump!"

"She said she needed to tell him something that was very important to their future. And Jerry's Roadhouse was a place where they wouldn't run into any of their friends. Kelly said she couldn't take the chance that someone might overhear."

"That sounds serious." Jennifer frowned. "What did Kelly tell Tommy?"

"She didn't tell him anything. Kelly died on her way to Jerry's."

Jennifer sighed. "That's awful! But doesn't Tommy have any idea what Kelly was going to tell him?"

"He hasn't got a clue. And his nightmares just keep getting worse, the closer it gets to Halloween."

"Kelly's birthday. That was the night Tommy was going to give her his engagement ring."

"Right. I've got to do something, Jen. Tommy's really hurting. You'll help me, won't you?"

"Yes. Of course I will. But . . . how?"

"All you have to do is talk to Kelly. Ask her what was on her mind the night she died, and tell Tommy what she says."

Jennifer's mouth dropped open and she turned to stare at Tim in utter disbelief. "You—you've got to be joking! That's really not funny, Tim!"

"I know it's not funny. And it's not a joke. I'm desperate, Jen. You told me you want to help Tommy, and so do I. And talking to Kelly is the only way we can help him."

"But . . . Kelly's dead! I can't talk to someone who's dead!"

"Why not? People do it all the time. They hold séances and they hear voices from the grave. Remember Whoopi Goldberg? She did it."

"You mean in *Ghost*?" Jennifer couldn't believe her eyes when Tim nodded. "But, Tim . . . *Ghost* was a movie!"

"Right. And this is a skit. Don't you see, Jen? If we do a séance for our skit, you can contact Kelly. And then Kelly can tell Tommy that she didn't commit suicide."

Jennifer frowned. "But what about the important thing that Kelly was going to discuss with Tommy?"

"We'll make up something. Maybe you could have Kelly say that she was having second thoughts about the wedding, that it was so much of a hassle, she wanted to elope instead."

"That might work." Jennifer looked thoughtful. "But I don't know if Tommy will believe that I really contacted Kelly."

"He'll believe it if you're convincing enough. And you're a good actress, Jen."

"But . . . why me?" Jennifer was still puzzled. "Why don't you get someone like Melanie? She's a much better actress than I am."

"But everyone knows that Melanie's an actress, and that makes her less convincing. You can do it, Jen. I know you can. And you're the only one I can trust."

Jennifer felt warm inside. It was good to know that Tim had confidence in her. "Okay. I'll do it if you think it'll help, but we've got a problem. I don't know how to hold a séance."

"Neither do I, but there's a psychic bookstore on Seventh Street. We'll go down there tomorrow and buy a couple of books. Remember, Jen . . . our séance doesn't have to be perfect. It just has to look real to Tommy."

"Right," Jennifer agreed, but she was already having second thoughts. Lexie's great-grandfather had a Yiddish word for a person who could be talked into anything, no matter how foolish it was. Lexie would say she was being a total schnook, and Lexie would be absolutely right.

Just as Jennifer expected, there was a crowd waiting for her when she got to her locker the next morning. It was clear that Tim had spread the word about their séance.

"I have to talk to you, Jen." Lexie rushed up to grab Jennifer's arm. "You're being a total schnook!"

"Are you talking about the séance?" Jennifer put on her most innocent expression.

"That's exactly what I'm talking about! You don't really believe in that stuff, do you?"

Jennifer nodded. She had to nod. Everyone was watching. "Of course I do. This is the best time of year to contact the souls of the dead, and everyone has questions about Kelly's accident. Tim and I are going to clear up the gossip surrounding her death, once and for all."

"You've got to be kidding!" Lexie's mouth dropped open in shock. "Are you telling me that you're actually serious about trying to contact Kelly's spirit?"

"That's right. Tim's going to help me, and we're going to hold our séance on Halloween night. I was really hoping that you'd be a part of our group."

"That's ridiculous! I don't understand you, Jen. How could you possibly expect me to participate in such an insipid, superstitious—" Lexie stopped in mid-sentence and stared at Jennifer. "Did you say that you're going to hold this séance on Halloween night?"

Jennifer nodded. She could tell that Lexie was catching on.

"Correct me if I'm wrong, but is this pagan ritual going to take place at the haunted lodge?"

Jennifer nodded again. "The spirits of the dead are very strong on Halloween night. I can almost guarantee that Kelly will speak to me, especially if all of her friends are there."

"I see." The corners of Lexie's mouth began to twitch. "Well . . .

I've never done the 'up table' thing before, but I guess there's always a first time."

"Great! I knew we could count on you, Lexie." Jennifer picked up her books and started to walk down the hall. She could tell that her friend was dying to ask questions, but Lexie managed to contain herself until they'd rounded the corner.

"Okay. Spill it." Lexie pulled Jennifer into an empty classroom. "This séance is your Halloween skit, right?"

"Not really. Since we have to do so much research, Miss Voelker agreed to grade it the same as a skit. But our séance is going to be totally authentic. I have no idea what's actually going to happen."

Lexie looked very suspicious. "And you're telling me that you and Tim didn't write a script for this séance?"

"How could we? We're almost positive that we can contact Kelly, but we don't know what she's going to tell us."

"Oh, that's good. That's very good!" Lexie cracked up. "Okay, Jen. I'll play along. Who else is going to be at the séance?"

"We're going to ask the whole drama class. We were all Kelly's friends."

"You're going to ask everyone except Brian . . . right?"

"Brian? We're going to ask Brian. Why wouldn't we?"

"Special effects. If Brian's part of the séance, he can't jiggle the table, or make a smoke screen, or play a tape of Kelly's voice."

"We'd never use cheap tricks like that! I told you, Lexie . . . this séance is going to be totally authentic."

Lexie grinned. "Of course it is. But when you tell us to shut our eyes, I'm going to keep mine wide open. I want to see exactly how you and Tim are going to pull this off."

Three

He'd agreed to take part in the séance. It would have looked strange if he'd been the only one to refuse. But he didn't like it, not one bit. Why couldn't they leave Kelly's death alone?

Naturally, there had been questions. There were always questions when a beautiful young girl died in a horrible accident, especially since Kelly's car had exploded on impact and no one had been able to recover enough of her body to conduct any tests.

He shook his head, forcing away the gruesome picture. They'd called in a special disaster team to search the area, but there hadn't been much to find. And then Kelly's parents had mentioned how depressed she'd been lately, and they'd looked for a suicide note. They hadn't found it, of course. They should have known that Kelly wasn't the type of girl to kill herself.

Sheriff Newsome had called him in and asked him the same set of questions he'd asked everyone else. Had Kelly been acting any differently lately? Had she ever mentioned suicide to him?

He'd answered the questions quite honestly. Yes, Kelly had seemed a bit depressed to him. She was stressed out about her SAT scores, and she'd been working really hard at the appliance store all summer, trying to save money. But Kelly had certainly never mentioned suicide to him.

After Sheriff Newsome had left, he had thought about Kelly,

pretty Kelly, so naive and loving. Her death was a terrible tragedy, but life had to go on.

It helped to look at the big picture. Time would pass and Kelly's tragic death would be almost forgotten. For the next few months, her classmates would shudder when they passed the spot where she'd died, and everyone would be a little more careful when the lights flashed and the crossing gates lowered. The garages would be busy for weeks, checking brakes and making sure that cars were in good running order, and the sound of a train whistle would bring tears to the eyes of Kelly's friends and family. Of course all that would pass as time erased the pain, and it wouldn't be long before Kelly's death would be relegated to the history of Foothill. A year from now, Kelly Bridges would be nothing more than a statistic in the courthouse records, and a name carved on a marble tombstone in the Foothill cemetery.

But Jennifer and Tim were stirring things up again by holding this ridiculous séance. He didn't believe in messages from beyond the grave, and trying to contact Kelly's spirit to ask her questions about her accident was in horribly bad taste. He'd really expected Miss Voelker to object . . . but she hadn't. And since the séance was part of Jennifer and Tim's skit, there was nothing for him to do but play along. He supposed they'd come up with some sort of stupid theatrics—Kelly's voice on a tape recording, or her image projected on a screen of smoke. Whatever they did, he'd have to take part, right along with everyone else.

He was sitting in the bleachers, overlooking the deserted football field. Football practice was over and he had the whole area to himself. This was one of his favorite places, and he came here often to think and dream of his future. Someday, perhaps even as soon as their first class reunion, these bleachers would be filled with people, all of them cheering for him. He needed the applause and the adoration, the grade-school kids clamoring for his autograph and the older residents shaking his hand and thanking him for putting Foothill on the map. That was the reason he'd been forced to kill Kelly. Perhaps she hadn't meant to do it, but Kelly Bridges had been holding him back from his destiny.

* * *

Jennifer hesitated as they approached the door of the Cosmic Eye. She knew she was being timid again, but she couldn't seem to help it. "Are you sure we have to do this? Maybe we should just make up the whole thing."

"No, Jen. Let's get a book and do it right. There might be someone in the audience who's been to a séance before."

Jennifer gave a resigned sigh. "Okay. You go in first and I'll be right behind you."

Tim turned to look at her and Jennifer gave him a nervous smile. She'd never been in a psychic bookstore before, and it was bound to be weird. On the drive here, she'd tried to imagine the interior of the Cosmic Eye.

It would be dark and gloomy inside, with black candles sputtering in the corners. There would be shelves of dusty books with strange titles and the odor of pungent incense would hang in the air. The owner, Zada Tilitch, would have piercing eyes and hair as black as a raven's wing. When they told her that they wanted to hold a séance for a Halloween skit, she'd accuse them of treating the occult lightly. She might be so angry, she'd put a spell on them, mumbling incantations in some long-forgotten language and jabbing sharp pins into little wax dolls that looked like them.

Jennifer shivered, and Tim reached out to take her hand. "Hey, Jen . . . You're not really scared, are you?"

"Me? Scared? Of course not!" Jennifer forced a smile. "Come on. Let's go. I want to get in and get out, as fast as we can."

"Don't worry, Jen. I'll protect you. You don't have to worry . . . unless you're a newt or a frog."

Jennifer laughed. They'd just finished reading *Macbeth* in English class and she remembered the witches' scene. "You mean, 'Double, double toil and trouble; Fire burn and cauldron bubble?' "

"Right. Remember the potion? 'Eye of newt and toe of frog. Wool of bat, and tongue of dog.' "

Jennifer made a face. "What is the wool of a bat, anyway?"

"I don't know, but it's got to be something gross. Come on, Jen. Let's go."

Tim opened the door and Jennifer's eyes widened as she followed him into the little shop. The inside of the Cosmic Eye wasn't at all what she'd expected! It was painted a sunny yellow, with white lace curtains on the big plate-glass window overlooking the street. There were lovely plants in baskets hanging everywhere and the walls were covered with books, all neatly dusted and arranged in alphabetical order. A round oak table and matching chairs sat in the center of the room, and there was a pleasant scent in the air. Jennifer realized that it was coming from a silver urn in one corner with a sign that read JASMINE TEA. PLEASE HELP YOURSELF.

"Feel better now?" Tim turned to her with a smile.

Jennifer nodded as she looked around. The little shop was charming. "I thought this would be creepy . . . but it's not!"

"Everyone thinks that, at first."

Jennifer whirled around, and her mouth dropped open as a woman came through a beaded curtain at the rear of the store. She had to be an employee. There was no way this lady could be the exotic Zada Tilitch!

"Miss Tilitch?" Tim smiled at her.

"That's me. Just call me Zada. It's easier. What can I do for you two?"

As Tim explained about their séance, Jennifer stared at Zada Tilitch. She was about forty years old, with frizzy blond hair, brown eyes, and round, wire-framed glasses. She was short and plump, and she was wearing a faded blue denim skirt, and a pink T-shirt with a picture of a guitar-playing cow on the front. Under the cow was a slogan in bold black letters that read I LOVE MOO-SIC.

When Tim was through with his explanation, Zada smiled at Jennifer. "You look shocked, dear. Did you think I'd have bats in my hair?"

"I guess I was expecting something like that. You seem to be very . . . uh . . . normal."

"God forbid!" Zada laughed. "Don't pass that around or I'll lose most of my customers."

Tim started to laugh and so did Jennifer. Zada had a good sense of humor, and there was something about her that made them want to tell her their secret.

"Come here and sit down at the table." Zada pulled out a couple of chairs. "I'll get you some tea and then you can tell me all about your séance. I can't help feeling that it's much more important than a simple Halloween skit."

Jennifer glanced at Tim, and he nodded slightly. There was no reason not to tell Zada the truth.

It took quite a while to explain everything, but when they were through, Jennifer felt as if a giant weight had slid off her shoulders. She took a deep breath and looked over at Zada. "So what do you think? Are we doing the right thing?"

"I think you mean well. And I agree that you should hold the séance. But I think it's only fair to warn you that this could turn out to be much more than you bargained for."

Zada looked very serious, and Jennifer frowned. "I don't understand. What do you mean?"

"If you follow the correct procedure, your séance could be successful."

"You mean you think we might actually contact Kelly's spirit?" Tim sounded surprised.

"It's possible. And you're holding your dress rehearsal on Friday?"

Jennifer nodded, and so did Tim.

"That'll be fine. I'll close the shop early and I'll be there."

"You mean . . . you're going to come to our séance?" Jennifer was puzzled.

"Of course. Dabbling with the occult can be dangerous, and it wouldn't be right to let you do this alone. An angry spirit has powers to transcend the boundaries between life and death. If Kelly's spirit is vengeful, she could wreak havoc upon those who call her from her rest."

"But . . . what could she actually do?" Jennifer shivered slightly.

Zada was silent for a long moment. It was clear she didn't want to say. And then she reached out to take their hands, clasping them tightly in hers. "If Kelly's spirit is strong enough, she could kill us all."

Four

It was the Friday before opening night, and Jennifer was tired. They'd read all the séance books that Zada had recommended and they felt they were prepared. But the warning that Zada had given them weighed heavily on Jennifer's mind. She was ninety-nine percent sure that Zada was wrong and nothing bad would happen at their séance. But that one percent chance that Zada might be right had disturbed Jennifer's sleep for two weeks running.

Now they were on their way to Saddlepeak Lodge. Jennifer sighed as she leaned back against the leather seat of the twins' white Jeep. Tim and Tommy had pooled their money to buy the used recreational vehicle, and since it had all-wheel drive and antilock brakes, it was perfect to use for the trip up the mountain.

"So what do you think of it, Jen?" Tim turned to her with a smile. This was his week to drive, and Tommy and Lexie were riding in the backseat.

"It's great!" Jennifer smiled back. "It's got all the special features of a truck, but it rides like a car."

"That's why we bought it. Tommy wanted a truck, and I wanted a car, so we got the Jeep instead. As far as I can see, there's only one drawback."

"What's that?"

"Tommy and I have to go on double dates. Would you mind that?"

Jennifer could feel her cheeks turning hot and she knew she was blushing. Was Tim asking her to go out with him, or was this just a general question to find out how a girl would feel about double-dating?

"Yes, you would mind? Or no, you wouldn't?"

Jennifer decided to treat it like a general question. It was safer that way. "I wouldn't mind at all. But there might be some times when a girl would rather be . . . uh . . . alone with her date."

Tim gave her a devilish grin. "I guess Tommy and I'll just have to take turns at times like that."

"Hey, Tim . . ." Tommy tapped him on the shoulder. "You want to stop at the Hilltop Grocery and stock up on some snacks? Lexie's hungry."

"Lexie's always hungry." Jennifer turned around to smile at her friend. "But you don't have to stop. My mother packed a whole duffel bag full of snacks."

Lexie groaned. "What did she pack? Rice cakes and trail mix?"

"Actually . . . no. Mom's off her health-food diet and she baked last night. I've got lemon poppy seed cupcakes, chocolate chip cookies, and a whole pan of fudge. And Dad threw in three different kinds of chips and some dip."

"Sounds good." Lexie licked her lips. "How about soda?"

"We've got that covered," Tim said. "There's ten assorted cases in the back. And everyone else is bringing food, too. We'll have enough supplies to last us for a week."

"We might need them!" Lexie sounded worried. "Did you hear the weather report?"

"Rain, and more rain," Jennifer said. "But they said there was only a forty percent chance."

"Not anymore. They upped it to sixty percent right before we left. My brother called from the station to tell me." Lexie's voice had the ring of authority. Her oldest brother was a highway pa-trol officer and he always kept her informed of any hazardous road conditions. "He said if it started to rain while we were on the road, we should be careful between mile markers eighteen and twenty-four. It's a rock-slide area."

"You don't have to worry. This baby'll go over anything." Tommy reached out to pat the Jeep lovingly. "Right, Tim?"

"Right. And it doesn't look like rain yet."

"Rain might not be all that bad." Lexie looked thoughtful. "If we have a real storm tomorrow night, it'll fit right in with our haunted lodge."

"That's true," Tommy said. "And Brian won't have to rig any fake thunder and lightning."

"Let's just hope the rain doesn't start until we've carried in all our—" Jennifer stopped and pointed out the window. "Look! They put up our signs!"

Tim pulled over to the side of the road, and they all got out to look at the sign. The shop class had cut a piece of plywood in the shape of a giant bat. It was painted black with Day-Glo red lettering that read FIVE MILES TO THE HAUNTED LODGE.

Everyone was smiling as they got back into the Jeep and headed back up the mountain. There would be five more signs, one every mile and one at the lodge, and they could hardly wait to see what other designs the wood-shop class had made.

"There's the next one!" Lexie pointed as they came around a curve. "It's a jack-o'-lantern! I think they did a really good job."

Another mile and Jennifer spotted the next sign. "It's a ghost! The kids are going to love this! But will they be able to see the signs in the dark?"

"Sure," Tommy said. "Ronnie rigged some batteries with timers so they'll light up. He drove up to look at them last night and he said they were pretty scary."

The next sign was a pointed hat, the kind a witch would wear. And the one after it was a black cat. But the best sign of all was the one at the entrance to the lodge. It was a giant skeleton holding a sign in its bony fingers that read WELCOME TO THE HAUNTED LODGE!

"Ohmigod! What's that doing here?" Lexie's eyes widened as

they pulled up the driveway and parked next to an old black hearse.

Tim laughed at Lexie's shocked expression. "That's the hearse from Pete's commercial. Central Motors let Pete drive it up here."

"It's eerie, seeing it here like this." Lexie shivered as she got out to walk past the hearse. "I just hope it doesn't give the kids nightmares."

Tommy laughed. "It won't. Kids love to be scared, and they know it's all in fun."

Tommy and Lexie went up the steps to the lodge, but Jennifer hung back to wait for Tim. She'd been feeling uneasy all day, and she'd decided to tell Tim about it. "Tommy just told Lexie that this is all in fun. But is it, really?"

"What do you mean, Jen?" Tim looked puzzled. "Of course it's all in fun. That's why we're doing it."

"I know most of it is, but how about our séance? Maybe I'm just having an attack of stage fright, but I can't shake the feeling that something bad could happen."

"Come on, Jen. There's nothing to worry about. You're just freaked over what Zada said."

"Maybe . . ." Jennifer wasn't convinced. What if it really was possible to contact Kelly's spirit? And what if her spirit was angry enough to kill them?

"Jen?" Tim dropped their bags at the side of the door and put his arms around her. "If you really don't want to hold the séance, we can cancel. We've got time to work up something else."

Jennifer stared up at him in surprise. That wasn't true! They didn't have enough time to work up another skit, and Tim knew it. And even if they managed to throw something together, their grades were bound to suffer.

"I'm serious, Jen. I don't mind . . . really."

Jennifer could feel herself blushing. Maintaining his straight-A average meant a lot to Tim, but he was willing to take a low grade to make her feel better. That meant he cared about her much more than she'd realized.

"Thanks, Tim." Jennifer hugged him. There was no way she'd let him sacrifice his grades just because she was freaked. "I appreciate the offer, but I'd rather do the séance. Everything'll be all right. I know it will."

But as Tim opened the door and Jennifer stepped inside the haunted lodge, she had the terrible feeling that nothing would ever be all right again.

Jennifer's uneasiness faded the moment they joined the excited crowd of students inside. There were twenty rooms on the second floor and an equal number on the third. They'd decided that the second floor should be the girls' domain, and Tim carried Jennifer's bag up the staircase to her room.

Tim placed her bag on the bed and turned to smile. "My room's right above yours. If you need me, all you have to do is throw something at the ceiling."

"Thanks, Tim. And if you need me, just knock on the floor."

After Tim had left to get settled in his own room, Jennifer unpacked the things she'd brought. They were going to hold their dress rehearsal with Pete, stay overnight in the rooms they'd chosen, and make sure everything was ready for tomorrow night's performance. Miss Voelker would ride up the next afternoon on the bus with the children, and then grade their performances.

Jennifer had chosen a room that faced the front of the lodge. When she was through hanging up her costume and unpacking her makeup, she walked to the window and pulled back the curtains so she could look out. A light rain was beginning to fall and Jennifer frowned as she thought of Zada. If it was raining hard, would Zada come to their rehearsal as she'd promised?

As Jennifer stood there, watching the raindrops splatter against the pavement, she noticed that Pete had moved the hearse to the parking lot at the side of the driveway so that the other students could unload their things. Lexie would feel better now that it wasn't parked right in front. Jennifer could understand why

Lexie had shivered when she'd seen the hearse. Her favorite aunt had died in September and Lexie's family had flown back east for the funeral. The hearse was a sad reminder that Lexie would never see her Aunt Leah again.

Surprisingly, the hearse didn't bother Jennifer at all. Perhaps she was finally getting over being so timid. But her imagination still kicked into high gear once in a while. It had happened today, when they'd arrived at the lodge, and she'd wanted to cancel the séance. If Tim hadn't snapped her out of it, they would have blown their grades and missed the chance to help Tommy.

There was a tap on her door and Jennifer went to open it. It was Tim, and she gave him a big smile. "Hi, Tim. Are you ready to go down and help?"

"I'm ready. Pete says it's cold downstairs. They turned up the heat and started a fire in the fireplace, but it'll take a while for a big place like this to warm up. Did you bring a jacket?"

"I've got my long parka coat, but that's kind of heavy. Won't my sweatshirt be enough?"

"No way. It's barely fifty degrees." Tim glanced at her Foothill High sweatshirt and frowned. "You'd better put this on, just in case."

Jennifer's eyes widened as Tim draped his Foothill High letter jacket over her shoulders. Did this mean what she thought it meant? At Foothill High, the students had decided to revive some of the customs of the fifties and sixties. When class rings were exchanged, it meant that a couple was engaged to be engaged. And letter jackets were much more than a simple award for doing well in athletics. When a girl wore a guy's letter jacket, it meant that she was dating him exclusively. What would Tommy think if he saw her in his twin brother's letter jacket?

"Thanks, Tim. But—" Jennifer stopped in mid-sentence and blushed. She wasn't sure how to ask Tim what the letter jacket signified.

It was as if Tim had read her mind, because he grinned at her. "Relax, Jen. You can tell everyone you just borrowed my jacket to keep warm. Unless you'd rather say something else?"

"Oh. Yes, that's fine." Jennifer knew she wasn't answering the question, but she wasn't sure what she should say. Rather than risk hurting Tim's feelings, she just thrust her arms into the sleeves and pulled the jacket close around her. It was wonderfully warm and smelled slightly of aftershave, a scent she found very pleasing. "Thank you, Tim."

"You're welcome.

Tim was grinning as they went down the stairs, and Jennifer hoped she hadn't given him the wrong idea. But wearing Tim's letter jacket made her feel very special, and she couldn't help smiling as they walked into the kitchen, where the other students had gathered.

Lexie didn't see them at first. She was busy, helping Susie and Tommy carve the pumpkins that Pete had brought in the back of the hearse. But when Lexie turned and caught sight of Jennifer in Tim's letter jacket, her eyes widened and she started to smile.

Jennifer shook her head slightly to let Lexie know that Tim's jacket didn't mean what she thought it did. Lexie's smile faded abruptly, and Jennifer thought she looked a bit disappointed.

Tommy didn't react to the letter jacket at all. He just handed her a hollowed-out pumpkin and cleared a space for them at the counter. Jennifer couldn't tell whether he just hadn't noticed that she was wearing Tim's jacket, or whether he really didn't care.

The art class had made some stencils and Jennifer took one from the box on the counter. She traced the stencil on her pumpkin with a black marking pen and handed it to Tim. She was tracing her third stencil when Tommy tapped her on the shoulder.

"Nice jacket, Jen." He winked at her. "Does it belong to anyone I know?"

Jennifer was about to tell him that she'd only borrowed Tim's jacket because she was cold. But then she noticed that everyone was listening. She didn't want to embarrass Tim, so she smiled and settled for telling the absolute truth. "It's Tim's jacket. And I think it's very nice, too."

Five

Lexie waited until they were carrying the pumpkins out to the lobby and no one was near enough to overhear their conversation. "You really blew it this time, Jen. Why didn't you tell Tommy that you weren't dating Tim?"

"I guess I should have, but I didn't want to embarrass Tim."

"Are you sure that's the only reason?" Lexie started to grin.

"Of course it is. Tim looked worried about what I was going to say, and everyone else was listening."

"Right. And you were more concerned about how Tim would feel than you were about giving Tommy the wrong impression. Doesn't that tell you something?"

Jennifer shrugged. "Not really. What do you think it tells me?"

"I think you like Tim much better than you like Tommy."

"You're crazy!" Jennifer scowled at her friend. "I told you before. I think I'm in love with Tommy."

But Lexie just laughed as she headed back to the kitchen for another load of pumpkins. "Think again, Jen. And this time, try to be honest with yourself."

All during dinner, Jennifer thought about what Lexie had said. Was it true? Did she like Tim more than Tommy? She certainly liked wearing Tim's letter jacket. Just knowing that it belonged to him made her feel toasty warm inside. But wouldn't she feel even better if she were wearing Tommy's jacket?

"You're really quiet tonight, Jen." Tim passed her the platter of sandwiches that the home economics class had made. "Are you worried about the séance?"

Jennifer passed the platter of sandwiches to Susie, who was sitting next to her, and then she leaned closer to Tim. "I'm not worried about the séance anymore. I'm just wondering if Zada's really going to drive all the way up the mountain in the rain."

"Maybe she won't have to drive."

Tim grinned, a sure sign that he was about to crack a joke, and Jennifer decided to beat him to the punch line. "You mean she might come on her broomstick?"

"Maybe." Tim was still grinning. "But modern witches don't use broomsticks anymore. Now they prefer to ride on—"

"Dust busters!" Jennifer finished the joke for him and they both cracked up.

"Okay, gang!" Pete stood up and clapped his hands for silence. "It's five-thirty and dress rehearsal's at seven. I've posted a schedule on the bulletin board by the registration counter. Make sure you know what time you're performing. Check your props, put on your costumes and makeup, and we'll meet down here in the lobby at six-thirty."

There was a flurry of activity as they hurried to put away the food and clear the table. Then everyone headed for the stairs to get ready for their rehearsal.

Jennifer felt the first flutters of excitement as she climbed up the staircase with Tim. "I checked the schedule and we're on last."

"I know. I asked Pete to do it that way. I wanted to give everyone else time to take off their makeup and get into regular clothes for the séance."

"That makes sense." They were almost at her door. She slipped out of Tim's letter jacket and held it out to him with a smile. "I guess I'd better give this back. Thanks, Tim. It's a great jacket. I really liked wearing it."

But Tim didn't take the jacket. He just grinned and stepped back. "If you like it, keep it. It looks really good on you."

Jennifer stared after him as he turned and walked down the hall. He wanted her to keep the jacket! But why? And for how long? She almost called him back to ask him, but she didn't. She just hugged the jacket close to her chest and carried it into her room.

He stared at the schedule and frowned. Tim and Jennifer were doing their séance last. That meant he'd have to worry about it through all the other performances.

The séance itself was no problem. There was no way the spirits of the dead could contact the living. He was quite sure about that. But the purpose for the séance was another matter. Were Jennifer and Tim suspicious about Kelly's death? Was the séance a trick to trap him into saying something he'd regret later?

Of course, he'd be very careful about what he said, but he couldn't sit there silently. If he didn't say anything at all, everyone would wonder why. He had to walk a fine line between reacting as one of the characters in the séance skit should and not revealing anything that might lead to further questions. So far, he'd managed that beautifully. Kelly hadn't told anyone their terrible secret and he'd silenced her forever before it could surface. But now Kelly's spirit was supposed to speak to them. And there was always the possibility that some smart person would start to put two and two together.

He paced the floor in his small room and wished he could think of some way to stop the séance. But he'd thought it all out and that just didn't seem possible. If he objected, there would be even more questions—perhaps the very ones that might lead to his downfall. If he'd only handled things differently back when it had all started!

The rain was pounding against the windowpane so hard it hurt his head. It had been raining then, too. It had rained all day, clearing for only a few hours in the early evening and then starting again, soaking them both.

He sat down on the corner of the bed, holding his aching head, and trying to think of something else. But memories of Kelly, images that he'd pushed from his consciousness, swirled in front of his mind. So beautiful, even with dripping hair and a wet dress plastered to her lovely body. So sweet. And so warm and loving. He could remember the way she'd smelled, a fresh scent that had reminded him of purple lilacs glistening with dew in the morning sun. And her smile. Those perfect teeth. Those generous lips that had clung to his. It hadn't mattered that she'd been out of her head on the allergy pills her doctor had prescribed, so dizzy and disoriented that she'd asked him to drive her home. The pills had made her giggle at everything, even the fact that neither one of them had a raincoat, and they'd been laughing as they'd dashed out to her car.

And then he was back, back to that wonderful, horrible night. It was the night that their fates had been sealed together forever.

They were in the cabin on Gull Lake. It was the closest place to get warm and he'd known that the family wasn't coming out this weekend. Kelly was wrapped in a blanket he'd taken from one of the beds. She was still shivering, sipping the cup of soup he'd heated for her.

"How's that?" He stepped back from the blaze he'd started in the fireplace and smiled at her. "Give it a couple of minutes, and it should be warm in here."

Kelly smiled at him and leaned closer to the fire. "It's nice. I think I'm warming up already."

"That's probably the hot soup." He smiled as he sat down on the couch next to her.

"Probably. Thanks for bailing me out tonight. You're really sweet."

He laughed. Kelly was bombed if she thought he was sweet. But she seemed very serious as she stared up at him.

"Why are you laughing? You *are* sweet!"

He was still laughing as she reached up to towel off her hair. But he stopped abruptly when the blanket slipped down to her waist.

There was no way that he could resist. She looked so beautiful in the firelight and she didn't seem to realize that the blanket had slipped. A guy would have to be made of stone to resist a beautiful, half-naked girl like Kelly. And no one would have to know.

Once he'd made up his mind, he moved quickly, pulling her close and kissing her warm, trembling lips. At first she resisted, trying to push him away. It was clear she hadn't really meant the invitation he was sure he'd seen in her eyes. She said something about the allergy pills and how dizzy she was. And then she told him that she just wanted to go home.

But it was too late to turn back. He'd been thinking about her all night and now she was here, alone with him. If she hadn't wanted this to happen, she wouldn't have asked him to drive her home.

He pulled off the blanket and pushed her down on the couch. Her body was beautiful in the firelight, and he could see tan lines from the bikini she'd worn at the lake. He reached out to trace them with his fingers and when she tried to stop him, he clamped his lips over hers and took possession of her mouth.

Any restraint he might have had disappeared in the fire of passion. This wasn't the time to think of consequences. That could come later, after he'd satisfied his blazing need. He paid no attention to her desperate struggles. She would be his tonight.

There was no one to hear her when she cried out. The cabin was set back from the main road and no one knew they were here. Beautiful Kelly, so warm and so loving. It was a night he'd remember for the rest of his life.

The phone rang once, bringing him back to the present with a jolt. It was a signal that they were ready to start the entertainment. He had to mask his feelings, go downstairs, and pretend to be part of the group.

There was time for only one more memory as he picked up his things and headed for the door. He hadn't lied to Kelly afterwards, when he'd held her in his arms and soothed away her tears. He'd told her that everything would work out for the best. And it had, now that she was dead.

The call came right as Tommy and Cheryl's skit was about to begin. They all heard the phone on the reservations desk ring, and a moment later Brian was calling for Pete over the loudspeakers.

"I'll be right back." Pete looked a little disgruntled. "Just relax for a minute, and we'll pick up right where we left off."

The phone call took a little longer than Pete had expected, and when he came back, he was frowning. "That was Miss Voelker. They're having a really bad storm in Foothill, and she called to see if we were all right."

"But it's barely raining up here." Cheryl pointed to the window where only a few drops were hitting the glass.

"We're almost twenty miles away." Tommy slipped his arm around her shoulders and gave her a little hug. "It'll take a while for it to get to us . . . if it does. Did Miss Voelker say it was headed our way?"

Pete nodded. "That's what she told me. She called the National Weather Bureau right before she called us. They told her it's supposed to blow over by tomorrow afternoon, just in time for the buses to drive up here."

"That's a relief!" Dale started to smile. "The kids would be really disappointed if we had to cancel our plans."

Tommy and Cheryl were just taking their places when the phone on the desk rang a second time. A moment later, Brian's voice came over the loudspeaker again. "Lexie? Your brother's on line one."

They all waited as Lexie hurried out to the registration desk to pick up the phone. She was gone for only a few moments, and when she came back she was frowning.

"My brother says there's a couple of big rock slides on the

road. Both lanes are blocked and no one can get through. He just wanted to know if we were all right."

Jennifer glanced at Tim. He looked just as worried as she felt. How about Zada? She'd promised to be here at six-thirty and it was almost eight. Was she caught in one of the rock slides?

"Does your brother think the buses can get through by tomorrow night?" Pete was frowning.

"He doesn't know, but he said to tell you to keep everyone here. The lodge is sandwiched in, right between two slide areas. It's the safest place we could be."

"Okay," Pete said. "We'll stay put."

"He says the road's a mess, and the rocks are still shifting so there could be more rock slides. He was just saying good-bye when the phone went dead."

"You mean we're cut off from everybody in Foothill?" Melanie began to look very nervous.

"That's right. And we're stuck here until they clear the road."

Just then there was a blinding flash of lightning, followed by a clap of thunder so loud that everyone jumped. The lights flickered once, and then they came back on.

"That was close!" Susie shivered slightly. "Does anyone know if this place has lightning rods?"

Tim nodded. "It does, and Tommy and I made sure they're all connected. We did the roof last summer."

"Do you think we should round up some flashlights and candles?" Melanie still looked worried. "If the storm gets bad, the lights could go out."

Dale shook his head. "Relax, Melanie. My uncle has the lodge on a backup generator system. It kicks in automatically if the power goes off."

"At least we won't be stuck without electricity!" Melanie gave a sigh of relief. "It's going to be bad enough if we're stuck up here by ourselves on Halloween night."

There was a crackle as Brian's voice came over the loudspeaker. "I think you're forgetting something, Melanie."

"What's that?" Melanie looked curious.

"Even if the buses don't get through, this is a great place to spend Halloween. We've got decorations, and food and drinks and entertainment. And that sounds like the makings of a great Halloween party to me!"

Six

They'd decided that Brian was right, and they were all in a much better mood when they went on with their dress rehearsal. The skits were good, Pete was enthusiastic about their performances, and everyone started having a wonderful time. They were having so much fun that they didn't really notice that the storm outside was getting worse.

"Okay, gang." Pete smiled at all of them. "The only thing left to rehearse is the séance, and everyone's taking part in that. Jennifer and Tim? You're on in fifteen minutes. Do you have any instructions for us?"

Jennifer had already told everyone what to bring for the séance skit. "The girls should get into their white dresses and the guys should change to dark clothes. We'll meet down here in fifteen minutes."

"What about the lights?" Brian spoke up. "Do you want them on?"

Tim shook his head. "We don't need them. We're doing the séance right here in the lobby, and the firelight is a perfect background. I'll just throw another log on the fire and it'll be perfect."

"The spirits don't like bright places," Jennifer explained. "They're much more receptive if the lights are low, especially if they cast a yellow or orange glow."

Melanie laughed. "Oh, sure. And if the lights are down low, we won't be able to see what you and Tim are doing in the shadows."

"No, Melanie." Jennifer shook her head. "That's not the reason. Tim and I will be part of the group, and we won't be doing anything except sitting here. I told you before. This is going to be an authentic séance with no tricks."

"Whatever you say." Melanie didn't look convinced as she headed for the stairs. But she stopped abruptly as she heard a banging noise at the front door. "I think somebody's out there. And it doesn't sound like a restless spirit."

Everyone gathered around as Pete went to the door and opened it. The sight that greeted them made everyone gasp. It was a woman wearing a rain slicker, and she was drenched to the skin.

"Zada?" Tim rushed up to take the two bags that Zada was carrying. "I don't believe it! You got through the rock slide!"

"I got through, but my car didn't. It's about five miles down the road. I had to climb over the rocks and hike up here."

"You'd better warm up by the fire." Jennifer helped Zada out of her raincoat and hung it on a hook by the door. Then she handed her a blanket and led her over to a warm spot in front of the big rock fireplace. "What happened?"

"I got caught between two rock slides. That's where my car is. I'm just lucky I could climb over the second one to get up here. Am I in time for the séance?"

"We were about to start."

"Good. Then my trip wasn't wasted. Just let me get into some dry clothes and I'll be ready. I brought some things for you to use."

Jennifer realized that everyone was staring at Zada, and she turned around to introduce her. "This is Zada Tilitch. She owns the Cosmic Eye bookstore, and she's going to help us with the séance. I didn't mention it before, because I didn't think she'd be able to get here."

"It sounds like you had a close call, Zada." Pete walked over to shake her hand. "You'll stay here, of course. If the buses with the kids can't get through, you can be our captive audience of one."

"That sounds like fun. Is there somewhere I can change to dry clothes?"

"I'll take you upstairs," Lexie offered. "There's plenty of rooms left. You can take a hot shower and dry your hair."

Zada looked a little worried. "How about the séance? What time are you holding it?"

"Whenever you're ready." Pete smiled at her. "We'll all take a break and have some hot chocolate. Just take your time and we'll wait for you."

Zada handed Tim one of her bags. "I won't need more than a few minutes. Why don't you unpack this, Tim? I brought some lilac-scented candles. They were Kelly's favorite and they might help attract her spirit to us. She loved lilacs."

"That's right!" Tommy looked surprised. "But how did you know?"

"I knew Kelly. She used to come into the store to visit me."

"I didn't know that!" Jennifer was shocked. "Why didn't you tell us before?"

Zada shrugged. "I didn't think it was that important. I've known Kelly for over two years."

"How did you meet her?" Tommy was curious.

"She waited on me at the appliance store, and she sold me the little refrigerator and microwave I have in the back of the shop. When she stopped by to see if everything was working properly, we started talking and we became good friends. Kelly came to see me at least twice a week."

Tommy was fascinated. "So you know a lot about Kelly?"

"Of course I do." Zada smiled. "Kelly was a lovely girl, but things weren't very good for her at home. She didn't feel that she could confide in her mother, so she used to come to me with her problems. She loved you very much, you know."

Tommy swallowed hard. "I know. Did you ... uh ... did you happen to see Kelly the night she died?"

"No. But she did come into the store that afternoon. She was very disturbed about something. When I asked her what was wrong, she said she couldn't tell me until she'd talked to you.

She promised to come in the next morning to tell me everything, but . . ."

Tommy nodded as Zada's voice trailed off. "But Kelly was dead by then. Do you have any idea what was wrong?"

"No, I don't. But Kelly had a secret she took to her grave, and that means her spirit is restless. I really believe that she'll take this opportunity to confide in us."

"You mean you think the séance will really work?" Tommy looked doubtful.

"I certainly do. I have a very strong feeling that we'll be communing with Kelly's spirit tonight."

There was an uncomfortable silence for a moment, and then Lexie took Zada's arm. "Come with me, Zada. The room next to mine's vacant."

That was the cue for everyone to troop upstairs, leaving Jennifer and Tim alone in the lobby. They didn't say much as they carried in the round, wooden table they'd decided to use for the séance, and arranged twelve chairs around it. They put out the candles that Zada had brought and then stepped back to survey the setting.

Both of them were silent for a moment, and then Tim slipped his arm around Jennifer's shoulder. "What's the matter, Jen? You look really freaked."

"I don't know. I just don't like this whole thing with Zada. She didn't tell us that she knew Kelly, and that makes me wonder if there's something else that she's holding back."

"Like what?" Tim shrugged. "Relax, Jen. Maybe this is all a part of Zada's act. It's possible she didn't know Kelly at all."

"But she was really convincing. And she knew that lilacs were Kelly's favorite flowers. I didn't tell her. Did you?"

"I don't think so, but it wasn't exactly a secret. It was even in the paper. Remember the article about Kelly's funeral? It mentioned that all her friends brought bouquets of lilacs to put on her grave because she loved them so much."

"You're right! I forgot all about that article. Zada could have read it."

"She probably did. And even if Zada did know Kelly, does it really matter?"

"I'm not sure. I guess not."

Tim smiled at her and Jennifer smiled back, but she was still anxious. Something was going to happen tonight, something bad, maybe even dreadful. And since Jennifer didn't know what it was, there wasn't a thing she could do to prevent it.

When he got up to his room, he thought about Kelly and the day she'd confided in him. She'd been so frightened he'd just wanted to take her in his arms and tell her that everything would be all right. Of course, he hadn't. It was a time to be firm, to tell her what she had to do and make sure that she did it.

"Relax, Kelly." He tried to sound casual, even though his heart was pounding hard. "You're right. It's a problem. But we can take care of it."

"How?"

Her voice was shaking and he smiled at her. She was so worried, she was acting like a little child who needed reassurance. "It's simple. First, we have to find out if it's true. I'll drive you over to a doctor in Crestview and he'll give you a test. If it comes back positive, we'll talk alternatives."

"I don't need to see a doctor. I already know it's true. And what do you mean by *alternatives*?"

He winced slightly. It was clear that Kelly was going to be difficult. "The way I see it, you've got two choices. Either you have the baby or you don't. And if you choose to have it, you've got another choice to make. You can keep it. Or you can give it up for adoption."

"It sounds so . . . so cold!"

Her lips trembled and he could tell that she was about to cry, so he put his arm around her shoulders. "Hey—it's not that bad. You know me. I'll go along with whatever you decide."

"Okay." She reached inside her purse for a tissue. "I know the smart thing to do, but I just don't think I can do it."

"You mean not having the baby?" He used the phrase deliberately, avoiding the word *abortion*. It had all sorts of negative connotations and this was the time for tact and diplomacy.

"Yes. I mean . . . it's not exactly against my religion or anything like that, but . . . I'm just not sure."

He nodded, the soul of understanding. "But wouldn't it be harder to have the baby and give it up? You'd have to leave town so people wouldn't know and you'd miss your senior year. That'd be hard to make up. And how about your college scholarship? Are you willing to let that go?"

"No . . . I don't want to lose that." Kelly sounded very uncertain. "I was thinking . . . maybe I could just stay here and keep on going to school. They wouldn't find out until Christmas. I could drop out then and have the baby."

He put on a smile, even though he felt more like scowling. That was exactly what he'd been afraid of. "But everyone would know. Do you really want that, Kelly?"

"No." Kelly shook her head. "That would be awful. But I'd get to keep the baby. And I'd only miss one semester."

"That's true. It's your decision, Kelly. I'll marry you now, if that's what you want. It's my baby, too. But I really hate to see you make a terrible sacrifice like that."

"Sacrifice? What do you mean?"

"You'd be just another statistic, a girl who got pregnant and dropped out. And don't forget that they'd let me stay in school. My parents would probably pay for a little apartment, but you'd be stuck there, staring at the walls and waiting for the baby to be born. You'd be all alone, Kelly."

"But my friends would come to visit. It wouldn't be that bad."

"They'd come . . . at first. But then they'd get busy with cheerleader practice, and basketball games, and rehearsing for the spring play. They'd be concentrating on homework, test scores, and plans for college while you'd be thinking about doing the laundry and cooking dinner. Your interests would be so different, you wouldn't have anything to say to your friends."

Kelly looked a bit worried. "Well . . . maybe that's true. But I'd have the baby to think about."

"That's just it, Kelly. The only thing you'd have would be the baby. The baby would become your whole life. You'd be wasting your intelligence, wasting your opportunity for a college scholarship, wasting all your chances for a better life. It wouldn't be good for the baby, either."

"I know you're right. But . . ."

"It would be hard for me, too." She was starting to cry again and he handed her his clean, white handkerchief. "I couldn't expect my parents to pick up the whole tab, so I'd have to work a couple of part-time jobs. My grades would slip, and I might even lose my scholarship."

"But you'd still get to go to college, wouldn't you? I mean . . . your parents really want you to go."

He nodded, a little tentatively. "I'm pretty sure that my parents would pay my tuition, but they wouldn't be happy about having to support all of us until I graduated."

"I guess you're right."

Kelly sounded very depressed and he reached out to give her a hug. It was time for a little kindness, along with the hard truths he was teaching her. "Maybe it'll all work out. One thing for sure . . . I know you'd make a really good mother."

"Thanks." Kelly gave him a small hint of a smile, but she didn't look happy. "Maybe I could take night classes. I know a girl who graduated from high school that way."

"Maybe . . . if you weren't too busy with the baby. Let's say you managed to do it. What would happen then? It wouldn't be fair to ask my parents to pick up the bill for your college expenses."

"I could work. I've always worked."

"That's true. But how much could you earn? You'd have to put the baby in day care and that would be expensive."

"I guess you're right." Kelly sighed deeply. "There's no way I'll ever be able to go to college if I keep the baby."

He didn't say anything. She was finally starting to talk sense.

"I don't want to make a decision right now, not until I can talk it over with someone I trust."

"Who?" He tried to be casual, but his whole body tensed. Kelly couldn't tell anyone she was pregnant!

"Don't worry." Kelly put her hand on his arm. "This won't get out. I promise."

"How can you be sure of that?" He tried to sound reasonable, even though he was beginning to panic. Something like this was bound to get out. Who did she think she was kidding?

Kelly was silent for a long moment. "Maybe you're right. Give me a little time to think it over."

"Sure, Kelly. Take as long as you want. Just call me before you talk to anyone, or do anything . . . okay? That's only fair. Don't forget that we're in this together."

"Yes. We are." Kelly looked very solemn as she got up to leave. "I'll call you before I do anything. I promise."

After Kelly had left, he'd sat there with his head in his hands. Could he trust her to call him before she told anyone else? He just wasn't sure. And could he really afford to take that chance?

He'd thought about it all that morning and into the afternoon. And then he'd made his decision. Kelly was frightened and very naive. She was bound to talk to someone. She couldn't handle something like this, all by herself. It didn't really matter who she told. No one in Foothill could keep a secret this big. It would come out, and his whole future was in jeopardy.

There was only one thing to do. He didn't like it, but there was no other choice. He had to silence Kelly before she talked. This was one secret that Kelly had to take to her grave.

Had he made the right decision? He winced as he remembered how he'd cut Kelly's brake line. She'd always parked her car by the big oak tree in her driveway. The yard was overrun with weeds and tall grass, and he'd had plenty of cover.

When he'd heard that Kelly was dead, he'd felt a stab of pity. Poor Kelly was gone and so was the unborn baby that no one could ever know about. He'd mourned them both, but he'd also been very relieved.

And now he was terrified again. The same fear that had forced him to kill Kelly was back in full force. He'd thought he'd ended it with her death, but he hadn't counted on Zada Tilitch, the psychic who claimed to be Kelly's confidante.

Even though Zada had insisted that she didn't know why Kelly had been so upset, he had his doubts. Kelly had told him that she needed to talk to someone. What if Zada had been that person? If Kelly had taken Zada into her confidence, would Zada reveal her secret at the séance?

Zada was a paid psychic who gave readings and held séances. Her reputation depended on giving a good show. If Zada could convince everyone that Kelly had spoken to her from the grave, it would be good for her business. She was bound to reveal Kelly's secret . . . if she knew it. And he couldn't take the chance that she didn't!

His position was clear. No one could know Kelly's secret. His very life depended on that. But what could he do? He shut his eyes and imagined a snowball, rolling down a hill. It started slowly, just a small compact ball the size of his fist. But as it rolled, it took on more snow, gaining speed and growing so large that no one person could stop it. The secret of Kelly's pregnancy was the snowball. He had to stop it now, before it could grow. He had to silence Zada permanently, before she could tell anyone else what she might know.

Seven

Zada was smiling as she stepped out of the shower. This séance was a wonderful opportunity for her. If it went well, and she would make sure that it did, her reputation as a psychic would be the talk of Foothill High. Tapping the teenage market was a natural. She didn't understand why she hadn't thought of it before. Teens had plenty of money and they were very concerned about their future. Before she left, she'd offer to do a couple of free readings, and they'd be hooked.

And then there were the parents. Zada's smile grew wider. When Jennifer had introduced her to the group, she'd listened carefully to the names. Lexie Sussman's father owned the town newspaper. If his daughter was impressed, there might be an opportunity for some free publicity. Tommy and Tim Jackson had connections, too. Their mother was president of the Foothill Ladies League. And then there was Dale Prescott, a state senator's son, and Cheryl Maloney, whose parents did a lot of fancy entertaining. The Maloneys might hire her to do readings at one of their parties, or lead a séance as an evening's entertainment.

Melanie Carpenter's mother was already a client, but she'd never told her husband and daughter. It would be a real coup if Mrs. Carpenter would bring her husband, the mayor, in for a reading. And then there was Ronnie Hughes. If he spread the word, it could lead to a lot of business. Ronnie's grandparents had raised a large family, and there were several generations living right here in Foothill.

Jennifer's parents wouldn't be interested. They had a reputation for being levelheaded. But Susie Romano might bring in some business, especially if her parents talked it up at the deli. And Brian Garvey's parents were naturals. Brian's younger sister had died of cancer last year, and if Brian told them that she had contacted Kelly's spirit, they might call to arrange a séance for themselves.

Most of Zada's leads came from checking the obituaries and she kept careful files. It always helped to be prepared, and there was usually something in the funeral notice that she could use in a séance. Kelly's had certainly been useful. That's how she'd learned that lilacs were Kelly's favorite flower. There had even been a picture, and she'd studied it carefully before she'd left the bookstore. If anyone asked questions about Kelly's appearance, she'd be able to answer them accurately. There was no way anyone would suspect that she hadn't known Kelly Bridges at all.

Zada knew they'd expect her to dress the part and she slipped into her black séance dress. It had wide, flowing sleeves, which came in handy for hiding things that would appear to materialize from thin air, and a voluminous, floor-length skirt.

Jewelry was a must and Zada clasped several pendants around her neck. She'd found an art student who'd made them for her, copying the designs from a book of celestial symbols. She'd wear a veil. It made her look much more mysterious and it had the added benefit of hiding her expression. And high heels were necessary if she wanted to appear tall and imposing.

Essential oil was next. Zada took the cap from a small bottle of patchouli, and wrinkled up her nose as she dabbed some on her wrists. Patchouli was rumored to be the same essence they'd used in Egyptian burial rites, and she'd be sure to mention that fact. It was probably true. The scent was strong enough to overpower anything, no matter how rank, and it always impressed the clients.

A glance in the mirror and Zada was satisfied. She looked dark and forbidding, just the way a psychic was supposed to look. She picked up a tattered leather book that she'd filled with scribbles and turned to head for the door. Zada Tilitch was ready. The séance could commence.

She was alone on the second floor. Zada had heard everyone else go down the stairs several minutes ago. She'd flick off the lights when she got to the head of the stairs and then she'd make her entrance.

Zada was smiling as she thought about their reaction. She'd go down several steps. Then she'd light her candle and call out for them. When they gathered at the foot of the stairs, they would be greeted by an eerie sight. A figure in black would be descending the staircase, holding a sputtering candle. At first they'd be frightened, but then they would realize who it was. That would convince them that things were not always as they seemed, and put them all into the proper mood for the séance.

Lightning stuck just as Zada was stepping out into the hallway. It was a perfect night for a séance. The lightning would make them all nervous and they'd be even more receptive when Kelly's spirit contacted her and asked to join them.

When Zada reached the top of the stairs, she snapped off the lights and listened. There was a group of students in the lobby, and although she couldn't hear what they were saying, she was sure that the topic of conversation was the séance.

Two voices floated clearly up the stairs and Zada smiled as she realized they belonged to Jennifer and Tim. They were alone in the kitchen, and they were definitely discussing the séance.

"I'm not sure about the séance, Tim. Zada's a professional medium. Maybe I should ask her to lead it."

"No, Jen. We've got it all planned out. Zada's expecting you to lead the séance, and you can't ask her to take over now. She said she was coming because she wanted to protect us in case something happened. And she was very definite about just wanting to watch."

Zada smiled, highly amused. She would be doing a lot more than watching, but they didn't know that. She had a few tricks up her sleeve that would make this séance an event they would talk about for years to come.

Jennifer would start the séance, and everyone would concentrate on her. That would give Zada time to set up her special effects. They would be very startled when the spirits called out for Zada, and Jennifer would be very grateful to have her take over. And then Zada would run the séance exactly the way she'd planned.

Zada's foot slipped a bit as she went down the first step. She wasn't used to wearing high heels and the stairs were highly polished. She steadied herself by clutching the handrail, but she was beginning to have second thoughts. It was dangerous to go down the stairs in the dark.

Zada was very careful as she went down the second step, and then the third. And then she heard the sound of someone breathing behind her. She whirled around, trying to see who was following her, but it was too dark.

Lightning struck again, and Zada caught a glimpse of a pale, disembodied face, but the flash of light was gone so fast she didn't recognize who it was. If someone followed her down the stairs, it would ruin her entrance.

Zada let go of the handrail and moved to the far side of the step. She steadied herself against the wall and whispered softly. "Go down and join the others."

But the figure didn't pass her as Zada expected. He just moved to the other side of the step with her. And then she felt hands gripping her shoulders.

"What are you doing?"

There was no answer, but before she could ask again, the person shoved her, pushing her forward down the stairs. Zada cried out as she fell, a scream of pure terror, but her cry was covered by a loud crash of thunder. And then she was tumbling head over heels down the long staircase, arms reaching out desperately, trying to grab something that would stop her fall.

But there was nothing to grab, only empty air, and Zada's head crashed into the newel post at the base of the stairs. The blow was so severe it snapped her neck, plunging Zada Tilitch into the same realm of darkness she'd spent her whole career pretending to contact.

*   *   *

They were all gathered around the huge stone fireplace, sipping mugs of hot chocolate. Jennifer glanced at her watch and frowned. "I wonder what's keeping Zada? It's been almost an hour."

"I'll ring her room." Brian stood up and headed for the reservation desk. "She looked really tired when she got here. Maybe she fell asleep."

Jennifer had a terrible feeling of foreboding as Brian rang the telephone in Zada's room. Zada had hiked five miles up the mountain so that she could be here for the séance. Surely she wouldn't have fallen asleep!

"There's no answer." Brian came back looking puzzled. "Do you think we should check on her?"

Tim stood up. "Come on, Jen. Let's go."

Jennifer's legs were shaking slightly as they walked across the lobby. The lights were off in the hallway and when they rounded the corner, she flicked them on. And then they both stopped, frozen in their tracks.

"Oh, my God! It's Zada!" Jennifer's voice came out in a frightened whisper. "Is she all right?"

Tim didn't answer. He just hurried to Zada and knelt down to check for a pulse.

Jennifer reached out for the wall to steady herself. Zada was very still. She looked like a crumpled rag doll at the bottom of the stairs, and her neck was bent at a very strange angle.

"Should I call for a . . ." Jennifer's voice trailed off. She couldn't call for an ambulance. The phone lines were down and there was no cell phone reception. But she couldn't just stand here shaking. She had to do something to help. "Tim? Do you want me to ask if anyone knows first aid?"

"First aid won't help, Jen." Tim looked very serious as he got up and walked back to her. "Zada's dead."

Jennifer opened her mouth to say something, but there was nothing to say. And then Tim was holding her tightly as she started to cry.

Tim held her for a moment and then he turned her around

and gave her a gentle shove toward the door. "Go back to the lobby and stay there with the girls. Tell the guys to come out here and help."

"Help?" Jennifer didn't understand. "How can the guys help Zada? She's dead!"

"The road's blocked, Jen. And it could be a couple of days before we can call someone to pick her up. We can't just leave her here at the bottom of the stairs."

"Oh. I see." Jennifer tried to move toward the door. But her feet didn't seem to be cooperating.

"Go, Jen." Tim gave her another shove. "You've got to tell them . . . okay?"

Jennifer took another step. This wasn't the time to be timid. Tim was counting on her. When she got to the door, she turned back, her eyes unconsciously memorizing the scene. "I think there's a tarp on the top shelf in the kitchen. Shall I have the guys bring it?"

"Good idea. Thanks, Jen. I'm glad you're not the type to fall apart in a crisis."

Jennifer carried the memory of Tim's words with her, all the way back to the lobby. And she was calm as she told everyone what had happened. Pete and the guys left to help Tim, and Jennifer even managed to comfort Susie, who couldn't seem to stop shaking. But during it all, while she was being calm and responsible, Jennifer's mind was whirling with unanswered questions. The lights had been off and it was possible that Zada hadn't known where the switch was. But she'd been carrying a candle and matches. Why hadn't she lit the candle so she could see? And why hadn't she held on to the handrail when she'd started to fall?

Suddenly, a thought popped into Jennifer's mind. It was so frightening that she gasped out loud.

"Are you okay, Jen?" Lexie looked concerned.

"I'm fine." But she wasn't fine, not at all. The pieces fit and she could imagine exactly how Zada's death had occurred.

Zada had been coming down the stairs in the dark, grasping the handrail to balance herself. She'd been planning something special for the séance, and that's why she was dressed in her long black dress and veil. She hadn't lit the candle because she'd wanted to make an entrance.

Someone had come up behind Zada while she was on the stairs. And Zada hadn't wanted that person to spoil her grand entrance. She'd decided to let that person pass her and she'd moved to the side, where the steps were narrower. But that person hadn't gone past her. This person had stayed right there in back of her, and pushed her down the stairs to her death!

But why would someone kill Zada? No one in their group had even met her before tonight. What possible reason could anyone have for wanting her dead?

The séance. Jennifer shuddered at the thought, but it was the only explanation that made sense. Zada was a psychic and someone had believed she'd use her power to contact Kelly's spirit. That someone had murdered her before she could reveal the secret that Kelly had taken to the grave!

"Jen? Did you hear me?"

Jennifer jumped as Tim touched her shoulder. She'd been concentrating so hard, she hadn't even heard him come into the lobby. "What did you say, Tim?"

"I said, Pete wants us to go ahead with the séance. It'll take our minds off what happened to Zada."

Jennifer glanced around, but no one was paying any attention to them. She moved closer to Tim and lowered her voice so they couldn't be overheard. "We can't do the séance, Tim. It could be dangerous. The séance is the reason Zada was murdered!"

"Murdered?" Tim put his arms around Jennifer and hugged her tightly. "You've got it all wrong, Jen. Zada wasn't murdered. She slipped on the stairs and fell. It's awful, but it was an accident."

Jennifer looked up, into Tim's face. He seemed perfectly sincere. "Are you sure, Tim?"

"I'm positive. Come on, Jen. Let's do the séance. Zada would want us to carry on."

"Well . . . okay." Tim was probably right. She'd been so upset over Zada's death, she'd imagined the worst.

Tim waited until she was seated and then he placed Zada's leather-bound book in her hands. "You should have this, Jen. I found it next to Zada's body. She was bringing it down for you."

As Tim went off to gather everyone for their skit, Jennifer frowned. She didn't want to lead this séance. She didn't even want be an observer. Despite Tim's assurances that everything would be all right, Jennifer had the terrible feeling that they ought to leave Kelly's spirit alone.

Her hands were shaking slightly as she held the book. Zada had told her that the book was a talisman. It contained ancient incantations that would protect her from harm. As she opened it, Jennifer half-expected to feel its energy. But nothing happened. Nothing at all. The book was just an old book.

Jennifer placed it, face-open, on the table. The strange symbols on its pages looked very mysterious and it made an excellent prop. Of course, the book was completely powerless. She had the ultimate proof: Zada had promised that it would protect anyone who possessed it, but it certainly hadn't protected her when she was falling down the stairs!

Eight

Melanie was frowning as she took her place at the table. "The storm is getting worse. Why don't we just forget about the séance and sit by the fire?"

"Good idea." Cheryl nodded. "Zada's not here and how can you hold a séance without a psychic? That's like putting on a circus without any clowns."

Dale laughed. "Unless we're the clowns. How about it, Jen? Are we the clowns?"

"No, we're not. And Zada wasn't here to lead the séance. She just came up here to watch me."

"You were going to lead the séance?" Melanie giggled. "Come on, Jen . . . you don't know anything about the occult."

"Yes, I do. I've done a lot of research and I've got Zada's book. Tim and I have been practicing almost every day."

"All right, gang. Let's have some cooperation here." Pete sat down in a wing chair next to the fireplace. "Tonight is a full rehearsal, and that means everyone gets the chance to do their skit."

Melanie looked a little embarrassed. "Okay. I'm sorry, Jen. I promise I'll cooperate. It's just that without your psychic here, I know we won't be able to contact Kelly's spirit."

"You mean you actually believed that Zada could do it?" Susie looked shocked.

"Well . . . actually . . . no, not really." Melanie shook her head. "But she was a psychic, and I thought she stood a better chance."

Lexie winked at Jennifer and then she turned to Melanie. "That's what I thought, too . . . at first. But when I really thought about it, I changed my mind. If anybody can contact Kelly's spirit, it's Jen."

"But . . . why?" Melanie looked doubtful.

"Because the spirits are attracted to a lively intelligence, an active curiosity, and a pure heart. Everyone knows that."

Melanie stared at Lexie for a moment. "Okay. I really think you're making this up, but let's start the séance and see."

Jennifer bit back a grin as she opened her séance book. Lexie had managed to say exactly the right thing. "All right, everyone. Tim will show you where to sit. I want you to put your arms on the top of the table and clasp hands while I light the master candle. We'll all stare into the flame for a moment and let our collective spiritual energy build."

"Do we hold hands through the whole séance?" Cheryl looked eager as she took Tommy's hand.

Jennifer nodded. "Yes. If anyone breaks the circle, the spirits will depart. Whatever happens, don't let go."

"Don't worry about that. I won't." Cheryl smiled up at Tommy. "Go ahead, Jen. You can start now."

It was clear that Cheryl enjoyed holding Tommy's hand. And Tommy didn't seem to mind. Just a week ago, Cheryl's blatant attempt to pick up on Tommy would have made Jennifer horribly jealous, but now she found that it didn't bother her at all. Was Tim responsible for her change in attitude? Jennifer was almost sure that he was, but she didn't want to make any decision about Tim and Tommy quite yet.

"Please don't close your eyes." Jennifer lit the master candle. "Concentrate on the flame, and try to remain calm and quiet. We must be perfectly receptive to the spirits who will join our table tonight."

She glanced around the table to make sure they were following her instructions. Everyone was watching the flickering candle flame . . . everyone except Tommy. Tommy looked very nervous. He was clenching his jaw and Jennifer could see the lines of tension on his forehead. Was he afraid of what might happen at the séance? Was he worried about what Kelly's spirit might tell them? There was only one way to find out, and that was to ask.

"Is there anyone here who is unsure about contacting Kelly's spirit?" Jennifer let the question hang in the air for a long, tense moment, but no one said a word. And then, just as she was about to go on with the ritual, Tommy spoke up.

"Maybe this isn't such a good idea." Tommy's voice shook slightly. "I'm not sure we should try to contact Kelly."

Tim turned to look at his brother in surprise. "But why? Come on, Tommy. It's only a skit. And we're certainly not hurting anyone."

"Yeah. I know. I didn't think it would bother me, but it just doesn't seem right. It's almost—uh—"

"Sacrilegious?" Lexie supplied the word.

"Yeah. Isn't holding a séance sacrilegious?"

"No." Jennifer was glad she had the chance to show that they'd done some research. "Spiritualism is a form of religion. It was very popular at the turn of the twentieth century. Disciples of spiritualism believed that it could prove there was life after death."

"You're sure it's not disrespectful to Kelly?" Tommy still looked concerned.

"Not at all. It's a way of showing how much we miss her, and how we all wish she could be here with us." Jennifer squeezed Tim's hand as she deviated from their plan. "I think we should all take a moment to say something to Kelly. Just imagine that she's sitting right next to you, and tell her what's in your heart. We'll go around the table so everyone can say something. Dale? Will you start us out?"

"I'd be glad to." Dale smiled at Jennifer. He was always ready to give a speech. "Kelly . . . I really admired you. You always had a kind word for everyone and it doesn't seem right to go through our senior year without you. I just want you to know that you'll live on in our hearts. You've had a real impact on our lives, and we're all better people for having known you."

Melanie nodded. "That's true. You were my friend, Kelly, and I just wish I'd had a chance to tell you how much I liked you. I'll never forget how you came to rehearsal early almost every night to help me learn my lines for the spring play."

"You helped me, too." Brian was next. "And I miss you every day, Kelly. You're the only one who ever laughed at my jokes."

Susie giggled. "And all of us know how awful Brian's jokes are. That was one of the great things about you, Kelly. You were always so careful that you didn't hurt anyone's feelings. You were a truly nice person. Ronnie? It's your turn."

"Hey, Kelly." Ronnie looked very serious. "I miss your smile. And I miss having you sit next to me in homeroom. I used to forget my notebook and you always picked it up for me. I probably would have flunked my junior year without you."

Cheryl was next and she shrugged. "What can I say? When I moved to Foothill, Kelly was already dead. I didn't even know her!"

"But you've heard me talk about her." Tommy gave her a nudge. "Come on, Cheryl. Everybody has to say something or the séance won't work."

"Okay, I'll try. But I'm really not sure what to say."

"Tell Kelly hello," Tommy urged her. "Say whatever's on your mind."

Cheryl took a deep breath. "Hi, Kelly. Everybody says you were very nice. Tommy really missed you a lot, at first. All he could think about was you. I hope you won't be jealous when Tommy starts dating again. I mean . . . he's all alone and it's not healthy for him to stay in love with a dead girl forever."

Just then a bolt of lightning crackled through the sky. It was accompanied almost immediately by a deafening roar of thunder so loud, everyone jumped.

"Maybe Kelly doesn't agree with you." Dale laughed, but he sobered quickly when Melanie poked him. "Sorry about that."

"It's your turn." Jennifer turned to Tommy, who took a deep breath.

"Kelly, honey . . . I know you're out there somewhere, and I want you to know that I still love you. I think about you every day, and I remember how sweet and warm and loving you were. Sometimes I can hardly stand it because I want to see you again, so much. Just yesterday, I picked up the phone and I started to dial your number. And then I remembered, and I felt so damn helpless. I just want you to know that I'll never stop loving you, Kelly . . . never."

There was a silence so deep that Jennifer could hear herself breathing. Tommy's little speech had affected her deeply and there were tears in her eyes. She knew she should say something. She was leading the séance. But then Lexie spoke.

"It's me, Kelly. Lexie Sussman. You always called me the voice of reason because I was so practical. I don't feel very practical tonight. I just feel sad that you're not here. And I'm hoping that somehow you can join us. I know that doesn't make sense, but I'm still hoping. If you're out there and you're listening to all this, please stick around. We need to talk to you again. All of us. Especially Tommy."

"Lexie's right," Tim said. "Please, Kelly. You've just got to contact us. Tommy misses you so much. I really think that if he could talk to you again, it would make him feel better."

Jennifer swallowed hard. It was her turn and she wasn't quite sure what to say. "Hi, Kelly. I've never led a séance before, but I'm going to do my best. We're your friends, Kelly. And we need to talk to you. I'll light the gold candle now and start the ritual."

Tim handed her the gold candle and Jennifer used the master candle to light it. Her hands shook slightly, but no one laughed or made any comment. Everyone seemed very absorbed in the ritual—even Pete, who was only here to critique it.

"The gold candle burns brightly. It is your guide and your beacon. Oh, spirit friends of our dear departed . . . slip through the curtain between life and death, and favor us with your presence."

There was another flash of lightning and Jennifer felt the tension rise. Everyone was watching her as she started to light the tall white tapers at the center of the table.

"Oh, spirits of darkness and spirits of light. Come to be with us on this night. We interrupt your rest to learn of life. We disturb your peace to help in our plight."

Tim squeezed Jennifer's hand as she finished lighting the tapers, and Jennifer squeezed back. "We will now invoke the spirit we wish to contact. Please try to visualize Kelly's face as we call her to us by name."

Zada had brought three lilac candles. Jennifer spoke the incantation as she lit the first one. "Kelly Anne Bridges, we summon you. From the realm of the living, your friends seek your help."

The first lilac candle sputtered, shooting out sparks. Someone gasped and Jennifer almost dropped the master candle. Zada must have brought special candles that sparked when they were ignited.

As the first candle began to burn and the scent of lilacs filled the air, Jennifer moved on to the second candle. "Kelly Anne Bridges, hear us tonight. Let your spirit soar into our midst."

The second lilac candle sparked brightly, but this time Jennifer knew what to expect. When it was burning steadily, she moved on to the third candle.

"We beckon to you, Kelly Anne Bridges. Come be with us now and fill our hearts with gladness."

The third candle sputtered once and burst into flame. All three candles were now burning brightly, and Jennifer went on with the ritual.

"Kelly Anne Bridges, favor us with a sign. Let us know that you hear us."

There was a long, tense moment. Jennifer held her breath and so did everyone else at the table. And then it happened. There was another flash of lightning and the table began to shake.

Jennifer almost jumped up in fear, but then she realized what must have happened. Even though they hadn't asked Brian for any special effects, he must have rigged the table. It jiggled wildly for a moment and then it moved, rotating slowly until the lilac candles were positioned right in front of Tommy.

"Kelly's spirit is here among us." Jennifer turned toward Tommy. "She has chosen you, Tommy. Kelly wants you to ask the first question."

Tommy's face looked very pale in the flickering candlelight. "Kelly? Are you . . . all right?"

The table leg rapped sharply against the floor. Just once. And then it was silent again. Tommy was frowning as he asked another question. "Once for yes, and twice for no? Is that right, Kelly?"

The table leg rapped once again. And then the table began to rotate until the lilac candles stopped in front of Tim.

"Me?" Tim looked startled. Brian was following his own script for the séance, and it was really putting them on the spot.

"Kelly . . ." Tim cleared his throat. "I hope this isn't too painful for you, but we need to know what happened on the night you died. Can you tell us, please?"

The table rapped sharply, just once. And then an eerie voice floated out of the darkness, coming from somewhere above their heads. "I will tell one of you, but not now. They are calling me and I must go."

There was another tremendous clap of thunder and then the table began to rise very slowly, giving them a chance to pull back their clasped hands. It rose almost a foot and then it stopped, hovering there in space.

"What shall we do?" Susie sounded frightened.

"Uh . . . nothing." Jennifer hoped her voice wasn't shaking. She certainly hadn't expected this! "Just wait and watch. And keep holding hands."

The table hovered in the air and then it began to spin. It spun faster and faster until the candle flames looked like a solid ring of light.

"Wow!" Tommy gasped as the table stopped spinning and began to lower again. It settled gently against the floor and then the flames began to go out, one by one, as if an unseen hand had pinched them from their wicks.

They sat in the darkness for a moment, stunned by what they had seen. And then Pete flicked on the lights and began to applaud. "That was fantastic, guys! I hope the kids can get up here tomorrow. This séance skit is nothing short of incredible!"

"Uh . . . thank you." Jennifer drew a deep, shaky breath. "I just think I should tell you that this didn't happen the way we expected. The séance . . . I think it was real!"

"Sure it was, and you're still in character." Pete grinned as he patted her on the back. "Come on, guys. Put away your props and clean up. We'll have a short critique session by the fireplace."

Jennifer waited until everyone was busy, and then she motioned to Tim. "Let's go find Brian. I want to compliment him on those special effects!"

Brian was in the kitchen and Jennifer hurried over to pat him on the back. "That was wonderful, Brian. The way the table moved was fantastic!"

"I still can't figure out how you did those candles." Tim reached out to shake Brian's hand. "Snuffing them out like that was really great!"

"And the voice from the loudspeakers. It really sounded like Kelly. But . . . I really wish you'd told us exactly what you were going to do. I almost jumped out of my skin when things started to happen."

"Yeah. Me, too." Brian looked completely freaked.

"You?" Jennifer started to frown. "But . . . why?"

"Because I didn't rig any of those things!"

Tim looked shocked for a moment, but then he started to laugh. "Come on, Brian. We're the only ones here. You can admit you're a special effects genius."

"That's true," Brian admitted. "But somebody else is even better. I'm telling you the truth, guys. I didn't do it."

"You didn't do anything?" Tim was skeptical.

"Not me. I thought you guys hired a pro to rig those things. And I was really mad that you didn't let me in on it."

"Wait a minute." Tim began to frown. "If you didn't do it, and we didn't hire anyone else, then who was in charge of the special effects?"

The question hung in midair, unanswered. They stared at each other for a long moment, and then Jennifer shivered. She wasn't about to say it, but she was beginning to wonder if it was Kelly.

Nine

He sipped his hot chocolate and stared into the flames of the massive, river rock fireplace. They'd critiqued everyone's performance and now they were all sitting around, just talking. Even though it was past eleven, no one seemed eager to leave the group to go upstairs. Perhaps they were all too rattled by the things that had happened at the séance.

Someone had just asked Jennifer how they'd managed to snuff out the candles, and she had shrugged. "I don't know. All I can tell you is, we didn't do it. And I don't know who did."

"Do you think it was Kelly?" He asked the question that was on everyone's mind.

Jennifer looked perplexed as she answered. "Maybe it was. I'm just not sure."

He managed to hide his grin, but he was impressed. Jennifer was still in character and she deserved an Academy Award for her performance tonight. She'd seemed genuinely shocked when the table had moved, and she'd actually jumped when Kelly had spoken. He'd seen her face when the candles had begun to extinguish themselves, and she'd looked every bit as spooked as the rest of them. She was acting as if she'd actually contacted Kelly's spirit.

Of course, that was impossible. He was sure of that. Some of the best minds of the century had tried to contact the spirits of the dead, and all of them had failed. Arthur Conan Doyle had spent years trying to prove that the spirit world existed, and he had failed. And if the great Harry Houdini had been unable to send a simple code to his wife from the other side, it was ridiculous to think that an amateur like Jennifer could actually talk to Kelly's spirit.

The séance was definitely a fake, but he knew he still had to be very careful. There was always the possibility that Kelly had talked to someone before she'd died. The séance could provide a way for that person to reveal Kelly's secret without exposing his or her identity. And he couldn't let that happen.

The grandfather clock began to chime midnight, and Melanie stood up. "I don't know about the rest of you, but I have to go to bed."

"Alone?" Immediately after Susie had asked the question, everyone burst into laughter. She blushed as she tried to explain. "I didn't mean it that way. I just meant . . . after everything that's happened tonight, I wouldn't go upstairs by myself!"

Melanie grinned good-naturedly. "It doesn't bother me. Kelly was a friend of mine. If she wants to haunt me, that's fine."

Jennifer watched as Melanie gave a jaunty little wave and headed for the stairs. Perhaps Melanie had the right attitude. Kelly had been their friend in life. There was no reason to think that would change, now that she was dead.

"She's right, you know." Jennifer turned to Tim. "If Kelly's spirit is here, she'd have no reason to hurt us."

Lexie nodded. "That's true. But I don't want to be alone and I'm willing to bet that no one else does, either."

"How about a little music?" Ronnie reached for his guitar. "I'm working on some old Beatles songs for my aunt and uncle's twenty-fifth wedding anniversary. You guys can sing along."

They were just starting the second chorus of "Here Comes The Sun" when Melanie burst through the doorway. She was wrapped in a robe and her hair was wet and dripping. Her face was the color of chalk, her eyes were wide and unfocused, and she was shaking so hard she could barely stand up.

Melanie leaned against the doorjamb, gasping. "I didn't believe it, but now I've got proof! Kelly is definitely here!"

The girls wrapped Melanie in a blanket and gave her a seat directly in front of the fire. They all took turns reassuring her, but it was still almost ten minutes before Melanie was calm enough to tell them what had happened.

"I went up to my room and I took a shower. I was just toweling off my hair when I noticed that there was something on my pillow. It was this pin." Melanie held it up so they could see the beautiful gold butterfly pin. "It was fastened to a note."

"Let me see." Tommy took the pin from Melanie's hand and his face turned pale. "This was Kelly's pin! How did you get it?"

"... I don't know. I told you. It was just there, on my pillow. ... I thought it was a present from one of you until I read the note."

"Let's see the note." Tim took it and unfolded the piece of paper. "It's written on Saddlepeak Lodge stationery. And it looks like Kelly's handwriting to me. It says, *My death wasn't an accident. It was murder. You were my friend. I'll tell you about it very soon.*"

"No way!" Cheryl was laughing as she turned to Jennifer. "You guys put that stuff on Melanie's pillow. It's part of your skit, isn't it, Jen?"

"No, it's not. And I haven't been upstairs at all tonight. I couldn't have put it there."

"Then Tim did." Cheryl turned to him.

Tim looked very serious as he shook his head. "Honestly, Cheryl . . . it wasn't me."

"Let me see that note." Lexie took the paper and examined it. "It really does look like Kelly's writing. But who put it in Melanie's room?"

Tommy looked very freaked as he answered the question. "Uh . . . I really hate to say this, but I think Kelly did."

"You're kidding, right?" Cheryl looked astonished. "I mean . . . think about it, Tommy. Do you really believe that Kelly came back from the dead to put a note on Melanie's pillow?"

"Yes, I do. I know it sounds crazy, but the pin convinced me. I gave it to Kelly for Christmas last year. And her mother—uh . . ."

"What?" Tim looked worried as his brother's voice trailed off. It was clear that Tommy was totally freaked. "What is it, Tommy?"

"Kelly's mother knew how much she loved that pin, so she decided to bury it with Kelly."

There was a stunned silence that seemed to go on and on, but finally Jennifer broke it. "Maybe Kelly's mother changed her mind. She might have decided to keep the pin, or give it to someone else."

"No way." Tommy looked grim as he shook his head. "I was right there when Kelly's mother placed that pin in her casket."

They stayed up until almost one in the morning, but finally everyone decided to get some sleep. When the group was breaking up, Pete called Jennifer and Tim over to the side. "Good work, guys. The extra bit you did with the note and the pin was great! When did you plant it?"

"We didn't." Jennifer shook her head. "I know everyone thinks it was part of the séance, but we didn't have anything to do with it."

Pete was still grinning as he turned to Tim. "Is that right, Tim?"

"Jennifer's telling the truth. We really don't know how that pin and note got on Melanie's pillow."

"Excellent!" Pete was so pleased, he laughed out loud. "You guys just never break character, do you? I can hardly wait to see what else you've got dreamed up for tomorrow."

Jennifer was frowning as she headed for the stairs with Tim. The rotating table, the candles that extinguished themselves, Kelly's voice, the pin and note on Melanie's pillow. They hadn't done any of that! And there didn't seem to be anything they could say or do to convince Pete.

When they stopped at Jennifer's door, Tim put his arms around her. "Pete doesn't believe us."

"I know. What are we going to do, Tim?"

Tim reached out to touch her hair. "I don't think there's anything we can do. Our séance is out of control. Pete thinks we're running the show, but we're not. Someone else is. Do you think it's Kelly?"

"I don't know." Jennifer shook her head. "I'm only sure of one thing. We started something at the séance tonight. And now I just wish we could stop it!"

Melanie was tired, but she couldn't seem to get up the nerve to go to bed. She could still see the mark on her pillow where the pin had been thrust, and it made her feel creepy inside. She really wished that Kelly had picked someone else to contact.

This wasn't part of Jennifer and Tim's skit. Melanie was sure of that. They'd looked just as shocked as everyone else when they'd seen the pin and the note. Kelly's spirit had come back from the grave to tell Melanie her secret.

Melanie's hands were shaking as she slipped on jeans and a sweatshirt. For all she knew the person who'd murdered Kelly might be right here at the haunted lodge. If Kelly told her who it was, she could be in terrible danger. The killer could decide to murder her before she had the chance to tell the rest of the group.

There was no way she was going to sit here and wait for the killer to appear. Melanie jumped up and headed for the door. She'd go downstairs and arm herself with the fireplace poker, and she'd stay awake until everyone else got up in the morning. If the killer came to her room, he wouldn't find her sitting here trembling like a frightened rabbit. She'd be downstairs, ready to sound the alarm if she heard anything unusual.

It was very quiet as Melanie grabbed her favorite snakeskin boots and slipped out of her room. She locked the door behind her and stayed close to the wall as she went down the stairs in the darkness. Everyone else was sleeping by now, everyone except the killer, and her. She wasn't frightened now that she had a plan. Everything would work out just fine.

The lobby was deserted, just as she had thought it would be. Melanie hurried to the fireplace, picked up the poker, and gave a sigh of relief. The poker was exactly the right weight. One swing and the killer would crumple. It was a perfect weapon for Melanie since she'd been the best hitter on the girls' softball team, two years in a row.

Melanie sat down on the couch, tucked her feet up under her, and listened to the sounds of the night. The lodge was old and it creaked in the wind. The rain was still falling, splattering against the windowpane, and the sound made Melanie glad that she was inside by a warm fire.

The fire was mesmerizing and Melanie's eyelids began to droop. The crackle of the logs and the hiss of the flames was very soothing. The leather couch was soft and it cushioned her body perfectly, cradling her like a baby in its mother's arms.

Rain outside, warmth inside, and soft, soft pillows. Melanie smiled a sleepy smile and stretched out, nestling her head against her arm. She'd just close her eyes for a moment to rest them. A minute or two would do her a world of good. If she took a quick little nap, she'd wake up refreshed and ready to stay alert for the remainder of the night.

A soft sigh escaped Melanie's lips as she slipped deeper and deeper into sleep. She didn't hear the stealthy footsteps as they approached her, and she didn't see the smile that spread across his face. She didn't even hear his satisfied chuckle as he opened the front door of the lodge and stepped out into the night.

Of course, he had to kill her. He'd known that the moment she'd appeared with the note. He didn't believe that Kelly had written it from the grave. There was another explanation, one that made much more sense.

Melanie's parents lived next door to Kelly's mother, and the two girls had been good friends. Kelly must have told Melanie her secret and now Melanie was about to reveal it. Since she was an actress, she'd decided to do it in the most dramatic way possible.

The butterfly pin had thrown him at first. It had almost made him believe in Kelly's ghost. But then he'd remembered that Melanie worked part-time at Hampton's jewelry store. It would have been simple for Melanie to buy another pin, just like the one that Kelly had loved, to make her story more believable.

Of course, Melanie couldn't actually prove that he'd killed Kelly. She was only guessing about the murder, trying to freak him out so much that he'd confess. That was why he had to eliminate her, before she could get any more fake messages from the "other side."

It didn't take long to get ready. All he needed was a heavy shovel and a pair of work gloves from the shed at the back of the lodge. He'd make it look like an accident. That way the rest of the group wouldn't get suspicious. He walked around to the front of the lodge, by the lobby window, and knelt down in the bushes. And then he made the sound that would bring Melanie outside in the rain.

At first she thought she was dreaming, but then she heard it again. It was a tiny, whimpering sound that she recognized immediately. There was a puppy outside the window, a poor little puppy in the cold and the rain. There was no way Melanie could stay inside by the warmth of the fire and ignore the puppy's pitiful cries.

"Hold on, baby. I'm coming." Melanie got up, pulled on her boots, and headed for the door. Puppies were her very favorite animals and this poor little thing would get soaked in the rain. Young puppies were very vulnerable and this one sounded weak and sick. Puppies could catch colds and die if they were exposed to the elements and she had to do something to help. She'd find him and bring him inside. Then she'd wrap him in a towel and heat some milk for him to drink. If she kept him warm, she could save his life.

Melanie shivered as she pushed open the door. The rain was coming down steadily and it had turned very cold. No wonder the poor little thing was crying! Who wouldn't cry if they had to stay outside on a night like this?

"Where are you, baby? Come on, boy." Melanie listened and she heard another cry. The puppy sounded young and very scared. The cries were coming from the area by the side of the lodge and Melanie hurried down the path to find him.

"Come on, puppy. Come to Melanie." She rounded the corner and stopped to listen again. For a moment everything was silent, but then she heard a small cry that seemed to come from the woodpile that was stacked against the wall. The puppy must have crawled under the logs to try to keep dry. He could even be stuck under there.

Melanie bent over to look, but all she saw were logs. She got down on her knees and whistled softly. "Here, boy . . . come out here so I can see you. I won't hurt you, I promise."

Just then there was a sound above her head and Melanie turned to look up. There was someone dressed in a rain poncho looming over her. "What are you . . . ?"

But she never had a chance to finish her question. A huge log toppled, crashing into her head. And then the rest of the woodpile followed, crushing the life from her body and half-burying her under a jumbled mass of firewood.

Ten

"My name isn't Mousie, it's Jennifer. And I've got tons of self-confidence. I've even got chutzpah and I'm going to prove it when Tim knocks on my door!"

Jennifer was very determined as she faced her reflection in the mirror. She was wearing her best pink sweater, the one everyone said brought out the color in her cheeks. It was true. Her cheeks were very pink, but that was probably because she was embarrassed about talking to herself in front of the mirror.

She'd spent a long time thinking after everyone else had gone to bed. She knew that she wasn't in love with Tommy any longer and she wasn't sure she'd ever really been in love with him. She'd just wanted to date him because he was so handsome and popular.

Tim was another matter. Jennifer liked him a lot and she wanted to date him, but she wasn't sure if he felt the same way about her. What could she do?

Jennifer knew exactly what Lexie would tell her. She'd say that there was only one way to find out. Jennifer had to stop being so timid and ask Tim exactly how he felt about her. But that was easier said than done, and Jennifer just hoped that Tim would get here before she lost her courage.

"I know he likes me. He wouldn't have let me use his letter jacket if he didn't like me. Lexie's right. I'm just going to come right out and ask him. The minute he knocks on my door, I'm going to . . ."

There was a knock on her door and she jumped. Tim was here! Chutzpah. She had to have enough chutzpah to ask him!

Jennifer didn't think. She just raced to the door and opened it. And then she pulled Tim inside, before she could change back into Mousie again.

"Hey . . ." Tim grinned down at her. "I thought the guys weren't allowed in the girls' rooms."

"They're not." Jennifer took a deep breath, and then she motioned to the edge of her bed. "Sit down, Tim. We need to talk."

"About the séance?" Tim sat down.

"No. About us. How much do you like me, Tim?"

"How much do I like you? Oh . . . about this much!"

Tim spread out his arms and Jennifer started to laugh. She couldn't help it. "Cut it out, Tim . . . that's what my dad used to do!"

"And he was crazy about you, wasn't he?"

"Sure, he was . . . but . . ."

"So am I," Tim interrupted her. "I think about you every day, and I'm happy when I'm with you. I don't want to date anyone else, just you, Jen. And I wish you'd hurry and get over that stupid crush you've got on my twin brother."

Jennifer felt a blush rise to her cheeks. Perhaps chutzpah wasn't all it was cracked up to be. She'd certainly gotten much more than she'd bargained for!

"Well? What do you have to say, Jen?"

Jennifer said the first thing that popped into her mind. "Uh . . . well . . . I'm over the crush I had on your brother."

"That's a step in the right direction." Tim started to grin again. "Now, how much do you like me?"

Jennifer opened her mouth and then she closed it again. Her knees felt weak and now that the moment was here, she was suddenly speechless. What if she said the wrong thing?

"What is it, Jen? Don't you like me as much as I like you?"

"No!" Jennifer managed to find her voice. "I mean . . . yes. I just don't want to say the wrong thing."

"You can't say the wrong thing, Jen. There isn't any wrong thing around me, as long as you're honest. Now, I'm not quite sure what you said. Was that a yes? Or a no?"

"I don't remember the question!" Jennifer started to laugh. "But I feel the same way you do, Tim. And I don't want to date anyone else, either."

Tim smiled. "Great! Then you should keep the jacket, because we're going steady, except for a technicality."

"What technicality?" Jennifer was puzzled.

"We haven't gone out on a date yet, so how could we be going steady?"

"Oh. I see. You've got a point, but what can we do about it?"

"I'm not sure. We can't go on a date while we're up here at the lodge. There's nowhere to go. Do you think a kiss would count the same as a date?"

Jennifer walked over and sat down next to him, on the edge of the bed. She felt very strange, kind of warm and quivery inside. "Yes. I think a kiss would count."

And then Tim was kissing her, his lips brushing lightly against hers. Jennifer sighed and snuggled closer, reaching up with her arms to clasp them around his neck. And then she said something very bold, something she'd never expected to hear herself saying in a million years. It was chutzpah, plain and simple, and Lexie would have been proud of her. "I'm not sure that one kiss counts. Let's do it again to make sure."

"Jen? We really should go."

Jennifer sighed. And then she smiled a happy, contented smile. "Go where?"

"Downstairs. They're probably wondering where we are."

"Oh." Jennifer looked up into Tim's wonderfully green eyes. "What time is it, anyway?"

"It's almost ten."

"Oh, my God!" Jennifer sat up so fast, she was dizzy. Of course, she was already dizzy from Tim's kisses, so it really didn't matter. "We'd better go downstairs right away! They're probably wondering where we are!"

Tim laughed as he helped her to her feet. "I think that's what I just said. Either that, or there's an echo in here."

"You did? Oh. I'm sorry, Tim. I guess I was kissing . . . I mean . . . thinking about something else. Check the hall, will you? I don't want anyone to know that we broke the rules."

Tim opened the door a crack. "All clear. Come on, Jen. Let's go."

But just as they were stepping out the door, they heard someone running down the hall. It was too late to go back inside and Jennifer groaned as she saw that it was Susie. Although she didn't really mean to gossip, Susie had the biggest mouth at Foothill High.

But Susie didn't seem to notice that both of them were leaving the room at the same time. She just grabbed Jennifer's hand. "Come on. We've got to hurry. Did you guys have any luck?"

"Uh . . . well . . ." Jennifer had all she could do to keep a straight face. They'd had a lot of luck! They were going steady! But somehow, she didn't think that was what Susie was asking. Instead of answering, Jennifer turned the question around. "How about you, Susie? Did you have any luck?"

"No. I checked the whole third floor, so you don't have to do that. How far did you guys get?"

Tim saw that Jennifer was about to crack up, so he took over. "Not very far."

"Okay. I'll do this floor and then I'll meet you in the lobby."

Susie raced off, and Jennifer turned to Tim. "What's going on?"

"I don't know, but Susie seemed really freaked. I think we'd better go down to the lobby and find out."

The moment Jennifer and Tim walked into the lobby, Tommy rushed up to them. "Hey, Tim. Did you find her?"

"Find who?"

"Melanie. Didn't you hear? No one's seen her since last night. I thought you guys were checking the second floor."

Tim shook his head. "Susie's doing it. Where do you want us to look?"

"Everybody else is searching the lodge. Why don't you two

start outside. It stopped raining and she might have gone for a walk."

"Okay. We'll report in right away if we find her."

Jennifer was frowning as they stepped outside. She doubted that Melanie had gone for a walk, all by herself. Tim must have been thinking the same thing because he looked worried.

"Her car's still here." Tim motioned toward the red Honda in the parking lot. "At least she didn't try to drive down the mountain."

"That's a relief! I thought she might have tried to go home. She did a pretty good job of hiding it, but I know she was really freaked by that note."

"Jen?" Tim pointed at the row of bushes that had been planted under the lobby windows. "Do those bushes look trampled to you?"

Jennifer moved closer. There were several broken branches right in the center of the clump, directly under the window. "It looks like someone was hiding in there."

"Someone . . . or something."

Jennifer shivered. Kelly's spirit? But spirits didn't trample bushes. They had no earthly substance, according to the books she'd read. That's why they could walk through solid walls and enter locked rooms. They weren't limited by earthly boundaries. "Do you mean . . . an animal?"

"Possibly. But it's unusual for a big animal like a bear or a mountain lion to come this close to humans. It was probably a dog. And since there aren't any prints, it must have happened before three in the morning."

Jennifer turned to look at Tim in surprise. "How can you tell?"

"It rained until three, hard enough to wash away any prints. After that, it turned into a fine mist."

"What were you doing up that late?"

"Thinking about you, hoping that you'd come up to knock on my door. And wishing that I had the nerve to go down and knock on yours."

Jennifer began to smile. She'd been blind not to notice that Tim really cared about her. She was about to suggest that he kiss her again, when she noticed another broken branch on another bush. And then another. And another. Leading right up to the corner of the lodge.

"Whatever it was, I think it went this way." Jennifer pointed out the trail of broken branches. "Come on, Tim."

As they stepped around the corner, Jennifer stopped and pointed at the woodpile. "Look at that, Tim! Somebody left their boots out here!"

Before Jennifer could walk any closer, Tim moved in front of her, blocking her view. He looked very grim as he turned her around so she couldn't see the woodpile.

"Tell the guys to come out here, Jen. And stay inside until we come back."

Jennifer nodded. And then she hurried toward the door. At first her horrified mind had refused to believe what was right front of her eyes. But now she knew, and the frightening image was firmly implanted in her mind. Those weren't logs at the very bottom of the woodpile. They were Melanie's legs, wearing her favorite snakeskin boots!

"Poor Melanie!" Lexie sighed. "She must have gone outside for more firewood and pulled out the wrong log so the woodpile collapsed."

"But why did she go outside for more firewood?" Tommy was puzzled. "There's a whole stack right here, next to the fireplace."

Susie thought about it for a minute, and then she shrugged. "Maybe she was worried that we'd run out."

"That doesn't explain what she was doing down here in the first place." Cheryl spoke up. "She said good night, and I saw her go into her room."

Susie shrugged again. "Maybe she couldn't sleep and she came downstairs to sit by the fire. She was pretty freaked about that note from Kelly."

"I'd better try to notify her parents." Pete stood up and

headed for the reservation desk. "The phones might be working, now that the rain's over."

They all waited anxiously, but when Pete came back he was
frowning. "No luck. The line's still down.. And my cell phone
still isn't working."

"Why don't we try to drive down to the Hilltop Grocery?"
Tommy suggested.

"Good idea," Tim said. "It's only three miles and their phone
could be on a different line. And even if it's not, our cell phones
might work down there."

Pete began to frown. "You'll never get through. Zada said
there was a rock slide between here and there."

"Then we'll move enough rocks to make a path." Tommy
looked very determined. "But Tim and I can't do it alone. Who's
coming with us?"

"I will." Dale stood up. "How about you, Ronnie?"

"Count me in." Ronnie walked over to grab his jacket.

"Me, too." Brian jumped to his feet. "Don't worry, girls.
We'll be able to dig our way through. We're all big, strong
guys."

Susie began to bristle. "Why is this turning into a totally guy
thing? Women are strong, too. I bet I can lift more weight than
you can."

"But you're a better cook than he is." Ronnie laughed at his
own joke. "You girls stay right here where it's nice and cozy.
You can whip up a hot meal for us when we get back."

Susie picked up a pillow and threw it at him, but he just
caught it and tossed it back. Then Tommy opened the door and
they all marched out, looking every bit as resolute as a small
army going into battle.

"There goes the male ego." Lexie grinned wryly. "I'm surprised they didn't ask us to knit them some socks while they
were gone."

"I wonder if they actually believe they can get through."
Susie was thoughtful.

"I think they do. They looked very determined." Jennifer
turned to Lexie. "Is there a Yiddish word for that?"

Lexie thought about it for a moment, and then she nodded. "It's called *meshuga*."

"*Mish-you-gah*?" Cheryl repeated the word.

"That's close enough," Lexie said. "It means *crazy*. And that's exactly what they are if they think they're going to move a ton of rocks, all by themselves."

Eleven

As the hours ticked by, Jennifer began to get worried. What was taking the guys so long? She knew that Pete was nervous about their prolonged absence, too. She'd seen him go to the window to look out at the road at least five times in as many minutes.

"Do you think we should go out to look for them?" Susie walked over to join Pete at the window.

"No, not yet. Give them another couple of minutes. If they're not back by three o'clock, we'll go looking for them."

They all nodded in unison and turned at precisely the same instant to look at the grandfather clock in the lobby. Their synchronized movements reminded Jennifer of a perfectly rehearsed cheer, and she almost giggled. But this was no laughing matter. It was possible there had been another rock slide and the boys were cut off from the lodge. Even worse, they could have been caught by the falling boulders, but Jennifer didn't want to think about that.

It seemed to take forever, but at last the grandfather clock in the lobby chimed three times. It took only a few moments to get their jackets and boots, and then they were ready.

"Okay. Let's go." Pete opened the door and they all stepped out, but Cheryl stopped so abruptly that Jennifer almost ran right into her.

"Do you hear that?" Cheryl sounded excited. "There's a car coming up the road!"

They all turned to look at the road. It was another perfectly synchronized turn, and this time Jennifer laughed out loud, she was so relieved. It was the Jeep. The guys were back!

Tommy was frowning as he pulled up in front of the lodge and they all piled out. "Sorry. We couldn't get through. There's a huge rock slide between here and the store."

"We tried to climb over, but the rocks were too unstable." Dale sounded disappointed.

"He's right. We almost caused another rock slide," Tim said. "But there's good news, too. We heard a bulldozer and it sounded like it was only a couple of miles away. All we have to do is wait until the road crew digs through to us."

Susie didn't look happy. "But when will that be? We could be stuck here until Christmas!"

"I don't think it'll take them quite that long." Brian laughed. "Come on, Susie. Look on the bright side. If we're going to get stuck, Saddlepeak Lodge is the perfect place. We've got food, water, heat, and electricity. What more could we want?"

"Cable TV." Tommy looked glum. "We're missing a whole day of college football."

"I love to watch football," Lexie said. "It's my favorite sport. I just wish I wouldn't always end up cheering for the wrong team."

"What do you mean?" Tommy turned to look at her.

"If I like a team, they lose. That's why I didn't try out to be a cheerleader. If I cheered for Foothill High, they'd lose every game."

Tommy looked doubtful, but Jennifer nodded. "It's true. My dad says Lexie has a real knack for picking losers."

"Hey, Lexie . . ." Tommy was grinning as he slipped his arm around her shoulders. "What are you doing for the next eight weekends?"

Lexie shrugged. "I don't know . . . why?"

"I want you to spend them with me. How about it? Do we have a date?"

Lexie shrugged again. "That depends. What did you have in mind?"

"I want you to watch football with me. I'll tell you which teams I want to lose and you can cheer for them."

"Okay." Lexie laughed as Tommy hugged her. "You've got yourself a deal."

Jennifer stared at Lexie in surprise. Her best friend had undergone an amazing transformation, right before her eyes. Lexie's cheeks were pink, her eyes were sparkling, and her smile was warm as she gazed at Tommy. Jennifer was wise enough to know the signs. Lexie was definitely interested in Tommy.

Was she jealous? Jennifer was relieved to find that she didn't feel the slightest twinge of envy. Tim was the one she wanted, not Tommy. Perhaps she hadn't really been in love with Tommy at all. She still liked him as a friend, but that was it. And Tommy seemed perfect for Lexie. But there was someone in the group who looked very jealous and it was Cheryl.

"I've got an idea." Cheryl spoke up. "Why don't we have another rehearsal? Our skit had some rough spots last night, and it'll give us something to do while we're waiting for the bulldozer to get through."

Jennifer almost laughed out loud. Cheryl's motive was perfectly transparent. She was in Tommy's skit and Lexie wasn't. It was a perfect way to get Tommy away from Lexie.

"That's a very good idea," Pete agreed. "If the buses with Miss Voelker and the kids are right behind the bulldozers, we could be giving a show tonight."

"In that case, we'd better do a full technical rehearsal," Brian said. "I haven't even tested some of my special effects."

"Okay." Pete glanced at his watch. "I'll give you twenty minutes to get into your costumes and makeup. Let's go over the whole production, from start to finish."

"Including the séance?" Susie started to frown.

"Of course."

"Uh . . . Pete?" Susie's voice was shaking slightly. "Do you think we could do things out of order, and start with the séance?"

"That's up to Jennifer and Tim. But why?"

Susie looked embarrassed and it was clear she didn't want to answer. "Uh . . . well . . . Melanie got that note from Kelly, and now she's dead. I know it's just coincidence, but . . . I'd rather do the séance in the daylight, that's all."

"That's okay with us, Pete." Jennifer decided to rescue Susie from further embarrassment. "We don't mind starting with the séance. Is that all right with everyone else?"

One by one they nodded, and Jennifer noticed that several of her friends looked relieved. The séance skit was starting to scare everyone, now that Zada and Melanie were dead.

But nothing unexpected happened at the séance. The table didn't rock or spin around and there were no ghostly voices. When it was over, everyone including Jennifer and Tim drew a deep sigh of relief.

"That was fine." Pete flipped his notebook shut. "But I guess the spirits don't communicate very well in the daylight."

Ronnie laughed. "That's okay. I don't think I could have survived another spinning table. Come on, everybody. Let's get into costume and rehearse the rest of our skits."

Jennifer and Tim had just finished putting their props away when there were shouts from the third floor. They hurried up the stairs to join the crowd that had gathered in Ronnie's room.

"The psychic duo strikes again, huh?" Ronnie grinned at them as they came in.

Tim frowned. "Do you mean us?"

"You bet I do! When I opened my suitcase, I found a note." Ronnie held up a piece of paper. "It was wrapped in this scarf, printed with lilacs."

"It's Kelly's scarf," Tommy explained.

"Here, Tim." Ronnie handed him the note. "Read it out loud."

Tim unfolded the note. "It's written on Saddlepeak Lodge stationery, just like the other one. And it says, *Ronnie—Talk to me at the séance tonight and I'll tell you everything.*"

"Very interesting." Ronnie was smiling as he glanced around

the room. "What do you think, guys? Are Jennifer and Tim playing more tricks?"

Jennifer shook her head. "You've got it wrong, Ronnie. Tim and I didn't write that note. I swear it!"

"Of course you didn't." Ronnie was still grinning. "Kelly wrote it . . . right, Jen?"

"I don't know who wrote it!"

"Excellent!" Pete started to clap and everyone joined in. "Good job, Jennifer. You're turning into a very convincing actress. This whole setup with the notes is great!"

Jennifer exchanged glances with Tim. Neither one of them knew quite what to say. Nobody seemed willing to believe that they hadn't written the notes.

"How about it, gang?" Pete turned to the other students. "Are you up for another séance tonight?"

"No!"

Everyone turned to look at Susie. All the color had left her face and she was trembling. "I don't think we should hold another séance, not after that note Ronnie got. What if something awful happens to him?"

"Susie, my love. I didn't know you cared." Ronnie burst into laughter. But when he saw that Susie was close to tears, he pulled her into his arms. "Hey, Suze . . . nothing's going to happen to me. And we've got to have the séance. I can hardly wait to see what these two jokers have got planned for me."

Tim shook his head. "You've got it all wrong, Ronnie. Jen and I don't have anything planned."

"I knew you'd say that." Ronnie chuckled. "You two guys are good! But I'm warning you . . . if that table starts spinning around again, I'm going to figure out exactly how you've got it rigged."

The lilac-printed scarf had brought back memories of her. Kelly had been beautiful, the last time he'd seen her. She'd been dressed in a simple cotton sundress, white with tiny sprigs of purple flowers in a repeating pattern. She'd looked so fresh and innocent that he almost hadn't believed what she'd told him.

Only the tears running down her cheeks had convinced him that she'd been telling the truth about their baby.

How could a night that had been so thrilling turn out to be such a disaster? He could still see her face in the light of the fire and feel the soft, satiny warmth of her skin. It should have been a happy memory for him, but it wasn't. Not now. Not after what had happened.

He leaned back against the pillow and closed his eyes. He still had ten minutes before he had to go downstairs and he needed to rest his eyes. He hadn't been sleeping well lately and he was very tired.

And then he saw Kelly's face again, as her car went out of control. Her mouth was open and she was screaming, begging for someone to rescue her. The car swerved down the hill, riding the lip of the ditch, heading straight for the crossing. And then the train rounded the bend, brakes squealing and sparking as they tried in vain to halt the tons of hurtling metal.

At the last instant, she turned to look out the window. And her eyes locked with his in a steady bond that no earthly force could break. And her beautiful lips formed the words that made up the restless terror of his sleep. *Murderer! I'll get you for this!*

He sat up with a jolt, sweating and feverish. It was the same dream, the same horrible message. But it was only a dream, nothing more. He hadn't been there to see the accident. Kelly had never seen him. He'd been miles away and there had been no way at all for Kelly to guess that he had killed her.

But did Kelly know the truth now, after her death? And was there some means for her to take her revenge? He shook his head in denial as he got up to pace the floor. There was no such thing as a ghost or a spirit. Dead was dead, and Kelly had ceased to exist on any plane. There was no possible way that the dead could hurt the living. But the living could hurt the living, and someone was trying to hurt him.

He frowned as he thought about Zada. He'd killed her because he'd thought she'd known Kelly's secret. But killing Zada hadn't stopped the threat. Someone else knew.

Melanie had received the note and he'd been sure that she was the one. But Melanie's death hadn't solved the problem, and now there was Ronnie. Someone knew Kelly's secret. He just wished he could figure out who it was!

Now someone was forcing him to kill again. Another note, another death. It was a horrible equation, but he had little choice. Did Ronnie know Kelly's secret? Was he the instigator and would the notes stop after his death? There was only one way to tell. He'd just have to kill Ronnie to find out.

Twelve

Ronnie was whistling as he opened the door to the formal dining room and carried in the props for his skit. He was in a very good mood. Jennifer and Tim had chosen him to receive Kelly's note, and he could hardly wait for the séance to see what else they had up their sleeves. It was clear they were going to have Kelly's spirit speak directly to him and he was more than willing to take part in their little drama. Of course, he'd act surprised when Kelly's spirit contacted him. Maybe he'd even make everyone think he was a little scared.

As he arranged his props on the dining room table, Ronnie began to smile. Susie's reaction to the note had been a real eye-opener. She'd actually been afraid that he might get hurt! And that meant she liked him much more than he had realized.

Ronnie's smile grew wider as he thought about Susie. He'd known her for years and their parents did business together. The bakery supplied all the bread that Susie's parents used in their deli. Susie was plump but that didn't bother him. He liked women with curves, and he'd always thought that most of the girls at Foothill High were too skinny. Susie was pretty, too, and she had a good sense of humor. Now that he thought about it, he wondered why he'd never thought of dating Susie before. They were already friends and their families got along just fine.

Just as soon as this Halloween weekend was over and they were back in Foothill again, he'd ask Susie for a date.

It didn't take Ronnie very long to arrange the plate and silverware he'd brought with him from the kitchen. There was only one place setting and it was at the head of the table. His skit was simple, but it was very frightening. Ronnie was playing a judge who'd sentenced a man to death by hanging. The man he'd sentenced had been innocent and he came back to haunt Ronnie, the judge who had condemned him.

There was only one thing that made Ronnie's skit tricky. In everyone else's skit, Brian was behind the scenes to do the special effects. In Ronnie's skit, Brian played the condemned man's ghost, and since he was on stage for most of the time, they had to rig everything by remote control.

The skit started with Ronnie at the head of the table, eating a solitary meal. There was a sound from above and Ronnie looked up to see the dead man swinging from a noose attached to the massive chandelier one floor above the table. As Ronnie watched in horror, the dead man dropped down from the chandelier with the noose still around his neck.

Naturally, they used a dummy, and after it fell, the lights went out. That gave Ronnie time to shove the dummy under the table so Brian could take its place. When the lights came back on, Brian moaned and got up to play the dead man's ghost.

The dummy hadn't worked at all last night. Ronnie had tugged on the hidden wire, but it hadn't fallen. They'd rigged it again, right after the performance, but Ronnie still wasn't sure it would work. He wanted to test it before tonight's performance.

Ronnie sat down at the table and reached for the hidden wire. There was a snap as the rope separated and the dummy came tumbling down. It was perfect and Ronnie grinned. They had it right, this time. The dummy looked very realistic and everyone who saw it fall would scream in terror.

Now that he'd tested the dummy, Ronnie had to hook it back up again. He grabbed the dummy's arms and dragged it over to the base of the narrow circular staircase that led to the mezzanine area overlooking the dining room.

Dragging the dummy up the stairs was impossible. Its arms and legs flopped around and got stuck between the balustrades. Ronnie finally gave up and draped the dummy over his shoulders, holding the legs in one hand and the arms in the other. It was called a "fireman's carry" and Ronnie had seen pictures of firefighters carrying people out of burning buildings that way. It looked easier than it actually was, and by the time Ronnie got to the top of the circular staircase, he was panting.

Ronnie rolled the dummy off his shoulders and let it fall to the floor with a thump. This was really a two-person job, but Brian was busy rigging things for the other skits.

"Hey! Is anybody around? I need some help in here!" Ronnie called out, but no one answered. That wasn't surprising. The dining room was set apart from the rest of the lodge by two sliding wooden doors and Ronnie had closed them when he'd come in.

Should he go back down the stairs to find someone to help him? Ronnie thought about it for a moment, but then he shook his head. He'd try to do it by himself, first. He might not need any help.

Lifting the dummy to the railing was awkward, but Ronnie managed to bend it in the middle and drape it over the rail. Now all he had to do was lean out, pull the wires in, and attach them to the dummy. Once the wires were in place, he could lift the dummy over the rail so it would hang down from the chandelier.

Ronnie was about to reach out for the wires when he thought he heard someone climbing the stairs to the mezzanine. He turned around with a smile on his face, expecting to see one of his classmates who'd heard him call out. But the footsteps stopped and although Ronnie waited for a moment or two, no one appeared at the top of the stairs.

"I must be hearing things." Ronnie frowned slightly as he turned back to the dummy again. "No one's there."

Ronnie reached out, but he couldn't grab the wires. They had tangled when the dummy had fallen and they were just out of his reach. He leaned out as far as he dared, but then something happened that made him realize that he'd better be extra careful. The sunglasses he always carried in his pocket slipped out and tumbled down to the dining room below.

"Uh-oh!" Ronnie shivered slightly as the lenses shattered on the marble floor. What if he lost his balance? Would his head shatter like the lenses of his sunglasses? The thought was frightening and Ronnie decided that there was no way he'd lean out any further without some sort of safety harness.

"Just look what you're putting me through." Ronnie gave the dummy a baleful look. "I do all the work and you just hang there, grinning."

Ronnie pulled off his belt, secured it to the rail, and buckled the end snugly around his leg. If he leaned out too far and lost his balance, the belt would keep him from falling. Ronnie felt much more secure as he leaned out and attempted to reach the wires again.

He was almost successful. His fingertips brushed against the tangle of wires, but he couldn't quite grab them. One more try and Ronnie was sure he'd be able to do it. He leaned out again, straining against the belt that held him securely. And then, just as he was about to grab the wires, he felt someone loosen the belt!

Ronnie didn't have time to think about who had loosened his belt. He didn't even have time to scream. He fell and his head hit the marble floor with sickening thud, and all the thoughts and memories and hopes and dreams that belonged to a boy named Ronnie Hughes were erased for eternity.

Tim and Jennifer sat on one of the couches, waiting for the rest of the group to arrive. The first to come in were Tommy and Lexie, and Jennifer grinned as she saw that they were holding hands. Lexie looked happy and so did Tommy. That made Jennifer happy, too . . . until Cheryl arrived.

Cheryl was smiling when she came in, but the moment she saw Lexie with Tommy, her eyes began to glitter dangerously. Jennifer held her breath. There was bound to be an ugly confrontation. But Brian walked through the doorway carrying a makeup case, just in the nick of time.

Brian took in the situation at a glance, and he walked over to Cheryl. "Hey, Cheryl. You're just the girl I want to see! You know a lot about makeup, don't you?"

"Of course I do. You know that."

Cheryl sounded sullen, but Brian pretended not to notice. "I need the advice of an expert. I'm supposed to be dead and I can't seem to get my makeup right. How about it? Can you fix me up?"

"I guess so." Cheryl gave Tommy and Lexie a withering look. "It's pretty clear I'm not needed around here!"

Tim squeezed Jennifer's hand and leaned over to whisper in her ear. "It's a good thing Brian came in when he did. I thought we were going to see fireworks."

"Hey, guys. . . . what do you think?" Susie was grinning as she came in. She was wearing a black hat with an ostrich plume that dipped down low over her left eye. The plume was dyed black to match the hat and it suited her perfectly.

"That hat looks great on you!" Jennifer complimented her. "Where did you get it?"

"I found it on top of a shelf in the linen closet. One of the guests must have left it behind."

Dale came in just in time to hear Susie's comment. "It doesn't belong to a guest. When my uncle bought this lodge, it had a clothing store in the lobby. That hat was on one of the mannequins."

"Do you think your uncle would let me buy it?"

Dale laughed. "You don't need to buy it, Susie. Just keep it. It really looks good on you."

"Are you sure?" Susie looked hopeful. "I mean . . . shouldn't you ask your uncle?"

"I don't have to ask him. I'm the one who packed up all the other stuff and gave it to charity. I just missed the hat, that's all. Consider it a gift from Saddlepeak Lodge."

"Thanks, Dale!" Susie gave him a delighted grin. "I just love this hat. It's totally me!"

Pete came in, carrying his clipboard. "Okay, everybody. Are we all ready to start?"

While the other students crowded around Pete, Lexie pulled Jennifer over to the side. "I need to talk to you, Jen."

Her friend looked worried and Jennifer began to frown. "What it is, Lexie?"

"It's Tommy. He asked me to the Thanksgiving dance. If I go with him, will that be a problem for you?"

Jennifer managed to hide a grin. "It certainly will!"

"Oh." Lexie looked very disappointed. "Well . . . I like Tommy a lot, but my friendship with you comes first. I'll just tell Tommy that I can't go to the dance with him."

Jennifer couldn't hide her grin any longer. This was working out even better than she'd expected. "Thanks, Lexie. Our friendship is very important to me, too. Just tell Tommy you won't go out with him unless it's a double date."

"A double date?" Lexie looked confused. "What do you mean?"

"It's Tim's week to drive the Jeep, and we're using it to go to the Thanksgiving dance. If you and Tommy want a ride, you'll just have to double-date with us."

Lexie started to grin. "Shame on you, Jen! You really had me worried for a minute."

"Listen up, gang!" Pete called out for order. "Is everybody ready to start?"

"We're ready," Susie called out. "But Ronnie's not here yet."

"He's probably in the dining room, rigging that dummy." Tim spoke up. "He said he was going to try it first, before the rehearsal."

"Okay. Since you've already rehearsed the séance, you two go and help him. Tommy and Cheryl can start their skit and you can join us whenever you're through."

Jennifer was smiling as she left the room with Tim. She was still thinking about the joyful expression on Lexie's face when she realized that Jennifer didn't care if she dated Tommy. It would be fun to double-date with her best friend. But the sight that greeted them when Tim pushed open the dining room door made Jennifer's happy smile disappear in a hurry.

"Oh, my God!" Jennifer stared at Ronnie's crumpled body in utter disbelief. And when she turned to Tim, there was genuine fear in her eyes. "Is he . . . ?"

Tim didn't say anything. It was clear that Ronnie was dead. No one could survive a fall like that.

Jennifer tore her eyes away from the gruesome sight and reached for the wall to steady herself. Tim would need her help. "Do you want me to get the guys?"

"Yes." Tim looked grateful as he stepped closer and gave her a brief hug. "Are there any more tarps?"

"I'll find one. And this time I'll come back with the guys to help you."

Tim shook his head. "Stay with the girls, Jen. Susie's going to take this really hard. She'll need you."

"Right." Jennifer turned to go. But then a terrible thought crossed her mind and she turned back to Tim with a worried expression on her face. "Ronnie got that note from Kelly. They're never going to believe that this was an accident!"

Tim looked very grim and Jennifer could tell he'd thought of that, too. They stared at each other for a long moment and then Jennifer sighed. "Do you think it was? An accident, I mean?"

"I don't know, Jen." Tim took a deep breath and then he said the words that struck terror into her heart. "Zada's dead and so is Melanie. And now Ronnie's dead, too. I really thought our séances were a fake, but now . . . I just don't know what to believe!"

Thirteen

"Okay, everybody. Calm down and let's talk about this rationally." Pete looked very serious as he faced them. "What happened to Ronnie was a terrible accident, but it was an accident."

Susie wiped her eyes with a tissue from the pack that Jennifer had given her. "Are you sure?"

"I'm positive."

"But what about the note he got from Kelly?" Dale began to frown. "Doesn't that prove that it wasn't an accident?"

"Of course not. Be reasonable, Dale. That note was just a part of Jennifer and Tim's séance, and it had absolutely nothing to do with Ronnie's accident. You don't really believe that Kelly wrote that note from the grave, do you?"

There was a long silence while everyone thought it over and the seconds ticked by without a sound. No one seemed willing to speak.

"Well? Do you?" Pete glanced around the room.

Tommy looked uncomfortable, but he was the one to answer. "No. I don't believe that note was from Kelly. She loved me and I loved her. We were planning to get married and spend the rest of our lives together. If Kelly could send notes from the other side, she would have written to me."

"But she didn't." The look Cheryl gave Tommy was sizzling.

"Maybe Kelly didn't love you quite as much as you thought she did."

Jennifer held her breath. The tension in the room was growing thicker by the minute. It was obvious that Cheryl was still fuming about catching Tommy and Lexie together and she was trying to hurt Tommy, any way she could.

Lexie turned to face Cheryl. "That's not true, Cheryl. Everybody knows how much Kelly and Tommy loved each other!"

"So I've heard." Cheryl shrugged. "But it didn't take Tommy very long to get over Kelly. He's been trying to pick up on me since the first day of school."

"That's only because you threw yourself at him." Lexie began to frown. "We all noticed it. And Tommy's too polite to tell you to get lost."

Cheryl put her hands on her hips. "I've never thrown myself at anybody in my life! And if I did, it certainly wouldn't be Tommy!"

"Oh, really? I saw you, Cheryl. And so did everybody else!"

"How about you?" Cheryl sounded outraged. "You're the one who's throwing herself at Tommy. I saw you trying to hold hands with him. You were practically slobbering at his feet!"

Jennifer glanced back and forth from Cheryl to Lexie as the two girls traded insults. She'd never seen Lexie get this mad before and Jennifer felt like a spectator at a tennis match, holding her breath as she waited for the sizzling backhand that would knock someone's head off. But before things could turn truly nasty, Brian stood up between Cheryl and Lexie.

"Simmer down, girls. The last thing we need is to fight with each other. We've got enough problems without that."

"Brian's right." Pete took charge. "Let's all try to act like adults. I think the best thing is to go right on with our rehearsal."

Jennifer spoke up fast, before Lexie and Cheryl could get started again. "Which skit is next, Pete?"

"Let's start with Dale and Susie. I want everyone to make a final check of their props. We'll all meet in the library in ten minutes."

Jennifer waited until everyone except Pete had left the room and then she hurried to his side. "Pete? I've got to talk to you."

"What is it, Jennifer?" Pete smiled at her. "Do you have a problem with the séance?"

"No. I mean, yes . . . in a way. I think we should cancel our séance skit."

Pete looked surprised. "But why? It's going very well. I think most of the class is really starting to fall for your act."

"I know." Jennifer was very serious. "That's the problem. Everybody's starting to believe in Kelly's ghost. And some of them are getting scared!"

"I realize that, but the best way to reassure them is to go on with your séance. If we stop now, it might cause someone to panic. When you plant the next note and the person who gets it doesn't die, everyone will start to relax."

"But we don't plant the notes! Someone else is doing that, and I don't know who it is!"

Pete laughed and patted Jennifer on the back. "Good girl! You're a real professional, getting back in character already. Come on, now. Let's hurry up or Dale and Susie might start their skit without us."

Jennifer was just opening the door to the makeup room, when she heard a muffled cry. Susie was standing in front of the lighted makeup table, staring down at something on the ledge.

"What's the matter, Susie?" Jennifer hurried across the room.

"You know what it is." She sounded freaked as she handed Jennifer a piece of lodge stationery. "It's another note from Kelly. It was wrapped around this lipstick in my makeup case."

Jennifer read the note aloud. "*Susie. My killer is among us. Be patient and I will tell you who it is.*"

"Look, Jen . . . these notes are very clever. But I really wish you and Tim had picked somebody else."

Jennifer opened her mouth to object. She was about to swear that they hadn't planted the note, when she remembered what Pete had said.

"I'm not mad at you, Jen." Susie sighed. "I know these notes are just a part of your skit. But look what happened to Melanie and Ronnie. They got notes from Kelly and they wound up dead!"

"That's true, but it's only coincidence. It's not like somebody actually killed them. You know what happened, Susie. Melanie pulled out the wrong log on the woodpile and Ronnie fell over the rail when he was rigging that dummy. They were accidents, pure and simple."

"I know that, but everybody's getting very nervous about the séances."

It was the opening she'd been waiting for and Jennifer took a deep breath. "That's exactly why we need your help, Susie. You know that our séance is only a skit, but some people actually think that I contacted Kelly's spirit."

"And you don't think you did?"

Jennifer hesitated and then she shook her head. "Of course not! And that's the reason Pete wants us to go right on with our skit. He wants us to prove that our séances aren't real."

"How can you do that?" Susie looked curious.

"It's simple. When everybody finds out that you got a note from Kelly, they'll watch you. And when nothing bad happens, they'll finally realize that there's absolutely nothing to worry about."

"I guess that makes sense. I see what you're trying to do, Jen."

"Then you'll help us?"

"What choice do I have?" Susie gave a rueful smile. "You and Tim chose me to be your guinea pig."

"I guess that's true. But being a guinea pig isn't all there is to it. You're also our fearless leader."

"No one's ever called me that before!" Susie started to laugh. "Okay, Jen . . . I may hate myself for this later, but I'll do it."

Jennifer reached out to hug her. "Thanks, Susie. You won't be sorry, I promise."

But as Jennifer followed Susie out the door, she hoped she could keep her promise. The notes from Kelly did seem to bring bad luck to anyone who received them. One thing was very certain: She was going to talk to Tim about it. Between the two of them, they'd keep a very careful eye on Susie until this Halloween weekend at the haunted lodge was over.

He sat in his room and tried to think. They'd all been very upset when they'd discovered that Susie had found a note from Kelly, especially when they'd realized that the lipstick was Kelly's color. Of course, anyone could have known Kelly's shade of lipstick. He wasn't concerned about that. It was the appearance of another note that upset him. It meant that killing Ronnie hadn't stopped the threat.

Who had written the note? He really had no idea and there wasn't any way to find out. It could be Susie. Kelly had worked only a block from the deli and she'd gone there for lunch several times a week. Kelly might have decided to confide in Susie and ask her for advice.

He'd always liked Susie. She was a warm, genuine person with only one fault and that fault would be her downfall. Miss Voelker had discussed something called the "fatal flaw." Hamlet's fatal flaw was indecision and it had caused his death. Captain Ahab was obsessed with the whale and that obsession had been lethal. Miss Voelker had used Midas as another example. His greed had killed him in the end. These were all literary characters, but Susie had a fatal flaw, too. She loved to gossip. All her friends had warned her that her big mouth would get her into trouble someday. Unfortunately for Susie, that day was today.

Fourteen

Susie straightened the collar of her white blouse with fingers that trembled slightly. She was more upset about the note from Kelly than she'd wanted to admit. She knew that Jennifer and Tim had planted the note as part of their skit. There was nothing spooky about that. But the notes were definitely bad luck, and she wished she'd never opened her makeup case to find it.

When Susie had shown everyone her note, she'd realized that a couple of her friends were beginning to believe that Kelly's ghost was real. They thought that the recent deaths hadn't been accidents at all, that Kelly's spirit was actually causing them!

Susie thought about it as she'd waited for their rehearsal to start. What possible reason might Kelly have for causing these "accidents"?

It wasn't difficult to find a motive for Zada's death. She'd been a psychic and she'd brought special aids to the lodge, to make the séance work. Perhaps Kelly hadn't wanted to come back and she'd been angry with Zada.

Melanie's death had seemed utterly senseless until Susie really thought about it. Melanie had asked to have Kelly's old locker, the one on the end right next to Tommy's. Kelly could have been mad about that. Perhaps she'd even been jealous that Melanie got to see Tommy so often in the halls.

Ronnie's death, however, was a complete puzzle. What had Ronnie ever done to Kelly? It took a moment, but then Susie figured it out. Ronnie had taken over Kelly's spot on the student council, a position he'd only gotten because Kelly had died.

Susie shivered as her thoughts turned inward. Had she ever done anything to make Kelly mad enough to kill her? She wasn't on the student council, she didn't have Kelly's old locker, and she'd never even thought of dating Tommy. Kelly would have no reason to be angry with her, unless . . .

Kelly's antique doll collection! Susie's face turned pale. She'd bought it from Mrs. Bridges right after Kelly's death, thirty dolls, all collector's items. Kelly's doll collection had been her pride and joy, and it had been much better than Susie's. Was Kelly angry at Susie for putting them all together so she could have the best doll collection in Foothill?

Susie shivered and goose bumps prickled her skin. Her great-grandmother had an old saying: When you shivered and goose bumps popped up on your skin, it was supposed to mean that a goose had just walked over your grave. But Susie didn't have a grave. She was still alive and she intended to stay that way. There was no way she was going sit here and shiver, afraid of a ghost that didn't exist!

Work was the best medicine. That was another of her great-grandmother's favorite sayings, and it seemed to be true. Susie sat down at the library desk and picked up her script. She'd go over her lines again. Even though she knew them perfectly, working on her lines would take her mind off Kelly's ghost and that silly note she'd found.

As she read over her lines, Susie began to feel much better. Dale had written the script and it was very good. She played a psychotic teacher who had murdered several of her former students.

The bodies of the former students were hidden in Susie's library and the five plastic skeletons, dressed in school clothes, looked very gruesome. They were sitting around the library table, tied to their chairs with fishing line. Several of them had books in their bony fingers and one even wore wire-framed glasses.

"Here's your blood, Susie." Dale came in, carrying a large plastic capsule. "Cheryl says it's guaranteed to work."

Susie held the capsule very carefully. She knew that if she squeezed it, the blood would splatter out. "But we've only got a couple of these. Do you think I should use it tonight?"

"Go ahead. We have to try it once before the actual performance. You brought extra clothes, didn't you?"

"Of course. Do you know if this stuff'll wash out?"

"It's supposed to. Cheryl read the instructions and it says it's guaranteed not to stain if you wash it out within twenty-four hours."

"Okay." Susie slipped the capsule into the pocket of her blouse. "How do the skeletons look?"

"Great." Dale walked over to stick a baseball cap on one of the skeletons and then he started to laugh.

"What's so funny?"

"I brought a pencil to stick behind one of the skeleton's ears. I forgot . . . skeletons don't have any ears!"

Susie laughed, too. "Don't worry, Dale. I'll wire it between a couple of finger bones. That'll do."

While Susie wired the pencil in place, Dale draped a letter sweater over the shoulders of another. "How's this?"

"It looks good, but whose letter sweater is that?"

"It's mine."

Susie's frown deepened. "Are you sure you want to use it? I mean . . . won't you feel kind of strange when you wear it again?"

"Why should I? It's just a plastic skeleton."

Susie turned away. For some reason, seeing the skeleton with a letter sweater really bothered her. Perhaps it was because Ronnie had been so proud of his letter sweater, and now he was dead.

"Hey, Susie." Dale walked up and put his hands on her shoulders. "If that sweater bothers you, I won't use it."

Susie forced a smile and shook her head. "No. It's perfect. It looks really gruesome."

"Okay. We'd better take our places. They'll be coming any minute. Let's knock 'em dead, Susie."

Susie frowned. She knew *knock 'em dead* was only a slang phrase, but it was an unfortunate choice of words, considering what had happened. Zada and two of Susie's friends had already been knocked dead on this Halloween weekend. Three victims and none of them even had a chance. Susie was going to be extra careful. She had to make sure that the same thing wouldn't happen to her.

Susie grinned as Brian dimmed the lights. The first half of their skit had gone very well. Everyone had gasped when she'd bashed Dale's head with the fake hammer and he'd fallen to the floor, presumably dead. Susie had left the room and Dale had given his solo performance, regaining consciousness and telling the audience how he was planning to trap his teacher, Miss Perkins.

Dale had given the audience the background story. Students had been disappearing from Roosevelt High. The missing students had been flunking out of school and their parents had assumed they'd run away from home. Dale didn't believe it. He suspected that Miss Perkins was responsible for the disappearance of his classmates and he was going to prove it.

Although Dale had been a good student, he'd deliberately flunked several tests. He'd also failed to do his homework and now he was on the teacher's list of flunking students. Just as he'd hoped, Miss Perkins had invited Dale to her home for a study session, all alone, at night. Dale had gone because he knew that several other students had attended one of her study sessions, never to be seen again.

During the first act, when Susie had hit Dale and he'd pretended to die, the library table had been hidden from view by a screen. Now that the room was dark, Susie and Dale quietly removed the screen. Then Dale took his place at the library table and Susie got back in character, holding a book in one hand and a ruler in the other. She was conducting a gruesome geography class for her dead students, and she would be quizzing Dale when the lights came back up.

"Now we'll have a short oral quiz on your homework." Susie's voice came out of the darkness. "Who wants to answer the first question?"

There was no answer and Susie gave an audible sigh. "All right, class. If there are no volunteers, I'll choose a student to answer. Name the continents, Dale."

No one spoke and Susie sighed again. "Dale? Give me your answer!"

There was a collective gasp as the lights came up and the audience saw the skeletons around the table. No one had seen the skeletons before. Dale had decided not to use them until this final dress rehearsal, and Susie was pleased to see that they had real shock effect.

Dale was sitting at the end of the table, his head buried in his hands. Susie marched over to him and held up her ruler.

"Answer me, Dale! Name the continents!"

But Dale was perfectly motionless and Susie raised her ruler higher. There was another gasp as the ruler came down to hit the table so close to Dale's hand, it looked as if she were actually hitting him. "You've failed another quiz, Dale. That is why I had to punish you. You were a *baaaaad* student! And bad students deserve to die!"

"No! I'm not a bad student, Miss Perkins!"

Susie pretended to reel in shock as Dale spoke. "You can't speak! You're dead! I killed you!"

Dale sat up a little straighter. "Yes, I'm dead. You killed me and I came back to tell you that you made a mistake. I was a good student, Miss Perkins. I can name the continents."

"Then do it!" Susie's voice was shaking and she looked slightly uncertain. "I think you're bluffing!"

Dale rose to his feet and smiled. And then he recited the names of the continents, one by one. When he had finished, he pointed his finger at Susie. "It's like I said. You made a mistake, Miss Perkins. You punished a good student. Why don't you admit it?"

"No!" Susie backed up as Dale started to move toward her. "That's impossible. Good teachers don't make mistakes."

"But you did, Miss Perkins. You killed me, and I didn't deserve to die."

Dale advanced and Susie retreated. For the first time she began to look very frightened. "I'm sorry I killed you, Dale. I'll make it up to you, I promise!"

"There's only one way to do that."

"How?" Susie's voice was shaking. "I'll do anything!"

Dale began to smile. "Your life for mine, Miss Perkins. It's the only way to atone for your mistake."

"Yes. I see that, Dale." Susie nodded slowly. "You are quite correct. I killed you in error and now I must make amends."

"Exactly! Go down to the police station and turn yourself in. They'll see that justice is done."

"No!" Susie shook her head. "I am the teacher. I will decide what is just and what is not!"

There was a gasp from the group as Susie darted behind the desk. They knew from previous rehearsals that she was supposed to pull out a drawer, take out a handgun, and pretend to kill herself. Susie knew it, too, but the prop gun wasn't where she was sure she'd placed it.

Susie stared down at the drawer for a moment. Where was her gun? She felt around in the back of the drawer and almost smiled in relief as she found it hidden under a pile of papers. Thank goodness she'd found it! Her carelessness had almost ruined Dale's skit.

But was this gun different? It seemed heavier as she lifted it out, but Susie didn't have time to think about that. Dale was shouting his line and she had to act quickly.

"No, Miss Perkins! Don't do it!"

Susie raised the gun and pointed it at her head. The blood capsule was already in her hand and she'd break it the moment she heard Brian's gunshot. Since the gun didn't actually fire, Brian would play a recording of a gunshot over the microphone and Susie's timing had to be perfect.

"I am a *baaaad* teacher!" Susie delivered her line in a fierce voice. "And bad teachers deserve to die!"

"No, Susie! No!"

Susie almost laughed as she heard Jennifer's voice. Jen was really getting into this skit. She'd even called Susie by her real name, not the name of the character she was playing. But Susie didn't hesitate. She was a good actress and good actresses went on with the show. She just put her finger on the trigger and began to squeeze it.

There was the sound of Brian's recorded gunshot, right on time. But at that exact instant, something horrible happened. There was another gunshot, directly on the heels of the first, so close that it sounded like one long explosion. It was so loud that several members of the audience screamed and covered their ears. But Susie didn't hear their screams. She didn't even hear the second explosion.

The sound in the library was deafening, echoing against the walls and bouncing back and forth between them. And then Susie was on the floor, blood spurting from her head in a sticky red river as the life flowed from her body.

"Fantastic!" Pete started to clap and everyone else joined in. "That was great, guys, much more realistic than the last rehearsal. Those blood capsules really work."

Dale was smiling as he took a bow, and then he reached down for Susie's hand. "Okay, Susie. You can get up now."

But Susie didn't grasp Dale's hand and pull herself to her feet as she'd done at the last rehearsal. She didn't even twitch as Pete called out her name.

"Susie? Come on, Susie. You don't have to be such a ham. The skit's over. It's time to take a bow."

But Susie still didn't move and Pete's grin faded as he walked over to her and knelt down on the rug. "Susie?"

But Susie didn't answer. She just stayed on the floor, motionless, in a pool of her own warm, red blood.

"Susie?" Pete sounded scared as he took Susie's hand and felt for a pulse. And then he looked up and the horrified expression on his face said it all. Susie wasn't acting. The second explosion had been a real gunshot. The fake gun wasn't a fake and their friend, Susie Romano, was dead.

Fifteen

"It's my uncle's gun." There was an expression of horror on Dale's face. "But I never realized he kept it loaded in his library desk! It's my fault Susie died. She was in my skit and I should have checked!"

Pete shook his head. "No, Dale. It's not your fault. It's not anyone's fault. I know it sounds cruel to say so right now, but Susie was responsible for her own death. We know what happened. I found the prop gun in the top drawer, and we all saw Susie pull out the second. She made a mistake that turned out to be fatal, but it was an accident."

Jennifer winced. She knew what everyone else was thinking and it was up to her to say it. "There's the note Susie got from Kelly. Do you think that . . ."

"No. Absolutely not!" Pete interrupted her. "That note has nothing to do with Susie's death. I don't want any of you to even consider it."

Jennifer took a deep breath. And then she blurted it out. "You're wrong, Pete."

Everyone turned to stare at Jennifer. It was the first time they'd ever heard her talk back to a teacher. She could feel herself starting to blush, but she knew she was right and she wasn't about to back down.

"I don't believe that Kelly's ghost murdered Susie. That's not what I mean at all! But finding that note and worrying about it could have made Susie careless."

"Jen's right." Tim slipped his arm around her shoulders and gave her a little hug. "Susie was really distracted after she got that note."

Pete didn't look happy, but he nodded. "Okay. You've got a point. But what can we do about it?"

"I think Jennifer and Tim should stop planting those notes." Cheryl sounded angry. "It's just causing trouble."

"But we can't!" Jennifer turned to face Cheryl. "Really, Cheryl . . . we'd stop in a heartbeat if we could, but we're not doing it!"

Cheryl rolled her eyes at the ceiling. "Sure. And the pope's not Catholic. Come on, Jen . . . admit it. The fun and games are over and your stupid skit's causing all sorts of trouble."

"We're not the ones causing trouble." Tim jumped in to defend Jennifer. "Jen and I don't like the notes, either. We'd stop them if we could, but . . ."

"I know, I know. You don't have to repeat it." Cheryl gave Tim a nasty look. "But if you're not writing the notes, who is?"

Pete held up his hands for silence. "Let's forget about the notes. They aren't important. It's our reaction that's causing all the trouble. I told Jennifer and Tim to go on with their séance, but maybe I made a mistake."

"You can't stop the séances." Brian's voice came over the loudspeaker. "It won't work."

Jennifer jumped and looked up at the speaker. She'd forgotten that Brian wasn't with them. "Why won't it work? Come in here and tell us."

There was a crackle as Brian shut off the microphone. A moment later, they heard him coming down the stairs from the manager's office. When he appeared in the doorway, he was frowning.

"Why can't we cancel, Brian?" Tim frowned right back at him.

"I told you. It won't work. Once you've summoned an angry spirit, you can't just send it away."

"You're making this up!" Cheryl turned to glare at him. "You're just trying to frighten us."

Brian shook his head. "No, I'm not. Zada brought some books with her and I read them last night."

"But . . . why?" Jennifer looked puzzled.

"Because I needed some answers. Something weird is going on here, and I wanted to find out what it was."

Everyone was silent for a long moment and then Jennifer asked the question. "Did you find out?"

"Yes. It's right here on page fifty-three." Brian opened one of the books. "It says, *Beware lest you summon an angry spirit, for it shall not go quietly. The living may not alter or even intrude upon such a spirit's chosen path without risking death.* I think we can safely assume that Kelly's spirit is angry . . . right?"

"Right," Tim said. "Kelly's spirit certainly seems to be angry. But that book just describes what's happening. We need to know what we can do about it."

"I was coming to that." Brian flipped open another book. "There's more right here. *An angry spirit must be acknowledged. Wrongs committed during the spirit's lifetime must be righted by those who remain behind. Only when the spirit is appeased, will it will slip back from hence it came.*"

"Oh, that's just great!" Cheryl sounded very sarcastic. "What do we have to do? Round up all the kids who were mean to Kelly in grade school, and offer them up as a living sacrifice?"

Brian didn't laugh. "Close, but not quite. We already know why Kelly's spirit is angry. She said she was murdered and she came back tell us who killed her. If we catch her killer, Kelly's spirit will be appeased."

"I guess that makes some kind of sense," Jennifer said. "But how are we going to do that?"

Lexie started to grin. "I know! We're going to switch the séance into one of those murder-mystery parties. You guys must have planned it this way."

"But we didn't!" Jennifer frowned. "Honestly, Lexie. I don't know anything about a murder-mystery party."

"Me, neither." Tim shook his head. "This is all Brian's idea."

Brian looked very serious as he shook his head. "It's not my idea, either. It's Kelly's. She's the one who wants us to find her killer. That means we've got to hold another séance. It's the only way that Kelly can tell us who killed her."

"Brian's right. We can't stop now. Let's go on with the séances." Tommy looked serious, too. "If somebody murdered Kelly, I want to know who it is."

Lexie nodded. "Me, too! But there's only eight of us left. Will it work?"

"It'll work." Brian sounded very certain. "How about it, Pete? Can we hold another séance?"

Pete shrugged. "Let's put it to the vote. How many want another séance?"

Tommy and Lexie raised their hands and a moment later, so did Cheryl. Jennifer hid a grin. It was clear that Cheryl wasn't going to be left out of anything that Tommy wanted to do.

"I'm in," Brian said. "How about you, Tim?"

"Sure. If everyone wants another séance, I'm willing to take part. But we can't do it without you, Jen."

Jennifer hesitated and then she nodded. "All right. Since I started the whole thing, I guess it's only right that I follow through. How about you, Dale?"

"Okay." Dale looked amused. "I'll cast my vote with the majority. But I think you should be in on it, Pete. I know this isn't really the time to bring it up, but the table's getting kind of empty."

There was a moment of silence and then Pete stood up. "All right. I'll take part. Get into your séance clothes and we'll meet around the table in fifteen minutes."

Jennifer was dressed and ready when Tim knocked on her door. But he didn't wait for her to answer. He just opened the door, crossed the room to where she was standing, and took her into his arms for a long, comforting kiss.

When the kiss ended, Tim looked down into her eyes. There was a gentle, caring expression on his face. "Are you okay, Jen?"

"I am now." Jennifer snuggled a little closer. "But I can't understand why Brian practically forced us into holding another séance. I talked to him yesterday morning and he told me he didn't believe in Kelly's spirit."

"Maybe he changed his mind."

"Maybe." Jennifer took Tim's hand and they walked toward the door. But she didn't really believe that Brian had changed his mind. There was another reason, and Jennifer just hoped that it wouldn't lead to even more trouble.

Everyone felt much better when they left the séance table. Absolutely nothing out of the ordinary had happened. There had been no knocks, no voices, no candles that mysteriously extinguished themselves. There was no evidence that Kelly's spirit had even heard them and that was just fine with Cheryl. She wanted Kelly's spirit to disappear so Tommy could concentrate on the living, particularly on her.

Cheryl grinned as she climbed the stairs. At least one thing had worked in her favor. Since she'd been sitting next to Tommy at the séance, Pete had paired them together. He'd told them there'd been too many accidents and he was starting a new policy. Everyone was now on the buddy system, and no one was allowed to go anywhere alone. Their buddies had to know where they were at all times, and anyone who got a note from Kelly had to promise to report to the group immediately. Tommy was Cheryl's buddy, Lexie was paired with Dale, Tim was Jennifer's guardian, and Brian and Pete had agreed to keep an eye on each other.

"I'll wait out here until you're ready." Tommy stood to the side as Cheryl opened her door. "Just call if you need me."

Cheryl turned to smile at him. "Don't be silly, Tommy. Why don't you just come in?"

"No." Tommy looked uncomfortable as he shook his head. "Guys aren't allowed in the girls' rooms. Go ahead, Cheryl. I'll wait right here."

"All right. Whatever you want." Cheryl managed to keep the pleasant expression on her face until she'd shut the door behind her. Then she started to scowl and she just barely resisted the urge to fling her shoe at the back of the door. What was wrong with Tommy? She'd expected him to jump at the chance to come into her room, and he had turned her down!

Could it be Lexie? Cheryl thought about it for a second and then she shook her head. Impossible! Lexie was short and skinny, without a sexy bone in her body. There was no way that Tommy could be seriously interested in her. Cheryl had been very jealous when she'd seen them holding hands, but now she realized that Tommy was probably just being kind to an unfortunate girl who obviously adored him.

Cheryl slipped out of her clothes and examined her figure in the mirror. She was much prettier than Lexie with curves in all the right places and a face that a model would envy. She was perfect for Tommy, but why had he turned down her invitation?

Kelly. Cheryl began to frown. Tommy was still thinking about Kelly. The séances had depressed him, bringing back painful memories of the girl he'd loved. Luckily, Cheryl had thought of a perfect way to take his mind off his former girlfriend.

It didn't take long to get into her bathing suit, a tiny white bikini that was sure to take Tommy's mind off Kelly. She slipped on a robe, no sense showing Tommy more than he could handle at the moment, and picked up her portable CD player. She'd already chosen the CDs she wanted to play and they were all mellow, romantic albums.

The next thing to pack was her sports bag. Cheryl hurried to the bathroom to get her scented bubble bath. She opened the medicine cabinet and then she saw it, a small gold class ring on the top shelf. There was a rolled piece of paper stuck through the band, and she gasped as she saw the initials on the ring. *K.A.B.* Kelly Anne Bridges. It was Kelly's class ring! And even before she unrolled the note, Cheryl knew it was a message from Kelly.

The handwriting was the same. She recognized it from the other notes. Cheryl frowned as she read the message. It said, *Cheryl—The killer is one of you. I will tell you who murdered me tonight.*

"Oh, sure!" Cheryl laughed and slipped the class ring back on the shelf. Jennifer and Tim were up to their old tricks and this time she'd been chosen. She wasn't nervous, not even a little bit, but Pete had made them promise to report any messages from Kelly and that meant a change in her plans for the evening.

Cheryl thought about leaving the note and the ring right there on the shelf. She could always claim she hadn't found them. But now that she considered it carefully, the note might actually help her. Tommy was waiting outside her room. He might decide to wait outside the spa, too. And if Tommy refused to climb into the Jacuzzi with her, all her plans for a romantic evening would be ruined.

There was a smile on Cheryl's face as she picked up the note and headed for the door. Jennifer and Tim might not realize it, but they'd done her a big favor. Because of the note, Tommy would be her captive audience tonight. He was honor-bound not to leave her. That would give Cheryl plenty of time to convince him that she was the perfect girl for him.

Tommy looked very serious as he unlocked the door to the spa. "Are you sure you'll be all right while I change?"

"Of course I will." Cheryl nodded quickly. "Just take the key and lock the door behind you. You can let yourself in when you come back."

As soon as Tommy had left the room, Cheryl started her preparations. Everyone had been very upset when she'd reported the note and Tommy had agreed when she'd suggested that he sleep in the adjoining room, so all she had to do was call out if there was any sign of trouble.

The rest of the girls had objected. Boys weren't supposed to be on the girls' floor. Lexie and Jennifer had even offered to stay in Cheryl's room, but Cheryl had turned them down. If Kelly's spirit tried to kill her, Lexie and Jennifer wouldn't be able to protect her. But Tommy might. He could reason with Kelly's spirit and convince her not to do any more harm.

Cheryl was grinning as she poured bath oil in the Jacuzzi and watched the bubbles form. After their interlude in the Jacuzzi, she was almost sure Tommy would never even set foot in the adjoining room. They'd keep the doors locked and closed. No one would have to know except them. And after one night with her, Cheryl was sure that Tommy would be hers for life.

Music was next, and she slipped Tommy's favorite CD into her player. She turned it on, but no sound came out of the speakers. A glance at the battery case and she knew what was wrong. One of the batteries was missing. She should have thought to check it before she'd left her room.

There were batteries in her room and she thought about going back to get them. But Tommy could be back any minute and she really didn't want to leave. Thank goodness there was a power source! There was an outlet on the far wall and a thick, black extension cord was rolled up neatly on the bench.

Cheryl hooked everything up and carried the CD player close to the Jacuzzi. She'd still have to climb out of the Jacuzzi to change CDs. It was too dangerous to touch the player while they were sitting in a pool of water. But she wouldn't have to walk all the way across the room to do it.

The CD player worked perfectly and Cheryl smiled as she sat down on the ledge of the Jacuzzi and took out her contact lenses. Removing them later might interrupt a very romantic moment, and she wouldn't need them tonight. Everything would be a blur, but that wouldn't matter. She didn't need to see to be sexy for Tommy. Then she climbed into the Jacuzzi and sighed in pleasure. The hot, scented water felt wonderful. She'd just leaned back and begun to relax when she heard the key in the door.

Tommy was here! Cheryl put on her sexiest expression and turned toward the door. There was a moment of wonderful anticipation that made her heart beat fast, and then the door opened.

"Hi, Tommy." Cheryl's voice was low and husky. But Tommy didn't reply and she giggled. Seeing her like this had made him speechless.

"Come on over here and join me." Cheryl reached out and brushed away some of the bubbles. "This Jacuzzi is just perfect for two."

But Tommy still didn't reply and her smile began to fade. What was wrong with him? Why didn't he say something?

"Tommy? Is everything all right?"

Cheryl sat up and squinted. And then she saw a shape moving toward the Jacuzzi and she smiled again. "Come on, Tommy . . . I'm getting lonesome in here."

Tommy still didn't say anything. He just walked closer and picked up the CD player.

"What's the matter? I put on your favorite album." Cheryl tried to sound pleasant, but she was really getting a little angry. Tommy knew you weren't supposed to pick up a CD player when it was running. It might scratch the disk, or jam, or something equally expensive to fix.

"What are you *doing*?" Cheryl gasped as he held the CD player in one hand and raised it like a football. "Tommy! Stop it!"

And then, before she had time to scream, the CD player was hurtling forward in an arc toward the water.

"Tommy! *Nooo!*"

Cheryl barely had time to scream before the CD player hit the surface of the water. There was a spark, a loud pop, and a sizzle like a steak thrown on a red-hot grill. And almost instantaneously Cheryl was just as dead as that steak, seared to death in a pool of bubbling, scented water.

Sixteen

Jennifer sat next to Lexie on one of the leather couches in the lobby. Even though she tried not to think of it, she knew she'd never forget the sight of Cheryl's dead body in the Jacuzzi. The boys had taken charge, telling Lexie and Jennifer to wait for them until they'd unplugged the CD player and taken Cheryl's body away. And Jennifer and Lexie were waiting, lost in their private thoughts and fears, staring at the fire in the huge stone fireplace.

Even though it was warm by the fire, Jennifer shivered. So many dead: Zada, Melanie, Ronnie, Susie, and now Cheryl. They'd started their Halloween weekend with twelve and only seven were left. Their number was decreasing, one by one. How many more would die before it was over?

Lexie tapped her on the shoulder and Jennifer turned. And then Lexie said something that made Jennifer shudder.

"If we don't do something, the dead will outnumber the living!"

"That's exactly what I was thinking," Jennifer said. "But what can we do? We can't even prove their deaths weren't accidents?"

Just then the guys trooped into the room. Pete was frowning and so were Dale and Brian. Tim was doing his best to look cheerful, but Jennifer could tell that he felt like frowning, too.

And Tommy's face was so white, it was clear he was still in shock.

"Everybody grab a seat." Pete sat down on one of the couches. "We need to talk about this."

Tim sat down by Jennifer and put his arm around her shoulders. He gave her a little hug and Jennifer was amazed at how she immediately began to feel better. The situation was still awful. Cheryl had died. But just knowing that Tim cared about her made everything seem less frightening.

Lexie patted the seat next to her and motioned to Tommy. "Come on, Tommy. Sit by me. And quit kicking yourself for what happened. It's not your fault. You weren't even there."

"But I should have been." Tommy was frowning when sat down. "I knew Cheryl got that note."

Lexie nodded. "We all knew. And you did your best to protect her, didn't you?"

"I thought so, but now I'm not so sure." Tommy sighed deeply. "I never should have left her alone. I thought locking the door would keep her safe . . . but it didn't!"

Pete leaned forward. "You locked the door to the spa?"

"Yes. And I took the key with me when I went to my room to change."

"Think hard, Tommy. Was the door still locked when you got back?"

"Yes. I unlocked it and went in . . . and that's when I found her."

"Cheryl was by herself in a locked room," Pete said abruptly. "That proves her death was an accident."

Lexie shook her head. "Not necessarily. Spirits can go right through locked doors. And even if there's no such thing as a spirit, there was more than one key to the spa, wasn't there?"

"Yes." Dale answered the question. "My uncle keeps a full set of keys in his safe. But they were locked up and I gave Cheryl the only key that was in his desk."

"How about the master key?" Brian began to frown. "Wouldn't that open the spa door?"

"Sure. And I showed everyone where it was, the first time we came up here. It was hanging on a nail in the manager's office and it said *master key* right on the label."

Jennifer shivered slightly. After she'd locked her door at night, she'd assumed she was safe. But she'd forgotten all about the master key. Anyone who'd grabbed it from the hook could have unlocked her door and walked right in. "Is the master key still there?"

"I don't know." Dale began to frown. "I'll go check."

They were all silent as they waited for Dale to come back. Jennifer knew they were thinking about how easy it would have been to unlock the spa door with the master key. A moment later, Dale was back and this time he was smiling. "It's still there. I guess Cheryl's death was an accident, after all."

Jennifer nodded, right along with everyone else, but she wasn't really convinced. If the killer had taken the master key, he could have returned it.

"Okay, guys. Listen up." Pete got to his feet and turned to face them. "I'm making a new rule. No one goes anywhere alone, not even to your rooms. We're going to bring down sleeping bags and spend the rest of the night right here by the fire. Any objections?"

One by one, they shook their heads. No one wanted to be alone after what had happened to Cheryl.

"Okay. Let's go get the sleeping bags." Pete motioned to Brian and Dale. "You two come with me. I want the rest of you to stay right here and wait for us."

But there was another shock when the group got back together again. When Pete had gone to his room to get his sleeping bag, he'd found a note taped to his mirror. It was in an envelope that had been fastened with a gold seal in the shape of a teddy bear.

"Kelly's seal!" Tommy stared at the envelope and his face turned white. "She ordered them from a catalogue. Kelly loved teddy bears."

Pete shrugged. "So do a lot of other people. I'm sure Kelly wasn't the only one to use gold seals shaped like teddy bears. If she got them from a catalogue, they're probably a popular item."

"But this seal has her initials on it." Tommy held up the envelope so they could all see Kelly's initials on the tummy of the teddy bear. "How many other people have Kelly's initials?"

"You've got a point," Brian agreed. "Go ahead, Pete. Open the envelope and see what's inside."

"It's a note from Kelly." Pete unfolded the piece of paper. "And it says, *Brian is right. My spirit is angry, but I would never hurt any of you. My killer pushed Zada down the stairs and made the woodpile fall on Melanie. He caused Ronnie's fall from the balcony and replaced Susie's prop with a real handgun. Now he has killed Cheryl and you must catch him before he strikes again. Be very careful, Pete. He will try to kill you, too, before I can tell you his name.*"

Jennifer shivered. "She's right, Pete! You have to be very careful. It's a good thing we're all down here together."

"I guess that means we'll have to hold another séance to find out who he is." Pete winked at Jennifer.

Jennifer's mouth dropped open. It was clear Pete thought they were responsible for the note. And he also thought they wanted to hold another séance. "No, Pete . . . we don't want to hold another séance!"

But Pete just grinned. He thought she was playing the part of a reluctant psychic. "Okay, Jennifer. We'll talk about it in the morning. It's late now and we all have to get some sleep."

It took a while, but at last the group had settled down, all in one room. Lexie and Jennifer had the couches and the boys had arranged air mats and sleeping bags close to the big, river rock fireplace. As Jennifer dropped off to sleep, she made a promise to herself. If Pete asked her to conduct another séance in the morning, she was going to refuse. She'd never do their skit again, not even when Miss Voelker and the kids got here. Zada and four of their friends were dead and Jennifer couldn't help feeling that the séances were to blame. Perhaps Brian was right and it was dangerous to stop, but she didn't see how it could get much worse than this.

*   *   *

Pete was thoughtful as he stared up into the darkness. The note from Kelly was very clever. He'd been about to suggest it when Jennifer and Tim had sent it to him, all by themselves. It was the perfect way to stop the panic that was beginning to build among his students. When they saw that he'd received one of Kelly's notes and he was perfectly all right, they'd begin to relax and realize that the other deaths were entirely accidental.

Had another student teacher ever been through anything like this? Pete doubted it. He was responsible for the drama class and four of his students had died. He'd done everything he could think of to protect them, but nothing had done any good. What would Miss Voelker say when she found out what had happened? Would she blame him for not doing his job? And how about the parents of the dead students? Would they accuse him of being negligent?

There was no way he could sleep after everything that had happened. He was too worried about whether people would blame him. Pete felt like pacing the floor in frustration, but he didn't want to wake any of his sleeping students. They were safe as long as they stayed together and this was the only time he didn't have to worry about them.

Pete stood up and walked quietly to the door. He needed a break and had a bottle of brandy stashed in the hearse. He wasn't much of a drinker but he knew that a shot of brandy would help him to relax so that he could sleep.

It was cold outside and he was shivering as he slid into the driver's seat. He turned on the engine and started the heater and then switched on the sound system. The hearse hadn't been used for its original purpose in quite a while and the previous owner had put in a great sound system. Pete had brought along some of his favorite music and he went through the disks, one by one. He didn't feel like listening to jazz or rock and blues would only depress him. That left classical and he slipped a CD into the deck.

As the strains of Segovia's classical guitar filled the air, Pete began to feel much better. His girlfriend played classical guitar.

She was a music major and she performed at a small club near the campus. Pete loved her and he'd decided to ask her to marry him when she graduated.

Pete opened the bottle and took a sip of brandy. Too bad he hadn't brought a glass, but the brandy was mellow and it was just what he needed. He took another sip and leaned back against the soft leather upholstery. It was good to be alone for a few minutes. He'd been on duty with his students since Friday afternoon and he was exhausted.

The heater sent out waves of comforting heat and Pete glanced at the clock on the dashboard. It was two in the morning, but he didn't feel like moving a muscle just yet. He needed another few minutes of pure relaxation before he went back inside.

Another sip of brandy and his eyes began to close. The music was great and a little nap wouldn't hurt. He hadn't slept soundly since they'd arrived at Saddlepeak Lodge, and it might be a while before he got a full night's sleep. He'd doze until the music stopped playing. That would be his cue to wake up. Then he'd go back inside, check on his students, and be on call for the rest of the night.

He'd been awake when Pete had gone outside. The others had been sacked out completely, and they hadn't even wiggled as he'd slipped out of his sleeping bag and tiptoed to the window.

He really didn't want to kill Pete, but he had no choice. After Pete had gotten that note from Kelly, he'd promised them all that they'd have another séance tomorrow. There was no way he could let that happen. Kelly's secret might be revealed at that séance and he had to protect himself.

There was an army-type rain poncho on the rack by the door and he slipped it on. If someone woke up and glanced out the window, they wouldn't be able to recognize him in the poncho. Then he let himself out the door and stood under the overhang, trying to think of the perfect way to accomplish what he had to do.

While he waited, he thought about Kelly. If she'd only cooperated and done what he'd asked, everyone would still be alive. The killings weren't his fault. They were Kelly's. And she was still causing him trouble, even after her death!

The dome light went on in the hearse and he moved a little closer so he could see. But when he realized what was happening, he began to frown. Pete was drinking! And Pete shouldn't be drinking when he was responsible for the safety of his students.

As he watched, Pete did something even more damning. He leaned back against the seat and shut his eyes. Pete was going to sleep out here and leave his students alone. Perhaps he'd be doing them all a favor by killing Pete. In times of war, sentries were executed for sleeping on duty.

He waited another few minutes and then he moved around to the back of the hearse. He knew what to do and it wouldn't be difficult at all. There were some rags in one of the garbage cans and he stuffed them into the tailpipe of the hearse. And then he stood there and watched, imagining how the fumes would back up and send Pete into a very permanent sleep.

It was a good dream, a wonderful dream, all about the life he'd share with his girlfriend. Pete's eyes flickered. He could almost touch her warm skin and smell her perfume. But that wasn't perfume he was smelling. It was something else. Pete opened his eyes and reached out to open the window to get rid of the invasive smell, but he was so tired that he could barely lift his arm.

He needed a little more sleep. Then he'd gather the energy to open the window. The darkness was closing in, much darker than the night outside. As Pete slipped into unconsciousness, he had one last, fleeting thought. The odor smelled a little like exhaust fumes. The note from Kelly. The other accidents. Was he about to become the sixth victim? But Pete was just too tired to hold onto that thought as he slipped into the permanent darkness.

He saw Pete's head roll back against the seat. His breathing slowed, growing more and more shallow, until finally it stopped. But he was patient and waited for another ten minutes, crouching on the far side of the hearse and peering in through the passenger's window.

He moved quickly then, pulling the rags from the exhaust pipe and stuffing them back into the garbage can. Then he dragged the can to the back of the hearse and jammed it up against the tailpipe. Everyone would assume that Pete had backed the hearse too close to the garbage can and when he'd started the engine, the exhaust fumes had killed him. It would be another accident, the sixth in a row. It would scare them all so much that Jennifer and Tim would refuse to hold another séance.

Seventeen

Jennifer gave a deep sigh of contentment. Someone was stroking her hair. When she'd been a small child, her mother had always come in to wake her that way, and Jennifer smiled and snuggled down a little deeper under the blankets. The touch was loving and gentle, and she felt warm and cherished.

"Jen . . . time to get up."

Jennifer sighed again and then she began to frown. The words were the same, but it hadn't sounded like her mother's voice. "Mom?"

"No, Jen."

There was a hint of laughter in the much deeper voice and Jennifer's frown deepened. It must be her dad, but why was he waking her? He always left for work early, at least an hour before she got up. "Dad?"

"No, Jen."

This time the voice actually laughed, a deep, rumbling sound, and her eyes flew open in shock. It was Tim! But what was Tim doing in her bedroom?

"Your hair's incredible, Jen." He reached out to stroke it, again.

"Sorry . . . I guess it's an awful mess." Jennifer began to blush. Her hair had always been horrible in the morning. "I'll brush it and tie it back right away."

"No. Don't do that." Tim smiled down at her. "It's so pretty this way. I think you should leave it loose. All those beautiful colors . . . it's like a rainbow."

Jennifer smiled in pure happiness. If she'd had any doubts about Tim, they were firmly erased by what he'd said. He liked her hair when no one else did. He'd just compared it to a beautiful rainbow! Tim was wonderful and they were definitely made for each other.

"You'd better get up, Jen. It's eight o'clock and the sun's out. It's a little warmer, too. Maybe they'll be able to get through to us today."

Suddenly it all came back: the haunted lodge, the séances, the notes, and all the horrible accidents. Jennifer's eyes lost some of their sparkle and she reached up to hug Tim. "Is everybody okay?"

"Everybody's fine. They're still sleeping, but Pete is up. I saw him outside in the hearse. He must be looking for something."

"Thank God!" Jennifer gave a huge sigh of relief. "I couldn't help worrying about him after he got that note."

"Me, too. Let's go up and change clothes, Jen. I don't want to wake the others just yet."

They went up the stairs. Tim waited in her room while she took a quick shower, and then she waited in his room while he did the same. Fifteen minutes later they were sitting in the kitchen, side by side at the long table, sipping steaming cups of hot chocolate.

"I'm so glad the sun's out!" Jennifer smiled as she glanced out the window. "I bet Pete is, too. He's been out there a long time."

"I know. I wonder if I should go out and help him."

"Let's both go." Jennifer pushed back her chair. "We can even take him a cup of hot chocolate."

As they stepped out the door, carrying a cup of hot chocolate for Pete, Tim began to frown. "I don't like this, Jen. He's still slumped over in the front seat. He was like that when I saw him early this morning."

"Maybe he fell asleep. He was really tired." As Jennifer

spoke the words, she felt her heart start to pound in fear. What if Pete wasn't sleeping? What if he was dead?

"Pete?" Tim tapped on the driver's window, but Pete didn't sit up. He didn't even move.

"Tap on the window again, Tim. He could be a really sound sleeper."

Tim knocked on the window and called his name, but Pete still didn't move. He turned to look at Jennifer and the fear she was feeling was mirrored in his face. That was when Jennifer spotted it, the empty brandy bottle on the floor of the front seat.

"I think I know what's wrong." Jennifer pointed to the empty bottle. "If Pete drank that whole bottle of brandy by himself, he's probably passed out cold."

Tim looked very relieved. "I'll open the door and check. Get ready to help me catch him, Jen."

"Okay. Let's take him into the kitchen and sober him up before the rest of the guys find out."

"Good idea. I don't want to see him fired, do you?"

"No." Jennifer shook her head. "I don't like it, but I can't really blame him. This whole weekend's been a terrible strain and he was just fine up until last night."

"Okay . . . here we go."

Jennifer stood to the side as Tim opened the door. But Pete didn't tumble out, groaning and holding his head, as both of them expected. He just fell into their arms as stiff as a board and Jennifer stared down at him in shock. "Tim . . . Pete's not drunk! He's . . ."

"I know." Tim didn't give her time to finish her sentence. "Go get the guys, Jen. I'll handle it until they get here."

Jennifer didn't say a word. She just turned around and hurried back to the lodge. And as she ran, words thumped through her head like a chant, in time with her steps. Another note. Another death. Another note. Another death. *When would it all stop?*

"Okay. We have to talk about this." Tim stood up in front of the river rock fireplace. They were all gathered together, sitting on the couches or on the floor and Tim was in charge. "There's only six of us left."

Everyone nodded. What Tim said was true. The only ones left were Tim and Jennifer, Tommy and Lexie, and Dale and Brian.

"What should we do?" Lexie sounded nervous. "These can't be accidents, can they? I mean . . . it's statistically impossible for any group to be so incredibly unlucky."

"I agree," Tim said.

"But that means there's a murderer on the loose, killing anyone who gets a note from Kelly!" Jennifer's voice was shaking. "And since we're the only ones here, the killer must be a member of our group!"

There was a tense moment of silence as they all glanced around, turning away the moment they met anyone else's eyes.

"No." Dale shook his head. "Look . . . we've known each other all our lives. We started first grade together and we're going to graduate together."

"Right . . . if we manage to live that long," Lexie said.

Jennifer couldn't help it. She giggled. Leave it to Lexie to see the humor in an impossible situation.

"Okay. I deserved that." Dale grinned at Lexie. "And I realize that what Jennifer said makes sense. But I just can't believe that one of us is a killer!"

Tommy jumped up. He looked very excited. "Hold it, guys! Maybe the killer isn't one of us. There's another alternative we haven't even considered."

"What's that?" Jennifer stared up at him hopefully. No one wanted to believe that the killer was right here in the room, perhaps even sitting next to them.

"What if this whole thing has nothing to do with Kelly's death? There could be another person here, hiding here at the lodge, someone who's so afraid of being discovered that he's killing us off, one by one."

"Good one, Tommy." Lexie giggled. "Do you really think Michael Myers from *Halloween* is holed up in the basement?"

Everyone cracked up except Dale.

Dale sighed deeply. "Very funny. Let's be serious. Tommy might have a point. There could be someone hiding in the lodge. We didn't check out every room when we got here."

"But why would anyone hide here?" Lexie asked the question. "It's miles from the nearest town!"

"You just said it," Brian stated. "Because it's miles from the nearest town. Think about it for a minute. If you wanted to hide out somewhere, what better place is there than this? It's miles from other people, it's heated, and there's food in the pantry. What more could you want?"

"Okay." Tim took charge again. "Let's assume that Tommy's right and there really is someone else here. Since the victims all received notes from Kelly, those notes must be setting the killer off."

"That's right," Dale said. "I think this is the time for all of us to be totally honest. Who's been writing the notes?"

"Not me." Jennifer shook her head. "Believe me, I'd tell you. This whole thing is getting really scary. But I swear I didn't write those notes and I don't know who did!"

Everyone turned to look at Tim, but he shook his head. "I didn't write them, either. And I don't know who did, unless . . . Brian?"

Brian shook his head. "Not me. I just do special effects. I thought you were writing them, Tommy."

"No way!" Tommy sounded outraged. "I didn't want Tim and Jen to do the séance in the first place. And I certainly didn't write any notes!"

Lexie patted him on the arm. "We believe you. And just for the record, I didn't write them, either. That leaves you, Dale."

"Not me." Dale looked baffled as he shook his head. "Then . . . how did they get here if none of us wrote them?"

There was silence for a moment and then Jennifer sighed. "Maybe Pete did. He was very encouraging about our skit, and he seemed to like the séances a lot. He might have tried to help by writing the notes."

"That's a possibility . . . I guess." Tim didn't sound convinced. "If you're right, there won't be any more notes."

There was silence again as everyone thought about Pete. And then Tim took charge again. "We're going to stick together at all times. No one goes anywhere alone. Got it?"

"How about the bathroom?" Lexie raised her eyebrows.

"We'll check it out first. Then you and Jen can go in together. The road crew should be here in a day or two and until they arrive, we're going to do everything in a group."

One by one, they nodded. Tim was right. But Jennifer didn't say what she was thinking. What if the killer got frustrated because he couldn't kill just one of them? What if he came out in the open and killed them all at once?

Someone was lying. He knew it. But no one in the group was willing to admit it. They'd even blamed Pete for the notes and there was no way that Pete could have written them. Pete had come to Foothill High this fall, a month after Kelly had died. Unless he'd talked to Miss Voelker about it, Pete would have had no way of knowing the shade of lipstick that Kelly had worn. He couldn't have known about her teddy bear seals, or the pin Tommy had given her for Christmas, or her scarf printed with lilacs. The author of the notes had known Kelly personally, and that meant he or she was a member of their group.

He didn't believe in Kelly's ghost. That was ridiculous! Someone here, someone very much alive, suspected that Kelly had been murdered. And until he figured out who that someone was, anyone who was unlucky enough to receive a note from Kelly would simply have to die.

Eighteen

It was one in the afternoon and the rain had started to fall again. Jennifer glanced out the window and sighed. It was turning into a gloomy day and there was still no sign of the road crew. Even the cheery fire they'd built in the fireplace did nothing to lift her spirits.

"I think I'll try to catch some sleep before it gets dark." Lexie sounded depressed, too. "Tonight's Halloween and that might set the killer off. I want to stay up all night, just in case."

"Good idea," Tim agreed. "Let's all take a nap. We'll be safe if we stay here together."

They all stretched out on the couches or on the floor, huddled together in a tight little group. Jennifer didn't feel like sleeping so she closed her eyes and tried to think of something pleasant, something that would distract her from the awful things that had happened.

Tim. Jennifer smiled. Why hadn't she realized that she was in love with him before this Halloween weekend? She'd assumed that he was only a friend, but she'd cared about him much more than she'd thought. Jennifer remembered something her mother had told her once, something she'd thought was ridiculous. Now, years later, her mother's words made a whole lot of sense.

"How do you know you're in love, Mom?" a twelve-year-old Jennifer had asked.

"Don't worry. You'll know." Her mother had laughed. "Just remember, Jennifer . . . the basis of true love is friendship."

Jennifer had frowned and asked the first question that had come into her mind. "What does that mean?"

"It means that if you don't have friendship, your love won't last."

Jennifer had nodded, but she remembered thinking that her mother was crazy. Friends were one thing and boyfriends were another. But now she understood what her mother had meant. She loved Tim, but he was also her friend. Tim was someone she could talk to, someone she admired, and someone who felt exactly the same way about her. He was kind and gentle, the sort of man she'd want for the father of her children. That was why she wanted to spend the rest of her life with . . .

Jennifer's eyes popped open in alarm. Her thoughts and feelings were leading her down a path she wasn't ready to take. She didn't want to get married quite yet. She wanted to wait, to live on her own, to be independent for the first time in her life. There was no way she'd go straight from her parents' house to an apartment she'd share with her husband. She wanted to finish high school and go on to college. And when she earned her degree, she wanted to start her career. Once both of them were established, it would be time to talk about marriage.

Jennifer shut her eyes again and smiled as she thought about married life. There they'd be, sitting side by side in the living room, after the children had gone to bed. They'd be talking and laughing at something one of them had said. Tim would be a research chemist and she would be an elementary school teacher. She would tell him about the students in her class and he would discuss the important work they were doing in his lab. They'd have lots of friends, people they'd met along the way. There would be friends from high school and college, teachers from her school, and coworkers from his lab. They'd have relatives, too. There would be two sets of parents, and Tommy, who would visit with his wife. Perhaps Tommy might even marry Lexie and then her best friend would become her sister-in-law!

The dream was so delightful, Jennifer giggled out loud. And then she felt something tickling her ear and she giggled again.

"Jen?" Tim's lips brushed her ear as he whispered, "Are you still awake?"

Jennifer blushed. It was a good thing that Tim couldn't read her mind! "Yes, Tim. I'm awake."

"Are you too nervous to sleep?"

Jennifer shook her head. "Not really. I was just thinking about something."

"It must have been something good. You looked really happy."

"It was." Jennifer blushed even harder and changed the subject before Tim could ask her what it was. "How about you? Aren't you sleepy?"

"Not really. But since we're both awake, why don't we stand guard?"

"That's a great idea." Jennifer threw back the blankets and stood up. "Come on, Tim."

They were very quiet as they tiptoed past their sleeping friends. Lexie was curled up in a ball on one of the couches and Tommy was on the floor, right next to her. Dale was next to Tommy, sleeping on his back and snoring softly. And Brian was next to him, completely covered by his sleeping bag.

"Look at Brian," Jennifer whispered. "I'd better fold back his sleeping bag. He can't get any air that way."

Tim watched as Jennifer reached out and folded back the sleeping bag. Then both of them gasped as they saw that the sleeping bag held a rolled-up blanket and the pillow, bunched up to look as if Brian had his head under the covers. Brian wasn't there!

Tim turned to Jennifer in alarm. "We've got to find him! He could be the killer's next target if he's gone somewhere alone!"

Brian wasn't in the kitchen or in his room. And his parka was still hanging on the rack by the door so he hadn't gone outside. They searched the spa and both floors of bedrooms, but Brian was nowhere to be found.

"Where is he?" Jennifer knew she looked worried.

"I don't know, but there's one last place to look. Let's try the manager's office on the mezzanine."

Jennifer and Tim headed up the stairs at a run. Brian had used the manager's office for his headquarters while they were doing the skits. It was the nerve center of the lodge with a bank of telephones and the microphone for the PA system, and Brian had adopted it as his private office.

"Do you hear a radio?" Jennifer stopped as they reached the mezzanine.

"I hear it. And I think it's coming from the manager's office."

The door was partially open and Tim glanced in. When he turned back to Jennifer, he looked worried. "Brian's sitting at the desk, reading a note . . . and it's written on Saddlepeak Lodge stationery!"

Jennifer's face turned pale. All the notes from Kelly had been written on Saddlepeak Lodge stationery. "It could be an old note. I know Brian kept them. Come on, Tim. Let's sneak in and read it. I want to make sure!"

Brian was staring at the note so intently, he didn't notice as they slipped in the door and tiptoed up behind him. Jennifer leaned closer so she could read over his shoulder, and what she saw made her start to tremble. The note was from Kelly, just as they'd suspected, but this was a new note, one they'd never seen before. Kelly had written that she was going to give herself a birthday present. She promised to name her killer at the stroke of midnight, tonight on Halloween!

Tim nudged Jennifer and then he pointed to the envelope that had held the note. Unlike the others, it didn't have a name. The envelope was perfectly blank and Jennifer frowned as she realized what that meant. This new note from Kelly, this certain death sentence for anyone who received it, could have been meant for any one of them.

Jennifer was about to ask Brian where he'd found the note, when Brian did something so crazy that she gasped out loud. As they watched, Brian picked up a pen and wrote his own name on the envelope.

Nineteen

Jennifer was too shocked to say anything. She just stood there and stared at the piece of Saddlepeak Lodge stationery that put Brian's life in terrible danger. Tim looked equally shocked, but he was the first to recover. She watched as he moved up closer to Brian and tapped him on the shoulder.

"Brian! What the hell are you doing?"

Brian swiveled around to face them. And then he gave a sheepish grin. "What do you think I'm doing? I'm smoking out the killer."

"But . . . that note'll put you in horrible danger!" Jennifer found her voice at last. "Don't do it, Brian. It's crazy!"

"I have to do it. I'm responsible for everything that's happened around here."

Jennifer frowned. "What do you mean? How are you responsible?"

"I wrote the notes. I got a sample of Kelly's handwriting and I forged every one of them."

Tim looked shocked. "But . . . why?"

"I wanted to make your skit more believable. That's the reason I rigged the table and the candles. And the notes were a natural. After all, Kelly's death was a little suspicious and I thought it would add to the drama of your séance."

"But the notes are death sentences!" Jennifer couldn't help raising her voice. "Everybody who got one is dead!"

"I didn't know that would happen. I thought they were all accidents, just like you did. I didn't realize that there was really a killer until Pete died."

Jennifer and Tim looked confused, and Brian went on to explain. "I know Pete was murdered. I was with him when he parked the hearse, and I know he didn't back up to that garbage can."

"You're sure?" Tim looked skeptical.

"I'm positive! That why I wrote this note to myself. I started this whole thing and now I've got to stop it!"

"Wait a minute." Jennifer's eyes narrowed. "I believe you when you say you wrote the notes, but how about Kelly's things? The scarf, the ring, the pin . . . how did you do that?"

"That was easy, too. Kelly wore Tommy's pin for her class picture. I took a copy of her picture to the jewelry store and picked out a pin that looked just like it. And Kelly wrote me a note once, with one of her teddy bear seals. I just steamed it off and used it again."

"How about the scarf?"

"She dropped it one day and I picked it up. I just never got around to returning it, that's all. And I knew her brand of lipstick. My sister wears the same color."

"How did you get her class ring?" Tim still didn't look convinced. "I know it was Kelly's. Her initials were engraved on the inside of the band."

"That took a little extra effort, but I managed to borrow it from Kelly's sister. I'll give it back when I get home."

"*If* you get home." Jennifer looked worried. "Don't send yourself that note, Brian . . . please! It's just asking for trouble."

"I know that. But I have to do something. I was just guessing, but I stumbled on the truth. Somebody really killed Kelly and now they're killing us to cover up the crime."

Tim and Jennifer were silent. They were so shocked, they couldn't think of anything to say.

"Hey, guys . . . I've got a plan." Brian did his best to convince them. "If I get a note from Kelly, the killer will go after me. Don't you see? It's the only way we can catch him."

"You can't do this, Brian." Jennifer shook her head. "It's too risky."

"No, it's not. We'll set a trap for the killer. You guys can help."

Tim reached out to take Brian's arm. "You've been watching too many cop shows. This is a real killer. He's killed six people already. I agree with Jen. It's much too risky."

"Look, guys . . . the killer's got to get rid of us. He can't let us go home and tell anyone what happened up here. So what are we going to do? Let him murder us all without fighting back?"

Tim glanced at Jennifer and she nodded. Brian had a point. The killer couldn't let them live.

"Okay." Tim sighed. "But this is going to take some careful planning."

Brian looked very serious as he faced them. "It shouldn't be that hard. I'll find the note when we all wake up from our nap. Then I'll come up here alone, and he'll try to kill me. Jennifer? Your job is to watch. And Tim? If anyone leaves the group, I want you to promise me you'll follow him."

"That might work if the killer is one of us, but what if he isn't?" Jennifer sounded worried. "What if Tommy's right and there's another person hiding up here? We'll all be sitting down in the lobby like lumps and you'll be up here, alone with the killer!"

"I've got that covered." Brian pointed to the microphone on the desk. "All I have to do is flick on this mike and call for help. You know how it works. I used it for all the sound effects when we rehearsed the skits. If you hear my voice on the loudspeaker, you can be up here in a flash."

Jennifer glanced at Tim. He looked every bit as worried as she felt. "But, Brian . . . isn't there some other way?"

"I don't think so. I've thought it all through and it should work in theory. Look at it this way. It's the only chance we've got of staying alive. Now let's go back down there so you can act totally freaked when I find that note."

They were all back in their sleeping bags again and Jennifer was amazed to see that Brian had actually managed to fall asleep. Either he was the craziest person alive, or he had nerves of pure steel. Tim appeared to be sleeping, too, and Jennifer wondered whether she was the only one who couldn't fall asleep. She'd just closed her eyes for what seemed like the millionth time when she felt a tap on her shoulder and turned to see Lexie with a finger to her lips.

"Jen?" Lexie leaned close to whisper. "I've got to talk to you . . . alone!"

Jennifer whispered back, "We could go over to that table in the alcove, but we shouldn't leave the lobby."

"Right." Lexie stuck out her hand and pulled Jennifer to her feet. "Come on, Jen. It's really important."

As soon as they'd pulled their chairs up to the table, Lexie started to frown. "Look, Jen . . . I've been your best friend for a long time, right?"

"Of course."

"And I'm still your best friend?" Lexie looked very relieved when Jennifer nodded. "Then that gives me the right to tell you something you probably don't want to hear . . . right?"

"Uh . . . okay." Jennifer braced herself. Lexie looked very serious.

"I woke up a while ago and you and Tim were gone. You don't deny that, do you?"

"No. I don't deny it. But . . ."

"I know that you probably wanted to be alone," Lexie interrupted her. "I can understand that. People in love always want to be alone. But I think it's incredibly meshuga of you to leave the group. You'll have plenty of time to be alone with Tim when we get back home. And right now you could be asking for trouble if you sneak away like that! Don't forget there's a killer out there."

"Yes, Mother Lexie." Jennifer started to grin.

"It's *Yiddishe mama.* That means 'Jewish mother,' and I know I'm acting like one. But I wouldn't be a true friend if I didn't warn you."

"Okay. But aren't you going to ask me what Tim and I were doing?"

"No. It's none of my business. But . . . I think I can guess!"

Lexie began to blush and Jennifer giggled. It was totally out of character for Lexie to blush and she knew exactly what her best friend was thinking. "It's not what you think, Lexie. Tim and I were upstairs in the manager's office, talking to Brian."

"Brian?" Lexie began to frown again. "He left the group, too?"

"He left first. Tim and I discovered he was gone and we went to find him."

"Brian's even more meshuga than you are!" Lexie's frown deepened. "What was he doing up there?"

Jennifer hesitated, and then she made up her mind. She could trust Lexie to keep a secret and a third pair of eyes would help when Brian put his plan into motion. "I'll tell you, but you have to promise not to tell anyone . . . not even Tommy."

"I promise."

"Brian was writing himself a note from Kelly."

"*What?*"

Lexie looked shocked.

"It's true. Brian wrote those notes from Kelly. He was just trying to add a little excitement to our skit, but those notes set off Kelly's killer. And since Brian feels responsible for all the awful things that happened, he decided to set a trap for the killer."

"What kind of a trap?" Lexie looked intrigued.

"He's going to find a note from Kelly. That'll make the killer concentrate on him. And then he's going to go up to the manager's office so the killer has the opportunity to catch him alone."

Lexie slapped the side of her head with her hand. "*Vey iz mir!*"

"*Vay is meer?*" Jennifer repeated it. "What does that mean?"

"It's something like 'woe is me' in Yiddish. So let me see if I've got this right. Brian's going to set a trap for the killer, using himself as bait?"

"Yes. If anyone leaves the group, Tim's going to follow them. And if the killer is someone who's hiding up here, Brian's going to call us on the loudspeaker."

"I see." Lexie sighed deeply. "And what will Tim do when this person tries to kill Brian?"

"Uh . . . I'm not sure. Catch him, I guess. We didn't really discuss that."

"*Vey iz mir!*" Lexie thumped the side of her head again. "Jen . . . that just happens to be the most important part."

Jennifer's face turned red. "You're right, Lexie. What do you think Tim should do?"

"He should arm himself. He's dealing with a dangerous killer. Where's the handgun Susie found in the drawer?"

"It's still in the drawer, but Pete took out all the bullets. And I don't know where he put them."

"Let's just pray the killer doesn't know where he put them, either!" Lexie shook her head. "Okay, Jen. The gun's out. How about a knife?"

"There's a knife rack in the kitchen."

"Good. Let's get a knife for Tim and hide the rest. How about other weapons?"

Jennifer thought fast. "There's the fireplace poker. Tim could hit him with that. And I think I saw a baseball bat in the storage room."

"Those are all good ideas, but I think Tim'll have to settle for hitting him with his fist."

"Why?"

"Because your time's run out. Brian just woke up."

"Uh-oh!" Jennifer groaned as she glanced toward the group around the fireplace. Lexie was right. Brian had crawled out of his sleeping bag and as she watched, he unfolded the piece of Saddlepeak Lodge stationery. The jaws of the trap had sprung and they weren't even ready!

TWENTY

He almost laughed out loud as he watched Brian unfold the note. Thanks to Jennifer and Lexie, he knew exactly what was going to happen. When they'd gone over to the table in the alcove, he'd moved closer so that he could hear them. They hadn't been paying any attention to him. They'd been much too interested in discussing Brian's plan to trap the killer.

It was an interesting plan and he might have fallen into their trap if he hadn't been prepared. But he was always prepared and now he had the knowledge to outwit them. His father would have admired his cleverness . . . if it hadn't involved a series of murders. Dalton Prescott had one failing as a politician: He was a law-abiding man. He'd be shocked if he knew that his only son, Dale, didn't mind climbing over dead bodies on his road to success.

Dale put a concerned expression on his face. He was getting very good at hiding his true emotions. Miss Voelker's drama class had been helpful and he was turning into an excellent actor.

He would go far in the political world. Dale was sure of that. The important thing was to make sure he didn't get caught. He'd gotten away with killing Kelly and he'd keep right on getting away with murder. He was going to let them think that their silly plan had worked, and then he'd kill them all.

As he looked around the group, Dale felt a small tug of re-
morse. These were his friends and he liked them, but killing
them was the only way out of this jam. Their deaths would look
like a horrible tragedy, with one lone survivor. Dale Prescott
would manage to get out of Saddlepeak Lodge alive.

Dale almost smiled as he imagined the stories in the newspa-
pers. The headlines would read TRAGIC HALLOWEEN WEEKEND AT
SADDLEPEAK LODGE. The people in Foothill would talk about it
for years. They'd praise young Dale Prescott for trying so
valiantly to save his friends' lives. Of course, Dale wouldn't succeed, but that wouldn't matter. Everyone would hail him as a
local hero. It would be just the boost his future political career
would need, and he'd be the only one left alive who knew the
truth about what had happened this fateful Halloween night.

"I don't understand you, Brian." Tommy frowned deeply.
"How can you laugh about something like this?"

"I'm laughing because I don't think it's real. This writing's
different."

"Who do you think wrote it?" Lexie asked the question, even
though Jennifer had already told her the answer. She was playing along, just as Jennifer had told her to do.

"I don't know. It could have been Ronnie, or Susie, or
Cheryl. We were all joking around about the séances and the
notes. I'm going up to the manager's office to get the other
notes, and we'll compare the writing."

"You're going up there alone?" Tim sounded very worried. "I
don't think that's a good idea."

Dale nodded. "Tim's right. Maybe we should all go with you."

"That's not necessary." Brian turned and headed for the door.
"You guys stay here. I told you before, this note's not real. I'll
just grab the other ones and bring them down here."

"Do you think I should go with him, just in case?" Tommy
stood up.

"No." Jennifer shook her head. She was following the plan
they'd worked out with Brian. "I'm sure Brian's right. He examined the other notes and he's very good with handwriting. If this

note isn't like the others, Brian doesn't have anything to worry about."

"Okay . . . if you're sure." Tommy gave a deep sigh and sat down. But after a few moments, he stood up again. "It's beginning to get dark. I'm going outside for more firewood while there's still enough light to see. We're going to need it if we're planning to stay up all night."

Jennifer felt her heart jump to her throat as Tommy went out the door. Tim had promised Brian that he'd follow anyone who left the group, but they'd had no idea it would be his own twin brother!

"Stay here. I'll be right back." Tim got to his feet. "I'm going to see if Tommy needs some help."

Jennifer and Lexie exchanged anxious glances. Could Tommy be the killer? He'd been grief-stricken when Kelly had died. At least everyone had *thought* he'd been grief-stricken. How could Tommy have killed the girl he loved? And how about Zada? Why had he murdered her? And Melanie and Ronnie and Susie. They'd all been good friends since grade school! And then there was Cheryl, the girl Tommy had seemed to want to date. And Pete, everyone's favorite teacher. It just didn't make sense!

There was a crackle from the loudspeaker and Jennifer and Lexie looked up. But the speaker was silent again. No cry for help. No word from Brian. Was everything all right in the manager's office?

That was when it happened, something so unexpected that Jennifer almost gasped out loud. Dale got to his feet and headed for the door.

"Dale! Where are you going?" Lexie's voice was shaking.

"To the kitchen." Dale stopped with his hand on the door. "I'm hungry and I'm going to make myself a sandwich."

Jennifer was so nervous, it took her a moment to find her voice. "You . . . you don't have to do that. I'll make you a sandwich."

"No way." Dale laughed. "I believe in women's lib and I can make my own sandwich. Besides, I need to stretch my legs. Do you girls want me to bring you back something?"

Jennifer shook her head. "No, thank you. I'm not hungry. But do you really think it's safe to go off alone?"

"I'm not worried." Dale turned to Lexie. "How about you? Would you like a sandwich?"

Lexie shook her head. "Uh . . . no, thanks. I'm not hungry, either."

"How about some water? A soda? A cup of hot chocolate?" Both Jennifer and Lexie shook their heads and Dale gave them a friendly smile. "Okay. I'll be back in a couple of minutes."

The moment the door had closed behind him, Lexie rushed over to Jennifer. "Okay, Jen. What do we do *now*?"

"I don't know. We never talked about what to do if two people left."

"Well, we can't just sit here." Lexie sounded freaked. "We've got to do something!"

"You're absolutely right. Let's go, Lexie. Since Tim's busy following Tommy, we'll just have to follow Dale ourselves!"

Tim stayed in the shadows, several feet behind Tommy. This simply had to be a mistake! Tommy couldn't be the killer, but he had promised to follow anyone who left and he would. They'd have to talk when all this was over. He'd tell Tommy that he'd never really doubted him and Tommy would say that he would have done the same thing, in Tim's place. Then they'd laugh about it and there would be no hard feelings or trouble between . . .

No! This couldn't be happening! Tim's eyes widened as he watched Tommy pick up a club-sized log and turn around to leave the woodpile. His twin brother was carrying the log like a weapon and he was heading around to the side door of the lodge. What was Tommy *doing*?

Heart pounding fast, Tim followed his brother inside the lodge and up the back stairs. Tommy was going toward the manager's office and he was armed with a club!

Tim could barely believe his own eyes. He'd told Jennifer that he was worried about Tommy's state of mind, but he'd never expected it to get this bad. He didn't believe for a minute that Tommy had killed Kelly. That was completely impossible. But

Tommy had been devastated when Kelly had died, and he'd never gotten over his love for her. His twin brother had been grasping at straws. Because he'd wanted so much to see Kelly again, he'd talked himself into believing that their séance had worked. And then, when Brian had pulled his stunt with the notes from Kelly, it had pushed Tommy over the edge.

At first Tommy had been amused by the notes from Kelly, but he'd come to believe they were real. And then he'd agonized over those notes, wondering why Kelly hadn't contacted him. In his crazed mind, he must have thought that Kelly had rejected him and now he was taking his revenge. Tommy had killed everyone who'd received those fake notes from Kelly, and now he was after Brian.

It was painful to contemplate, but Tim had to face reality. His brother was carrying a club, a lethal weapon. And he was climbing the stairs to the manager's office to find Brian. Tommy was completely insane. That was the only explanation. His insane twin brother was going to kill Brian and he had to find a way to stop him!

Tim held his breath as Tommy hesitated at the door to the manager's office. Perhaps Tommy wouldn't go in. Perhaps there was some other reason he'd picked up the club from the woodpile. Perhaps . . . but no. Tommy was turning the doorknob and going into the manager's office!

There wasn't time to think. There was only time to act. And Tim acted quickly, using the element of surprise. Before Tommy could raise the club from his shoulder, he jumped his twin brother, grabbing the club and attempting to wrestle him to the floor.

"Hey!" Tommy whirled around with deadly intent, but when he saw who had jumped him, he dropped his club in shock. "Tim? Hey, bro . . . *what are you doing?*"

But before Tim could answer, something happened that made them all stop dead in their tracks. There was a tremendous crash of thunder and the generator went out, plunging the room into semidarkness.

*   *   *

Jennifer put her eye to the crack in the kitchen door and then pushed it open. "He's not here! We've lost him, Lexie!"

"He hasn't had time to go very far. Listen . . . maybe we can hear him."

Both girls stepped back into the hallway and listened. And then they heard it, the sound of footsteps on the stairs.

"Hold on a second." Lexie dashed back into the kitchen and pulled two knives from the butcher-block holder. She handed one to Jennifer and then she motioned to the stairs. "Now we're armed. Let's follow him!"

"Which way did he go?" Jennifer stopped when they reached the landing and leaned back to whisper. If Dale was the killer, she didn't want him to know that they were behind him.

"Up there!" Lexie whispered, too, as she pointed to the second set of stairs. "I can hear him on the third floor!"

Heart pounding in fear, Jennifer climbed to the third floor, Lexie close behind her. But when she reached the top of the stairs, she heard footsteps running toward the back staircase. "He's going down again! Let's go!"

When they reached the back stairs, they heard a door bang shut on the landing. Dale was on the mezzanine, the same floor as the manager's office!

Jennifer's legs were trembling as they tiptoed down the stairs and eased open the door. But before they could step out onto the mezzanine, there was a bolt of lightning, an ear-splitting crash of thunder, and a sizzling pop as the lights went out.

"Oh, my God!" Jennifer was so frightened she forgot to whisper. "What was *that*?"

"I think lightning just struck the generator. Come on, There's no time to waste!"

Jennifer tiptoed onto the mezzanine, peering into the gathering darkness. They hadn't gone more than a few feet before she saw a shadowy figure ahead in the semidarkness. He was bending over by one of the potted palm trees that were placed at regular intervals on the mezzanine.

"There he is!" Jennifer's voice was a frightened whisper.

"I see him. I think he's tying his shoe."

Jennifer's eyes were adjusting to the dim light and she could see him more clearly now. "What should we do?"

"Let's go around the other way. If we can make it to the manager's office before he gets there, we can warn Brian. He's a sitting duck in there!"

Jennifer followed Lexie as they reversed their direction. The mezzanine was built in a circle, overlooking the lobby, the dining room, and the library. When they passed the spot where Ronnie had fallen, Jennifer shuddered. If Dale had killed Ronnie, he would surely kill Brian if they didn't get to the manager's office in time.

Dale felt like shouting out in triumph. His plan had worked. He'd heard Tommy and Tim come up the back stairs and he knew they were in the manager's office with Brian. Now the girls would join them and soon he could put the second half of his plan into motion.

Jennifer and Lexie were just passing the section of the mezzanine that overlooked the library. He could hear their soft footsteps on the carpet. As soon as they went into the manager's office, he'd be ready to act.

Dale pulled the master key out of his pocket. This was a little like shooting fish in a barrel, but he didn't have time for any more games. He'd lock them all in the manager's office together. They didn't know there was no way to get out, once he'd locked the bolt from the outside. At first they'd think they were safe behind the closed door, but eventually they'd realize that they were prisoners. Doomed prisoners. Prisoners who would die before this Halloween night was over so they'd never be able to tell the story of how Dale Prescott had murdered them all.

Twenty-One

"You thought *I* was the killer?" Tommy was so shocked his mouth flew open. "Tim! You should have known better than that!"

"What was I supposed to think? You left the group right after Brian got that note and you took a club from the woodpile. And then you came up here to the manager's office!"

"You bet I did! Somebody had to protect Brian!"

Brian shook his head. "No, Tommy. It was all a trap to catch the killer. I sent myself that note so that we could lure him up here."

"You really thought it was *me*?" Tommy still looked shocked.

"I hoped it wasn't." Tim winced a little. He thought about lying to his brother and saying he'd never doubted him, but he just couldn't do it. "Sorry, Tommy . . . I know I shouldn't have suspected you, but I figured you'd gone off the deep end. And you were the only one to leave the group."

"I guess that's true." Tommy began to grin. "So you thought I was going to murder old Brian here and you jumped me. For a little guy, you pack some muscle, bro."

"Thanks." Tim grinned back. Tommy wasn't mad at him and he felt very relieved.

"Hey . . . we're forgetting something!" Brian spoke up.

Tim and Tommy turned and spoke in unison. "What?"

"The killer. It's got to be Dale, unless you buy that seventh-person theory. And I don't."

"Me, neither." Tommy shook his head. "I just said that to give us some time to . . ."

"Oh, my God! The girls are down there with Dale!" Tim ran for the door, but the moment he turned the knob, the door crashed open and Jennifer and Lexie tumbled in. At first Jennifer didn't even notice Tim and Tommy. She just ran over to Brian and threw her arms around him.

"Brian! Thank God you're all right!" Jennifer hugged him tightly. "Dale's the killer and he'll be here any minute! Do you have any weapons?"

"I've got two. And they're right over there!"

Brian was grinning as he pointed, and Jennifer whirled around. And when she saw Tommy and Tim, she threw herself in Tim's arms and started to cry. "I was so worried about you! I was worried about everybody! And now we're safe. We're all safe right here!"

Dale was humming a little tune as he went down the stairs. It would take them a while to realize they were locked in. He wished he could see the expressions on their faces when they realized it, but he couldn't afford that luxury. He had things to do and places to go, and the first place was the walk-in cooler. He'd been the one to suggest that they store the bodies there. And now he would move them all and place them in various rooms of the lodge. It had to look natural or someone might get suspicious and start asking questions. After being so very careful thus far, he'd be negligent if he took a silly chance like that.

The cooler was kept at a constant temperature and Dale shivered as he stepped inside. They were all there and he gave a little wave at he faced his former friends.

"You first." Dale dragged Susie's blanket-wrapped body into the kitchen and took off the wrapping. Then he propped it up on the counter, right next to an open box of doughnuts. "Maybe I did you a favor, Suze. Now you don't have to diet anymore. Eat all the chocolate-covered doughnuts you want!"

Dale was laughing as he went back inside the cooler again. Pete was next and he dragged his body into the library, unwrapping it and putting in a nice reading chair. "Here you go, Pete. Pick any book you like. You told us you loved to read."

"Hey . . . Cheryl." Dale dragged her body out of the cooler. "Where shall I put you?"

It took a minute, but then he had it, and he was smiling as he dragged Cheryl's body over to the service elevator. He unwrapped her and carried her in.

"There you go, Cheryl." Dale pressed the button for the top floor and laughed as he closed the doors manually. "There's no power right now, but this is your last chance to move up in the world."

Ronnie was next and Dale wasn't smiling as he dragged his body into the lobby. He'd liked Ronnie a lot and he'd been a good friend. Dale was thoughtful as he unwrapped Ronnie's blanket and put him on one of the leather couches. What final thing could he do for Ronnie? It took a moment, but then Dale had an idea that made him laugh out loud, all the way to the cooler.

"You wanted a girl, Ronnie." Dale was puffing with exertion as he carried Melanie's body into the lobby. "And you always said that Melanie was pretty. Well . . . here she is, and I can guarantee that she won't leave you for another guy!"

Dale unwrapped Melanie's body and lifted her up, right next to Ronnie. It looked like they were nestled together on the leather couch, and that made him feel good.

"How about you, Zada?" Dale hurried back to the cooler for Zada's body. It was the last one and he was exhausted by the time he'd dragged her out. "I didn't know you, so I'm not really sure what I can do for you."

It took some thought, but at last Dale had it. He carried Zada to the séance table, unwrapped her, and propped her up in a chair. The candles were still on the table and Dale almost lit one, until he remembered. Zada would have to conduct her séance without an open flame. "Go ahead, Zada. Now that you're dead, you ought to be able to contact one of your fellow spirits."

When he went back to the kitchen to close the cooler door, Dale realized that his stomach was growling. He'd missed breakfast his morning and that meant he'd done all this work on an empty stomach. "Mind if I have a doughnut, Suze? Or do you want them all?"

Dale was grinning as he took a chocolate-covered doughnut out of Susie's box. She wouldn't mind. She'd always been generous about sharing her food.

As Dale munched, he had a very disturbing thought. Tim was an A student at the top of his class and the rest of them were no slouches, either. What if they figured out a way to escape, and they told everyone what he had done? But they couldn't escape from a locked room with security bars on the window. There was nothing they could do, no way they could spoil his perfect plan.

"You can't escape! I'm smarter than any of you!" Dale laughed in satisfaction. And that thought made him feel so good, he ate another of Susie's doughnuts.

"Okay. We're ready." Tim gave Jennifer one last hug. "We're going to find him and capture him."

Jennifer managed a smile, but she felt more like crying. They'd discussed it all and there was no other choice. The boys had gathered their weapons: a sharp letter opener for Brian, a heavy brass vase for Tim, and Tommy's club.

"Stay here and wait." Tommy put his arm around Lexie's shoulders. "And don't open the door to anyone except us."

"We won't." Lexie hugged him back. And then she pointed to the two knives she'd brought from the kitchen. "Don't worry, Tommy. If he tries to break in here, we'll carve him up like a Thanksgiving turkey!"

"Good girl!"

As Tommy hugged Lexie, Jennifer smiled. Perhaps her dream of a best friend who was also her sister-in-law might come true. But only if the boys captured Dale and got back here safely.

"Ready?" Tim motioned to Brian and Tommy. "Let's go!"

Jennifer watched as they moved toward the door. Her heart

wanted Tim to stay, but her mind knew that they had to defeat Dale. It was like Tim had said. Dale wouldn't just leave them here. He'd try to kill them and they had to capture him before he could make his next move.

"Good hunting, Tim." Jennifer put a smile on her face. Even though she'd never experienced it firsthand, she thought she knew how girlfriends and wives must feel, sending their men off to war. But Tim didn't leave. He just stood there at the door, turning the knob and pushing against it.

"What's the matter?" Lexie sounded worried.

"I don't know." Tim turned around with a frown on his face. "The door won't open."

"It must be stuck." Tommy put his shoulder to the door, but it wouldn't budge. "This is weird!"

"Let me see." Brian moved up to the door, but instead of trying to force it open, he got down on his hands and knees and examined the lock. When he turned back to look at them, he was scowling. "Dale locked it from the outside. There's another bolt. I can see it. And it's encased in a steel sleeve. I hate to say it, but there's no way in hell we can open it from this side."

Dale was humming as he worked at the huge gas furnace by the light of a powerful flashlight. He'd resented it at the time, but now he was grateful that his uncle had asked him to supervise the men when they'd installed it. He'd asked them about safety and they'd told him that there was only one way to make the system back up. Of course they hadn't known they were providing him with the tools for murder.

The red button on the furnace was the manual override and the blue button would turn on the gas. There was an automatic shutoff if the pilot light was out, but he'd figured out how to defeat that. The gas would hiss out, seeping into every nook and cranny of the lodge, building up until the deadly concentration was at its peak.

Dale frowned slightly as he thought about his friends. When they smelled the gas and realized what was happening, they'd open the window. But that would only buy them a little time.

There was no escape from the manager's office. His uncle had installed security bars after someone had tried to break in last summer. Eventually, they'd all lose consciousness, even if they crowded together at the open window. And that was when he'd execute the final stage of his plan.

He'd climb the hill in back of the lodge with his uncle's high-powered rifle. And when the time was right, he'd fire a round into the kitchen. There was plenty of metal in there with the stainless steel countertops, the restaurant-sized stove, the huge refrigerator, and the ceiling rack that held pots and pans. His shot was bound to create a spark. His friends would be dead by then, or at least unconscious. They wouldn't feel a thing when Saddlepeak Lodge blew up like a giant bomb.

Dale smiled as he took out the notebook in his pocket and glanced at his calculations. He owed the success of his plan to Brian, who had tutored him in math. He'd figured out the number of cubic feet and the answer had told him how long it would take for the fumes to reach peak concentration. Once he turned on the gas, his friends would have twenty minutes to live.

He reached out and touched the red button for the manual override. It was time to start the countdown. But then he remembered one other thing that Brian had taught him. It wouldn't hurt to go over his calculations once more. This was even more important than a final exam and Brian had told him to always check his work.

Dale walked over to the janitor's worktable and sat down on a stool. One final check, one more opportunity to discover any mistakes. When that was complete he would be fully prepared to become a local hero.

Twenty-Two

"I think it's safe to assume he plans to kill us." Brian sat behind the desk. "Does everyone agree?"

One by one, they nodded. Dale had killed all the rest of their friends and it was a safe assumption. Then Tommy gave a short, little laugh. "Okay, Brian . . . tell us something we don't know."

"All right. I will." Brian sat up a little straighter. "He knows about the dead bolt and the security bars on the window. He thinks we're trapped up here, and that might just buy us some time."

"To do what?" Jennifer frowned.

"To plan our escape." Tim turned to face them. He'd been standing at the window and he motioned to Tommy. "Take a look at these bars. They're attached to the wooden frame and I think we might have some termite damage."

Tommy hurried over to the window to look. And when he turned back, he was grinning. "Tim's right. That wood looks rotten. If we dig it out a little with those knives you girls brought, I think we can remove it."

"And the bars would come off with the frame?" Lexie looked hopeful.

"Maybe . . . if they're not set in concrete."

"What are we waiting for?" Brian pushed back his chair and grabbed the knives. "Let's give it a try."

It didn't take long to loosen the frame. The wood was riddled with termite holes. But just as Tommy was about to pull it out, Jennifer ran over to stop him.

"Not yet! It's going to make noise and we can't let Dale hear us. If he knows what we're doing, he'll come in here to kill us!"

"Right," Tim said. "We know the frame's loose and we know we can remove it. That's enough for now. Let's figure out how we're going to get out this window. It looks like it's at least twenty feet to the ground."

"We'll make a rope!" Lexie grabbed one of the lace curtains and pulled it down. "These curtains are perfect."

Jennifer turned around to look at her in shock. "But the curtains are lace. They'll tear."

"No, they won't. We'll twist them up and tie a knot every foot. Get the other curtain, Jen. I'll twist and tie the knots."

"I hate to raise this question, but do you know how to tie knots?" Brian looked concerned.

"Of course I do. I was a Girl Scout. I earned a badge for tying knots."

They all watched as Lexie fashioned the rope. When she was through, it looked so sturdy that even Tommy was satisfied. But after Lexie had attached it to the heavy oak cabinet next to the window, everyone could see that it would be much too short.

"Don't worry. It'll be fine." Tommy looked at the rope and then he glanced down at the side of the building. "If we dangle from the end, it'll be less than a ten-foot drop."

Jennifer reached out to steady herself on the edge of the desk. There was no way she could jump ten feet. She wasn't even sure she could climb down the rope in the first place! But this wasn't the time to tell the others about her fear of heights.

"What's our plan?" Brian turned to Tim.

"It's very simple. Tommy'll pull out the window frame. He's the strongest one here. Then he'll climb down the rope and jump to the ground. Lexie will go next and when she jumps, Tommy'll catch her."

Lexie nodded and Tim handed her the keys to the Jeep. "The minute Lexie hits the ground, she'll run to the Jeep and drive it over to the window. Brian'll be the next one out. Then Jennifer. And then me."

"No!" Jennifer thought fast. She couldn't let them know that she was afraid to climb down the rope. Tim would be brave and foolish, and he'd refuse to leave without her. "Let me be last, Tim. If you go first and you catch me, Tommy can get in the driver's seat. Then we'll be all ready to go."

"Okay, that'll work." Tim smiled at her. "Are we ready?"

"Almost. Is there any way you can play some loud music, Brian? We don't want Dale to hear us."

"I've been thinking about that and I've got something better than loud music. Miss Voelker videoed last year's spring play and I've got the audio of Kelly's part right here. I pieced the words together and I used it that first night at the séance. Remember how freaked Dale got?"

Tommy clapped him on the back. "That's perfect! I just wish we could play it over the speakers. Then Dale could hear it all over the lodge."

"We can," Brian said. "The sound system has a battery backup. All I have to do is flick the switch. There's only one problem. The audio I have runs a minute max. I can loop it so it repeats, but there's no time to piece together anymore."

"That doesn't matter." Tim sounded confident. "We'll be out of here before Dale realizes that it's a recording."

Lexie started to cough. "We'd better hurry! I smell gas and I think Dale's trying to asphyxiate us."

Jennifer's face turned pale. She'd been smelling a strange odor, too. Lexie was right. It was definitely gas.

"Okay, let's go!" Brian pressed the button on sound system and Kelly's voice started to play at a deafening volume. And then things started to happen very fast.

Tommy grabbed the bars and pulled out the window frame with one giant effort. He tossed it aside like it was a matchstick and climbed out to slide down the rope. Tim was acting as their leader and the moment he heard his brother land, he motioned to Lexie. "Go, Lexie! Go!"

Jennifer held her breath as Lexie went over the sill and out into the darkness. She heard Tommy grunt as he caught her, and then it was Brian's turn.

Brian didn't hesitate. He just climbed out, grabbed the rope, and slid down. Tommy grunted again and Tim motioned to Jennifer. "Go, Jen."

"No!" Jennifer felt the panic begin to start. "I told you before. You first!"

"You're sure? I saw you on that ladder. I know you're afraid of heights. You've got to promise that you won't choke up on me!"

"I won't. I promise!" Jennifer tried to keep her voice from shaking as she said the words Tim wanted to hear. She knew she couldn't climb down the rope, not in a million years, not even if she died up here. But she knew that Tim wouldn't leave her if he had any doubts, and she had to make sure that he got to safety.

And then Tim was gone and she leaned out the window, watching as he slid down the rope. He held out his arms, and the tears ran down her cheeks as she gave a little wave. "I can't, Tim! I just can't do it!"

Tim was shouting. The tape of Kelly's voice was so loud she couldn't hear him, but she knew what he was saying. He was begging her to climb out the window and jump into his arms.

"Go without me! Please, Tim! Go! Now!"

But Tim didn't move. He just stood there holding out his arms. And then she heard it, the sound of glass breaking on the floor below. There was an almost inhuman bellow as Dale reacted to Kelly's voice, but it wouldn't be long before he figured it out. When he did, he'd come up here to stop the tape. And they'd still be out there, waiting for her! If she didn't conquer her fear and climb out the window, Mousie Larkin would be responsible for killing them all!

I NEED TO TALK TO YOU. I HAVE A SECRET AND I MUST TELL YOU. JUST YOU. YOU ARE THE ONLY ONE I CAN TRUST. YOU ARE THE ONLY ONE WHO CAN KNOW HOW MUCH PAIN HE CAUSED ME. YOU ARE THE ONLY ONE WHO CAN KNOW THE HORRIBLE THINGS HE DID TO ME. HE KILLED ME! HE KILLED ME!

Dale let out another bellow of pure rage and threw the oval mirror against the river rock fireplace as hard as he could. Kelly was here! The séance had worked! She was screaming, screeching, accusing him of killing her!

I NEED TO TALK TO YOU. I HAVE A SECRET AND I MUST TELL YOU. JUST YOU. YOU ARE THE ONLY ONE I CAN TRUST. YOU ARE THE ONLY ONE WHO CAN KNOW HOW MUCH PAIN HE CAUSED ME. YOU ARE THE ONLY ONE WHO CAN KNOW THE HORRIBLE THINGS HE DID TO ME. HE KILLED ME! HE KILLED ME!

Dale stopped, a heavy glass vase in his hand. And then, even though he wanted to block out the words that Kelly was screaming, he made himself listen very carefully.

I NEED TO TALK TO YOU. I HAVE A SECRET AND I MUST TELL YOU. JUST YOU. YOU ARE THE ONLY ONE I CAN TRUST. YOU ARE THE ONLY ONE WHO CAN KNOW HOW MUCH PAIN HE CAUSED ME. YOU ARE THE ONLY ONE WHO CAN KNOW THE HORRIBLE THINGS HE DID TO ME. HE KILLED ME! HE KILLED ME!

Dale's hand was shaking as he set down the vase. Kelly was still screaming about how he'd killed her, but she was saying the same things, over and over again. Why? What did it mean?

The moment he thought about it, he had the answer. It was a tape. They'd put a tape of Kelly's voice on the loudspeakers to trick him. The tape was looped so it would keep playing, but he'd figured it out. He knew it was only a recording. Kelly wasn't really here. She wasn't actually accusing him of anything. Kelly was dead and buried and he'd been listening to a recording of her voice.

Even though he knew he was right, the recording was still making him crazy. Dale put his hands over his ears, but that didn't help. Nothing helped. Kelly's voice was coming from the speakers and it was so loud, he couldn't think. And he had to think clearly so that he could finish his work and get out of here.

He climbed up and pulled the wires on the speaker. But he could still hear Kelly's voice. They'd hooked up the recording to the PA system and he had to stop it!

*   *   *

Jennifer forced herself to climb out on the ledge. Her knees were shaking and she felt like fainting, but she knew she had to go down that rope before Dale came through the door. She shut her eyes and grabbed the rope. There was no way she dared to look down, not even at Tim's loving face and his outstretched arms, and the anxious eyes of her good, loyal friends. And then she began to climb down.

It seemed to take forever, hand over hand, slipping down to the first knot, and the second, and the third. There were seven knots and she counted each one of them until finally she was hanging in midair at the very last knot of the rope.

"Jump, Jen! Now!"

It was Tim's voice. She heard it clearly even though the sound of Kelly's voice was still loud in her ears. And she made her shaking hands relax, releasing her hold on the rope. As she fell through the air, Jennifer experienced a floating sensation. It was almost as if she were wrapped in a cocoon of love and trust and faith. And then she was cradled in Tim's loving arms and she reached up to wrap her arms around his neck as he ran with her to the Jeep. She'd done it! She'd conquered her fear! And now they would all be safe!

The windows were down in the Jeep and they heard Kelly's voice as Tommy drove away. *NOW I'M GOING TO TAKE MY REVENGE! YOU MURDERED ME, DALE!*

"Nooooo!" Dale's voice came out in an anguished howl as he unlocked the door and barreled through. He had to shut it off! The sound of Kelly's voice was driving him crazy!

But where was the switch? The room was dark, as dark as a tomb. He had to shut it off, but he couldn't find it unless he had light.

That was when Dale remembered that his uncle's manager smoked cigars. He always kept a fancy gold lighter on the desk and Dale felt around in the darkness, trying to locate it. He smiled as his fingers touched the cold metal surface.

Dale didn't stop to think. He just flicked on the lighter, creating a spark and then an open flame. Almost immediately, there was a tremendous explosion that rocked the very foundation of the lodge. The fireball it created sent flames that seemed to shoot up to the sky itself. And Kelly's voice came to an abrupt and very timely end.

Dale didn't know that Kelly's voice had stopped playing. He wasn't around to enjoy the silence he'd given his life to create. Dale was now engulfed in a much greater silence, a total stillness that was deep and unending, the perpetual silence of death.

Epilogue

They were all sitting in the Jeep, huddled under blankets to keep warm. They had been parked there all night, waiting for daybreak and hoping that the bulldozers they heard in the distance would finally break through the rock slide.

Lexie tapped Jennifer on the shoulder. "I've been thinking about it, Jen. You were meshuga to wait so long. I thought you'd never climb out that window!"

"Neither did I." Jennifer sighed. "I just kept thinking about how far down it was and telling myself, *vey iz mir, vey iz mir.* And through it all I was worrying about whether the tape would fool Dale, but he was an even bigger schnook than I thought."

"At least you finally showed some chutzpah! I'm proud of you, Jen!"

"Me, too." Tommy grinned at Jennifer and then he turned to Lexie. "Those words were Yiddish, right?"

Lexie nodded and Tommy started to smile. "I know one Yiddish word. It's *tuchus*!"

"*What?*" Lexie's face turned bright red. "Where did you hear *that*?"

"We were fixing the roof on a guy's house last summer, and I heard him tell his wife that he was crazy about her *tuchus*. Is it some kind of food?"

Lexie couldn't keep a straight face. She laughed so hard, tears of mirth ran down her cheeks. "I'm not going to tell you. But I think they had a very good marriage!"

They were all laughing, imagining the worst, when Tim held up his hand. "I think the bulldozer's about to break through. It sounds much closer now."

"Then it's time to make a decision." Jennifer turned to face the group. "People are going to ask questions about what happened up at the lodge. What do you think we should say?"

There was another silence, while they all considered it carefully. They'd talked about it after they'd heard the explosion and seen the giant fireball light up the sky. The lodge had blown up and Dale was dead. Should they tell the authorities exactly what had happened? Or would it be kinder to all the families if they thought their loved ones had died in the explosion?

Brian had raised another point. If they told everyone that Dale was a serial killer, his father's political career could be ruined. Dalton Prescott was a good man and he made an excellent senator. If people knew the truth about his son, they might not vote for him.

"We've had all night to think about it." Tim took a deep breath. "Let's make our decision. Brian? You go first."

Brian cleared his throat. "I think we should say it was an accident and we don't know how it happened. There was a big explosion and we were lucky to be outside at the time."

"Sounds good to me," Tommy agreed. "It's clean, it's simple, and there's no evidence left to prove us wrong. I keep thinking about Kelly's family. They're finally beginning to get over her death. If we tell them that she was murdered, it's going to cause them even more grief."

"I agree with Tommy," Lexie said. "And don't forget that we're not actually lying. The lodge did blow up with everyone else inside."

"Jen?"

"I agree. If we tell everything that happened, no one will believe us anyway. It's so weird, it sounds like we made it up."

"Okay. It's unanimous." Tim smiled at Jennifer. "But we

have to make a pact. It'll be our secret, just the five of us. And if we need to talk about it, we'll be there for each other."

"Agreed." Jennifer reached out to put her hand on Tim's. And then Tommy put his hand on hers, and Lexie put her hand on Tommy's, and Brian reached out to touch Lexie's hand to seal their pact.

"I'm really glad we decided to say it was accidental." Brian gave a big sigh of relief. "I sure wouldn't want to try to explain that audio!"

Lexie turned to look at Brian in surprise. "What's to explain? You told us how you made it. Miss Voelker videoed the spring play and you just pieced Kelly's words together."

"That's true, but it's not what I mean. Do you remember the last thing Kelly said as we drove away?"

"I'll never forget it." Jennifer shivered. "It was really chilling. Kelly said, *Now I'm going to take my revenge. You murdered me, Dale!*"

"That's right. And the minute I heard her, I started to believe that your crazy séances really worked. It practically proves that Kelly was protecting us from the other side."

Jennifer frowned. Brian had teased them about their séances before, but this time he sounded totally serious. "I don't understand, Brian. I was in the spring play. And I know that Kelly used all of those words in her lines."

"You're wrong, Jen. Kelly used every word except one. On the tape she said, *You murdered me, Dale.* And there was no character in the spring play named Dale!"

Slay Bells

This book is for Trudi Nash.
With special thanks to: John, Rudy, & Amber,
and my personal Santa Claus.

Prologue

Winter in Minnesota was beautiful. Lazy snowflakes drifted down outside the window, covering the dirty slush in the parking lot with a lacy blanket of pristine white. The cars were dusted with what looked like powdered sugar, and the reflected lights from the Christmas trees by the main entrance made the snow glisten with brilliant flashes of color. The scene was worthy of a Christmas card, but he deliberately sat down with his back to the view. It was two weeks before Christmas, and Christmas made him sad.

The Christmas music didn't help. There were speakers everywhere, even in the employees' lounge, and the tape had been running, over and over, all day. It was intended to put the employees in a cheerful mood for tomorrow's grand opening, but it wasn't working for him.

There was a time when he'd loved Christmas carols. He'd even gone caroling when he was in the high school chorus. But now the familiar music reminded him of last Christmas, the Christmas his grandmother had died. He could still remember the paralyzing fear he'd felt when they'd carried her off to the hospital. But he hadn't shown that fear. He'd been determined to be strong for his grandfather.

His lunch break was almost over. In less than ten minutes, he'd have to put a smile on his face and join the rest of the employees. He leaned back in his chair, trying to relax, and thought about the way this area used to look, when his grandparents had owned the land. He was sitting smack dab in the middle of what used to be his grandmother's vegetable garden, and the bedroom he'd used, when he'd stayed with his grandparents, had been right about where the Christmas tree at the center of the mall now stood. Those had been happy times, times he remembered with joy. He'd spent a lot of time at the farm, and he'd learned to love everything about farming. His parents thought he was crazy, but he'd always said he wanted to take over the land, once he'd graduated from college, and turn Gramps and Grandma's farm into a real showplace.

His hands unconsciously clenched into fists as he thought about how the Crossroads Corporation had bought the farm. They'd descended like vultures, a week after his grandmother's funeral. He hadn't been there. He'd left the day before, to go back to school. The slick-talking real estate agent had taken advantage of his grief-stricken grandfather, and convinced him that they were making him a wonderful deal. Poor Gramps, who'd been showing the first symptoms of Alzheimer's, had believed him and signed on the dotted line.

When he'd found out about it, he'd tried to stop the sale. But Gramps had been the sole owner of the land, and he hadn't yet been diagnosed with Alzheimer's. Now, almost a year later, Gramps was in a nursing home. Alzheimer's was usually a cruel disease, but in Gramps's case, it was a kindness. Gramps would never realize how badly the Crossroads Corporation had cheated him. But his grandson did. And it was eating him up inside, just like the cancer that had killed his grandmother.

Five minutes left. He got up to pour himself a cup of coffee, and leaned back in his chair again. Under any other circumstances, he might have enjoyed working at the Crossroads Mall. It was a beautiful building, and the surrounding countryside was gorgeous. The mall was built at the intersection of three state highways, and it served three Minnesota cities. Prairie Falls, twelve miles to the east, was the home of Prairie College. Students at Prairie would be sure to shop at the mall, and they made up a large proportion of the area's population. And Portersville, fifteen miles to the west, was the county seat. Since people would have to drive right past the mall to go to the county courthouse, they'd stop in to do their shopping. Two Rivers, at the apex of the triangle, attracted plenty of tourists. It was Shane Winter's hometown, and Shane had become one of the hottest new stars in Hollywood. Just to prove that he hadn't forgotten his Minnesota roots, Shane was coming out to the Crossroads Mall to promote the opening, and that meant the tourists would come here, too.

He turned around to glance out the window again, and his heart caught in his throat as he recognized the big pine tree they'd decorated at the edge of the road. It was his favorite tree, the great grand-daddy of all pines. He could remember crawling under its massive branches in the winter, and peeking out at the icy world. It was always dry and cozy under the big pine tree. Its branches were so thick, no amount of snow could reach the ground.

Tears came to his eyes and he blinked them back. The pine tree wasn't his any longer. It belonged to the Crossroads Mall. And the mall had ruined everything. The flowers his grandmother had planted around the house were covered over with asphalt, and the grove of apple trees that Gramps had grafted had been bulldozed to make way for the mall garage. The farm he'd loved was completely gone.

Gramps had always promised that the family farm would be his someday. He'd even written it into his will. Of course that didn't count for much now. There was no way he could reclaim his inheritance unless the mall failed, and the property was auctioned off to the highest bidder.

"Fat chance!" He said the words aloud, and gave a bitter laugh. People were eager to find ways to spend their money and this mall was the biggest shopping center in central Minnesota. The multi-plex movie theater would do a booming business, and the beautiful restaurant on the upper level would become *the* place to go and be seen. There was no way the mall could fail. Air-conditioned in the hot, muggy summer, and heated in the stark, frigid winter, the Crossroads Mall would provide a pleasant environment that everyone would enjoy. It was bound to be a huge success, and there wasn't a damn thing he could do about it.

Despair washed over him, and he gave a deep sigh as he listened to the next song on the tape. It was a children's song, "Santa Claus Is Comin' To Town."

> *You better watch out; you better not cry;*
> *Better not pout; I'm telling you why:*
> *Santa Claus is comin' to town.*
>
> *He's making a list and checking it twice;*
> *Gonna find out who's naughty and nice:*
> *Santa Claus is comin' to town.*
>
> *He sees you when you're sleepin';*
> *He knows when you're awake;*
> *He knows if you've been bad or good;*
> *So be good for goodness sake.*

He raised his eyebrows as he listened to the words. He'd never really noticed it before, but the Santa in the song was vengeful. The first line was a warning. *You better watch out.* It sent a clear message to everyone who listened. Santa would get you if you weren't good. Santa saw you, and he put your name on a list. If you were good, you got presents. But if you were bad, Santa would . . . what? Punish you?

Suddenly, he had an inspiration. Perhaps he should be Santa this year, and punish the people who'd hurt his grandparents. It was an intriguing idea, and he began to smile for the first time today. It wasn't a nice smile, but Santa didn't have to be nice. Did he?

One

Diana Connelly caught sight of her reflection in the plate glass window of the Alpine Ski Shop, and stopped to stare. She'd pulled her hair back this morning, and fashioned it into what she'd thought was a smart, sophisticated twist at the back of her neck. During the day, wisps of reddish blond hair had escaped, and now there were tight little curls all over her head. With her bright blue eyes, and light skin with freckles, she looked like Little Orphan Annie.

A good-humored giggle escaped Diana's lips. She often laughed at herself. She knew she should brush her hair before anyone else caught sight of her, but she'd left her purse in a locker in the employees' lounge, and she didn't want to walk all the way to the other end of the mall. There was only one thing to do. Diana pulled off the band that held the rest of her hair in place, and let it spring loose to tumble down in a curling mass around her shoulders.

Diana gave one more glance at her reflection, and shrugged. There really wasn't any solution for her curly hair. She'd spent a fortune on products that promised to tame unruly hair, but none of them seemed to work on her. She had inherited her grandmother's hair, and that was scary. Grannie had a permanent perm, and she always looked as if she'd stuck her finger in an electrical socket.

There was a bench in front of Elaine's Boutique, and Diana limped over to sit down. When she'd accepted this temporary Christmas job, they hadn't told her she'd have to dress up in green tights and a green jerkin, and skip around the mall all day! If Diana had known that she was going to be one of Santa's elves, she might have reconsidered. The mall was huge, and Diana knew exactly how huge. Her father owned the construction company that had built the mall, and she'd spent all last summer as his assistant, making sure everything was completed according to code.

As she kicked off her shoes to massage her aching feet, Diana spotted Cindy Swanson, her college roommate, walking toward her from the other end of the mall. Actually, walking wasn't the correct word for what Cindy was doing. Hobbling would be more like it. But seeing Cindy hobble made Diana feel much better. Cindy was a physical education major, and she was always giving Diana grief about not exercising enough.

"Brutal!" Cindy sighed as she sank down on the bench. "Sue missed her calling. She should have been a Marine drill instructor."

Diana laughed. Sue Langer was the head cheerleader at Prairie College, and she'd just put the elves through a grueling rehearsal. It hadn't been easy to skip around the mall three times with smiles on their faces.

"Sue's really in great shape." Cindy looked very envious. "I watched her the whole way and she didn't even break a sweat."

Diana nodded, and then she parroted the old adage her grannie had taught her. "Women don't sweat. Horses sweat, men perspire, and women glow."

"Well, I'm definitely glowing." Cindy laughed and her whole face lit up. For a moment, she looked very pretty. Cindy wasn't at all beautiful in the traditional sense of the word. Her light brown hair, which was really very nice, was cut so short, it made her face look thin. Her deep brown eyes were set just a little too wide, but her nose was perfect and she had the kind of cheekbones models would kill for. Cindy was petite. She wore a size three, and she didn't weigh more than a hundred pounds.

But Cindy knew how to intimidate people. She had a personality that made all of her friends treat her like a live hand-grenade.

Cindy was a no-nonsense person, and she always said exactly what she was thinking. If she didn't like something you did or said, she told you. Straight out. Right then and there. With no pulled punches. Diana knew that Cindy didn't mean to hurt anyone by her sharp comments, but sometimes, she did.

Diana had been intimidated, at first. Cindy had looked and acted like a very tough person. That misconception had lasted for almost two weeks, and it might have lasted much longer if they hadn't found the kittens.

Cindy and Diana had been walking home from class when they'd heard small, crying noises coming from a neighborhood dumpster. They'd lifted the lid and found two very young kittens, curled up in a pitiful ball, inside. Cindy hadn't said a word. She'd just piled up a couple of broken cinder blocks to stand on, and jumped in to rescue them. Then she'd taken them home, and smuggled them into their "no pets" building.

The kittens had been too young to eat solid food, but Cindy had mixed up a concoction she'd said would work, and she'd fed them every three hours with an eyedropper. Naturally, Diana had asked if she could help, and Cindy had taught her exactly what to do. When the kittens were old enough to get along on their own, Cindy had canvassed the neighborhood to find a home for them, refusing to give them away separately since they were so cute together. And she'd actually cried when she'd handed them over to a family who'd promised to love them and take good care of them.

The episode with the kittens had opened Diana's eyes, and she'd realized that Cindy's sharp tongue was a defense against her very sentimental nature. Cindy cried when she saw a sad movie, and she got all mushy when she saw a couple holding hands. Kids got to her, too. Diana had caught her cooing to babies, and reading stories to the kids in the neighborhood. It was a side of Cindy that very few people saw, but Diana was hoping that someday Cindy would drop her tough act, and let everyone see what a sweet, caring person she was.

Cindy waved a hand in front of Diana's eyes to get her attention. "Why are you staring at me with that sappy expression on your face?"

"Oh . . . uh . . ." Diana was ready to give an excuse, but then she decided to be honest, instead. "I was just thinking about the kittens, and what a nice person you are."

"Shh!" Cindy glanced around to make sure there was no one close enough to hear. "Don't blow my cover, huh? As far as the rest of the world's concerned, I'm a bitch in training."

"But . . . why?" Diana was puzzled.

"It's easier that way. It gives me an excuse for not dating."

Diana frowned. "Sorry, but I don't get it."

"If I'm a bitch, everyone'll think that's the reason the guys don't ask me out. I don't want them to find out the real reason."

"What real reason?" Diana was still puzzled.

"I'm ugly." Cindy looked upset. "That's the real reason I never have any dates."

"But you're not. You're very pretty when you smile. If you'd smile more often, maybe . . ."

"No way!" Cindy interrupted her. "If I smile all the time, I can't be a bitch. Don't you see, Diana? It's a lot better to be an unpopular bitch than it is to be an unpopular ugly girl."

Diana opened her mouth, and then she closed it again. Cindy's logic left a lot to be desired, but this wasn't the time for a lecture. It was best to change the subject. "Speaking of bitches . . . I haven't seen Heather. Isn't she here?"

"She's here."

Cindy's eyes began to glitter dangerously, and Diana winced. Cindy hated her older brother's ex-girlfriend. Heather Perkins was a junior, and she'd been dating Cindy's brother, Jay, since the beginning of the school year. Back then, Jay had been the star quarterback of the Prairie College football team, and Heather had attended every game. Everything had been great while Jay had been playing, but he'd been injured in late October, and the coach had taken him out for the rest of the season.

The minute Heather had heard that Jay was benched, she'd dumped him for the new quarterback, a senior who drove a new

Porsche. Both Cindy and Diana agreed that Jay was better off without Heather. She was a spoiled, rich girl who'd only been going with him for his celebrity status. But Jay had been hurt by the breakup, and that had made both girls fume. Then, just before Thanksgiving, everything had turned around again.

Heather's new boyfriend had bombed during his first two games. The college paper had called him Mr. Velcro, because he couldn't seem to get rid of the ball before he was sacked. He'd been replaced by a walk-on freshman who'd managed to pull off a miracle. Prairie State College had won a bowl bid, and they'd be playing on New Year's Day. Of course everyone knew that they didn't have a prayer of winning, not without a seasoned quarterback.

That was when the second miracle had happened. Jay's injury had turned out to be less serious than everyone had thought, and the coach had told the college paper that Jay would be fully recovered in time for the big bowl game. Now Heather was interested in Jay again, and Diana and Cindy were sure that the only reason Heather had taken a job at the mall was to try to win him back.

Cindy's eyes were still glittering and Diana shivered. Cindy despised Heather with a passion. "There's something you're not telling me, right?"

"Right." Cindy nodded. "Let's just say it helps to have a daddy who owns a big piece of the mall."

Diana immediately caught Cindy's drift. "Heather's not an elf like us?"

Cindy didn't say anything. She just gave a very unladylike snort.

"I take it that's a no." Diana sighed. Of course Heather wasn't an elf. With her daddy's connections, Heather could get a much better job. "Is she working in one of the stores?"

"Are you serious?! Daddy's little girl wouldn't let her lily-white fingers touch a cash register. That's too much like real work."

"I guess you're right." Diana nodded. "What's she going to be doing, then?"

"Heather's got the best job here. She's the Crossroads Mall's Christmas Angel."

Diana tried to conjure up an image of a Christmas Angel, but all she could think of was the time she'd played an angel in a grade school pageant. Her costume had consisted of a white sheet draped around her body, cardboard wings covered with aluminum foil, and a foil-covered halo that had kept slipping over her left eye. "Does Heather have to wear a costume?"

"Of course. She's got a gorgeous white dress with sparkles all over it. And a real diamond tiara that looks a little like a halo."

"No wings?" Diana raised her eyebrows.

"Well . . . sort of. She wears this little jacket that's really lacy around the back of her shoulders. And it sticks out on both sides. I think it's supposed to be her wings."

"Well, at least it's not typecasting." Diana laughed. "We all know that Heather's no angel."

"Truer words were never spoken. Aren't you going to ask me about her job?"

"Okay." Diana nodded. "Does Heather have to skip around the mall like us?"

"Nope. No skipping."

"How about those heavy trays of cookies?" Diana looked hopeful. "Does she have to carry one of those?"

"Nope. No cookies."

Diana frowned. She was running out of ideas. "A punch tray? They said they'd be passing out punch."

"Nope. No punch . . . except for the one I'd love to give her right between her baby blues."

Diana grinned. "Me, too. But tell me . . . exactly what does Heather have to do as the Christmas Angel?"

"Nothing." Cindy gave an emphatic nod as Diana's mouth dropped open. "Its true! Heather doesn't have to do anything at all. The Christmas Angel sits on a gold velvet throne next to Santa. That's it."

Diana felt her anger rise. "Heather gets paid for sitting, and we have to bust our buns, skipping all over the mall?"

"You got it. Of course Heather gets a half hour longer for lunch than we do."

"But . . . why?"

"Because her job is such hard work." Cindy's tone was sarcastic. "Sitting all day on a gold velvet chair is horribly exhausting. Heather would never be able to survive without a full hour for lunch."

The two girls exchanged annoyed glances. It wasn't really jealousy. Neither one of them would have minded if one of their friends had landed the job, but the idea that Heather, who'd never worked a day in her life, had landed the cushiest job of all, rankled beyond belief.

There was a moment of silence, broken only by the sound of the Christmas music playing over the loudspeakers. Then Cindy cleared her throat. "Well . . . let's both try to keep Heather away from Jay. I don't want to see him get hurt again."

"I'll do my best," Diana promised. "But Heather's not so easy to sidetrack."

"True." Cindy looked depressed. There was another moment of silence as both girls listened to the refrain from "Joy To The World," and then Cindy began to smile. "Did you hear? Shane Winter's coming out here tonight, to rehearse."

"I heard." Diana tried to be casual, but she couldn't help smiling as she thought about Shane Winter. She was hoping that he'd remember her. Of course, she'd changed quite a bit since Shane last saw her. Her family used to live next door to the Winters, and she'd been the skinny, red-haired kid who'd peered through the fence to spy on him when he'd sat on the porch swing with his dates. Back then, Shane had been the object of all Diana's fantasies, and she still felt a warm, tingling thrill when she saw his face on the screen, or listened to one of his albums. Diana knew she was being unrealistic by hoping that Shane would come back to his old hometown and fall madly in love with the girl who used to live next door, but that sort of thing happened in the movies all the time.

Diana thought about how she'd changed since Shane had last

seen her. She was much prettier now than she'd been in junior high. Everyone said she had a very good figure, and her teeth were nice and straight, now that her braces were off. Her hair even looked good right after she brushed it, and she'd brush it and put on makeup, right before Shane was due to . . .

"Diana? Hey . . . Diana!"

Diana blinked, and she felt herself start to blush as she realized that Jay was standing next to her.

"Oh, don't mind Diana." Cindy exchanged a grin with her older brother. "She was dreaming about Shane Winter again."

"I was not!" Diana crossed her fingers to negate the lie, and glared at her roommate. There were times when Cindy could be a real pain.

But Cindy just kept on grinning. "Sure you were. You always get that mushy expression on your face when you play one of his songs."

"I . . ." Diana struggled for something to say. This was embarrassing, especially since Jay was staring at her. "I used to live next door to him."

Jay nodded. "I know. Cindy told me. Do you think he'll remember you?"

"I doubt it." Diana shrugged, as if she didn't care. It was the furthest thing from the truth and she hoped she was being convincing. "I look a lot different now. I was only thirteen when Shane left town."

"He'll probably remember. I bet you were a cute kid."

Jay give her a very warm smile, and Diana blushed again. Cindy's brother was very handsome. He was tall and broad-shouldered, but there wasn't an ounce of fat on him. It was all muscle. And with his sun-streaked brown hair and dark brown eyes with incredibly long lashes, he was what Diana's grandmother called a "dish." He was nice, too, and Diana could tell he loved his younger sister. Cindy was totally different when Jay was around. She dropped her tough act and turned into a regular person.

If circumstances had been different, Diana might have been very interested in Jay. But they weren't. And she wasn't. Her heart belonged to Shane Winter, and it had ever since she'd been that skinny kid in junior high. Of course, Diana dated. The other girls were always lining her up with somebody's brother or cousin or friend of a friend. Diana usually had a good time, but she hadn't found one single date who even came close to measuring up to her memory of Shane.

"Were you?"

Jay was smiling at her, and Diana tried to concentrate. What was the question? Oh, yes. Jay had asked if she'd been a cute kid.

"I wasn't cute." Diana shook her head. "I was skinny, and my hair was even redder than it is now. My dad used to call me his little matchstick."

Jay laughed. "Well, you're not skinny now. And your hair is beautiful. I like it down like that."

"Uh . . . thank you." Diana started to blush again. She'd never been any good at handling compliments. She felt like pointing out that her hair was frizzy, and she hadn't brushed it for several hours, but she'd read an article just last week about how to accept compliments. You were supposed to say thank you, and nothing else.

Cindy turned to her brother. "Are you just here to flirt with Diana? Or are you here in your official capacity as head honcho of the college work team?"

Jay laughed, he was obviously used to his sister, but Diana blushed even harder. There were times when she wished she could gag Cindy with a pair of her old sweat socks.

"I'm here officially. Sue needs you to help in the giftwrapping booth. We've got three hundred stuffed toys to wrap before the Tree Lighting Ceremony tomorrow night."

Just then the speaker system crackled, interrupting the strains of "Have Yourself A Merry Little Christmas."

"All Santas report to the costume area for fittings. All Santas, on the double."

"All Santas?" Diana looked puzzled. "There's more than one Santa?"

Jay nodded. "The guys are taking turns playing Santa. We're doing it in shifts. It's a hard job, Diana. The costumes are heavy, and Santa has to be on his toes for the kids. I didn't think any of us should do it for more than four hours at a time."

"So we won't know who Santa is?" Cindy looked intrigued.

"Absolutely not. That's part of my plan. If you elves don't know who's inside the Santa costume, you can't slip up and use Santa's real name."

Diana nodded. "That's a good idea. Are you going to play Santa, too?"

"You bet. And I'm late for my costume fitting." Jay turned to go, but before he left, he reached out to touch a lock of Diana's hair. "Leave your hair down, Diana. It really looks great that way."

Cindy waited until her brother had left, and then she grinned at Diana. "Ho, ho, ho!"

"What's that supposed to mean?"

"Jay never said anything about your hair before. I think he's beginning to get interested in you."

"You're dreaming." Diana felt a blush rise to her cheeks again, and she turned away so Cindy couldn't see it. She'd been thinking the very same thing. If she didn't know better, she'd swear that Jay had been trying to pick up on her. Of course, that was ridiculous. Jay was a really sweet guy, and he was only being nice to his sister's roommate.

Cindy was frowning as they got up from the bench and started to walk toward the gift-wrapping booth, and Diana knew she was in for a lecture.

"Look, Di. You're my friend, and I'm telling you this for your own good. It's stupid to get this hung up on a movie star."

"I'm not hung up!" Diana sighed deeply. "I told you before. Shane Winter's not just a fantasy. I actually *know* him."

"Correction. You *knew* him. But that was a long time ago, and this is now. Does my brother have a chance with you?"

"Your brother's very nice." Diana sighed again. "I like him, okay? But you're the one who's hung up on a fantasy if you think he's interested in me."

"Maybe. And maybe not. Be honest with me, Di. If Jay asked you out, would you go?"

"I . . . I don't know." Diana shrugged. "But I'm sure he won't ask me out. I'm absolutely certain that the only reason Jay pays attention to me at all, is because I'm your friend."

Diana was very relieved as they reached the gift-wrapping booth, and Cindy started talking to the other elves. Nan Eldridge, Heather's roommate was there, and so was Betty Woo, a girl they knew from their English class. Naturally, Heather was conspicuously absent. Wrapping packages was work.

"Hey, girls . . . look at this!" Sue Langer opened one of the boxes, and pulled out a small, stuffed animal. Its eyes were on crooked, and it was covered with a bright green fuzz that looked as if it had been sprayed on.

All four girls looked at it for a long moment, and then Diana asked the question that was on everyone's mind. "What kind of animal is it supposed to be?"

"I think it's a frog," Cindy made a guess.

Sue held the stuffed animal up and turned it around and around. She didn't look convinced. "How can you tell?"

"Well . . . it's sort of crouching, and it doesn't have any ears. And it's green."

"That's good enough for me." Sue stuck the toy back in the box and handed out rolls of paper. "I wonder where they got these cheap little things. They look like they came from a carnival booth."

Diana picked up a box and flipped it over to read the stamp on the bottom. "They're from Hong Kong. And this one says, 'fargile.' "

"What?!" Sue cracked up. "You're kidding, aren't you?"

Diana shook her head, and held up the box so Sue could see. "Nope. It says 'fargile.' I think it's supposed to say 'fragile' except they got the letters reversed."

"Maybe not." Nan spoke up. "Fargile might be its name. Does anyone know what 'frog' is in Hong Kongese?"

Sue began to laugh. "They don't speak Hong Kongese, Nan. Hong Kong is on the coast of China. They speak Chinese."

"I knew that." Nan looked a little sheepish. "Hey, Betty. Do you know the Chinese word for 'frog?' "

Betty nodded sagely. "Of course. It's flog."

That cracked everybody up, and it was a good five minutes before they could start wrapping the boxes. Diana's job was to tie the bows, but her mind wasn't really on her work. She was too busy thinking about what Cindy had said. Was she so blinded by her fantasy of Shane that she was ignoring the real world? There was only one way to tell. Shane was coming out here to rehearse tonight. Diana was determined to look at him honestly, and decide once and for all, whether Cindy was right.

Two

It was so cold, his breath came out in frosty clouds, and he shivered a little as he walked out to the garbage area in back of the mall. One of the industrial-sized dumpsters was already open, and he smiled as he tossed the roll of red foil paper into the bin. He'd decided who Santa should punish first, and that made him feel good. Now all he had to do was come up with a perfect method.

He'd liked her at first, until he'd found out that she'd driven out to the farm last fall, and sweet-talked his grandfather into debt. She'd been canvassing the area to raise money for a children's play area, and she'd talked his poor, confused grandfather into signing a pledge on the installment plan.

Gramps wasn't to blame. He'd had no idea what he was signing or what it would end up costing him. He'd forgotten that he'd signed the pledge, and when the bills had come, he'd torn them up and thrown them in the trash. The whole thing had been turned over to a collection agency, and the interest on the money had grown fast. The final bill had come to almost a thousand dollars, and it had been taken out of the estate by the probate judge.

She was totally oblivious to the bad thing she'd done, but that didn't matter. The net result was still the same. She'd cheated him out of money that should have been his, and it had gone to the very mall that had robbed him of his land.

His hands were clenched into fists, as he turned to walk back inside the mall. She'd been very bad, taking advantage of Gramps. She definitely deserved to be punished, and Santa would just have to do it.

"That didn't take as long as I thought." Jay smiled at Diana as she handed him the last of the gift-wrapped packages. "Are you sure you wrapped them all?"

Diana nodded. "Three hundred and one boxes. I counted them as I brought them out."

"Three hundred and *one?*" Jay looked puzzled as he placed the last of the packages under the huge Christmas tree. "Where did the extra one come from?"

"We found it under the counter, already wrapped and tagged. I guess somebody got an early start."

"But there were only three hundred boxes. I was here when the shipment came in. I wish we could find that extra box to check it."

"Why?" Diana was puzzled.

"It might be a phony. Someone could have used an empty box to demonstrate how to wrap a package."

Diana looked worried. "I hope not! It'd be a real shame if we passed out the presents tomorrow night, and one of the kids got an empty box."

"That's exactly what I was thinking." Jay nodded. "Do you think we could tell which one it is by the weight?"

"That won't work. Those stuffed frogs are really light. But don't worry, Jay. I can find it. I remember carrying it out with the first load, and it's different from all the others. It's wrapped in red foil paper with a green ribbon."

It took almost a half-hour to find the package. They were all stacked up around the tree, and the red foil package was at the bottom of one of the stacks. Diana was the one to spot it, and she sat down on the floor at the base of the Christmas tree to pull it out. "Here it is! Do you want to open it?"

"You can do it. You found it."

As Diana examined the box, Jay sat down next to her. It was romantic, huddled down here, under the huge Christmas tree, with the scent of pine surrounding them. Someone had turned on the lights to test them, and the tinsel shimmered as it reflected the multi-colored bulbs.

"It's pretty down here, isn't it?" Jay's voice was hushed.

Diana nodded and she felt her heart beat faster, as Jay pulled off a piece of tinsel and wove it into her hair.

"I used to crawl under the Christmas tree when I was a little kid. I loved to look up at all the lights. I remember falling asleep under there once, and my father had to pick me up and carry me to bed."

Diana's heart beat even faster. She'd done the same thing, with one difference. Her mother had been the one to carry her up to bed. She turned to Jay and smiled. "I used to think that Christmas was magic. And I didn't understand why we couldn't leave the tree up all year long."

"Sounds like a good idea to me." Jay reached out for another piece of tinsel and wove that one in, too. "Maybe we ought to start a tradition. We could buy a live tree in an enormous pot, and decorate it for every season."

Diana nodded. "We could put on red velvet hearts for Valentine's Day, and little flags for the Fourth of July. How about Easter? Would we have bunnies?"

"That would work. And we could mix in some of those fancy hand-painted eggs. There'd be Shamrocks for St. Patrick's Day, and a whole tree full of ghosts and goblins and jack-o'-lanterns for Halloween."

"Bat," Diana reminded him. "You forgot the witches and the bats. But how about Thanksgiving? I'm not sure I want a tree full of turkeys."

Jay nodded and slipped his arm around her shoulders. "You've got a point. But we could string cranberries into garlands, and drape them over the tree. And we could drill holes in walnuts and hang them from the branches like ornaments. There's only one holiday that's really got me stumped."

"What's that?" Diana snuggled a little closer. It felt good to be hugged.

"New Year's Eve."

"Oh." Diana's mind spun in circles. What could they use for New Year's Eve? Party hats were too big, and champagne bottles were too heavy. Then she thought of it and she began to grin. "We'll sprinkle the whole tree with confetti and hang party favors from all the branches. We'll get some little silver horns, and wind-up noise makers, and long curly streamers made out of colored paper. It'll look great! And when we have our New Year's Eve party, everyone can grab something to use from the tree!"

Jay hugged her even closer and bent down to kiss the tip of her nose. "That's the best idea I've ever heard! Does that mean we're all set for New Year's Eve?"

"Uh . . . New Year's Eve?" Diana tried not to look shocked. What had she said?

"The party. With the tree," Jay reminded her. "We'll set it up in the living room of my apartment, and invite everybody we know. You don't have other plans for New Year's Eve, do you?"

"Uh . . . no, not exactly." Jay raised his eyebrows, and Diana swallowed hard. She didn't really want to tell him what she'd planned for New Year's Eve, but some instinct made her blurt it out. "I always watch the Times Square celebration on television."

Jay smiled and gave her another hug. "No problem. We'll do that, too. Our party'll be lots of fun, Di. You'll see."

"Yes. It will be." Diana smiled, but she had her doubts. Jay said they'd ask everyone they knew, and that included Heather. It was a little strange, planning a party, and not knowing whether she was going to be Jay's date, or not. But rather than bring up that question right now, she glanced down at the box on the floor. "Shall I open this now?"

Jay nodded, and Diana picked up the box. It was a good wrapping job, and the package was even tagged. She opened the little gold foil folder to look inside, but it didn't say "From The Crossroads Mall," like all the other ones they'd wrapped.

"What's the matter?" Jay noticed her worried expression.

"This box has a different tag." Diana turned the box around so Jay could see. The tag read, "TO SUE, FROM SANTA." "Do you think it's a package for Sue Langer?"

"Did I hear my name?" Jay and Diana looked up to see Sue standing by the tree. She was staring at them with an amused smile on her face. "You two look like you've been decorated, instead of the tree."

Diana blushed, and scrambled to her feet. "I know. We've been crawling around, looking for this package. It's an extra one and we were afraid it was empty, but then we noticed that it's got your name on it."

"My name?" Sue took the package and rattled it. "It sounds empty, but maybe . . . oh, my God!"

Jay and Diana stared at Sue in confusion as she began to blush. She looked excited and embarrassed at the same time.

"What is it, Sue?" Jay looked curious.

"Well . . . I think it might be a surprise package from Ronnie."

Diana nodded. Ronnie Knollwood had been dating Sue for the past three years, and everyone could tell they were wild about each other. "Don't keep us in suspense, Sue . . . open it."

"I would, but I don't think Ron wanted me to get it until tomorrow night. He's meeting me here, and then we're going out to celebrate our third anniversary. I met him at the Christmas dance, when I was a freshman."

"Do you think it's an engagement ring?" Jay raised his eyebrows.

"I don't know. It's too big for a ring box, but Ronnie loves to surprise me. He could have put the ring box inside a bigger box to fool me."

"Are you going to wait until tomorrow night to open it?" Jay looked disappointed.

"That would be torture." Sue turned to Diana. "Do you think we can rewrap this, if I'm really careful when I open it?"

Diana nodded. "Sure. Ronnie'll never know the difference. Go ahead, Sue. I'm dying to know!"

"All right, but you two can't tell anyone. I want Ronnie to think I'm surprised."

"It's a deal." Jay nodded. "Let's get back under the tree and open it, just in case somebody else comes along."

Diana noticed that Sue's fingers were trembling slightly when she opened the package, but she managed to slit the tape neatly with her fingernail and keep the foil paper in one piece. Then she lifted the lid of the white cardboard box, and frowned as she looked inside. "It's empty!"

"Are you sure?" Diana leaned over to peer inside the box, which was lined with tissue paper. She spotted a folded piece of paper, and pulled it out. "Here, Sue. It must be a note from Ronnie."

Sue unfolded the paper, but she looked very puzzled as she read the words that were written inside. "It says, *You better watch out; you better not cry.* And it's not Ronnie's writing. What does it mean?"

"I don't know." Jay looked just as puzzled as Sue. "That's a weird thing to write in a note."

"Listen to that!" Diana hushed them as "Santa Claus Is Comin' To Town" started to play over the loudspeaker. "Those are the words in the note!"

After the first verse had finished playing, Jay nodded. "You're right. But why would anyone write down part of the lyrics and wrap them up a box?"

"Especially *those* lyrics." Sue looked worried. "*You better watch out? You better not cry?* That's kind of scary."

Jay slipped his arm around Sue's shoulder and gave her a little hug. "Relax, Sue. It's obvious the package wasn't meant for you. It's probably a joke for someone else named Sue."

"That must be it." Sue slid out from under the tree and stood up. Then she leaned down to grin at them. "You two look cute under there."

After Sue had left, Jay draped a friendly arm around Diana's shoulders. "She called us cute. Nobody's called me cute since I was four years old."

"But you *are* cute." Diana giggled, and tossed some tinsel at him.

"No, I'm not." Jay picked up a strand of tinsel and wound it around his finger like a ring. "I'm handsome. My mother told me I was."

"But doesn't your mother wear glasses?"

They were both laughing, when they heard footsteps approach. Then someone called out, "Hello? What's going on under there?!"

Diana froze as she recognized Heather's voice. She turned to Jay with a worried expression, but he just grinned. A second later, Heather's arm shoved aside a low-hanging branch, and her face appeared in the gap it had left. There was a very shocked expression on her face as she stared at them.

"Hi, Heather." Jay grinned even wider. "We're just checking out the tags on the packages. Care to join us?"

Heather put a smile on her face as she turned to Jay. "No, thanks. I have to get ready. The *Night News* team is coming out to do a whole segment on me. Why don't you meet me when I'm through, and we'll catch a bite to eat?"

"I can't, Heather. I already took my break."

Heather shrugged. "After work, then. I really need to talk to you."

"Sorry, but I've got other plans."

Jay was still grinning, and Diana noticed that he didn't look the least bit sorry. Was he finally over Heather?

"Okay. Catch you later." Heather turned to Diana. "Sue wants you in costume. You'd better get over there right away."

Diana was frowning as Heather left. She'd been fitted for her elf costume hours ago, and Sue hadn't said a word about needing her when she'd been here. Diana suspected that Heather was just making up an excuse to get her away from Jay, but it wouldn't hurt to check.

"I guess I'd better go." Diana started to move out from under the tree, but Jay slid out first, and offered her his hand. He pulled her to her feet and dusted the tinsel off her hair.

"Did you drive out here with Cindy?"

Diana nodded. "We came in her car. Mine's in the shop . . . again."

"Tell Cindy to meet me at Embers when we're through. I'll buy you both a burger."

"Okay," Diana agreed quickly. She loved the burgers at Embers. But then she remembered what Jay had told Heather, and she frowned. "I thought you had plans after work."

"I do. I'm meeting you at Embers."

Jay was grinning as he walked away. So was Diana, as she hurried off in the opposite direction. Then Diana remembered the expression in Heather's eyes, and her smile faded quickly. Heather had lots of influence at the college, and she was a dangerous enemy.

Diana shivered and walked a little faster. When Heather had found them sitting under the Christmas tree, she'd stared at Diana as if she'd been a bug she wanted to crush. What would Heather do when she found out about the New Year's Eve party that Diana was hosting with Jay?

Three

Diana's suspicions were right. When she'd arrived at the costume area, she'd found that Sue hadn't asked Heather to get her. But Sue had been very glad to see Diana, and she'd immediately put her to work getting the Santa costumes ready to wear.

When the costumes had been brushed and hung on hangers, Diana and Cindy had started in on the wigs and beards. They had to be combed out and placed on Styrofoam heads so they wouldn't get tangled.

"Why did they rent four costumes?" Diana was curious. It seemed like an unnecessary extravagance.

"They're hot and heavy." Cindy explained. "This way each guy has his own costume and it can air out between wearings. How far along are you?"

"I'm all done with Jay's." Diana pointed to Jay's wig and beard. She could hardly wait to see him in costume. "Who are you doing?"

"I just finished Dave Atkin, and I'm starting on Hal Bremmer."

"Did it give you a thrill to do Dave's?" Diana grinned at Cindy. Dave was a handsome sophomore.

"Not really. Dave doesn't know I'm alive. He's going with a gorgeous girl in the drama department."

"How about Hal?" Diana was curious. "Do you know him?"

386 Jo Gibson

"Sure. He's in my history class. I'm not sure if I like him, though. He bumped my grade down to a 'B' when he aced the last test. Our professor grades on a curve."

Diana set Larry Fischer's wig on its stand. Larry was Jay's best friend, and they shared an apartment. "Is Larry going out with anybody right now?"

"He's dating some girl from Duluth, and Jay says his share of the phone bill is astronomical. He always calls after the rates go down, but . . ."

"Get into your elf costumes, quick!" Sue came racing into the costume room. Her face was flushed, and she looked excited. "The crew from *Night News* is here, and they want to tape all the elves, skipping around the mall!"

"They want *us?*" Diana was surprised.

"That's what they said. Come out to the Christmas tree the second you're ready. I've got to round up the rest of the girls!"

The door banged closed behind Sue, and Diana turned to Cindy with a puzzled expression. "I wonder what happened? Heather told me the *Night News* crew was going to do a whole segment on her."

"Maybe they couldn't get her on tape." Cindy laughed. "Isn't there some old superstition that says you can't take a picture of the devil?"

"Once more, gang!" Sue shouted out. "Twice around the tree and then gather in front of Santa's throne."

Diana did her best to keep the smile on her face, but it wasn't easy. They'd skipped the length of the mall twice, and now they had to skip some more. She hoped that the cute cameraman was getting good footage, because there was no way she could do it again. Even Sue was beginning to get slightly breathless.

As Diana skipped past Santa, she tried to figure out who he was. He was sitting on his throne, so she couldn't tell anything from his height, and the beard and mustache covered his face. She couldn't even see the color of his eyes behind his gold wire-framed glasses. But then she noticed that Santa was wearing a tinsel ring. It was Jay!

Jay seemed to know she'd recognized him, because he gave a little wave. And when they had skipped around the Christmas tree the last time, he motioned her over to sit directly at his feet.

"Cut!" A guy in a *Night News* sweatshirt motioned to the cameraman. Sue had told Diana that he was the field director. "Is Tracy ready?"

"I'm here."

Diana stared in awe as Tracy Thomas, the *Night News* anchorwoman, walked to a spot in front of the Christmas tree. She was just as glamorous in person as she was on television. She nodded to the guy in the sweatshirt as he cued her, and then she began to speak.

"We're here at the new Crossroads Mall at the intersection of Highways Twelve and Fourteen. The mall doesn't open until tomorrow morning at ten, but there are over a hundred employees here today, getting ready for the opening. *Night News* is going to give you a sneak preview of this lovely new shopping area in the Morrison County countryside, so tune in at ten for all the details."

Tracy fluffed her hair as the cameraman panned the mall. Then she flashed a smile as the camera focused on her, again. The field director gave her a signal, and she started to speak again.

"Here we are at the new Crossroads Mall, and Christmas is definitely in the air." Tracy began to walk over to the group around Santa as she continued her speech. "The mall was completed only last month, in a cooperative venture by three Minnesota cities, Prairie Falls, Portersville, and Two Rivers. And I'm told there's plenty of fun in store for the shoppers who attend the grand opening. Let's find out from the man himself, Santa Claus!"

Tracy stepped up to Santa's throne and smiled at Jay. "Hello, Santa. Can you tell us about some of the activities planned for tomorrow?"

"Ho, ho, ho!"

Diana grinned as Jay gave his merriest laugh. His voice was

so deep, she might not have recognized it if she hadn't seen the tinsel ring on his finger.

"Mrs. Claus has been very busy in the kitchen, and she's made cookies and punch for everyone who comes to the grand opening."

"I'm sure the mall will be very crowded tomorrow." Tracy smiled at Jay. "Will parking be a problem?"

"Ho, ho, ho! Not at all." Jay laughed again. "Just pull up to the valet sign and my helpers will park your car for you. Then hop on Santa's sleigh-ride shuttle and we'll bring you right up to the main entrance."

"That's very convenient. How many stores will be open, Santa?"

"The Crossroads Mall has twenty-four stores that are opening tomorrow, with another fifteen planned for the first of the year. There's a wide variety of merchandise, and each and every store has a complimentary gift for you. And if you attend the grand opening and enter the winter sweepstakes . . ."

"Yes, Santa?" Tracy looked excited.

"Just come with me." Jay stood up and gave her his arm. "The grand prize is right over here."

Jay and Tracy walked over to the two shiny, red snowmobiles which were displayed on podiums. When they got there, Tracy clapped her hands. "This is the grand prize?"

"That's right. If your name is drawn, you'll win this pair of his and her snowmobiles, generously donated by the Crossroads Mall Corporation!"

"I'd love to win those!" Tracy smiled at the camera as they began to walk back. "You just convinced me, Santa. I'll definitely be here. But how about my little niece and nephew? Will they get a chance to meet you?"

"Yes they will, Tracy. I'll be right here in Santa's Village, and I'm looking forward to meeting all the kids."

Tracy nodded. "Now, Santa . . . I don't want you to give away any secrets, but one of your elves told me there'd be a surprise for the kids at the Tree-Lighting Ceremony tomorrow night."

"Oh, *ho!* That's right, Tracy. And I know exactly which elf told you. It was this cute little red-headed imp right here, wasn't it?"

Diana giggled as Jay pointed to her, and then she blushed as the cute cameraman turned his lens her way. She slapped her hand over her mouth, and managed to look comically distressed.

"That's all right, little elf." Jay reached down to pat Diana's head. "I was going to tell them anyway. Do you kids at home see all those presents piled under the tree? If you get your mommy and daddy to bring you out to the Grand Tree-Lighting Ceremony at eight o'clock tomorrow night, you'll get an early Christmas present from the Crossroads Mall!"

"Thank you, Santa." Tracy reached out to shake his hand, and then she turned to face the camera again. "We hope to see you all tomorrow at the grand opening of the Crossroads Mall."

"Cut!" The field director rushed up to Tracy. "Great job, Tracy! I think we've got everything we need."

"But how about me?"

Diana turned to look at Heather, who was sitting on her gold-cushioned chair. She was dressed in her angel costume, and she looked mad enough to spit.

"I thought you were going to interview me!"

The director smiled at Heather. "Don't worry, sweetie. We've got you in the long shot, and you'll be on the show."

"But you told me you were going to . . ."

Heather's objection was interrupted by a flurry of activity at the mall entrance. Four people came in, brushing the snow off their coats, and stomping their boots. Tracy turned to look, and then she nudged the cameraman. "Cover me, Paul. That's Shane Winter!"

Diana watched as Tracy and her crew hurried down the walkway to meet Shane's group. There was a limo driver in full uniform, an older man carrying a leather briefcase, and a gorgeous brunette in a full-length mink coat. Shane was standing in the center of the group, and Diana gasped as he turned her way.

He was even more handsome than he'd been when he'd lived next door to her!

She was in such a daze, Diana didn't even notice as the other elves got to their feet and raced over to stand in a circle around Shane Winter and his group. Cindy gave her a little nudge. "Aren't you going to go over and say hello?"

"No." Diana turned to frown at her. "I told you before . . . he probably won't even remember me."

Before Diana had time to object, Cindy got up and hauled her to her feet. "You can refresh his memory. Come on. Let's go."

"But, I really don't think I should . . ."

"Sure, you should." Cindy pulled her down the walkway, and shoved her to the front of the group. "Hey, Shane! Look who's here! Do you recognize her?"

Diana knew she was blushing beet-red. The bright lights were on and she knew that the *Night News* cameraman was getting this all on tape. She vowed to smother Cindy with a pillow when they got back to their apartment, and did her best to look calm and composed. "Hello, Shane. I'm sure you don't remember, but I used to live . . ."

"Little Red!" Shane grinned at her. "How could I ever forget you? You made my life miserable, all through high school."

Tracy laughed and pulled Diana closer, right into the glare of the lights. "How did she do that?"

"Little Red lived next door to me. And she used to peek through the hedge and spy on me when I sat on the front porch with my dates. She made some of the girls so nervous, they refused to date me."

"Is that true?" Tracy turned to Diana.

Diana thought fast. She didn't want Shane to go into detail. She'd simply die if he told about the time she'd howled like a wolf to scare Shirley Mielke away. "I'm afraid it is. I practically ruined Shane's love life. Of course . . . there was a lot of love life to ruin."

Tracy laughed, and so did Shane. And then Tracy started to ask him about his high school days. Diana took advantage of the opportunity to slip to the back of the crowd. She looked around for Cindy, but her roommate had made a quick exit to the other side of the crowd.

"Nice job, Diana. You've got a real flair for comedy."

Diana whirled around to find Jay standing right behind her. He'd changed to jeans and a college sweatshirt, but the tinsel ring was still on his finger.

"Thanks." Diana knew she was still blushing. She wanted to tell him that she really hadn't intended to be funny, but she remembered the article she'd read on accepting compliments gracefully, and she decided to compliment him, instead. "I thought you made a wonderful Santa."

"Really?" Jay looked pleased. "We drew straws to see who'd do the interview, and I picked the short one. When did you realize it was me?"

"I'm not sure. I knew pretty early, though." Diana grinned up at him. Jay didn't seem to realize that the tinsel ring had given him away, and she wasn't about to tell him.

Just then the bright lights went out, and the field director stepped up to stand beside Shane. They had a brief conference that Diana and Jay couldn't hear, and then he turned to the group with a smile on his face. "We're going to tape one more segment. I want the elves on the floor by the Christmas tree. Shane's agreed to sing a song, and they'll be the audience. What are you going to sing, Shane?"

"Let's do 'Blue Christmas.' " The man with the briefcase stepped up. "Shane always sings that to a beautiful girl."

"How about me?"

Heather stepped forward to smile at Shane, and Diana almost laughed out loud. There wasn't a shy bone in Heather's body.

"You'll do just fine, honey." The man with the briefcase smiled at her. "What are you? Some kind of fairy?"

Heather shook her head. "I'm the Christmas Angel. If we wheel the baby grand out by the tree, I could sit on top."

"That'll make a nice shot." The field director looked pleased. "What do you think, Shane?"

Shane shrugged. "Sounds good to me. Let's do it now. The weather's getting nasty out there, and Allison and I have plans for tonight. Right, Allison?"

"Right."

The beautiful brunette in the mink coat gave Shane a very intimate smile. If Diana'd had any doubts about Allison's relationship to Shane, that smile would have erased every one of them. But she hadn't read anything about Allison in any of the fan magazines. Didn't the press know that Shane had a girlfriend?

It didn't take long to set up for the segment. The boys wheeled out the piano and Heather climbed up on top. The field director spread her skirts in a perfect circle around her, and nodded for Shane to take his place at the piano.

"Hold it." The man with the briefcase hurried up to the piano. "We need a blanket."

Diana turned to Cindy, who was sitting next to her on the floor. "Why do they need a blanket?"

"They have to mute the piano. Shane's going to lip-synch his song. His manager told me he always lip-synchs his concerts."

Diana was puzzled. "Do you know why?"

"I'm not sure, but I'm going to watch him like a hawk. Do you remember if he played the piano in high school?"

Diana shook her head. And then something occurred to her that made her frown. "My parents were friends with his parents, and we used to go over to his house a lot. I don't think they had a piano."

"Exactly! I don't think he knows how to play. Maybe he doesn't really sing, either."

Diana's eyes widened "Do you think he's pulling a Milli Vanilli?"

"Maybe. Nan's studying vocal music, and she told me his speaking range doesn't match his singing range at all."

"But that happens sometimes, doesn't it?" Diana looked a little worried. All her dreams would be dashed if Shane turned out to be a complete fake.

"It happens, but it's unusual."

Cindy was silent for a moment and then she reached out to pat Diana's hand. "Will you be really upset if your idol turns out to have feet of clay?"

"I don't know," Diana answered her honestly. "Maybe he won't. And if he does, I'll just have to deal with it somehow."

Diana watched Shane carefully as they got ready to tape the segment. When Allison was busy talking to the man with the briefcase, Shane slipped his arm around Tracy's waist and said something that made her blush. They looked at each other for a long moment, and then Tracy nodded. But the minute Allison turned her attention back to Shane, he quickly dropped his arm and gave her an innocent smile.

"I wonder what he said?" Diana was curious.

"I know," Betty Woo spoke up.

Cindy turned to look at Betty in surprise. "But how did you hear from this far away?"

"I read lips. It's something I picked up when I was a kid. I used to sneak downstairs to watch television, but I couldn't turn up the volume because my parents thought I was in bed. I didn't realize it then, but lip-reading really comes in handy."

"Tell us!" Cindy began to grin. "What did he say?"

"He said, *I'm staying at the Portersville Inn, room 213. Be there at midnight. If you're as good as you look, I'll give you an exclusive.*"

"Are you sure?" Diana turned around to stare at Betty.

"I'm sure. He's very easy to read. Most actors are."

All during the taping of Shane's segment, Diana did her best to hang on to her dream. When Shane's song was finished, she turned to Cindy with a question in her eyes.

"Sorry, Di." Cindy gave a deep sigh. "I took six years of piano, and Shane didn't play 'Blue Christmas.' It wasn't even close."

"But . . . maybe he wasn't trying to play 'Blue Christmas.' It didn't really matter what he did. The piano was muted and they didn't do any close-ups of his hands on the keys."

"Okay. Let's put it to the test." Cindy took Diana's arm and led her over to the man with the briefcase. "Hi. Can you tell us where Shane's staying? Her parents want to call and say hello."

"I'm sorry girls, but I can't give out that kind of . . ." The man with the briefcase stopped, and stared at Diana. "Wait a second. Aren't you the girl who used to live next door?"

Cindy nudged Diana, and she nodded. "That's right. I'm Diana Connelly."

"Then I guess it's okay, but you've got to promise not to tell anyone else. I don't want Shane to be mobbed by autograph hounds."

"We understand." Cindy nodded solemnly. "And we promise to keep it a secret."

"We're at the Portersville Inn until tomorrow night. Tell your parents to ask for Joe Harmon. I'll make sure they get through to Shane."

"Thanks a lot, Mr. Harmon. We really appreciate it."

Cindy took Diana's arm and pulled her over to a bench near the center of the mall. "You look sick. Wait right here. I'll get you some water."

Diana sat down on the bench and sighed. She'd thought that she was in love with Shane, but she'd been caught up in a fantasy. Shane wasn't the type of man she'd thought he was, and she felt like a silly fool for dreaming about him all these years.

"What's wrong, Di?" Jay walked up and sat down beside her. He looked very concerned as he handed her a cup of water, and he put his arm around her shoulder. "Cindy said you felt sick. Is there anything I can do?"

Diana took a deep breath, and cuddled closer. Suddenly she felt much better. "I think I'm all right now. Thanks, Jay."

"You probably overdid it with the skipping." Jay smiled down at her. "You gave me a scare, though. You looked so miserable, I asked Cindy if someone had died."

Diana nodded. Jay was right. Someone *had* died. Her dream of Shane had suffered a painful death, but now that the last of her illusions was gone, Diana felt free for the first time in her life.

"Do you still want to go out for that burger? Or would you rather go home and rest?"

Diana looked up into Jay's concerned face, and gave him a radiant smile. "I'd love a burger. And don't worry about me. I feel just fine now. I think it was just a case of delayed growing pains."

Four

"Come on, you two." Cindy ran up to the bench. "They're getting ready to show the edited version of the tape."

"How did they do it so fast?" Diana was curious.

"They've got an editing bay in the *Night News* van, and Paul let me watch. That's why I sent Jay over with your water."

"Paul?" Diana began to grin as they got up and followed Cindy to the large monitor that had been set up by the Christmas tree. Cindy had dropped her bitch act completely, and she was already on a first-name basis with the cameraman.

"Paul Murphy. He's from somewhere right around here, and he's a junior at the University of Minnesota, majoring in film studies."

"He's a student?" Jay was surprised. "I didn't know the *Night News* hired student cameramen."

"They don't, not usually. Paul's instructor got him a summer job there last year as a gofer, and he worked his way up."

"What's a gofer?" Diana was puzzled.

"Oh, you know. Paul had to *go for* sandwiches, and *go for* coffee, all sorts of stuff like that. But then he filled in when one of the regular cameramen got sick. And he did such a good job, they hired him to work as an extra cameraman on all of his school breaks."

Diana nodded. Cindy had certainly found out a lot about Paul in a very short time.

"Hi, Paul." There was a huge smile on Cindy's face as she waved to the cameraman and led the way to the front of the crowd, where Paul was saving seats for them. "This is my brother, Jay, and my roommate, Diana."

"Santa." Paul grinned at Jay. "Nice job, guy. Have you ever thought about turning pro?"

Jay laughed and shook his head. "No way. That suit's too hot."

"I bet it is." Paul nodded, and turned to Diana. "You were great, too. I got a couple of nice shots of you. You're almost as photogenic as Cindy."

"Uh . . . thank you." Diana wasn't really sure what to say. She'd never thought of Cindy as being photogenic. But she was saved from further comment when Paul grinned and held up the tape.

"Catch you in a couple of minutes. I have to give this to Morrie."

Cindy watched Paul leave with a smile on her face. Then she turned to them to explain. "Morrie's the field director. Well . . . ? What do you think?"

"I like him." Diana nodded. She knew exactly what Cindy was asking. "How about you, Jay?"

Jay nodded, too. "Nice guy. As your older brother, I give you my blessings."

"Thanks a lot!" Cindy laughed, but when Jay turned to talk to Larry Fischer, who was sitting right behind them, Cindy leaned close to Diana and lowered her voice. "Wait until you see Heather. You're gonna die laughing."

"Why?"

"She looks fat!" Cindy nodded, as Diana looked dubious. "I'm not kidding. Paul told me that's why no one wears pure white on television. It's too contrasty and it makes you look as big as a house under the lights. Not only that, the camera adds about ten pounds."

"Did I look fat?" Diana was concerned.

"Of course not. You look cute, you'll see."

Just then the lights dimmed, and a moment later, Paul came back to sit next to Cindy. Then the large monitor next to the screen came on, and Diana began to smile as Tracy's image appeared.

Watching the tape was fun, especially when Jay whispered that her hair looked beautiful. And Cindy was right. Heather did look fat. Jay's Santa Claus imitation was perfect right down to the last "Ho, ho, *ho,*" and Cindy looked absolutely gorgeous when she appeared on the screen. The tape had just finished when Cindy nudged Diana and pointed toward the entrance of the mall. Two highway patrol cars had just pulled up, and their red lights were flashing.

There was a moment of silence, as everyone turned to look at the two officers who were getting out of their cars. Then Jay turned to Diana with a frown. "There must be something wrong. They don't use their lights unless it's an emergency."

The silence lasted for another second, and then everyone started to talk at once. Paul jumped to his feet, and turned to Cindy. "Later, okay? This could be something big."

They all watched as Paul grabbed his camera and headed off after Tracy at a run. A fire? A death? An accident? Diana felt her heart beat a rapid tattoo in her chest as they joined the crowd that was heading toward the entrance.

"It's okay, folks." The older officer did his best to calm the crowd as he came in through the plate glass doors. "But the weather's getting real nasty out there, and we came out here to warn you."

The younger officer nodded. "The weather bureau just posted storm advisories. There's a big one coming in, and it's going to hit hard. We came to lead you out."

Tracy Thomas stepped up to the officers, and Paul was right behind her. "How bad is it supposed to get, Officer . . . ?"

"Daniels." The older officer answered her unspoken question. He didn't seem to be fazed at all by the fact he was on camera. "They say it's going to be a full-scale blizzard. We can't let you drive out unless you've got chains or snow tires. The road out there is a mess. That means you'll have to double up so we can evacuate everyone."

Shane stepped up to the younger officer. "How about four-wheel drive? I'm Shane Winter and I can't get stuck out here. I have to fly back to L.A. tomorrow night."

"You should be able to make it, Mr. Winter." The young officer swallowed hard. He was obviously flustered at being this close to a major star.

The older officer frowned. "That depends. How heavy is your vehicle?"

"It's a Cadillac stretch limousine." Shane's driver spoke up.

"You should be able to make it." The older officer nodded, and then he turned to the crowd. "We've got another officer on the way, so let's split up into three groups. If you need to get to Portersville, gather over here on my right. People headed for Two Rivers, line up on my left. Officer Goetz will take the group for Prairie Falls. We need to know the type of vehicle you have."

Jay, Diana, and Cindy moved to the Prairie Falls group, along with the rest of the college students. Cindy looked worried as she turned to Diana. "Sorry, Di. My car won't make it."

"You didn't put on the snow tires Dad bought for you?" Jay turned to Cindy with a frown.

"I was going to take my car in last week, but I was so busy studying I . . ." Cindy sighed deeply. "Forget the excuses, Jay. I goofed. I should have done it right away."

Jay slipped his arm around Cindy's shoulders. "Don't worry about it. My truck's got four-wheel drive. You and Di can ride with Larry and me. It'll be a little crowded, but we'll make it."

"Thanks, Jay." Cindy looked very grateful, but before she could say any more, Larry rushed up with a clipboard.

"Will you help me, Jay? I told Officer Goetz we'd make a list of everyone who needs a ride."

Jay looked down at the clipboard and frowned. "All these people need rides?"

"That's right." Larry nodded. "And most of them have little kids they need to get home to."

Diana peeked over Jay's shoulder, and her eyes widened as she saw that the first side of the page was almost completely filled with names. "We'll help, too. Is there another clipboard?"

"Officer Goetz has a couple up there at the table." Larry pointed toward the front of the line.

Diana nodded. "Okay. Cindy and I'll get a list of available cars and the number of passengers they'll hold. That should make it easy to match the people who need rides with the cars we have."

"Good idea!" Jay gave her a little hug. "Let's get started. This should be a snap."

But it wasn't. Diana sighed as they finished, and brought their clipboards up to Officer Goetz's table. Since they hadn't had much snow this winter, almost everyone had put off switching to their snow tires. And they didn't find a single vehicle with chains. There were a half dozen vans and trucks with four-wheel drive, but most of the drivers had car-pooled to the mall this morning, and they didn't have room for extra passengers.

"Di?" Jay tapped her on the shoulder. "There's a woman on our list, Gloria Olsen. She's eight months pregnant, and she's got two kids in day care. She's really nervous about getting stuck out here. And then there's a janitor with a heart condition. He's got medicine he has to take at night. And another man's wife is in the hospital. He's worried and he wants to visit her tonight. I know I promised you a ride, but . . ."

"It's fine with me, Jay," Diana interrupted. "I don't mind if you drive them home."

Jay shook his head. "That's not it. I thought I'd let them use my truck. I don't really need to get home tonight, and neither does Larry. Cindy said to go for it, but are you sure you don't mind?"

"I'm positive."

"You're a good sport, Diana." Jay gave her a hug. "I'll go give them my keys."

Diana was smiling as Jay hurried off through the crowd. She didn't mind being snowbound at all, as along as Jay stayed here with her.

"Di? I've got great news!" Cindy wove her way through the crowd until she'd reached Diana's side. "You said you'd stay, didn't you?"

"Of course. What's the great news? Is Paul staying, too?"

Cindy shook her head. "No. He has to go with the news van. But guess who's leaving?"

"Shane? I heard him say he had to fly back to L.A. tomorrow night."

"Oh, he's already gone." Cindy made a disgusted face. "He didn't take anybody else with him in that big stretch limo, either. Paul told me he said it would be too much of an inconvenience."

Diana shrugged. Surprisingly, the news that Shane was selfish and irresponsible didn't bother her at all.

"Maybe I shouldn't have told you." Cindy began to look a little worried. "Are you upset?"

"Not a bit. I'm completely over Shane. The whole thing was just a silly fantasy."

Cindy nodded. It was clear she approved. And she began to beam again. "Back to the good news. I just found out that someone else is leaving. Nan just told me that Heather's new car has four-wheel drive!"

Diana's smile grew until it was even bigger than Cindy's. Thank goodness Heather was leaving! But just then, Officer Goetz called for silence, and everyone gave him their attention.

"Okay, folks. I've got four sets of keys here, thanks to Jay Swanson. He started the ball rolling." Officer Goetz picked up a set of keys. "These are from Hal Bremmer. His Dodge pick-up has chains and he says it'll hold four if you squeeze."

Cindy and Diana clapped along with the rest of the crowd. Hal had done the right thing.

"And this belongs to a new Ford Explorer." Officer Goetz held up another set of keys. "Sue Langer says it'll hold eight."

Cindy and Diana applauded again. It was nice of Sue to lend out her new car.

"And here's another set of keys from Dave Atkin. His father's an investor and he owns the Crossroads Pub. Dave has a classic

Lincoln with snow tires, and he's willing to lend it to six people who need rides. These college kids are great, aren't they folks!"

Everyone applauded, and Cindy grinned at Diana. "Good for Dave. But you noticed who didn't give up her keys, didn't you?"

"Everyone noticed." Diana motioned toward Heather who was actually starting to look a little embarrassed.

"Okay, folks." Officer Goetz called for attention again. "Raise your hands if you still need a ride. Let's get these keys redistributed right away."

Diana noticed that there were still a lot of hands, and she exchanged worried looks with Cindy as Officer Goetz counted the number of people who were left. "Oh-oh. I wonder what he's going to do."

"All right." Officer Goetz nodded. "I can take four people with me. It's against regulations, but I figure this qualifies as an emergency. Unfortunately, we still have almost forty people left. Does anybody have any suggestions?"

"I do!" Heather stepped up to the front of the crowd. "My father leased five delivery vans with four-wheel drive. I just called him, and he's given me permission to turn the keys over to the carpool. They're all gassed up, and they're in the mall garage. And I'm throwing in the keys to my car, too. I'm staying here so that the people who really need to get home, can go."

Cindy turned to Diana with a frown. "Damn! I should have known she'd do that."

"But that's not like Heather." Diana was puzzled. "She's never cared a bit about other people."

"Of course not. But Paul's getting it all on tape, and she knows we're staying. She saw Jay hand over his keys. Heather wants Jay to think she's just as generous as he is."

"Right." Diana nodded.

"But that's not the real reason." Cindy winked at Diana. "There's no way Heather is going to leave you alone out here with Jay. She still wants him back, and that means she has to keep her eye on the competition."

*   *   *

Fifteen minutes later, Diana and Cindy stood with the group of people who were staying. There were only seven of them, and they were all college students. Diana and Cindy, Jay and Larry, Hal, Sue, and Heather.

"I wish we could stay." Nan waved as she climbed into the van with Betty Woo. "But my mom's sick, and I have to take care of my little brother."

Betty nodded. "And I'm house-sitting for the Forresters. They'd be really upset if it turned cold and the pipes froze. But I really feel like I'm deserting all of you."

"Don't worry about it." Jay smiled at the two girls. "Just make sure someone comes out here to get us when the roads are clear."

"Hey, Cindy. I'll see you later." Paul leaned out of the window of the news van and waved.

Cindy waved back, but Diana noticed she didn't look happy. It was too bad that Paul wasn't staying.

Gradually, the caravan began to move. Officer Goetz was at the rear, and he gave a little toot on his horn as he passed them. No one had anything to say. The silence was only broken by the howl of the wind and the sound of sleet hitting the plate glass windows.

They stood like statues looking off into the distance as the caravan crossed the parking lot and pulled out onto the road. Even Heather was silent as they huddled in the doorway, under the overhang, and watched as the last set of taillights disappeared in the blowing snow.

Jay opened the door and they all trooped in. Their footsteps sounded hollow and empty in the giant open space and the sound of the Christmas music playing over the loudspeakers seemed forlorn now that everyone had left.

"Well . . ." Jay cleared his throat. It was a surprisingly loud sound in the empty mall. "Cheer up, everybody. We're snowbound, and there's nothing we can do about it. I guess we'd better make the best of it."

Dave nodded. "Good idea. Is anybody hungry? I've got the keys to the Crossroads Pub, and my dad said to help ourselves."

"I think I should call home first," Diana spoke up. "My parents might be worried if they hear we're stranded out here."

Cindy laughed. "It's not *if*, it's *when*. Your parents always watch the *Night News*, don't they?"

"Always." Diana nodded. "Why don't we all call home and tell our parents we're fine? Then nobody'll worry about us."

Jay nodded. "Good idea, but we'll have to use a land line. Our cells don't work way out here. Make your calls, and then we'll all meet at the Crossroads Pub. And lighten up, gang. This is going to be fun!"

"Right!" Sue smiled her best cheerleader smile. "There's plenty of food and we can stuff ourselves silly. And there's a bed for everyone at the furniture store. Just think about how lucky we are. If you have to get snowbound, this is the perfect place!"

Diana nodded along with everyone else, but she strongly disagreed. Sue was partially right. The mall would be the perfect place to be snowbound . . . if Heather had left.

Five

The Crossroads Pub had a friendly atmosphere with its wood-paneled walls, oak tables with captain's chairs, and stacks of pewter mugs behind the bar. There was a wooden sign on chains over the door, and the room was decorated to resemble a British pub, with antique family crests on the walls and framed pictures of famous British soccer players. It was a fairly small space, seating only thirty, and the intimate, almost cluttered atmosphere was a welcome change from the emptiness of the giant mall outside.

Diana could smell the bratwurst sizzling on the grill in the kitchen, and she smiled across the table at Jay. "Sue was right. This is fun. Do you think Dave needs any help in the kitchen?"

"I don't know. Let's go ask him." Jay stood up and so did Diana. "Better take your mug with you. He says it gets hot back there."

The kitchen smelled wonderful, and Diana walked over to the grill to inspect the plump sausages. They were a beautiful brown color and juice drizzled out to sizzle against the coals. She walked over to Dave and gave him her best I-haven't-eaten-in-a-month look. "How long until we eat?"

"Less than ten minutes. If you want to help, slice open some of those buns and spread them with the coarse-ground mustard."

"What can I do?" Jay looked just as hungry as Diana felt.

"Get the crock of pickles out of the cooler and fill a couple of those green glass jars."

"I want to help, too." Cindy appeared in the doorway, and grinned as she walked over to inspect the sausages. "God, it smells good in here!"

Dave grinned. "I know. Dad gets the sausage fresh from a little shop in Wisconsin. And St. John's monastery bakes the buns, especially for us."

"But who makes the pickles?" Jay came out of the cooler, carrying a huge earthen-ware crock of pickles. "They're the best I've ever tasted."

"My aunt makes them for us. She uses my grandmother's recipe."

Diana came over to peer into the crock of pickles. There were at least a dozen garlic cloves floating on top, and she grinned. "At least we won't have to worry about vampires."

"I didn't know you were superstitious." Jay looked surprised.

"I was just joking." Diana was a little embarrassed. "I'm really not superstitious at all."

Cindy laughed. "Oh, no? You won't walk under a ladder, and you made me go three blocks out of my way so a black cat wouldn't cross our path. Face it, Diana. You're definitely superstitious."

"No, I'm not." Diana began to blush. Cindy had a big mouth. "It makes perfect sense not to walk under a ladder. Something might fall on you. And what's the big deal about walking a couple of extra blocks? You're always saying I should exercise more."

Cindy turned to her brother. "Right. You heard her, Jay. She's not superstitious. This is from the girl who totally freaked out when I bought black candles for Halloween."

"I just don't like the smell of licorice, that's all. And the candles you bought were scented."

"Oh, sure." Cindy grinned at her brother. "Did you know that Diana rubs a rabbit's foot right before she takes a big test? And she even goes through a little ritual, every night before she goes to bed. She's got a set of miniature Guatemalan dolls in a tiny box on her bedside table, and she takes them out and gives each doll something to worry about. She says the dolls do the worrying for her, and that helps her to sleep better."

Diana took a step toward Cindy. She was all primed to dunk Cindy's head in the vat of pickles, but then she noticed that Jay wasn't laughing. He just looked very interested.

"Where do you buy dolls like that, Diana?"

"I . . . I think I got mine from a catalogue." Diana did her best to stop blushing. She still wanted to kill Cindy for violating her privacy.

"They'd make great gifts." Jay looked totally serious. "I'd like to order some."

Dave nodded. "Me, too. You could give them to almost anyone, and they demonstrate a very sound psychological principle."

"They do?" Cindy stared at Dave in astonishment.

"Absolutely." Dave looked serious as he turned to Cindy. "My psych professor was talking about the effect worry has on sleep patterns. It's really disruptive. Haven't you ever had trouble sleeping because you were worried about something? Like a mid-term? Or a killer final?"

"Well . . . sure." Cindy still looked a little dubious. "But I don't see what that has to do with Diana's little dolls."

"It's simple. Diana tells the dolls her worries. And by verbalizing them, she takes off some of the pressure. Since her anxiety is lessened, she can sleep better. And it's a well-known fact that well-rested people are much more efficient."

Diana had all she could do not to say, *I told you so!* to Cindy. But she didn't, because that would seem childish. She just grinned, and started to spread mustard on the buns.

"These are ready to come off the grill." Dave signaled to Jay. "Bring that big platter over, will you?"

Jay grabbed the platter and headed for the grill. Then he turned back to Cindy. "If you want to help, you can put pickles in those big green jars."

Cindy walked over to where Diana was working, and lowered her voice so that Jay and Dave wouldn't hear. "I'm sorry,

Di. I never should have told them all those personal things about you. I guess I just wasn't thinking."

"You're apologizing?" Diana turned to Cindy in surprise. Cindy never apologized.

Cindy nodded. "Yeah. I am. I started thinking about how it would feel if somebody did that to me. And I probably would have killed them. Are you still mad at me?"

"No, I'm not mad anymore. But you *do* have a big mouth."

Cindy winced. "I know. But I'm going to watch it, Di. Really, I am."

"Okay." Diana smiled at Cindy. And then she said the first thing that popped into her head. "You've never promised to try to watch your mouth before. What's got into you, anyway?"

Cindy began to blush. It was so unusual, that Diana couldn't help staring.

"I don't know. I guess it was something Paul said. We were talking in the news van, and he mentioned that he used to go with a girl who had a big mouth. The reason he broke up with her was because she told her friends some of the personal things he'd said to her."

Diana nodded, and waited for Cindy to go on.

"We started talking about how some things are private, and how much it hurts if another person you trusted violates your privacy. And that's what I just did, except I didn't even realize what I was doing, until after I'd done it."

Diana smiled. Cindy had only known Paul for an hour or so, but he'd obviously caused her to think very seriously about herself.

"Why are you smiling?" Cindy looked confused.

"Oh, I don't know. I was just thinking about how much I like Paul. He's perfect for you, Cindy."

"I know." Cindy sighed. "I wish he'd stayed behind. I gave him my phone number, but maybe he's got a whole collection of girls' phone numbers. Do you think he'll call me?"

Diana took a deep breath. That was a difficult question. If she said yes, Cindy would be terribly disappointed if Paul didn't call. But if she said no, Cindy would be horribly depressed. There was only one thing to do, and that was to tell the truth.

"I don't know, Cindy. I hope he does. He seemed to really like you. But I don't know him well enough to guess what he's going to do."

"Me neither. That's why I asked. I guess I'll just have to wait and . . ." Cindy stopped and frowned. "Did you hear something?"

"No. What did you think you . . ."

Diana stopped in mid-sentence as she heard a noise. It sounded like a muted pounding and it was coming from somewhere outside.

"I hear it. But I don't know what it is." Diana hurried over to Jay and Dave. "Cindy and I heard someone pounding, outside. Is there a back door to the Pub?"

Jay turned to Dave. "Oh-oh. I locked the front entrance when we came in. Maybe somebody's trying to get in."

"The loading dock!" Dave led the way through the storeroom. "We were supposed to get a delivery tonight. Those big rigs are heavy, and one of the drivers might have made it through. We'd better check it out."

Dave unlocked the heavy metal sliding door and Jay helped him push it up. They peered out into the blowing snow, but there was no truck outside.

"Hello? Is someone out here?" Jay cupped his hands around his mouth and shouted as loud as he could. "Hello?"

"Over there!"

Jay pointed, and Diana caught sight of a parka-clad figure stumbling toward them. Dave and Jay jumped off the dock and hurried to help the stranded truck driver.

"Oh, my God!" Cindy looked scared. "But where's his truck?"

Diana gave the only possible explanation. "He must have gotten stuck on the road, and walked in. It's a good thing you heard him, Cindy. He could have frozen to death out there."

"I'm going to get some coffee." Cindy was turning to go back to the kitchen, when Dave and Jay pulled the truck driver up on the loading dock. She took one look at his face, and her eyes widened in shock. "Paul!"

Cindy and Diana rushed to help, and in a few moments, they had Paul seated in the warmest part of the kitchen, right next to the grill. He leaned back in his chair, and gave a deep sigh of relief. "Thanks, guys. I thought I was a goner out there. All the doors were locked."

"I'm going to unlock the front entrance right now." Jay nodded. "Someone else might make it through, and try to get in."

"Did you come in the news van?" Cindy noticed that Paul had brought his video camera case.

"No. I talked them into letting me do a human interest segment on the people who were stuck at the mall, but they couldn't spare the van. I talked Officer Goetz into letting me drive one of the delivery trucks. He didn't think you should be trapped out here without an emergency vehicle. But I ran into a snow drift I couldn't get through. There was no way around it, either, so I had to leave the truck about a mile down the road. I've got to call and tell him I made it."

Dave nodded. "I'll do it. You just rest up, and have some more of that hot coffee."

"This fire sure feels good!" Paul took another sip of his coffee and grinned at Diana and Cindy. "I didn't think I'd ever warm up again. It was really cold out there."

Diana noticed that Cindy's face was white, and she could tell that Cindy was thinking about what would have happened if she hadn't heard Paul pounding at the door.

"We're certainly glad you made it!" Diana smiled at Paul. "But now you're stuck out here, too."

Paul nodded. "I guess I am."

Diana had the urge to laugh. Paul didn't seem a bit concerned that he was stuck at the mall with them, and she didn't think it had anything to do with the human interest segment he was supposed to do for the station.

Just then Dave came back with a grin on his face. "Officer

Goetz says congratulations. He also told me he advised you against even trying to get through."

"That's true." Paul looked a little embarrassed. "But I told him that I had to see Cindy, and I convinced him that it was an emergency."

"What emergency?" Cindy looked puzzled.

"Remember when you gave me your phone number?"

Cindy nodded. "Sure."

"Well, you forgot to write down your area code."

The communications room was locked, but he was resourceful. He'd found a full set of keys in the security office, and he now had access to every part of the mall. It was late, and almost everyone had found a place to sleep. The furniture store had plenty of beds.

He glanced around and smiled as he saw the empty walkway. He was the only one out, and no one would be able to observe what he was about to do.

The room was dark, but he didn't switch on the lights until he'd locked the door behind him. Then he walked to the box labeled, "telephone," and began to systematically unplug the wires, labeling them as he went. He would cut off their link to the outside world. It was very important that no one interfere with his plan. But when he had finished, he would hook everything back up again so the whole world would know exactly what had happened.

Icy snow rattled against the plate glass window. The sound pleased him. It reminded him of muted snare drums, the kind they used for funerals of state. On the twenty-fifth anniversary of President Kennedy's death, they'd replayed footage of his funeral. The muted snare drums had impressed him even more than the riderless horse. Of course this wouldn't be a funeral of state. She didn't deserve that honor.

She hadn't been frightened when she'd opened his present, but that didn't matter. She was only the first, and it would take them a while to figure out the pattern. Of course, they'd think it was an accident. He'd planned it that way. They would all be accidents. And they'd be so horrible, no one would ever want to come out to the Crossroads Mall again. It might take a few months, but the mall would close without the huge crowds of customers that the owners had expected. The big chains would be the first to pull out, and without them, the mall would have huge empty spaces with no revenues. No one would drive out here to patronize the smaller stores, not when their goods were easily obtainable elsewhere. Eventually, all the stores would close, turning this huge complex into a ghost mall. The investors would suffer, just like he had suffered, and they'd end up salvaging what little they could to cut their losses.

Land was the only constant. The land was stronger than any brick and concrete edifice that man could build. Grass would push up through the asphalt, and tiny trees would grow in the cracks. Walls would crumble and birds would build their nests in the rubble. It would take years, but the land would reclaim this place. And it would be his land, the land his grandfather had intended for him. It was his Christmas present, the only one he really wanted, and Santa would make sure he got it.

Six

Everyone else was sleeping soundly, but Sue Langer was wide awake. Part of the problem was the daybed she'd chosen. It was very pretty with its white metal frame and blue and white flowered sheets and comforter, but it wasn't very comfortable. Sue smiled as she considered writing a warning and taping it to the frame. *If you want your guests to sleep all night, don't buy this bed!* Of course she'd never actually write a note like that, but there really ought to be some way to sleep on a bed before you bought it.

Sue plumped up her pillow and turned on her back, but that didn't help. Neither did rolling on her stomach, or on her side. She just wasn't sleepy, and when she closed her eyes, they popped right back open again.

They'd tried to shut off the Christmas music, but the door to the communications room had been locked. They couldn't even get in to change the tape, so they had to hear the same songs over and over. Sue didn't really mind. She loved Christmas carols. But they made her miss Ronnie terribly.

She'd tried to call Ronnie at work, but he'd been out on a delivery. Naturally, she'd left a message for him on his voice mail, but she missed him so much, she wanted to hear his voice. The lights in the store were dim, and she couldn't see her watch, but she'd heard the grandfather clock in the dining room section chime eleven times quite a while ago. It had to be close to eleven-thirty by now, and Ronnie got off work at eleven. Perhaps she should try to call him one last time. He'd be home by now.

Sue sat up on the daybed and slipped into her shoes, careful not to wake anyone else. Then she walked quietly through the furniture store and went out the door into the mall. As she passed the main entrance, she shivered a little. It was unlocked, and that gave her an uneasy feeling.

After Paul's experience, Jay had insisted they leave the main door unlocked, just in case some unlucky truck driver broke down on the road and made his way to the mall. That was also the reason they were leaving on the lights. A stranded motorist might see them from the road, and head for the mall to take shelter. It all made perfect sense, but Sue was nervous about that unlocked door. She was used to double-locking her apartment door at night.

Sue stopped as she came to the giant Christmas tree, and stood for a moment, enjoying the sight. There was something very romantic about a Christmas tree, and she wished that Ronnie were here to enjoy it with her. Getting snowbound at the mall would have been wonderful then.

"Silent Night" was playing over the loudspeaker, and Sue smiled as she walked on to the bank of pay phones just past the Crossroads Pub. She'd probably heard "Silent Night" about a hundred times today, but she loved it so much, she didn't mind. She'd met Ronnie at Christmastime, and she thought of "Silent Night" as "their" song. If they had a Christmas wedding, she might even ask the organist to play it when she walked down the aisle.

Sue put in her quarter and dialed Ronnie's number, but there was no dial tone. The phones had been working fine when they'd all called their parents, but the storm must have knocked down the lines. She tried another phone to be sure, but that one didn't work, either. They were cut off out here at the mall, with no way to talk to the outside world.

For a moment, Sue almost panicked, but then she realized that she was being ridiculous. They weren't going to be stuck here forever, and the Highway Patrol Officers had promised that the plows would be out, just as soon as the storm let up. They were perfectly all right, out here at the mall. They had plenty of food and water, and the building was well heated. They were really lucky they were here, where they had all the essentials to wait out the storm.

Dave had left the pub unlocked, and Sue went in to pour herself a chilled mug of beer. Perhaps it would relax her so she could sleep.

As Sue slid onto a bar stool and sipped her beer, she thought about how much Ronnie would like the Crossroads Pub. He loved to play darts and there were two boards mounted in wooden cabinets on the wall. Perhaps Ronnie would form a dart league, and they'd play out here a couple of nights a week. It would be a nice place to hang out.

Thinking about Ronnie began to make Sue feel sad. Although they had separate apartments, they spent most of their time together. Now Ronnie was in Prairie Falls, and she felt a little lonely, out here by herself. Diana had Jay, whether she realized it or not. And Cindy seemed to be fascinated by Paul. Heather had been flirting with Dave and Larry, attempting to make Jay jealous. She'd even tried to pick up on Hal Bremmer, but Hal had just smiled at her in that quiet way of his, and told her he wasn't interested. The other girls had someone to talk to, but she didn't have anyone. She was all alone and she missed Ronnie terribly.

Her beer mug was empty and Sue refilled it from the tap behind the bar. Then she sat back down on her stool and thought about what Ronnie would do when he got her message. One thing was for sure. He'd miss her as much as she missed him. He might even get in his car and try to drive out here.

Sue took another drink, and began to smile. She was sure Ronnie would try to get through. He'd do his best to convince the Highway Patrol that his full-size Blazer would make it through the snow. Of course they wouldn't let him try. Part of their job was to protect people from themselves.

What would Ronnie do when they told him he couldn't go

through the road block? Sue took another sip of her beer, and noticed that her mug was almost empty. The beer was making her slightly woozy, but that didn't matter. If she got a little tipsy, she could always sleep on one of the red leather booths in the pub. It was bound to be more comfortable than the daybed.

Sue refilled her beer mug, and moved to the booth. She was feeling nice and mellow, but her thoughts about Ronnie kept her awake. If Ronnie really wanted to get to her, he might try to borrow her uncle's snowplow. When Ronnie was determined to do something, nothing could stop him.

There was a smile on Sue's face as she thought about Ronnie and her uncle. Uncle Nate would think up all sorts of perfectly legitimate reasons why Ronnie shouldn't use one of his big snowplows, but he'd eventually give in. After all, Ronnie worked for him all last winter, plowing the county roads.

Sue was so convinced that Ronnie was on his way, she decided to go out to the double-glass doors by the entrance and watch for him. Wouldn't Ronnie be surprised when he drove up in the snowplow and saw her standing there? She'd tell him she couldn't sleep because she'd missed him so much. Then they'd come back here so he could warm up, and she'd fix him something to eat.

It took quite a while for Sue to walk to the employees' lounge to get her parka out of the locker. By the time she'd slipped it on and headed for the front entrance, "Silent Night" was playing on the loudspeakers again. She smiled as she pulled open the doors and stepped outside, into the frozen air. The wind wasn't blowing as hard as it had been, and only an occasional flurry of snow skittered across the parking lot. She could hear the loudspeakers from out here, and this time the song was "Oh, Little Town Of Bethlehem." The reflection of the Christmas lights on the snow was so beautiful, Sue felt her spirits soar. Glistening spots of color were everywhere. Red, blue, orange, green, yellow, and white. They flashed on and off, sparkling against the snow, until Sue began to feel dizzy from watching them. Then a big gust of wind whipped up, and she stepped back under the overhang where she was partially sheltered from the blowing snow.

Sue stood under the overhang and stamped her feet. She was beginning to get very cold, and she wondered if she was being silly. Perhaps Ronnie wasn't coming, after all. Uncle Nate might have convinced him to wait until morning so that he could make the trip in the daylight.

The tips of her toes felt numb, and Sue wished she'd worn her boots. Her tennis shoes provided no warmth at all, and her feet felt like blocks of ice. Sue stamped her feet again, and peered out at the road. There were no lights. Nothing was moving out there on the highway. Was it possible that not even a snowplow could get through?

Sue turned toward the door, feeling foolish. She'd wanted Ronnie to come out here so much, she'd talked herself into believing that he was on the way. The cold had sobered her thinking, and brought her to her senses. Ronnie was probably in bed right now, sleeping after his long day's work. He wouldn't be foolish enough to start out here at midnight. He'd come tomorrow, in the middle of the day, when it was warmer.

She was about to pull open the door and go back inside, when she thought she heard the sound of sleigh bells. Sue stopped and listened. Was her imagination working overtime? But then she heard them again. They were loud and distinctive, and she couldn't help hearing them over the sound of the wind. But where were they coming from?

Sue stepped out a few feet from the door, to stare up at the overhang. There were six heavy planters on top of the narrow balcony. Larry's father had designed the building, and he'd told her all about the planters. In the spring, they'd hold flowering apple trees, and they'd be replaced in the summer with gardenias. When autumn came, they'd be filled with chrysanthemums, but right now, in honor of the Christmas season, they held miniature pines which were decorated for Christmas.

As Sue stared up at the planters, she heard the sleigh bells again. It wasn't a figment of her imagination. Someone was up on the overhang . . . but who? And why?

Just then a shadowy figure stepped into her line of sight. Sue gasped, and then she started to laugh. It was Santa, wearing his full costume, and he held a set of sleigh bells in his hand. It was very clear that she wasn't the only one who'd had too much to drink. One of the guys had dressed up in his Santa costume and come out here to put on a show!

"Hi, Santa." Sue walked a little closer, a smile spreading over her face.

"Ho, ho, ho!"

Santa's voice was deep and merry, and Sue laughed out loud. He walked over to lean against a planter, and grinned down at her as he rang the sleigh bells again.

"Come on, Santa." Sue began to get a little worried. She could tell that Santa was bombed by the way he'd lurched against the planter. "You'd better come down from there. You might fall."

"Ho, ho, ho!"

Sue moved closer, and stared up into his face. She couldn't tell who it was. The beard and mustache covered too much of his face.

"Come on, Santa. The show's over. You have to come down now. How did you get up there, anyway?"

"Ho, ho, *ho!*"

Santa gestured toward a door at the other end of the overhang, and Sue nodded. Of course. The gardeners had to get out on the ledge to take care of the planters, and Santa had found the access door.

"Come down, Santa. Right now!"

Sue frowned as Santa shook his head. He was being very stubborn. She hoped he wouldn't topple off the overhang, but he probably wouldn't hurt himself, even if he did. There was a deep drift of snow beneath the overhang, and it was at least three feet deep. But it was cold out here, and she had to get him down before he passed out and froze to death.

How could she get him down, when he didn't want to cooperate? Sue decided to try flattery and trickery. Since he thought he was Santa, she'd appeal to his best Santa instincts.

Sue took a deep breath, and waded into the icy snowbank. The cold seeped through her legs and feet, but she gritted her teeth and kept on going until she was almost directly beneath him. She'd have to change shoes when she got back inside, but it would be worth it if she could get him to come down.

"Come down, Santa." Sue grinned at him. "I've been a good girl all year. I want to sit on your lap so I can tell you what I want for Christmas."

Santa laughed, and Sue gave a sigh of relief as he got to his feet. She hoped he knew how to get down by himself. She certainly wasn't going up there to help him! But instead of walking toward the door, Santa turned to grin at her.

It was the strangest grin that Sue had ever seen, and she drew in her breath, sharply. Santa was supposed to be kind and benevolent, but this Santa's grin looked evil. His eyes seemed to bore into her as if they could read the fear that was beginning to grow inside her, and the twinkle lights reflecting off his face made him look almost demonic.

She stepped back instinctively, but she stumbled in the deep snow and fell to her knees. Then Santa gave a horrible, demented laugh, and pushed against the heavy planter with both arms.

Sue opened her mouth to scream as the planter started to move. She scrambled frantically to her feet, but it was too late. She was trapped, immobile, in the waist-deep snow. All she could do was stare up in horrible fascination as the heavy planter toppled from the edge of the overhang, Christmas lights winking on and off, directly toward her head. It struck in a grand burst of Christmas color, but all Sue saw was eternal darkness as her lifeless body crumpled, and her blood stained the pristine white snow with bright red poinsettia-colored splotches.

Seven

He was still laughing as he entered the mall again, and locked the service door behind him. There was no need to check to make sure she was dead. The heavy pot had crushed her skull. No one could live through trauma like that.

The costume room was at the opposite end of the mall, but he was very cautious as he hurried down the walkway, ducking into store doorways whenever he thought he heard a sound. There could be someone else with insomnia, and he didn't want to run into anyone while he was wearing his costume.

He breathed a deep sigh of relief as he reached the costume area, and slipped inside. He locked the door behind him, and changed to street clothes as fast as he could. Then he hung up the costume and brushed the snow from the red velvet material. It would dry before morning and no one would be the wiser.

In less than ten minutes, he was back at the furniture store. He tiptoed past the living room section where two of them were sleeping on sofa beds, and took a detour to glance at the grand-father clock in the dining room section. It was one-twenty in the morning. His night's work had taken almost two hours, but it had been very productive. One had been punished. And Santa would punish another, tomorrow night.

When he reached the bedroom section, he moved stealthily past the sleepers and got into bed again. He'd prepared a story in case someone had missed him, an excuse about having to get up to use the restroom. But there was no need to utter the lie. From the even breathing of the other sleepers, he was certain no one had noticed that he'd been gone.

He gave a satisfied sigh as he found a comfortable position and snuggled down under the blankets. He was going to rest well tonight. He had begun to take his revenge, and the feeling it had given him was sweet. As he closed his eyes, "Santa Claus Is Comin' To Town" began to play on the speaker system, and he drifted off to sleep with a contented smile on his face.

Diana woke up as someone whispered her name. She rolled over, opened her eyes, and blinked in confusion as she saw Jay standing by her bed. For a moment, she didn't know where she was, but then she remembered. They were all snowbound at the mall.

"It's almost eight," Jay whispered so he wouldn't wake the others. "How about a cup of coffee?"

Diana gave a quick nod, and got out of bed. She slipped into her shoes and followed Jay past the other sleepers to the mall outside. She waited until they were three doors down from the furniture store, and then she spoke. "Coffee sounds wonderful, but where do we get it?"

"We make it. Let's brew a big pot so there's plenty when everybody else wakes up."

Jay motioned toward the escalator, and they got on to ride up to the second floor. Jay had stepped on behind her, and he was standing so close, Diana could feel the warmth of his body. She had the urge to lean back and enjoy the comfort of his arms, but she didn't. She just smiled and rode up, watching their reflection in the mirrors that lined the escalator walls.

"Where are we going?" Diana stepped off the escalator, and waited for Jay to catch up to her.

"To the restaurant. I checked it out, and it's open. I was going to make the coffee myself, but I wasn't sure how to use their coffee machine."

"So you woke up a female to do it for you?" Diana tried to look stern, but her eyes were twinkling.

Jay nodded. "Yeah. But I wasn't being sexist or anything like that. I just figured you might know more about coffee machines than I do."

"Why did you pick me?" Diana couldn't hide her grin as Jay led her into the main part of the restaurant.

"Because . . . oh, I don't know." Jay grinned back, but he looked a little embarrassed. "I guess I just wanted you with me. It was lonesome, being the only one awake."

Diana's grin grew wider. He'd wanted her, not just any female. "Okay. Show me that coffee machine and we'll see if we can figure it out."

"Right this way." Jay led Diana into the restaurant kitchen, and motioned toward the coffee machine. "Do you know how to work one of these?"

"Sure. The reservoir's always filled with hot water. All you have to do is put coffee in the basket and pour cold water through the hole in the top. The water you pour in forces the hot water out, and it drips down through the grounds."

"You figured that out just by looking at it?"

There was an expression of awe on Jay's face, and Diana laughed. "Not really. It's just like the one my dad has in his office."

In less than five minutes, they both had steaming cups of coffee, and Diana had put on another pot. They wandered out into the main part of the restaurant, and peered out the huge plate glass windows at the snow.

"I think it's letting up a little." Jay looked hopeful. "What do you think, Di?"

Diana shook her head. Everything outside the window was completely obscured by a swirling wall of white. "I think you're just trying to cheer me up. I can't even see where the highway's supposed to be."

"Then I guess we're stuck here." Jay didn't look at all upset. "Did you have plans for the weekend?"

"I was supposed to go to my cousin's baby shower tonight. I'd better call and tell her I'm not going to make it."

"But we all called our parents last night. Wouldn't your folks have told your cousin that you were snowbound out here?"

Diana frowned slightly. "I don't think so. They were invited to the shower next weekend for the relatives. I'm not sure they even know about this one."

"There's a phone over there." Jay pointed toward the reservations desk. "Go ahead, Di. I don't think anyone's going to be upset if you make a local call."

Diana walked over to the phone and lifted the receiver. Then she turned to Jay with a frown. "There's no dial tone."

"Maybe you have to dial nine to get an outside line."

Diana dialed nine, but nothing happened. "It's not working. Do you think the phones are out?"

Jay nodded. "That's certainly possible. The storm dumped a lot of heavy snow, and one of the lines might have snapped. Let's try the pay phones. They might be on another line."

Diana and Jay carried their coffee cups along as they tried several banks of pay phones. None of them worked.

Finally, Diana turned to Jay in frustration. "What am I going to do? I promised I'd be there early. I was supposed to help with the refreshments."

"Don't worry, Di." Jay slipped his arm around her shoulders. "If your cousin was watching television last night, she'll know you're stuck out here."

"I know that. But maybe she wasn't watching. I'd feel a lot better if I could talk to her and explain."

Jay nodded. "I understand. If it'll make you feel better, we'll try the pay phones outside. One of them might be working."

It didn't take long to get into their parkas and boots. Diana shivered as Jay pulled open the door and they stepped out into the blowing snow. It was a lot colder than it had been yesterday, and little bits of ice blew against her cheeks, stinging and turning them red.

"Here. You'd better take this." Jay leaned close so she could hear him over the howl of the wind, and handed her a long, green woolen scarf. As Diana wrapped it around her face, she caught the faint scent of perfume, and she wondered if Heather had made it for him. That didn't seem likely. Heather wasn't the type to knit. But there was only one way to find out for sure, and that was to ask.

"Nice scarf." Diana smiled, even though the scarf was wrapped around her mouth and he couldn't possibly see her smile. "Did someone make it for you?"

Jay nodded. "My grandmother knits. She gave it to me for Christmas last year, along with a pair of mittens. I've got those, too, if you want to wear them."

"No, thanks. I've got these pink ones my grandmother made." Diana slipped them on and grinned. "I guess we'd freeze if our grandmas didn't spend hours on these things. My grandma used to even knit a rope to hold my mittens together, so I wouldn't lose them."

"You mean that long piece of yarn that went up one of your sleeves and down the other? With a mitten attached to each end?"

"That's it!" Diana giggled. "My grandma made my mittens like that until I was in junior high."

Jay nodded, and reached into his pocket to pull out his mittens. "Consider yourself lucky. My grandma still does it."

"Oh, no!" Diana cracked up as Jay separated his mittens and showed her the braided rope of yarn that held the left to the right. Then he motioned toward the side of the building, and they waded through the snow to get to the phones.

Diana dropped in a quarter and held the receiver to her ear. But even through the thick scarf she could hear that there was no dial tone.

"It doesn't work?"

Diana shook her head and moved to the next phone, but she couldn't get a dial tone there, either. These phones were just as dead as the ones inside.

"At least we got some fresh air." Jay took her arm and they started back toward the entrance. But then he stopped and let out a muttered exclamation.

"What is it?" Diana stopped, too, and looked where Jay was pointing. It was impossible to see very far because the wind was whipping up flurries of loose snow, but she did catch sight of a Christmas tree, half-buried in a deep snowbank.

"You stay here." Jay pushed her under the shelter of the overhang. "I'll check it out."

"No. I'm coming with you. If I stop moving, I'll freeze to death."

Diana tucked her hand under his arm and they started off together, wading through a huge pile of snow to get to the tree. When they arrived at the half-buried Christmas tree, both of them were puffing.

"One of the planters must have fallen off the overhang." Jay pointed to the tree. "That tree came from up there . . . see?"

Diana turned around to look. When she'd walked through the entrance, yesterday, she'd noticed that there were six trees in the planters. Now there were only five.

"The winds must've been really bad last night. It's just lucky that no one was walking underneath when . . . oh, my God!"

There was panic in Jay's voice, and Diana started to turn around. But Jay blocked her view, and gave her a little push toward the entrance. "Don't look. Just go get the guys . . . quick!"

"But . . . what is it?" Diana tried to turn again, but Jay wouldn't let her.

"Please, Diana. Just do what I say. Keep the girls inside, and send out the guys on the double. Tell them it's an emergency. And have them bring some blankets."

Diana shivered, but it wasn't from the biting wind. There was something terribly wrong. She opened her mouth to ask what the emergency was, but she knew Jay wouldn't tell her. He was determined to get her away from here, but she was so frightened by the desperate tone in his voice, she couldn't seem to move.

"Diana . . . go! Go now!"

Jay gave her another little shove, and Diana took a shaky step. That seemed to break the spell, and she stumbled awkwardly toward the entrance.

Her fear seemed to evaporate, once she got inside the door.

The mall was familiar and warm, a safe haven from the storm. Diana turned to glance out the plate glass door. And at that exact moment, the wind stopped blowing.

Diana could see Jay clearly, standing by the huge mound of snow. He was staring down at something sticking up from the snowbank, and he looked horrified. Then the wind picked up again, obscuring Diana's view, but not before she'd seen exactly what was protruding from the mound of snow. And the sight made her run for the furniture store as fast as her shaking legs would carry her.

As she delivered Jay's message and urged the guys to hurry, the image Diana had seen floated on the very edge of her consciousness, too horrible to be real. But it was there, nonetheless, etched permanently into her brain. Jay had been standing there motionless, looking down at something half-buried in the snow, something frightening and dreadfully gruesome.

He'd been staring at a human arm!

Eight

Once everyone had learned about Sue's awful accident, none of them had felt like being alone. They'd spent the entire day going from phone to phone, to see if any were functional. There were over three hundred phones in the mall and they'd checked them all, including the ones in the stores and the offices. None of them had been working, and there was no way they could report Sue's death.

When darkness had begun to fall, they'd all gathered in the Crossroads Pub. No one was very hungry so they'd picked up deli food at the grocery store on the main floor, and they'd arranged it on a platter. Jay and Larry had gone to the juice stand on the promenade level, and come back with several bottles of apple cider. They'd heated it with nutmeg and cloves, poured it into mugs, and stuck a cinnamon stick in each one. Now they were all sitting around the big, round table in the center of the room, sipping hot apple cider and eating sandwiches, trying to avoid thinking about what had happened. It wasn't working. Sue's horrible death was on everyone's mind.

Diana sighed, and everyone turned to look at her. She took a deep breath, and said exactly what was on her mind. "I know you guys don't want to talk about Sue, but I have to ask a question. It's important."

"Okay." Jay nodded. "Go ahead."

"What did you do? Wrap her in the blankets and leave her in the snowbank?"

"No." Jay looked around at the other guys, but none of them seemed to want to elaborate. "We . . . uh . . . we put her in a safe place."

"Outside?" Diana frowned. She knew it didn't make sense, but the thought of Sue, outside in the cold, was really disturbing.

"No. We didn't leave her outside." Paul spoke up. "We talked it over, and we decided that it was better to bring her inside."

"But why?"

Hal cleared his throat. He looked very uncomfortable. "Uh . . . animals. We thought maybe they might . . . you know."

"Oh." Diana winced as she caught his meaning. "I understand. But where did you put her?"

"Does it matter?" Jay looked very uncomfortable.

The emotional part of Diana wanted to drop it. Jay looked really upset. But her practical side took over.

"I'm sorry, Jay, but it *does* matter. What if we open a door and . . ." Diana swallowed hard. "You know what I mean. And that's why I think you have to tell all of us where you put Sue's body."

Jay thought about it for a moment, and then he nodded. "Okay. This is going to sound kind of weird, but we put Sue's body in the best place we could think of. She's in the meat case in the grocery store."

"The meat case?" Diana stared at Jay in shock.

"This whole situation gives me the creeps," Heather suddenly exclaimed. "Especially what Paul did!"

"Me? What did I do?" Now Paul began to frown.

"You taped the whole thing, and I think that's irresponsible journalism!"

"No, it's not." Cindy glared at Heather. "Paul was just doing his job. He explained the whole thing to me. Since the police couldn't come out here, Paul used his camera to make a record for the police. They can watch the tape and see exactly where Sue was when she died."

Heather had the grace to look slightly embarrassed. "Oh. That's different. But there's something I don't understand. What was Sue doing out there in the first place?"

Everyone exchanged glances. They'd been wondering the same thing. Finally, Diana spoke up. "Maybe she couldn't sleep?"

"But it was freezing cold outside. If she couldn't sleep, why didn't she just walk around the inside of the mall?"

"I think I might know the answer to that." Dave gave a troubled sigh, and they all turned to look at him. "I didn't say anything before, but there was a half-empty beer mug on the counter when I came in here. Did any of you get up in the middle of the night to have another beer?"

One by one, they shook their heads, and Dave nodded. "That's what I thought. Sue must have had trouble sleeping so she came back here to drink. Let's assume she had one too many, and she stepped outside to try to sober up. The lights were on, and she waded out into the snow to look at the Christmas trees on the overhang. And then a strong gust of wind came up, and the tree fell, and . . . well . . . you know the rest."

Diana nodded, along with everyone else. She didn't want to voice her objection now, but there was a big hole in Dave's theory. Sue could have had too much beer. That much was true. And she could have stepped outside to clear her head. But Diana didn't believe the planter had toppled in a strong gust of wind. She'd seen the way the planters were attached to the overhang, and it would have taken much more than a strong wind to move them. And the one that had fallen was the one in the middle, the one that was protected the most from the wind.

Jay looked concerned as he leaned close to whisper in Diana's ear. "You look worried. Is something wrong?"

Diana shook her head. She didn't want to alarm Jay. Not yet. Not until she'd thought everything out. But there was another big hole in Dave's theory. Sue had been wearing her expensive new tennis shoes, the ones she'd bought for cheerleading. And there was no way she would have waded out into the snowbank with her new cheerleading shoes, not unless she'd had a very good reason.

Suddenly, a thought occurred to Diana, and she began to shiver. She glanced up at Jay, but he was listening to something Cindy was saying. That was good, because she didn't want him to notice the panic that was spreading through her whole body. She'd just thought of a new theory, a theory that made much more sense. Someone else had been outside with Sue. Diana was sure of it. And that someone had lured her out into the deep snow, and pushed the planter down from the overhang to kill her!

Santa smiled as he sat in the locked security office and worked on his list. They were all beginning to relax now, after the shock of Sue's death. Several of them had wandered off to do various things in the mall, and that made his work much easier. It was hard to cut out the one he wanted from the herd, when they were huddled together like frightened sheep.

Of course, they were oblivious to his grand plan. They had no idea that there would be more accidents. Only he knew that. Santa knew everything, including exactly who the next victim would be. He was making a list and checking it twice, going to find out who was naughty and nice. And the next victim had been very, very naughty.

He never would have known, if Gramps hadn't told him. It had been in the summer, five years ago, when Grandma was still alive. A couple had slipped off the road in the rain, and they'd walked to the farmhouse, asking for help.

Gramps had been suffering from a summer cold, but he'd never been able to refuse anyone in trouble. He'd fired up the tractor and spent the better part of an hour pulling the young man's car up onto the road. The girl had stayed in the farmhouse, talking to Grandma. She'd been friendly and sweet, and he had no quarrel with her.

But the young man had done something very bad. He might not have known it, but that was no excuse. When he'd driven back to the farmhouse to pick up his date, he'd found her sitting at the kitchen table with Grandma, copying down some of the priceless recipes that had been in their family for generations. Instead of waiting for her to finish, he'd insisted she leave with him right away. And when she'd objected, he'd told her that if she was that interested in recipes, he'd buy her a Betty Crocker cookbook!

Grandma's feelings had been hurt. She'd complained that the young man was terribly thoughtless and he didn't deserve such a nice girl. To make matters worse, the next day Gramps had started coughing and his cold had turned into pneumonia from standing out in the rain so long. It had taken him two long months to recover, and they'd had to pay a hired man to help out when Gramps was sick. The young man deserved to be punished for causing all that trouble, and Santa would make sure he paid with his life.

He got up from the desk and pulled out the top drawer of the filing cabinet. Inside, he found the roll of green foil Christmas paper he'd picked up at the Hallmark store on the upper level, and he carried it over to the desk.

As he started to wrap the present, he hummed a few bars of his favorite Christmas song. He'd watched the girls in the wrapping booth and learned how to taper the corners to make it look professional. It was an honor to get a present wrapped by Santa himself. In the old children's fable, the elves did that task.

He didn't know how to form a perfect bow, but the Hallmark shop had made it easy with premade bows that simply stuck on the package. He chose a big gold one, shaped like a multipointed star, and peeled off the little strip of paper that protected the taped surface. Then he stuck it on the top of the package and smiled. It was a perfect gift, extremely well suited for the person who would receive it. Now his only problem would be getting it out to the tree, unobserved.

Once he'd turned out the lights in the security office, he opened the door and peeked out. He could see the huge Christmas tree from here, and no one was in sight. There would be an element of risk when he carried the package down the walkway, but life was full of risks, and he'd prepared for this one. If someone spotted him, he'd tell them he'd found the package in the employees' lounge. There would be no reason to doubt that little white lie.

A moment later, the deed was accomplished. The present sat in a central spot under the tree, foil paper glittering brightly under the twinkling lights. They'd all agreed to meet here at eight to plan what they'd do for the rest of the evening, and they'd be sure to notice the present. It would be opened, and the note would be read. And then Santa would punish his next victim.

"I suppose you think I'm crazy." There was a worried expression on Diana's face as she looked up at Jay. They were sitting on a bench on the promenade, and she'd just finished explaining her theory to him.

"No, Di. I don't think you're crazy." Jay put his arm around her shoulders and smiled down at her. "But I do think you're borrowing trouble."

"Then you don't believe me?"

Jay sighed, and pulled her closer. "Sure, I believe you. And it could have happened the way you say. But it also could have happened the way Dave explained it."

"But why did that particular planter fall? And why was Sue standing right beneath it, getting her new cheerleading shoes all wet?"

"I don't know." Jay shrugged. "I don't think we'll ever know. Only Sue could tell us that."

"Do you really think Sue would have waded through the snow in her new shoes?"

"No. Not if she'd been sober. But maybe she wasn't. And maybe she didn't even think about her shoes. People do all sorts of strange things when they're bombed. Remember Evan Collier?"

"Of course I do." Diana nodded. Evan was a straight "A" student, a nice, quiet guy who went to church every Sunday, and wrote letters to the school paper, complaining about the loose morals of his classmates. Just last month, Evan had gotten so bombed at a party, he'd taken off all his clothes and gone swimming in the college pool. And when Mrs. Iverson, the girls' swimming coach, had threatened to call the campus police, Evan had pulled her into the water and kissed her.

Jay was looking at her with a question in his eyes, and Diana sighed. "Okay. You made your point. I guess Sue could have forgotten she was wearing her cheerleading shoes. But how about the planter? I still don't see how the wind could have pushed it off the ledge."

"Neither do I, not if it was secured the way you think it was. But it's possible one of the gardeners knocked it loose when he was planting the Christmas tree. That would explain why it was the only one to fall."

Diana frowned, but then she nodded. "I guess it could have happened that way. But do you really think Sue's death was an accident?"

"Let's leave that up to the police to decide. They're the experts, not us."

"Okay." Diana nodded, and she felt as if a heavy weight had been lifted off her shoulders. Jay was right. The police were the experts. And the highway patrol would come out here, just as soon as the roads were cleared. They'd call in a team of detectives, and they'd be the ones to decide if there had been any foul play.

Jay leaned down and kissed her softly, his lips barely brushing her forehead. Then he glanced at his watch and stood up. "I'll walk you back to the Christmas tree, and then I've got something I have to do."

"What?" Diana looked up at him with shining eyes. He'd kissed her again! Jay's first kiss had landed on the tip of her nose while they'd been sitting under the Christmas tree, and this one had brushed her forehead. Diana warned herself not to read too much into what had happened. Jay had given her two friendly kisses, nothing more than that. But her knees felt weak, she was slightly breathless, and she couldn't help wondering what a real kiss would be like.

Jay looked very uncomfortable. "I promised Heather I'd meet her by the fountain. She said she had to talk to me about something terribly important. It's probably nothing, but . . . well . . . I've been avoiding her lately, and I guess it won't hurt to just listen to what she has to say. I owe her that much . . . right?"

"Mmmm." Diana nodded, and kept her expression carefully neutral. But as they rode down the escalator and walked toward the Christmas tree in the center of the mall, she was frowning slightly. Everyone except Jay knew that Heather was trying to get him back. Unfortunately, Jay seemed oblivious to that fact.

Jay grinned as he spotted Cindy and Paul sitting on a bench by the Christmas tree. "Hi, guys. Take care of Diana for me, will you? I'll be back in a couple of minutes."

"Sure. No problem." Paul nodded, and gestured toward his video camera. "I was just going to do a little spot with Cindy, and it always helps to have an audience. You don't mind, do you, Diana?"

"No. Of course not." Diana's frown deepened as she watched Jay walk away. She wished there was some way she could stop him from meeting Heather, but she didn't want to let him know that she was worried.

"What's the matter, Di?" Cindy saw Diana's frown. "Is there something wrong?"

"Not yet, but there might be. Jay's meeting Heather at the fountain."

"Oh, oh." Cindy looked worried. "Why is he meeting *her?*"

"She told him she had something important to discuss with him. I don't think she told him what it was."

Cindy rolled her eyes. "My brother's an idiot! He never should have agreed to meet her!"

"Time out." Paul glanced from Cindy to Diana and then back again. "You're both upset, and I don't know why. What's going on, anyway?"

Diana looked embarrassed, but Cindy turned to Paul with fire in her eyes. "Heather's a bitch! She used to be Jay's girl-friend, but she dumped him for another guy. And now she's dumped the other guy. Heather's going to pull every dirty trick in the book to try to get Jay back."

"Oh. I get it." Paul slipped his arm around Cindy's shoulders. "And you're hoping that Jay will be smart enough to steer clear. Is that right?"

Cindy nodded, but she still looked worried. "When it comes

to women, Jay's not exactly known for his brain power. I just wish I knew what was happening at the fountain."

"That's easy." Paul patted his video camera. "I've got a long lens I can use. Do you want me to get the whole thing on tape?"

"No! Don't do that!" Diana looked shocked.

"Why not?" Cindy began to grin. "It would serve Heather right!"

Diana shook her head and looked very serious. "That's true. I'd tell you to go for it if Heather was the only one involved. But it really wouldn't be fair to Jay. He's got to handle this on his own, without any interference from us."

"But I thought you liked him." Cindy was puzzled. "Don't you want to save him from Heather?"

"Of course I do! But spying on him isn't the answer. It would mean that I don't trust Jay to do the right thing, all by himself. And I do trust him."

Paul lifted his eyebrows, and nodded. Then he turned to Cindy with a smile. "I think Diana's absolutely right. And I also think she's falling in love with your brother."

"Really?" Cindy looked delighted. "But how can you tell that?"

"Diana trusts him. You heard her say that. And she won't stoop to using dirty tricks to trap him. That means she really cares about him. Is that right, Diana?"

Diana could feel herself blushing. Her face felt hot, and she knew her cheeks were turning bright pink. "It's true. I *do* care about Jay. But falling in love . . . well . . . I'm just not sure about that."

"Yet," Cindy prompted her, "you're not sure about that *yet!* But you will be before we get out of here. I'm willing to bet on that."

Paul laughed, and gave Cindy a little hug. "You're just like Yente in *Fiddler on the Roof.*"

"I remember her." Cindy looked pleased. "Yente was the matchmaker."

"That's right. And that's exactly what you are, Cynthia Swanson!"

Cindy laughed as Paul hugged her, but Diana's mouth dropped open in shock. Cindy hated the name, Cynthia. She'd threatened to kill anyone who called her that, but she didn't seem to be a bit angry with Paul.

Right then and there, Diana decided to play matchmaker, too. Cindy might not know it, but she was falling in love with Paul. And people who were falling in love needed time alone. She stood up and grinned at them. "I'll be back in a couple of minutes. I need to go get my sweater."

"You're cold?" Cindy looked concerned. "It's got to be eighty degrees in here. Are you coming down with the flu, or something awful like that?"

"No. I'm just a little chilly, that's all."

"We'd better go with you." Paul started to get to his feet. "I promised Jay we'd take care of you."

"Don't bother. I'm just going to run to the furniture store. I left my sweater in there. You two go on with what you were doing."

Diana turned and headed down the walkway. When she got about halfway to the furniture store, she turned to look back. She'd done a good job as a matchmaker. Paul and Cindy were sitting close together on the bench, his arm around her shoulders, and her head nestled close to his chest.

It didn't take long to get her sweater, but Diana purposely took another few minutes, walking around the furniture store, looking at the various displays. They were all arranged like little rooms with walls that were open on one side. She stopped by a display of a child's room, and began to smile. The whole room had a dinosaur theme. The bedspreads on the bunk beds were printed with frolicking dinosaurs, and so were the curtains. The rug had a giant dinosaur woven into its center, and the toy box was even shaped like a dinosaur.

Diana smiled as she dreamed of tucking two little boys in bed, kissing them good night, and handing each one a dinosaur pillow to cuddle. She knew she wanted to have children someday, and she smiled even wider as she remembered what Cindy had told her. Jay was very good with children, and he'd done volunteer work at the campus children's center all last summer. If she married Jay, their children would have a wonderful father.

Diana blinked and shook her head. She was definitely getting ahead of herself. Here she was, thinking about marrying Jay and having children, and he was at the fountain with Heather!

As Diana turned to leave the furniture store, she wondered if Cindy's first instinct had been right. Diana had held fast to her principles when she'd refused to let Paul spy on Jay and Heather with his video camera. But right now, she really wished she knew exactly what was happening at the fountain!

Nine

They were all sitting around the Christmas tree, and Paul's video camera was on. He'd brought over a dozen one-hour tapes with him, enough to record anything interesting that might happen. He'd told them the station might be interested in knowing what it was like to be snowbound at the mall, and they'd agreed to let him tape their activities whenever he wanted. Everyone was very excited about the possibility of selling it to the station as a news feature. The station paid good money for features, and they could divide the profits.

"I think we should call it, 'Snowbound Seven.'" Paul began to smile. "It's a catchy title."

Cindy turned to Paul with a frown. "It's catchy, but it's wrong. How can we call it 'Snowbound Seven' if there's eight of us?"

"That's true. But only seven of you will be on tape. I'll be behind the camera."

Diana smiled as Jay put his arm around her shoulders. He hadn't mentioned anything about his meeting with Heather, but it was obvious that her plan to win him back hadn't worked. Jay was here, right by her side. And Heather was sitting between Larry and Hal.

"I'm ready." Hal grinned at Paul. "What do you want us to do first?"

Paul thought for a moment. "The first thing I need is a shot they can use for a bumper card."

"A what?" Hal looked puzzled.

"A bumper card is a shot they use to advertise the show. Haven't you ever watched a movie on television?"

"Sure." Hal nodded.

"There's a shot they use, halfway through the commercials to remind you they're going back to the movie. Sometimes it's a still from the movie and there's a voice-over that says something like, *The Friday night movie will continue, right after these important messages.* That's the bumper card."

"I've seen it." Hal nodded again. "When it comes on, it means you've got time to fix popcorn before the movie actually starts. Why do they use those, anyway?"

Paul laughed. "Federal regulations allow only so many minutes of commercials in one stretch. But if the station puts on a bumper card, it counts the same as going back to the movie. It breaks up the string of commercials, and the station can run another batch."

"And more commercials mean more money?"

"Exactly!" Paul gave Hal an approving look. "The stations don't exist to entertain you. They're a business, just like any other business. The movie, itself, doesn't bring them any profit. They make their money from selling air time to advertisers, and they want to run as many commercials as they can."

Hal nodded. "I get it. And I understand why we need a bumper card. What kind of shot do you want to use?"

"I need something that establishes how empty the mall is, and how alone you are, way out here. Any suggestions?"

"I've got one." Cindy looked eager. "How about if everyone grabs one of those presents and sits under the tree, looking sad? You could tape us from a long way back to show that there's nobody here except us."

Paul nodded. "That's great, Cindy! I want everyone to pick up a package. Hold it on your lap, and sit very close, huddled together, as if you're lonely. Then give me your best forlorn look . . . like this."

Diana stared as Paul put on a forlorn face. He looked just like a sad-eyed basset hound. Cindy was staring at him with open admiration, and Diana almost laughed out loud. Cindy was fascinated with Paul, and Paul seemed to be just as fascinated by her.

"Come on, Diana." Jay handed her a package and took one himself. Then he put his arm around her shoulders and gave her a little squeeze. "Now look sad."

Diana did her best to look forlorn, but her eyes were sparkling and her heart was thudding a million miles a minute.

She glanced over at Heather, and felt like grinning as she caught Heather's angry stare. Heather was fuming. Diana lowered her eyes and looked as sad as possible, under the circumstances. Heather had tried to get Jay back, and Heather had failed. Everyone here could plainly see that Jay preferred her instead.

He watched carefully as the packages were taken. And he almost smiled as Santa's present, the one wrapped in green paper, was chosen. No one was looking at the tags right now. They were too busy following the instructions, scrunching together in a group and looking forlorn. It would have been inappropriate to laugh, even though his heart was singing with joy.

This turn of events was a pure delight. Not only would he exact his revenge, he'd have a record of it for the rest of his life. He could watch the tape over and over, and relive these wonderful memories.

It was a very good shot. Everyone looked very sad. And it would have made an excellent bumper card. Of course the station wouldn't need a bumper card because this tape would never be aired. The station wouldn't even know that it existed. Santa would make sure of that.

A warm glow spread through his body as the video camera whirred away. Too bad he couldn't wear his red velvet suit. It would make this moment even more enjoyable. But taking a risk like that would be very foolish, and Santa was much too clever to expose his identity at this point in the game. He was one of them now, and he'd continue to blend into their group until the very end. Only then would he reveal his secret, and bask in the glory of his success.

"Cut!" Paul was smiling as he put down his camera. "Okay, everybody. You can put your packages back now."

Diana nodded, and picked up her package to hand it to Jay. It was the first time she'd ever actually looked at it, and she frowned slightly as she noticed that it was wrapped in green foil paper. She didn't remember any rolls of green foil paper in the wrapping booth. And she was sure they hadn't used any star-shaped bows. Then she noticed the tag, and her frown deepened. It was a different type than the tags they'd used.

"What's the matter?" Jay looked concerned.

"Probably nothing, but . . . I don't think we wrapped this package."

Jay took the present, and flipped open the tag. "This is strange. It says, *To Dave. From Santa.*"

"To me?" Dave leaned over, and grabbed the package. "I'm going to open it!"

Suddenly Diana remembered Sue's package, and the weird message inside. Sue had opened it. And now Sue was dead. She shivered, and turned to Jay with fear in her eyes.

"No. You'd better not." Even though Diana didn't say anything, Jay seemed to know exactly what she was thinking. He reached out for the package, but Dave pulled it back.

"Oh, no, you don't. It's for me. You saw the tag. My name's on this present."

"But you don't know if this present's for you." Jay tried reasoning with him. "There's a million other guys out there named Dave."

"But I'm the only one here right now. It's fate. And I'm going to open it."

As Dave tore off the paper, Diana noticed that Paul was taping again. She held her breath as Dave lifted the lid on the white box inside.

"Oh, oh! I guess I've been a bad boy this year. Santa gave me an empty box."

"No, he didn't." Heather reached inside the box and picked up a piece of paper. "Santa left you a note. Shall I read it?"

Paul nodded, and Heather smiled at the camera before she began to read. "It says, *Better not pout; I'm telling you why: Santa Claus is comin' to town.*"

"Weird!" Dave took the piece of paper, and glanced down at it. "Heather's right. That's what it says. Okay, Santa . . . even though I'm stuck out here with a bunch of crazy friends who leave me empty boxes with crazy notes inside, I promise that I won't pout."

"Any idea who left you that note?" Paul prompted from behind the camera.

"Maybe." Dave turned to look at Heather. "I seem to remember that a certain young lady, who shall forever remain nameless, accused me of pouting when she turned down my invitation to our high school prom."

Heather's eyes widened in surprise. And then she shook her head. "You're talking about me! But I don't remember saying that."

"You did. And it obviously left a deep psychological scar. I still remember every word you said."

Jay laughed at the shocked expression on Heather's face. "Don't leave us hanging, Dave. Tell us!"

"She said, *Sorry, but I'm waiting for Steve Rawlins to ask me.*"

"Well, I was!" Heather gave a deep sigh. "And he asked me the very next day. I did you a favor, Dave. If I'd promised to go to the prom with you, I would've just had to cancel."

Dave nodded. "Right. It was pretty obvious that Heather thought Steve was a more prestigious date than I was."

Heather began to look very uncomfortable as everyone turned to stare at her. "It wasn't that. You just don't understand. Steve was the class president, and he got to pose for all sorts of pictures. If I'd gone with you, nobody would have paid any attention to me."

"Spoken like a true social climber." Dave turned to the rest of the group. "Do you want to know what else she said?"

Diana shook her head. It was pretty obvious that Dave had an axe to grind. "No, that's enough. That happened a long time ago, Dave. We really don't want to hear any more."

"Oh, but I want to tell you." Dave grinned, but it wasn't a nice grin. "Heather said, *Stop pouting, Dave. It makes you look even uglier.*"

"Well . . . it did make you look uglier!" Heather began to frown. "Really, Dave. I don't know why you're bringing all this up now. I certainly didn't mean to hurt your feelings. I was just being honest."

Dave licked his finger and chalked an imaginary mark in the air. "That's one, Heather. And this present's the second one. What are you trying to do? Permanently damage my psyche?"

"Of course not! You're just mad at me because I wouldn't kiss you last night. That's why you're being mean. And you're dead wrong about that stupid present. I didn't give it to you!"

Dave opened his mouth to argue, but Diana spoke up. "I believe you, Heather. I'm sure you didn't give Dave that present."

"You are?" Heather turned to her in surprise. "Why?"

Diana thought fast. She didn't want to embarrass Heather by telling everyone the real reason. If Heather had wanted to say something to Dave, she wouldn't have bothered writing a note, putting it in a box, and wrapping it up with his name on it. Heather was much more direct. She would have come right out and said it to his face.

"It's simple." Diana grinned as she thought of a perfect way to phrase her answer. "It's just not your style to be sneaky."

Heather nodded. "That's absolutely right. I'm glad *somebody* around here knows that!"

"I agree." Jay spoke up. "There's no way Heather could have wrapped that package."

Heather turned to Jay with a million-watt smile. "I'm so glad you believe in me, Jay."

"That really doesn't have anything to do with it." Jay didn't smile back. "But I know you didn't wrap that package."

"How do you know that?" Cindy looked doubtful.

"Just look at her nails." Jay reached out and grabbed Heather's hand, holding it up so everyone could see her long acrylic nails. "I got a good look at that package. It was wrapped in foil, the kind that tears very easily. If Heather had tried to wrap it, there would have been rips all over the paper."

Heather was clearly miffed as she snatched her hand back. There was fire in her eyes as she turned to Diana and pointed. "She could have done it. She's got short nails. And so does your baby sister."

Diana opened her mouth to protest her innocence. Heather was a bitch. She'd just defended Heather, and now Heather was trying to shift the blame to her! But before Diana could say anything, Jay squeezed her hand.

"They didn't do it, either." Jay shook his head. "Cindy was with Paul all day. And Diana was with me."

"Diana wasn't with you all the time." Heather gave a smug little smile. "You were with me at the fountain . . . remember?"

"Of course I remember. It's pretty hard to forget all the nasty lies you tried to make me believe about Diana. But we don't need to go over that again. I already told you how I feel."

Heather looked slightly embarrassed, but she plunged ahead anyway. "Okay, but Diana wasn't with you then. And that's when she could have wrapped that package."

"Wrong." Cindy spoke up. "Diana was with us."

Diana turned to Cindy in surprise. She hadn't been with them the whole time. She'd deliberately spent at least thirty minutes in the furniture store, so that Paul and Cindy could be alone.

"Let's just forget it, okay?" Dave looked contrite. "I'm sorry, Heather. I didn't mean to give you a hard time. I guess I'm just getting jumpy, cooped up out here."

Heather nodded. "That's okay, Dave. And I'm sorry, too, for hurting your feelings."

There was a moment of silence as everyone stared at Heather in surprise. Was it possible that being snowbound was having a positive effect on her personality?

"Well, don't look at me like I'm crazy!" Heather sighed, and tossed her hair back over her shoulder. "I just decided I'd try to be nice until we get out of here. Otherwise, somebody's probably going to kill me."

"We appreciate your supreme effort, Heather." Dave started to laugh, and one by one, they all joined in. Heather even giggled, and she didn't seem at all upset that the joke was on her.

When the laughter had died down, Jay held up his hands for silence. "Dave was right. We're all getting a little jumpy. I think we need some recreation. Any suggestions?"

"Too bad we can't watch a good movie," Diana spoke up. "It might make us forget all about the fact that we're snowbound. The multi-plex was going to show that new Tom Cruise film, tonight."

Heather looked interested. "You mean, *Show-Off?* I'm dying to see that one!"

"Me, too." Cindy nodded. "Diana and I were going to catch the midnight show, right after we got off work. And if we weren't too tired, we were going to go for the triple feature. *Show-Off* at midnight, *My Time* at two-fifteen, and *They All Ran Home* at three-thirty."

"The theater's open that late?" Paul looked surprised as he walked over with his camera.

"They were running a special for the grand opening." Diana explained. "Five dollars to get in, and you could stay all night."

Paul glanced at his watch and started to grin. "What time was the first show supposed to start?"

"Nine forty-five," Cindy answered his question. "And they were going to give out free popcorn."

Paul turned on his camera and motioned to Cindy. "Go ahead, Cindy. Lead the way to the theater. I think you're all in for a big surprise."

Ten

"The lights are on!" Diana stood in the lobby of the Crossroads Theater, and gazed up at rows of lights that lined the ceiling. "But none of us turned them on. How did that happen?"

Hal laughed at her shocked expression. "Relax, Diana. They're probably on a timer. A lot of businesses do that."

"Come on. Let's go sit down in theater four." Paul gestured for them to follow him. "That's where *Show-Off* is supposed to run."

Cindy looked puzzled as they all trooped into theater four. But the minute she sat down, she turned to Diana with a grin. "I get it. Paul's doing another bumper card to show how isolated we are out here. He's going to tape us sitting in the Crossroads Theater, waiting for a movie that's not going to start."

"Not quite." Paul glanced at his watch again. "It's nine forty-four, and something should happen, right about . . . now!"

Cindy gasped as the lights began to dim. Then she turned to Paul in surprise. "How did you know that was going to happen?"

"Hal figured it out earlier. Everything's on a timer. Now watch and see what else is going to happen."

"Oh, my God!" Cindy almost jumped out of her seat as the curtain rolled back, and the music began to play. She gasped again as the screen came alive with a commercial for popcorn, and she turned to Paul with alarm. "Someone's here, running the projector!"

"Relax, Cindy. Nobody else is here." Paul sat down next to her and leaned back in his seat. "Most multi-plex theaters are run by computer. And the projectionist set everything up before we got snowbound. The movies'll run, right on schedule, until someone comes out here to reprogram the computer."

"So we can watch movies all night!" Jay started grinning. "Let's hear it for Paul!"

Everyone clapped, and Larry shouted out, over the applause. "Nice going, Paul!"

"Hey." Paul looked slightly embarrassed. "I didn't do anything except tell you to come here. But I do have one favor to ask . . ."

"Anything." Cindy nodded eagerly. "What is it, Paul?"

Paul gestured toward the screen where a giant bowl of popcorn was revolving slowly, glistening with butter. "It's this popcorn commercial. It looks so good, I can almost taste it. Do you think you guys can figure out how to run the popcorn machine?"

They all watched *Show-Off* together, and when it was over, everyone trooped to the lobby to see if they could figure out how to run the popcorn machine. Cindy took one look at it, and started to grin. "It looks almost the same as the one we had in high school. And I used to make popcorn for the basketball games. Do you want me to try to make it work?"

"Sure. I'll help." Diana hurried behind the counter and began searching for the popcorn. Luckily, it came in pre-measured bags and the machine had instructions printed on the side. In no time at all, they had buttered popcorn.

"But we need something to drink." Heather found a stack of cups next to the soft drink machine, and put one under the spout. She pressed a button, and gave a little squeal as her cup filled up with orange drink and ice.

"Candy, anyone?" Hal dangled a ring of keys he'd found in a drawer in the manager's office. "One of these ought to unlock the snack case. We'd better write up a tab, though. We don't want to cheat the theater."

"I'll do it." Larry picked up a notebook and pen, and started to write down their names. "Who wants what?"

There was a flurry of activity as Hal unlocked the case and they all chose snacks for the next movie. Jay grinned as he grabbed a bag of gummy bears.

"You actually *like* those?" Diana looked shocked.

"They're my favorites, especially the red ones. What do you want?"

"Anything with chocolate. I'm a chocoholic. I love chocolate-covered caramels more than anything else in the world!"

"More than kisses?"

Jay was grinning at her, and Diana felt a blush rise to her face. "Uh . . . well . . ."

"Never mind." Jay reached inside the snack case again. "You can have both. That way you don't have to choose. Which do you want first?"

"I . . . I don't know." Diana glanced around. Thank goodness no one was eavesdropping on their conversation!

"I'll start you out with the caramels, and I'll give you the kisses in the middle of the movie . . . okay?"

"I . . . uh . . ." Diana was so embarrassed, she didn't know what to say. She glanced down at the candy Jay was holding in his hand, and then she blushed even more. He had a roll of chocolate covered caramels. And a big box of Hershey's Kisses.

"Oh. *Hershey's* Kisses!" Diana spoke without thinking. "I thought you were talking about . . . uh . . ."

Jay looked puzzled for a moment, but then he caught on and he started to laugh. Larry and Dave turned to look at them, and Diana wanted to sink right through the floor.

"Jay! Please stop!" Diana knew she looked just as desperate as she felt. "If you keep on, they're going to ask you why you're laughing!"

Jay chuckled as he led Diana into the theater. They took seats in the sixth row of the center section, and Diana sighed as she stared at the darkened screen. She was horribly embarrassed, but she had to know.

"Jay?" Diana looked up at him.

"Yes, Diana?"

"You won't tell, will you?"

Jay shook his head. "I promise I'll never say a word. But I might stoop to blackmailing you."

"Blackmailing me?" Diana looked worried. "Exactly what do you mean?"

"If I keep your secret, you have to give me a kiss."

"It's a deal." Diana nodded quickly. She was so grateful that Jay had agreed not to tell, she was ready to give him anything he asked for. She reached down for the pile of candy on the seat and handed him the box of kisses. "Here. You can open it right now if you want to."

Jay started to laugh again. Then he slipped his arm around Diana's shoulders, and pulled her close. "That's not what I had in mind, Di."

"Oh!" Diana felt the heat rise to her face again. She felt terribly stupid for misunderstanding. "I . . . I . . ."

Jay held his finger to her lips, and Diana's heart started to pound very fast. Then she sighed as Jay leaned down and brushed his lips against hers.

At first it was just a light, friendly kiss, the kind her dates had given her at the door when they'd said good night. It felt wonderful, and Diana snuggled closer. Jay's lips were soft, but they were also firm, a strange contradiction that she'd never noticed when anyone else had kissed her. She pressed her lips a little harder against his, and closed her eyes as a delightful shiver rippled through her body.

Diana gave way to her instincts. Without any conscious thought, she reached up to wrap her arms around Jay's neck. He tightened his arms around her, and held her pressed close against him, so close she could feel his heart beat faster and faster as the kiss went on.

Now he was nibbling at her lips, little nips that made her gasp and open her lips slightly. Jay groaned, deep in his throat, and his kiss changed character. It was harder, and he took control of her mouth, probing with the tip of his tongue. It was warm and then hot, like a searing fire, and Diana felt a trembling sensation that started at her toes and rushed all the way up to the very top of her head.

It was impossible to think. Her mind was jumbled, her thoughts in a tangle. All she could do was feel as his fingers spread over her back, rubbing, caressing, making her skin tingle. And then her hands were moving, too, her fingers exploring the soft hair at the back of his neck.

Gradually, as if from a great distance, Diana heard a low noise. It swelled and grew, louder and louder, until she recognized what it was. Someone was clapping. No, it was more than one person. It sounded as if a whole rowdy crowd was applauding and cheering, whistling and stomping their feet.

Jay must have heard it, too, because he started to laugh. He gave her one last kiss, a light touch of his lips that promised much more at a later time, and then he let her go.

"Thank you." Jay stood up and bowed. And then he pulled Diana to her feet.

"Oh, no!" Diana gasped as Jay turned her around. Cindy and Paul had taken seats behind them, and they were whistling and clapping.

"Encore, encore!" Cindy grinned at them. And then she pointed to Paul. "And just in case you want to relive these precious moments, we've got it all on tape."

"You didn't!" Diana gave Paul a horrified look.

"No." Paul smiled at her. "Cindy wanted me to, but I told her it wasn't fair to tape you when you thought you were alone."

Diana sat back down. She was almost weak with relief. At least their kiss wouldn't be on the tape.

"Where's everyone else?" Jay sat down next to Diana, and put his arm around her shoulders.

"We all split up," Cindy explained. "Larry went to see a Madonna movie, Hal decided he wanted to watch some sci-fi thing, and Dave's watching a thriller. Heather said she was going to hole up in theater six and relive her childhood. They're running Disney classics all night."

"Are you staying here with us?" Diana turned to Cindy.

"No, but we'll meet in the lobby right after the next movie is over. Paul wants to see *Guts*. That's the new war flick with Mel Gibson. If you need us, we'll be in theater three."

As Cindy and Paul left, Diana tried not to laugh. Cindy hated war movies with a passion. She thought they justified senseless killing. She'd told Diana she'd rather die than go to a movie that glorified war. But she'd been all smiles as she'd left to see *Guts* with Paul.

Jay turned to Diana with a frown. "I don't get it. Cindy hates war movies."

"Right."

"But she's going to see a war movie with Paul?"

Diana grinned at him. "Right. With Paul."

"I see." Jay nodded slowly. "The movie doesn't matter, but Paul does."

Just then the giant bowl of popcorn disappeared, and the preview for the main feature came on, a western called *Powder Horn*.

"Oh, good! A western!" Jay looked delighted for a moment, but then he turned to Diana. "Wait a second. We got the wrong theater. You wanted to see *My Time*."

Diana shrugged. "That's all right. We can catch it later. Let's watch this one."

"Okay . . . if you're sure. Do you like westerns?"

"Not really."

"Then why don't we go to . . ." Jay stopped, and began to grin. "The movie doesn't matter, but I do?"

"You got it!" Diana grinned, and snuggled up very close as they began to watch the movie.

Eleven

Dave held his breath as the gorgeous blonde opened the basement door, and started down the steps. *Fatal Vacation* wasn't really that scary, but he came embarrassingly close to screaming as the axe murderer hurtled out of the shadows. Of course it didn't really matter if he screamed. That was one of the advantages of being alone in theater five. He could talk back to the characters on the screen, and no one would tap him on the shoulder to complain that he was spoiling the movie for them. He could boo when something dumb happened, and he could cheer when the hero saved his girlfriend. He could change seats as many times as he wanted, and he could even stand up in the front row if he needed to stretch his legs. If he wanted to smoke, he could light up. If he felt like drinking, he could have a cold sixpack right next to him on the seat. And if he had a girl with him, they could even . . .

Dave groaned out loud. He really shouldn't think about that. He'd only get frustrated. Diana was with Jay, Cindy was with Paul, and the only girl left was Heather. There was no way that Dave wanted to get mixed up with Heather. She was still dumping on guys, just like she'd done in high school.

Thinking about Heather made Dave feel a little guilty. He really shouldn't have brought up all that old stuff from high school. His psych professor had said it was healthy to vent your anger, but not at someone else's expense. Sure, he'd apologized, but he shouldn't have jumped all over her in front of everyone else. Heather couldn't really help the way she was. A child's personality developed early, and Heather had been pampered since the day she was born. She was Daddy's little girl, and she'd always had everything she'd ever wanted. Heather still thought she could have everything she wanted. And right now, she wanted Jay.

Dave sighed. He really felt sorry for Heather. He could see the writing on the wall, and he knew she was in for a shock. Heather still believed she could get Jay back, but she couldn't. He'd seen Jay and Diana together, and there was real chemistry between them. Heather might not know it, but she had lost. What would she do when she found out?

Dave considered the various options. Heather might cope by using denial, telling herself that she hadn't really wanted Jay in the first place. She could also rationalize the whole thing by saying that if Jay was interested in someone like Diana, he wasn't the man she'd thought he was. But what if Heather couldn't cope with Jay's rejection? What would happen then? She could become terribly depressed, perhaps even suicidal. If that happened, she'd need help.

There was a smile on Dave's face as he contemplated how grateful Heather would be when he offered to help her. He'd no longer be the guy she'd turned down when she was in high school. He'd be her dearest friend, and she would see him in a totally new light. She might even experience transference.

Dave's smile grew wider. Transference was a psychological term referring to the special kind of relationship that often existed between a psychologist and his patient. Heather would come to think of him as the most important person in her life. And he would be. Perhaps she'd even grow to love him, just like he'd loved her all these years.

There was a scream, and Dave was rudely snapped out of his fantasy. The blonde looked terrified as she faced the axe murderer, and Dave felt her panic as he stared at the evil glint in the madman's eyes. The scene was so real, he actually shouted. "Don't just stand there! Run for your life!"

It was almost as if the blonde had heard him, because she whirled around and started to run. There was a chase through a parking lot, the madman slashing at her with his axe. But this was no ordinary dumb blonde. She crawled under a tarp on a pickup truck, and hid there while he passed by.

The scene switched to police headquarters where a handsome man was trying to convince a grizzled police sergeant that his girlfriend was in terrible danger. Dave tuned out, and leaned back in his seat again, reaching out for a handful of popcorn. It was a real kick watching this movie all by himself. It was his private showing and they were running it just for him.

Now the blonde was back on the screen, peeking out through the tarp at the parking lot. The axe murderer was still out there, lying in wait by the side of a camper, but she didn't know it. She started to wiggle out from under the tarp and Dave shivered. He loved thrillers, but it gave him a creepy feeling to be the only one in the darkened theater. Every sound was magnified, and he felt as if he were actually part of the movie.

"Don't do it! He's right by that camper!" Dave shouted out another warning, but this time the blonde didn't listen. She dropped to the pavement, and began to inch her way past the parked cars, straight for the camper where the madman was hiding.

The music began to build, and Dave held his breath. Then the madman jumped out, and the blonde screamed. They'd probably cast her for her ability to scream. It was the best movie scream Dave had ever heard.

"Run!" Dave knew he was being ridiculous by shouting instructions at the blonde on the screen, but this movie was getting to him. He could feel his heart pounding in fear as the blonde whirled and ran toward the building. She tried one door, but it was locked. And then another. And another. The fourth door opened, and she slipped inside, locking it quickly behind her.

But the maniac killer had seen her duck into the building! He tugged at the door for a moment, and then hurled himself at the wooden surface. No luck. The door held firm. Dave knew what was coming, but he still gasped as the mad killer picked up his axe, and swung it at the door with a horrible thud.

Wood splintered as the madman repeatedly struck the door with his axe. The blonde stared at the shattering door for a moment and then she turned to run. Dave could see that she was in an empty theater, a theater a lot like this one. She emerged from behind the darkened screen, and raced for the seats to huddle down behind them as the madman battered at the wooden door. The lock wouldn't keep him out for very long. The maniac was chopping the door into matchsticks.

Dave glanced behind him. The blonde on the screen was hiding behind the seventh row, exactly where he was sitting. He clenched his fists and resisted the urge to actually get up and run as the door splintered, and the murderer hurtled into the theater.

There was an ominous undertone to the music now. It was growing louder and louder, and Dave actually covered his eyes and peeked out through his fingers as the madman approached the back of the screen. He knew it was only a movie, but the setting was so real, Dave felt as if he was in terrible danger.

The madman wasn't after him. He wanted the blonde. Dave tried to remember that, as the insane killer came closer and closer, his demented expression filling the screen.

The axe whistled down with a mighty force, and Dave gasped. But it struck the back of the screen, slitting it neatly. The blonde was whimpering, huddling beneath the seat, and Dave felt like whimpering, too.

And then the killer was there, coming up the aisle, stalking his prey. Dave hunched down in his seat, and winced as he came closer and closer. He was almost at the seventh row now, the row where he was sitting. And then the movie became reality as Dave felt the killer's heavy hand on his shoulder.

Dave screamed as loud as he could. He was too scared to run, but his head swiveled around and his eyes were wide with fright. And then he came back to the real world with a rush as he saw one of the guys in a Santa suit, standing behind him.

"Jesus! You scared the hell out of me!" Dave's voice was shaking. "What are you doing in that suit, anyway?"

"Ho, ho, ho!" Santa smiled, and shook his head.

"Oh, I get it. You got bored watching movies, and you decided to walk around to all the theaters and make a personal appearance. Is that right?"

"Ho, ho, ho!"

Santa just kept smiling, and Dave smiled back. "Okay . . . let me see if I can figure out who you are. Jay?"

Santa was still smiling, but he shook his head. Dave tried again. "Larry?"

Again, Santa shook his head. Dave nodded, and began to laugh. "Hal! I should have known it! You look good in that suit, guy!"

But Santa shook his head again, and Dave frowned. "Paul? What did you do? Get tired of taping and try on one of our suits?"

"Ho, ho, ho!"

Santa was clearly amused at Dave's failure to identify him, but Dave was beginning to get freaked. Then he remembered the girls, and he started to grin. One of them had decided to get in the act and put on a Santa suit. With all that padding, and the mustache and beard, a girl could play Santa and no one would know it.

The lights in the theater were dim, and Dave couldn't really tell who it was, but he decided that Cindy was the most likely candidate. She'd told him that she hated her elf costume. And she was always claiming that women could do anything that men could do. It would be just like Cindy to dress up in one of their Santa suits to prove that she could play Santa as well as a guy.

"You're right, Cindy." Dave grinned as he nodded. "You make a perfect Santa. You've got the voice down perfectly. And that's why you won't say anything except *Ho, ho, ho* . . . right?"

But Santa's head shook from side to side, and Dave raised his eyebrows. "You're not Cindy?"

Again, Santa indicated that Dave was wrong, and Dave gave a deep sigh. "Okay . . . if you're not Cindy, you have to be . . . Diana!"

The minute he said it, Dave knew he was right. Jay had probably talked Diana into dressing up in his costume to see if she could fool them. And she had. She made a perfect Santa.

"Did you go to any of the other theaters?" Dave grinned as Santa indicated no. "So I'm the guinea pig, huh? You figured if you could get by me, you could fool everybody else. Come on, Diana. Take off the wig. I know it's you."

"Ho, ho, ho!" Santa laughed again, and indicated that Dave was wrong. "Ho, ho, ho!"

"Okay. You're not Diana." Dave began to grin. If Santa wasn't Diana, there was only one person left. "You really fooled me, Heather. But why are *you* playing Santa? I thought you really got off on being the Christmas Angel."

"Ho, ho, ho!"

Santa shook his head again, and Dave frowned deeply. "Now, wait a minute. There's only eight of us out here. If you're not one of us, who the hell are you?!"

"Ho, ho, ho!"

This time, Santa's voice sounded very ominous, and Dave began to feel the first stirrings of panic. Santa was standing very close to him, so close that he seemed ready to pounce. There was a horrible scream from the loudspeakers. The maniac axe murderer had found the blonde, but Dave didn't dare glance at the screen, not with Santa grinning at him. It was an evil grin, a grin that scared Dave so much, he would have bolted from his seat and run for his life if he'd been able to get past the looming figure of Santa.

"Hey, whoever you are, you look great." Dave knew he was babbling, but he couldn't help it. He had to keep Santa talking until he could figure out some way to escape. He sat up a little straighter in his seat, and wondered if he was fast enough to leap over the row of seats.

Dave took a deep breath, all prepared to chance it. And then, before he could move a muscle, Santa turned on his heel and walked back up the aisle again, going out through the exit.

"Jesus!" Dave let out his breath in a shuddering sigh of relief.

His knees were shaking, and he was dripping sweat. The Santa he'd seen had really scared him.

The blonde was screaming on the screen again, and Dave felt like screaming, too. Some nut had waltzed right into the theater, dressed up in a Santa suit. He wasn't sure what the strange Santa had wanted, but it couldn't be good.

The blonde screamed again as Dave pulled himself to his feet. Her beautiful blue eyes were wide with horror, but it seemed insignificant now that Dave realized that the Santa he'd seen wasn't one of their group.

As Dave hurried up the aisle, the music built to a swelling crescendo, but Dave didn't turn to look back. The movie was tame compared to what was actually happening out here at the mall!

Santa was nowhere in sight as Dave peeked out the exit. The lights were on in the lobby, and he could see that no one was there. The thought of walking across the lobby made his knees start to shake again. Santa could be hiding behind the refreshment counter, or lurking in one of the alcoves that lined the walls. What if Santa jumped out to tackle him as he walked by? The thought scared him half to death.

Dave took a deep breath and prepared to move. He couldn't stay here, hiding in the theater like some kind of coward. There was safety in numbers, and he was all alone. He had to get them all together so that they could search for this weird Santa, and find out who he was and what he wanted.

Where should he go first? Dave tried to remember what movies they'd all decided to watch. Larry had gone to the Madonna movie, but that was playing in theater one, all the way across the lobby. Cindy and Paul had said they were going to watch *Guts,* but that was in theater three and it also meant he'd have to walk across the lobby, alone. Hal was watching some sci-fi thing, and Dave had no idea where that was playing. And Jay and Diana had left without mentioning which movie they'd chosen.

Heather. Dave's face turned white as he realized that Heather was all alone in theater six. Santa could be in there right now, terrorizing her. It was up to him. He had to save the woman he loved. And he did love Heather, despite her faults. He'd loved her for years and she didn't even know it!

The thought of Heather screaming in fear drove Dave nearly insane. He didn't need the others. He'd save her himself.

Dave took a deep breath, and opened the door all the way. No one in sight. He was about to step out to head for theater six, when all the lights in the lobby went out. The only illumination came from the very front of the lobby, where it faced the mall. But Dave was at the back, where the shadows were deep and menacing.

Over the sound of his heart hammering loud in his chest, Dave heard a scream. Was it the blonde from his movie? Or was it Heather?! Standing here, quaking in fear, wouldn't give him the answer. He had to go to theater six and find out.

His eyes were beginning to adjust to the dark as he inched his way along the wall until the refreshment stand was right in front of him. The ready light on the popcorn machine was on and it cast an eerie red glow over the darkened counter. The deep-fat fryer was also plugged in, and Dave could smell the odor of fat heating up for french fries.

It would be stupid to face Santa unarmed, and Dave ducked behind the counter to find a weapon. There were piles of napkins and packets of salt stored on the shelves behind the counter, but they were useless. He could forget the plastic knives and forks, too. They'd only break. But there was a metal box right under the hot dog grill and that looked promising. It was filled with hot dog skewers and one of them would make a nasty weapon.

Dave grabbed one of the sharply pointed metal rods, and stood up. He was armed and ready to save Heather. But as he turned to leave the counter, he got a nasty shock. There was a large, bulky figure standing at the end of the counter. Santa was here! And the evil grin on Santa's face was enough to make Dave's teeth start to chatter in fright.

As Santa hurtled forward, Dave didn't have time to think. He just reacted and stabbed out with the skewer. The sharp metal point speared Santa in the stomach, but the costume was heavily padded. Santa just laughed as he pulled out the skewer, tossing it to the floor with a clatter. And then he lunged at Dave with a fierce growl.

Dave opened his mouth to scream, but he couldn't. The air whooshed out of his lungs as Santa knocked him into the counter with a powerful tackle. And then Santa was shoving him along the long counter, straight for the popcorn machine at the end.

He tried to fight back, grabbing handfuls of the red velvet suit, but Santa had the strength of a maniac. Dave gasped for air, but he was wheezing so badly, he couldn't seem to draw any oxygen into his tortured lungs. The red light on the popcorn machine loomed larger and larger as Santa barreled him toward it. And then Santa gave a mighty shove, and stepped back. But Dave was going too fast to catch his balance. He slipped on some water that had been spilled on the floor and stumbled against the popcorn machine's metal surface.

There was a deafening crack, and sparks flew to light up the darkened interior of the lobby. But Dave didn't hear the crack. And he didn't see the sparks. His body spasmed as two hundred and twenty volts arced through his body, and the person who had been Dave Atkin only moments before, fell to the floor in a smoldering heap of charred flesh.

Santa stepped over the body and grabbed the broom that stood at the corner of the counter. He quickly chopped at the wires that had run from the deep-fat fryer to the popcorn machine, and severed them cleanly. He tucked the wires in his pocket, and then he walked to the box on the wall behind the counter, clicking the circuit breaker back in place. But he didn't turn the lights back on. That would ruin Santa's grisly surprise.

There was a smile on Santa's face as he hurried out into the mall. There was plenty of time to change into his street clothes. The movies still had at least twenty minutes to run. He'd be just as shocked as everyone else when they discovered Dave's body.

As he changed out of his costume, he anticipated what they would say. What a terrible accident. There must have been a short in the circuit, something wrong with the wiring. Poor Dave. If only he hadn't spilled that water on the floor and then touched the metal cabinet of the popcorn machine.

Only Santa knew that it hadn't been an accident. He'd punished Dave deliberately, because he'd been bad. Santa was keeping a list of all the bad boys and girls, just the way it said in the song. And there would be more accidents and more deaths before Santa was finished with his work.

Twelve

"That was really a good movie!" Diana sighed happily as the credits rolled on the screen. The villain had gone off to jail, and the cowboy had married his girlfriend at the end of the movie.

Jay smiled down at her. "Are you sure you're not just saying that?"

"No. I liked it. Maybe I'm developing a taste for westerns . . . especially ones with happy endings. What should we watch next?"

Jay shrugged. "You humored me last time so it's your choice. I'll go to any movie you want to see."

"Okay." Diana nodded. "Let's go out to the lobby and see where everybody else is going."

"You want to watch a movie with the group?" Jay looked disappointed.

"No. I figured we'd pick the film that nobody else wanted to see."

They were laughing as they walked up the aisle and pushed open the door to the lobby. But their laughter stopped abruptly, as they saw that the lobby was dark.

"Do you think they set the timer wrong?" Diana moved a little closer to Jay. It was eerie being out here in the lobby without any lights.

"I don't know. Maybe someone turned off the switch by mistake. I'll feel around and see if I can find it."

"No!" Diana grabbed his arm. "Don't leave me here!"

Jay chuckled. "What's the matter, Di? Are you afraid of the dark?"

"No . . . but I'd much rather come with you." Diana felt a little foolish as she hung on to his arm, but something about the darkened lobby scared her. She could see the dim rectangle of light by the exit to the mall, but it was almost completely dark where they were standing. There was a strange smell in the air, too. It was a combination of odors that she couldn't quite identify, but it reminded Diana of the time she'd singed her hair with a curling iron.

"Hello? What happened to the lights?"

It was Cindy's voice and Diana immediately felt better. At least they weren't alone. "We're over here . . . by the door to theater four."

"Hang on. We're coming."

Diana recognized Paul's voice, and she peered through the darkness, watching for Paul and Cindy to appear. It took a while. They must have been moving very carefully so they wouldn't bump into the benches or statues, but at last they materialized, less than two feet away.

"Hey . . . is anybody here?"

It was Heather's voice, and Diana didn't really want to answer, but she did. "Over here. By theater four. Where are you, Heather?"

"I'm by theater six, all the way in the back. What happened to the lights?"

"I don't know." Diana recognized Larry's voice, coming from a long way off. "Don't move, Heather . . . I'll come over to you."

"Hal?" Jay called out. "Are you here?"

"I'm by theater one . . . where are you?"

"We're over by theater four," Jay called out again. "Where's Dave?"

"I don't know. Maybe his movie lasted longer. Do you know

where the lights are? There must be a master switch here some-where."

"Hold on a second," Jay called out. Then he gave Diana's hand a squeeze and lowered his voice. "If you're all right now, I'm going to try to find the lights."

Diana nodded. And then she realized that Jay couldn't see her nod in the dark. "Go ahead. I'll stay here with Cindy and Paul."

"Okay, Hal." Jay raised his voice again. "I'm coming your way. I'm going to inch along the wall and see if I can find a switch."

"I'll meet you halfway." Hal sounded amused. "I just hope I don't trip over one of those statues and break my neck."

Diana shivered as Jay disappeared into the gloom. She could hear his hand sweeping across the wall, searching for a light switch. It was strange, standing here in the dark, with nothing but her sense of hearing to rely on. Every sound was magnified in the silence. She could even hear Paul and Cindy breathing.

They stood motionless for what seemed like hours, Jay and Hal calling out to each other every few feet. And then Jay gave a shout of triumph.

"I just found a switch! Shall I turn it on?"

"Go ahead. Try it." Hal's voice sounded strangely muffled.

There was a click and bright lights flooded the lobby. Diana gave a huge sigh of relief, and then she started to applaud. Everyone joined in and there was cheering and whistling. It was strange how being in the dark could be so terrifying. The lobby had seemed huge and frightening only moments before, but now, with the lights back on, it was perfectly familiar and not at all scary.

"Thanks for saving my life." Hal came up to Jay and clapped him on the back. "I thought I was a goner, for sure."

Jay looked puzzled. "Why? What happened?"

"See that tree?" Hal pointed to a large ficus tree in a brass planter. "I got hung up in that thing, and it almost strangled me."

They stood in the middle of the lobby, congratulating Jay on finding the switch. Everyone was smiling, and they all felt as if they'd averted disaster.

"Now I know what it feels like to be blind." Heather shuddered slightly. "I've never been so scared in my life!"

Diana nodded. She'd been frightened, too. But then she realized that Dave wasn't with them. "Where's Dave?"

"He said he was going to see some thriller," Cindy spoke up. "But he didn't say where it was playing."

"He was in theater five." Heather sounded very sure of herself. "I saw him go in."

"I'll go get him." Larry offered. "Maybe his movie isn't over yet."

They all watched as Larry walked to theater five and opened the door. He went in, but a moment later he came back out, looking puzzled. "He's not there. And the movie's over."

Diana felt her heart start to pound in sudden fear. "But where is he? Do you think he's all right?"

"Don't worry, Diana." Jay put his arm around her shoulders. "I'm sure Dave's fine. Maybe his movie got out early."

"But he knew we were all supposed to meet here, after the show." Cindy looked worried, too.

"He'll show up," Paul did his best to reassure her. "If the lights were out when he came out of the theater, he might have gone to get a flashlight."

Larry nodded. "That makes sense. I'm going out to the mall to see if I can spot him. He's going to be mad if he misses the next feature. We were going to watch *Creature From Another Time*. It's supposed to be a classic horror flick."

"Oh, save me!" Cindy made a face. "I read a review of that. It's got some kind of giant slug that sucks the air out of people. You couldn't pay me to watch a movie like that!"

Jay winked at Diana, and then he turned to Cindy with a perfectly straight face. "But it's supposed to be very imaginative. Paul and I were talking about it just this afternoon. Paul said he could hardly wait to see it."

"He did?!" Cindy's mouth dropped open, and she turned to Paul in alarm. "I'm sorry, Paul. I didn't know you liked films like that. Of course, I've only seen a couple, and I guess I shouldn't criticize them without seeing more. As a matter of fact, I'd love to go to *Creature From Another Time* with you. It'll probably be great!"

Paul grinned at the anxious expression on Cindy's face, and then he reached out to give her a hug. "Relax, Cindy. Jay was putting you on. I don't like monster movies, either."

"Gotcha!" Jay grinned at his sister.

"Rat!" Cindy retaliated by sticking out her tongue at Jay. And then she looked terribly embarrassed because she'd done such a childish thing. "Really, Jay . . . you're completely impossible!"

"I know." Jay patted her on the head. "Will you forgive me if I buy you a big box of Milk Duds?"

Cindy nodded, her good humor restored. "Maybe. But make it two boxes. And if you throw in a giant orange drink, you've got yourself a deal."

"Done!" Jay was laughing as he led the way to the refreshment stand, but he stopped short as he came within a foot of the counter. "Do you smell smoke?"

Diana wrinkled up her nose, and frowned. "It smells more like hair burning. We'd better check the popcorn machine. Maybe it ran out of oil."

"I'll do it." Jay lifted the board and slipped through to the other side of the counter. "No. It's not the popcorn machine. It's off. But it really smells awful back . . ."

Diana felt her heart hammer hard in her chest as Jay's voice trailed off. He was looking down at something behind the counter, and his face had turned chalk white.

"Jay?" Diana's knees started to tremble. "What is it?!"

Jay didn't say anything. He just swallowed hard. Diana began to shiver as he raised his eyes to hers. There was an expression of horror in his eyes that made her feel faint.

Jay took a deep breath, and swallowed again. Then he cleared his throat, and turned to face Paul. "Go find Larry. Get some blankets and come back here. Hal? I need your help."

"Sure." Hal nodded quickly. "What do you want me to do?"

"Take the girls out by the Christmas tree. And then come back here."

"What is it?" Diana's voice was shaking as Hal took her arm. "Please, Jay . . . I'm not going to leave until you tell me!"

Jay swallowed again. He still looked sick. "It's Dave. He's back here. And he . . . uh . . . he had an accident."

"Is he . . . ?" Diana couldn't finish the sentence. If the sick expression on Jay's face was any indication, she already knew the answer.

Jay nodded. "He's dead. You girls go with Hal. And stay right by the Christmas tree and wait for us. We'll come to get you just as soon as we can."

"Come on, Diana." Hal's voice was gentle as he nudged her toward the exit to the mall. "You can't help Jay by staying here. It'll just make things harder."

Diana nodded, and started to walk to the exit with Heather and Cindy. But she carried the image of Jay's grief-stricken face with her, and she blinked back tears all the way through the mall.

Thirteen

They were all gathered in the Crossroads Pub. It had been Diana's suggestion since the pub was the coziest place in the mall. Jay had just finished telling them how Dave had died, and Heather had burst into tears.

"Do you think it was . . . uh . . . he didn't suffer, did he?" Heather choked out the words.

"No." Larry shook his head. "It was instantaneous, Heather. I'm sure of that."

"Good. I'd hate to think that he . . ." Heather blinked back tears, and cleared her throat. "You know what I mean."

Cindy frowned. "But I thought you didn't like Dave. Why should you care if . . ."

"That's not true." Heather interrupted her. "I *did* like Dave. I just didn't want to date him, that's all. But now I wish I'd gone to that stupid thriller with him. If I'd been with him, maybe he wouldn't have gone out for popcorn. And then he'd still be alive!"

Heather looked so miserable, Diana didn't even mind when Jay slipped his arm around her shoulders. It was clear that Heather felt guilty about the way she'd treated Dave in the past.

"Look, Heather . . ." Diana searched for some words of comfort. "Any one of us might have used that popcorn machine. Jay and I talked about getting more popcorn . . . didn't we, Jay?"

Jay nodded. "That's right. Diana almost went out for a re-fill."

Heather turned to look at Diana, and Diana could read the ex-pression in her eyes. Heather was thinking, *Too bad you didn't. Then it would have been you, instead of Dave.* But Heather did-n't say anything. She just snuggled up to Jay and leaned her head against his shoulder.

"I don't know about you guys, but I'm having a beer." Paul broke the uncomfortable silence. "Anybody want to join me?"

Cindy nodded. "I do. Why don't you draw a couple of pitch-ers. And be sure to get a mug for Heather. She needs to pull her-self together."

"That's a good idea." Jay took his arm from Heather's shoul-der, pushed back his chair, and stood up. Diana couldn't help but notice that he looked very relieved. "I'll get the mugs."

"So, Heather"—Cindy gave Heather a perfectly innocent smile—"do you feel better now?"

Heather glared at Cindy. She knew Cindy had come up with the excuse Jay needed to break up their embrace. She looked as if she wanted to say something scathing, but all she did was nod.

"Why don't you try to use the phone behind the bar?" Cindy turned to Diana. "Maybe it's working now."

Diana tried not to grin as she got up and headed behind the bar where Jay was standing. Cindy knew the phone wasn't working. She'd tried it when they'd first come into the pub. It was just a way to get her back with Jay while Heather was left behind, sitting at the table with Cindy.

"Come over here, Heather." Cindy motioned to the chair di-rectly across the table from her. "I want to know all about the Christmas play. I missed it, but everybody said that you were fantastic."

Diana watched as Heather slid over to talk to Cindy. Cindy was a true friend, and she was also absolutely brilliant. Cindy knew that there was no way Heather could resist bragging about her starring role in the sorority play.

As Heather began to tell Cindy about the costumes she'd worn and the character she'd played, Diana picked up the phone. There was no dial tone, but she hadn't expected one. The lines were still down, and with the storm raging outside, they wouldn't be fixed anytime soon.

"Hey, Di." Jay looked happy to see her as he came back with an armload of chilled mugs. "You want to help me carry these to the table?"

"Sure." Diana picked up a serving tray and began to arrange the mugs on its flat surface. "Jay? Can I ask you a question?"

Jay nodded, and Diana took a deep breath. She didn't really want to ask, but she had to know. "It's about Dave. Exactly how did the accident happen?"

"I don't know." Jay sighed deeply. "The popcorn machine must've had a short. His hand was still touching it when I found him."

Diana looked puzzled. "Are you sure?"

"Yeah. Why?"

"The popcorn machine's only one-ten. I could understand it if he'd been using the deep-fat fryer. That's a two-twenty circuit. But the popcorn machine? It would have given him a nasty jolt, but it shouldn't have killed him."

"Maybe the popcorn machine was plugged into the wrong outlet."

"That's impossible." Diana shook her head. "The deepfat fryer has a different kind of plug. And it was hardwired to a dedicated outlet."

"Are you sure?" Jay began to frown.

"I'm positive. I was right there when the electrician ran in the lines. I asked him why he was doing it that way, and he said it was a safety feature so no one could plug a one-ten appliance into a two-twenty circuit."

"Then I don't understand it at all." Jay's frown deepened. "Unless . . ."

"Yes?" Diana held her breath. She really hoped that Jay could come up with a reasonable explanation.

"What if Dave had a heart condition? One-ten might kill you if you had a weak heart."

Diana nodded. "That's possible. But did he? I never heard him say anything about it."

"Maybe he didn't know." Jay slipped his arm around Diana's shoulder and gave her a little squeeze. "It won't do us any good to speculate. The only one who can tell for sure is the county coroner."

Diana nodded and forced a smile. "Well . . . we'd better get these mugs to the table before they start asking what we're doing back here."

"Right." Jay put his finger under her chin and gave her a light kiss on the lips. "We'll talk later, Di. I really don't want to think about it right now."

As Jay picked up a pitcher of beer, Diana hefted the tray of mugs, and began to step out, around the bar.

"Wait a second." Jay put his hand on her arm. "Will you sit next to me when we get back to the table?"

Diana grinned as she nodded, but she couldn't resist pushing her luck. "I'd love to sit next to you . . . but why?"

"Because Heather's getting a little too . . ." Jay sighed and looked embarrassed. "I think she's trying to pick up on me, again. And I don't want to hurt her feelings, but I'd much rather be with you than anyone else."

Diana gave him a brilliant smile. She felt like shouting in triumph, but she managed to hold her excitement in. This wasn't over. Not by a long shot. Heather was persistent, and she'd try to lure Jay away again. But for now, it was more than enough to hear Jay say that he preferred being with her.

They sat up late, and talked until they couldn't keep their eyes open any longer. They were all reluctant to go back to the huge furniture store and go to sleep in their separate sections. Even though no one mentioned it, they were all thinking about Dave's body stretched out next to Sue's in the cooler. Finally, Larry suggested that they sack out at the pub, together.

Everyone went in a group to collect their bedding, and they stood for a while at the huge plate glass window, looking out at the blowing snow. As usual, Paul was taping them. They'd gotten so used to seeing him with his camera on his shoulder, they didn't even react any longer.

"I don't think it's blowing over." Jay frowned as he tried to see the highway through the blowing snow.

Larry nodded. "It looks worse to me. I can barely see the Christmas tree by the front entrance, and it's only thirty-seven and a half feet away."

"Thirty-seven and a half?" Cindy turned to Larry in surprise. "Is that a guess, or do you really know?"

"I really know. My dad designed this place and I remember the placement of the trees from the blueprints."

"I didn't know your father was an architect." Heather looked at Larry with new respect. "Has he won any awards?"

"Sure. He won the Golden Chimney last year."

Jay started to laugh. "The *what?*"

"I'm not kidding." Larry had a grin on his face, but he shook his head. "I know it sounds ridiculous, but there really is a Golden Chimney award. It's for designing the best heating system in a self-contained building of over five stories. He also won the Truesdale for that big industrial complex just south of Minneapolis."

"Your father's Clayton Fischer?" Paul looked impressed when Larry nodded. "We did a spot on him last year. He designs schools, too, doesn't he?"

"Sure. He did a multi-purpose building for McAlister College. That won another award, but I don't remember the name. We've got a whole shelf full of statues and stuff at home."

"That's fantastic." Heather's smile was warm as she turned to Larry, and Diana nudged Cindy. Perhaps Larry would be the next in Heather's long line of guys. "Are you going to be an architect, too?"

Larry shook his head. "Not me. If I can't make it as an artist, I'll probably end up building dollhouses."

"Dollhouses?" Heather wrinkled her nose. "Why would you want to do that?"

"They're not really dollhouses, Heather. That's just slang for the miniature models that architects use. Every detail has to be perfect and they're all done to scale. Didn't you see the miniature they did of the mall before it was built?"

Heather nodded. "Sure. Everybody saw it. It was on display at the county courthouse. But it still seems kind of silly to me."

"How about if I told you that the model of the mall cost my father over fifteen thousand dollars?"

"Oh." Heather began to look interested again. "I didn't realize that they were so expensive. How long does it take to build one?"

"About a month, maybe two. And the materials don't cost more than a hundred dollars or so. It's almost all profit. You're paid for your skill in reading blueprints and translating them into something concrete that people can look at."

"Have you ever built a model?" Paul moved in for a closer shot as he asked the question.

"I did a couple. And I've done a lot of what they call artist's renditions. They're framed watercolors of the structure from various angles."

"And they're expensive, too?" Heather moved over so that she was closer to Larry.

"They're much cheaper . . . only a couple hundred dollars. But you can knock them off really fast. I did six for my dad during Thanksgiving break, and it was no sweat."

As they walked back to the pub, carrying bedding and clothes, Cindy leaned close to Diana. "What do you think? Does Heather have a new victim?"

"Looks like it." Diana grinned. "She was really impressed with Larry's dollhouses, once she found out how much they were worth."

Cindy grinned. "That's a lucky break for you. Now maybe she'll concentrate on Larry, and forget all about my big brother."

"Maybe." Diana nodded, but she had her doubts. Heather was the kind of person who liked to keep more than one guy on the string. While it was clear that Heather was definitely interested in Larry, Diana was sure that he wasn't her number one priority. Diana still had a mental picture of what had happened earlier tonight, when Jay had put his arm around Heather's shoulder. She could recall the exact expression on Heather's face as she'd cuddled up to Jay and rested her head on his chest. If Heather's smug expression had been any indication, Jay was still right there, at the head of her list.

He was tired and he'd done enough work for tonight. Santa had accomplished exactly what he'd set out to do. The bad boy had been punished, and now it was time for him to rest up for his next task.

As he snuggled under one of the furniture store's most expensive quilts, he smiled up into the darkness. The storm wouldn't last forever, and he had to hurry if he wanted to accomplish everything before the roads were cleared.

He gave a deep sigh, and plumped up his pillow, moving to a more comfortable position. He would rethink his list in the morning, copy it over, and move the names into proper position. Some of the worst offenders needed to be punished immediately. Those names would go to the top of Santa's list. The others could move down near the bottom, and wait their turn. Once he had a clear order of priority, he'd know exactly who Santa's next victim would be.

There was a smile on his face as he pulled the covers up to his chin and listened to the music on the loudspeakers. Sleigh bells were jingling, and "Santa Claus Is Comin' To Town" was about to play. It was his song, the song that had given him such wonderful purpose. They all thought Dave's death was an accident, a result of faulty wiring at the theater refreshment stand. It was another strike against the Crossroads Mall, a reason for people to avoid this place where accidents seemed to happen so frequently. Santa was the only one who knew that Dave's accident hadn't been an accident at all, and Santa would never tell. If there was one thing that Santa knew how to do very well, it was how to keep a secret.

Fourteen

"Diana? Wake up, Diana."

"No, Mom . . . not yet." Diana burrowed a little deeper under the covers, and tried to go back to sleep. But her mother was very persistent. Was it time for school already?

"Come on, Di. It's morning. Wake up."

Diana groaned, and tried to open her eyes. That wasn't her mother's voice. It must be Cindy, waking her up for her eight o'clock class. But Cindy's voice was very deep, even though she was almost whispering. And the hand on her arm felt much bigger than Cindy's hand. And why was she sleeping in her clothes?

"Diana . . . please. I need you."

Diana's eyes fluttered open and she recognized Jay's face in the dim light. Without thinking about what she was doing or why she was doing it, she reached up to wrap her arms around his neck, and pulled him down for a kiss.

At first the kiss was sleepy, a mere brushing of lips and a snuggling together that made Diana feel very safe and warm. But then Jay kissed her back, and Diana felt a shiver of delightful anticipation that made her tremble and press herself even more tightly against him. She still felt safe and warm, but there was a new emotion added to the mix. She wanted more than simple kissing, more than simple hugging. She wanted Jay to slide under the covers with her, and . . .

"Oh!" Diana sat up, blinking. She'd suddenly remembered where she was, and it was lucky that no one else was awake. They were sleeping in booths at the Crossroads Pub, and that was much too public a place for the intimate thoughts that were running through her mind.

"Forget where you were?"

Jay was grinning down at her, and Diana blushed as she nodded. Luckily, the lights were dim, and he couldn't see that her face was bright red with acute embarrassment.

"Maybe we should have slept in the furniture store . . . all by ourselves."

Diana's blush deepened as she smiled up at Jay and shook her head. "Actually, I think it's a really good thing we didn't!"

"You're very beautiful when you're sleeping . . . you know that?" Jay reached out to touch her face in a one-finger caress that traced the shape of her lips. "You looked just like an innocent little girl. Until you pulled me down to kiss you. Then you weren't quite so innocent."

Diana giggled. "That was *your* fault. At first I thought you were my mom, waking me up for school. And then I thought you were Cindy."

"You kiss your mom and my sister like *that?*"

"Of course not! I knew it was you by then." Diana shivered slightly. She still had the almost overwhelming urge to pull Jay under the covers with her and kiss him again and again. Since this wasn't the time and place for something like that, she threw back the covers, jumped up quickly, and slid her feet into her shoes.

"Wait a second, Di." Jay took her arm and turned her around to face him. "You wanted to, didn't you?"

Diana considered playing dumb and asking him what he meant. But she knew exactly what he'd been asking about, and that would be less than honest.

"Well, I . . . Yes, I wanted to." Diana whispered the words, and somehow, that made them even more intimate. Then she drew a deep breath, and sighed. "Let's go make coffee. I need a cup to clear my head."

"It's already made. I thought we could carry it out to the Christmas tree and talk. Unless you'd prefer to . . ." Jay let his voice trail off and gestured toward the booth where Diana had been sleeping.

Diana didn't have any trouble catching his train of thought. She was tempted. It would be wonderful to snuggle down under the covers with Jay, but she shook her head. "No way. The others'll be getting up soon. I think coffee by the Christmas tree is a much better idea."

"Okay."

Jay looked a bit disappointed, but he smiled agreeably as he led the way to the coffee machine. Diana got two mugs from the shelf. They were bright blue with "THE CROSSROADS PUB" imprinted on the side in gold letters, and Jay filled them almost to the brim.

They were very quiet as they tiptoed past the sleepers, and went out the door to the mall. When they were a few doors away, Jay turned to her and smiled. "It's great to have coffee in the morning with you. It starts the day off right. Maybe we ought to do it all the time."

"That would be nice." Diana smiled back, but her mind was racing a million miles a minute. Was Jay talking about meeting her every morning at the college cafeteria? Or did he have a more intimate arrangement in mind? She cautioned herself about jumping to the wrong conclusions, and kept right on walking toward the huge Christmas tree in the center of the mall.

"How about right here?"

Jay gestured toward a bench facing the Christmas tree, and Diana glanced at her watch as she sat down. It was a little strange, sitting in front of the Christmas tree at eight in the morning. Of course it was impossible to tell it was eight in the morning without any windows facing the outside. It could have been eight at night, and she never would have known the difference with the lights on the tree twinkling brightly and the Christmas carols playing on the loudspeakers.

"Is something wrong?" Jay reacted to her pensive expression.

"No. Not really." Diana shook her head. "I was just thinking how timeless it is inside the mall. The lights are always on and the music's always playing. It's almost like another world."

Jay nodded. "It's an artificial world, almost like being inside a space capsule. And you're right about how timeless it is. If we didn't have our watches, we wouldn't know what time it really was. I wonder why they didn't put a big clock on the wall."

"My dad told me why. It's psychology. There aren't any clocks in casinos, either. They want you to lose track of the time. The longer you're out here at the mall, the more money you might spend."

"Makes sense." Jay nodded. And then he looked sad. "Dave would have known that. He was a psych major."

They were both silent for a moment, remembering the last time they'd seen Dave. And then Diana shivered as she recalled exactly what had happened.

"What is it?" Jay slipped his arm around her shoulders.

"The package." Diana's voice was shaking. "I forgot about it last night."

"The present Dave found?"

Diana nodded. She felt very shaky as she put her fear into words. "It was just like Sue's. And both of them opened their presents and read the notes . . . and then they died."

Jay took a moment to think it over. "It's got to be a coincidence. I mean . . . it's not like someone murdered them or anything like that."

Diana turned to look at Jay and his eyes mirrored her fear. For a moment they just stared at each other as the terrible suspicion started to grow. And then "Santa Claus Is Comin' To Town" started to play over the loudspeakers, and Diana shivered so hard, her teeth began to chatter. The innocent children's Christmas carol sounded suddenly ominous, and Diana knew she'd never be able to listen to it again without hearing its dark undertones.

"No." Jay shook his head as if he were trying to shake off the thought. "It's impossible, Diana. We've been watching too many thrillers on television, or reading too many detective novels."

"Are you sure?" Diana really wanted to believe him, but the seed of suspicion had been firmly planted.

"I'm positive. Don't forget . . . I was the one who found Sue. And I found Dave, too. I'm sure they were both accidents. It's kind of eerie out here, cut off from the rest of the world. We're just imagining the worst."

Diana took a deep breath, and released it in a shuddering sigh. "You're right. I guess things just got to me. Maybe I'm not awake yet. But it is kind of strange about the presents . . . isn't it?"

"It's strange." Jay's voice was flat, with no emotion, as if he didn't want to scare her. "And it's even stranger if what you say about the construction is true."

Diana sat up a little straighter. "It *is* true. And I know the popcorn machine wasn't plugged into the two-twenty line. I turned it on. If something had been wrong, it would have shorted out right away, and then I would have been the one to . . ."

Diana stopped and shivered again. She could have ended up like Dave! The same thought must have occurred to Jay, because his face turned pale.

"Let's not think about that. And when everybody else gets up, let's warn them to be very careful. We're cooped up in here, and we might be getting a little stir-crazy. We're probably all accident prone, and we sure don't want any more accidents!"

Diana nodded. She was sure that Jay was just saying that to make her feel better. But it was better to think that Sue and Dave's deaths were accidents than it was to believe the alternative!

They were frightened again, and when they were afraid, they tended to stick together. He didn't get a break until late afternoon, when they'd all calmed down a little and split up.

He looked around carefully as he let himself into the security office. It was too bad that Santa wasn't invisible. Then he couldn't be followed. But Santa didn't have that power so he had to be very alert.

Once he was inside the office, a huge smile spread across his face. His plan was going very well, and he felt almost euphoric as he took his list from the center desk drawer and began to read the names. Who would be the next to get a personal visit from Santa?

As he checked the list, one name jumped out at him, emerging from the river of other names like the big trout that had snapped at Gramps's hand-tied flies.

A sparkling river had run through Gramps's farm, providing food for the table and fun for Gramps. And Gramps had shared his sport with his grandson. They'd spent hours together, tying flies at the kitchen table and putting them in Gramps's tackle box. Each lure he'd tied had been especially designed to catch the big trout Gramps had called Professor Pisces. He could still remember those crisp, chilly mornings at the farm, hopping out of bed before daybreak to pull on his waders and make the trek to the river with Gramps. They'd walked carefully through the woods, guided by the beam of Gramps's old flashlight, stepping over fallen logs and pushing through the underbrush until they'd reached the river's bank. They'd perched on the huge granite rock that lay half-submerged in the water, and shared the Thermos of hot chocolate Grandma had fixed for them. And then they'd spent all day trying to catch Professor Pisces.

He pressed his pen to the paper so hard, it almost tore through. The happy days of fly casting with Gramps had all taken place before the contest. After that, fishing was ruined. And he'd just written down the name of the person who was to blame.

The contest had been in all the papers, and he'd begged Gramps to enter. It was a father-son contest, but grandfathers and grandsons could enter, too. Gramps hadn't wanted to enter, but Grandma had talked him into it. It would be fun for the boy, she'd said. And the boy deserved a little fun in his life.

He still remembered how excited he'd been, and how sure he'd been that they would win. There weren't really any rules. You just fished all day, in any of the designated spots, and brought your catch in to be weighed at the local butcher shop before dark.

When they'd gathered that morning, to check in for the contest, almost all the other contestants had crowded around to admire the delicate flies that lined Gramps's tackle box. There had been only one exception, one father-and-son team who'd looked at the flies and turned up their noses. While the son had smirked, the father had bragged that they'd ordered their flies from an expensive fishing catalogue, the finest that money could buy. And then the son had announced that they were sure to win the contest.

During the morning session, the man and his son had fished right next to them, and it was clear that they didn't like to lose. Although it was supposed to be a friendly contest, the man and his son had gotten angrier and angrier with each fish that Gramps had pulled from the river. And then the sun had reached its highest point in the sky, and one of the contest officials had come around to announce the lunch break.

They'd put down their poles, and left their tackle boxes by the side of the river to mark their spots. Picnic tables had been set up under the trees, and they'd found a nice, shaded spot to enjoy the lunch that Grandma had packed for them. Everyone else had been very friendly, but the man and his son hadn't taken part in the conversation. They'd sat by themselves, glaring at Gramps. And then the father had leaned close to whisper to his son. The son had left the table for a couple of minutes, and when he'd come back, he'd been grinning. And then the contest official had announced that lunch break was over, and the afternoon session had started.

They'd walked back to their spot, and Gramps had opened his tackle box, looking for his favorite fly. But he hadn't reached inside to pull it out. He'd just groaned, like someone had kicked him in the stomach.

He'd rushed to Gramps's side, feeling fear rush over him in a wave. Was Gramps sick? But Gramps had pointed to the tackle box, and he'd groaned, too, when he'd looked inside. The tube of glue they'd carried to make repairs had burst open, and every single one of Gramps's hand-tied flies was covered with sticky adhesive.

The father and son had come over to ask what was wrong, and Gramps had shown them the tackle box. The father had patted Gramps on the shoulder. What an unfortunate accident! He'd offered to let Gramps borrow one of his flies, but Gramps had said that wouldn't be fair. He still had one fly left, and he'd fish with that.

Naturally, they'd lost the contest. And the father and son had won. But after they'd gone home, he had looked at the tube of glue very carefully, and he'd seen the hole that someone had punched in it. He'd remembered how the boy had left the picnic table and come back grinning. And he'd known exactly what had happened.

Gramps had stopped fishing after the contest. He'd put his tackle box up in the attic and he'd never looked at it again. There had been sadness in his eyes when he'd walked out to his clear, sparkling river and stared down at the water. Grandma had tried to get him to tie new flies, but he'd told her that all the fun had gone out of it. And now it was over. Gramps's river was gone.

They'd dammed up the river when they'd built this place, and the shallow trickle that was left provided the water for the large fountain that decorated the front lobby of the mall. The boy had ruined Gramps's favorite sport. And the mall had turned his sparkling river into a concrete fountain, where giggling girls tossed in pennies to make wishes. It was a tragedy, but Santa would take his revenge. He'd punish the naughty boy and the mall, all at once.

Fifteen

Hal had suggested they get all dressed up with clothes borrowed from stores in the mall to have dinner at the Crossroads Bistro, and they were all seated at the very best table in the restaurant with a view of the surrounding countryside. Of course the view wasn't exactly what they would have liked. It was snowing again, and the winds were blowing so hard they could barely make out the lights on the Christmas tree at the entrance to the mall.

"This was a great idea, Hal." Diana looked over at him and smiled. Hal had even done the cooking, and the meal was delicious. "You're a fantastic cook."

Hal grinned, but he shook his head. "Thanks for the compliment, but I don't deserve it. The chef had the entrees in the freezer. All I had to do was turn on the oven and bake them."

"That might be true, but none of us would have thought to do it." Cindy patted Hal on the back. "And I've never had Beef Wellington before. It's delicious!"

"Mine's great, too. And I've never had it before, either." Jay started to smile, but then he realized what Hal had said and he began to frown. "You didn't have any trouble with the oven, did you, Hal?"

Hal was clearly puzzled as he shook his head. "No. It worked just fine."

"Thank God!"

Jay looked very relieved, and Hal looked at him strangely. But then he nodded. "Oh. I get it. But you didn't have to worry about me. I made sure the floor was perfectly dry, and I wore rubber gloves when I turned on the switch."

Paul opened the second bottle of red wine, and filled their glasses. Then he picked up his camera, and nodded to Jay. "Let's have a toast."

"To Hal." Jay raised his glass. "He planned a great evening to cheer us up, and we're grateful."

Diana raised her glass, and so did Cindy and Heather. Larry followed suit, and he even added the traditional response. "A speech from the man who made all this possible. Come on, Hal. Say something."

"Thanks, guys. But it's really no big deal." Hal had a big grin on his face as they started to applaud. He stood up and bowed, and then he sat down again. "I just thought we needed a night out . . . to get our minds off everything bad that's happened."

Everyone nodded, and Diana spoke up. "You were right, Hal. And I'm glad you convinced us to dress up. I just hope I don't spill anything. This dress has to go back on the rack before anyone misses it."

"Not necessarily." Paul shut off his camera. "Why don't you girls do a little promotion piece for the store where you got your clothes. That way the management will probably let you keep them."

Heather looked excited. "He's right! It'll be free publicity for the store and they always love that. Let's model the clothes for Paul's documentary, and see if the store offers to give them to us."

"Do you want to go first?" Paul nodded to Heather as he switched tapes in his video camera.

"Sure." Heather looked smug as she turned to Cindy and Diana. "Just watch me. And when it's your turn, do exactly what I did. I'll do the commentary, since I've had acting experience."

Cindy and Diana exchanged glances. Heather was showing off again, but she probably knew a lot more about modeling than they did. If Paul was right, and they could get these expensive clothes for free, it would be fantastic!

"We'll work the modeling into our dinner scene." Heather stood up and took charge. "As soon as Paul starts taping, I want Jay to tell me how fabulous I look. That's my cue to stand up and show off the dress."

Jay glanced at Diana. They both knew that Heather was trying to look as if she were still Jay's girlfriend, but it really wasn't worth arguing about. Diana gave Jay a quick wink to tell him it was all right with her, and he grinned as he winked back.

"All right. Is everyone ready?" Heather glanced at her reflection in the mirrors that lined the dining room wall, and fluffed her hair. When everyone nodded, she motioned to Paul. "Okay, Paul. Let's roll."

Diana tried not to grin. She'd noticed that Paul had been taping the whole thing, from beginning to end. He'd captured Heather being bossy, and that was fine with her.

"Isn't this fun?" Heather smiled brightly at the camera. "I just love getting all dressed up and going out to dinner at the Crossroads Bistro, especially when the food is this fabulous! What are you having, Jay?"

"Beef Wellington." Jay grinned as he went along with the scene. "It's the best I've ever tasted."

Diana bit back a giggle. Jay had just told them all that he'd never had Beef Wellington before.

"Say, Heather . . ." Jay looked thoughtful. "Is that a new dress? It's really gorgeous!"

Heather stood up and turned around. The skirt whirled out around her hips in a graceful arc, and she smiled at Jay. "This lovely dress is from Elaine's Boutique, right here at the Crossroads Mall. Fashion experts agree that it's impossible to go wrong with basic black, and this designer creation combines style with comfort. Notice the loose, flowing design and the graceful lines of the skirt. You can add a touch of jewelry for color, or cinch in the waist with this stunning gold belt, also from Elaine's. Do yourself a favor and drop in at Elaine's Boutique at the Crossroads Mall to see the latest in fashion."

Cindy couldn't help it. She burst into applause. After a moment, so did everyone else. Heather bowed and sat down. She looked very pleased with herself. "Okay, Diana . . . it's your turn. We'll need an introduction from someone."

"I'll do it." Jay grinned at Diana. "Should I tell you how incredibly beautiful you look?"

"No!" Heather looked embarrassed as everyone turned to stare at her. "I mean . . . you could, but you already introduced me. We should give someone else a turn. How about you, Hal?"

"Me?" Hal looked shocked. "But I don't know anything about women's fashion!"

"You don't have to. Just tell Diana you like her outfit. Then she'll get up and twirl around, and I'll describe what she's wearing. Ready, Paul?"

"I'm ready. Go ahead, Hal."

Hal wiggled his eyebrows as he turned to Diana, and Diana almost lost it. He was even better than Groucho Marx.

"You really look good tonight, Diana. Of course you always look good, but that's really a stunning . . . uh . . . thing that you're wearing. The color makes your eyes glow like sapphires."

"Thanks, Hal." Diana managed to keep from giggling as she tried to remember what color sapphires were. "I went shopping this afternoon at Elaine's Boutique."

As Diana got up to turn around, Heather described her outfit. Diana kept smiling, and somehow she managed to twirl around without losing her balance.

"Okay. I guess that'll do." Heather gave her a nod when she sat down again. "Cindy? You're next. You can introduce her, Larry."

Larry nodded. "Okay. But I've got a question first. What color are sapphires?"

"Search me." Hal started to laugh. "I just thought it would sound good. It was a line from one of those late-night movies. Of course, that was an old black and white movie, so I just guessed."

Heather rolled her eyes to the ceiling. "Honestly, Hal. Everybody knows that sapphires are blue. But it worked because Diana's outfit is sort of a blue-green color."

"Lucky for me."

Everyone cracked up except Heather, and she was frowning when she turned to Larry. "Go ahead. And don't mention any precious stones unless you know what color they are."

"Ready?" Larry turned to Paul, and waited until he nodded. Then he cleared his throat. "Hey, Cindy. You look totally fabulous. It's quite a change from your usual jeans and faded Ts. Where did you get that dress?"

Cindy laughed as she stood up and whirled around. "It's from Elaine's Boutique. I'm going to buy all my clothes there from now on, because Elaine's assistants are so helpful. If you're like me, and you're a total idiot when it comes to fashion, they'll give you expert guidance. To tell you the truth, I never dreamed I could look like this! Isn't that right, gang?"

Jay whistled, and so did Hal and Larry. And Diana applauded. Heather was just opening her mouth to speak, when Cindy went on.

"I'm going to let our fashion expert, Heather Perkins, take over now. She has to describe what I'm wearing because I don't know the difference between a camisole and a cummerbund."

"Really, Cindy! You didn't have to admit that you were that stupid!" Heather groaned and rolled her eyes toward the ceiling again. "You can edit that out, can't you, Paul?"

Paul nodded. "Sure. Go ahead, Heather. Describe Cindy's outfit."

Diana watched Paul's expression as Heather described what Cindy was wearing. He was grinning and Diana hoped that he'd leave Heather's comment in. Heather was running true to form and it would be wonderful to see her bitchiness on tape, even if that snide little comment she'd made got edited out before Paul tried to sell his tape to the station.

"Well? What did you think?" Heather finished her description and turned to Paul.

"Very good." Paul nodded. "I'm sure Elaine's will give you the clothes."

"You want to know what I think?" Jay grinned at Heather.

"Of course." Heather wore a smug smile. It was clear she expected Jay to compliment her on the wonderful job she'd done.

"I think my entree's getting cold. Let's eat!"

After dinner was over, there was the usual discussion of what they should do for the evening. No one felt like going to another movie, not after what had happened last night.

"How about bowling?" Paul looked thoughtful.

"That's a great idea!" Jay grinned at him. "Does anyone know how to work the machinery?"

"I do."

Everyone turned to Larry in surprise, and he shrugged. "I worked down at the Portersville Bowl when I was in junior high."

"The Portersville Bowl?" Cindy grinned. "Wasn't that the place they called the Toilet Bowl?"

Larry nodded. "Yeah . . . it wasn't exactly a showplace. But I did learn a lot and I'm sure I can get us started."

"Bowling!" Heather shuddered slightly and wrinkled up her nose. "Could we think of something a little more *refined?*"

Cindy grinned at Heather. "Nope. The orchestra's not playing tonight, and there's miles of snow between us and the opera house. Come on, Heather . . . be a sport."

"Well . . ." Heather gave a long-suffering sigh. "All right. I'll go along and watch. But I just had my nails done, and I don't want to even *think* about participating."

Sixteen

"Oh, my God! I can't believe I did that!" Heather jumped up and down and threw her arms around Cindy. "What's that called again?"

"A strike. You got a strike. You're a natural, Heather. I told you you'd love bowling."

Heather looked a little sheepish. "I know you did. And I do. But it really is hell on my nails."

"Why don't you cut them off?" Cindy suggested. "You can always have them done again later."

Diana held her breath, waiting for the explosion. Heather's long, highly polished nails were her pride and joy. But the anticipated explosion didn't come. Instead, Heather smiled at Cindy and nodded.

"Good idea. Does anybody have nail clippers?"

"I do." Diana found her nail clippers in the pocket of her purse, and handed them over quickly, before Heather could change her mind. Heather was certainly different, now that she was enjoying herself. Was it possible that she was actually human?

"How about a team tournament?" Jay suggested. "We could have the boys against the girls."

Diana shook her head. "That won't work. There's one more of you than there is of us."

"That's okay." Cindy grinned at her brother. "I'll bowl twice. That'll make it even."

Jay shook his head. "I don't think that's a very good idea. We wouldn't want to wear you out."

"Oh, you don't have to worry about that. Just get your team organized. And say a little prayer while you're at it."

While the guys went to the racks to find bowling balls, Diana turned to Cindy. "Jay looked really upset when you said you'd bowl twice. What was all that about?"

"He knows my average. That's why he's worried."

"It's that bad?"

"No. It's that good. I was the Prairie Falls teen champ for three years running. If I haven't lost my stuff, we're going to beat the pants off them!"

"That's great, Cindy!" Heather smiled, but she looked a little worried. "I just hope I don't spoil things for us. Maybe that strike I got was just beginner's luck."

Cindy shook her head. "Don't worry. You'll do just fine. I'll give you pointers as we go along."

"Are you ready?" Hal walked over to join them.

"Almost." Cindy started to write their names on the transparent grid that was showing on the overhead projector. "I just wish we had a trophy or some prizes. That'd make it more fun."

Hal gestured toward the case of trophies on the wall. "I don't suppose . . . no, we'd better not. They belong to the bowling alley."

"How about using some of those stuffed toys under the tree?" Diana suggested. "We could make up little plaques to hang around their necks."

Hal nodded. "Good idea. I'll go get eight of them. Four for the winners and four for the runners-up."

"Wrong." Cindy shook her head. "You only need three for the winners. I'm bowling twice, remember?"

"I'll help you, Hal." Heather put her bowling ball on the rack, and hurried to catch up with Hal.

"She sure seems different." Cindy turned to Diana. They were both amazed that Heather had offered to help. "Do you think it's permanent?"

"I don't know. She cut her nails, and she seems to love bowling. And she pulled her hair back into a ponytail without even checking the mirror. Those are very good signs."

"True." Cindy nodded. "Well . . . let's just cross our fingers and wait. I didn't think I'd ever say it, but there may be hope for Heather yet."

It was a sudden death play-off, with one ball for each contestant. The boys had gone first, and now it was time for the girls to bowl. The boys had proved to be a lot tougher to beat than Cindy had thought. Paul was an excellent bowler, and so was Jay. Even Hal had held his own, although he claimed he'd never done much bowling. The boys would have won, hands down, if it hadn't been for Larry. Although he had a very good average, his game was really off tonight.

"Uh, oh." Cindy winced as Larry threw his first strike of the night. "We've got our work cut out for us. We all have to bowl strikes if we're going to win."

Heather nodded, and gave a deep sigh. "It's all my fault. I really blew my last three frames."

"That's okay, Heather." Diana patted her on the shoulder. Heather really did look miserable. "It's just a game . . . right, Cindy?"

"Diana's right. And you did incredibly well for a beginner. Is your arm getting sore?"

Heather rubbed her arm and nodded. "It is kind of sore. But we need strikes to win, and I've got to try."

"Come on, girls," Larry called out to them. "It's too late to plan strategy. Why don't you just admit you lost and save yourselves the trouble. There's no way you can all bowl strikes."

Cindy bristled. "Oh, yeah? Says who?"

"Says me." Larry put his hands on his hips and his grin held a clear challenge.

Jay walked over to intervene. "Hey, Larry. Don't give the girls a hard time. We're not out to prove anything here."

"That's right." Paul walked over to join them. "This is just a friendly tournament. It doesn't really matter who wins."

Even Hal got into the act as he walked over to take Larry's other arm. "Take it easy, Larry. We're supposed to be having fun."

"Okay, okay." Larry shrugged them off. "But there's no way they can win. Maybe Diana and Cindy can pull off strikes in the pinch, but Heather's going to bomb. She's a waste."

Cindy walked back to join Diana and Heather. She was shaking her head. "Competition really changes Larry's personality. Jay used to be on a dart team with him, but he bowed out when Larry got nasty with the other teams. He told Jay he was using psychology to rattle them, but Jay thought it was more like a personal attack."

"But what Larry said is true." Heather looked very depressed. "I don't think I could bowl a strike if my life depended on it."

Heather's words set Diana's mind whirling. If Larry was using psychology on them, there had to be some way to turn it around. Suddenly she had an inspiration, and she turned to Cindy and Heather. "We can use psychology, too. Let's think of somebody we absolutely can't stand, and pretend they're standing right in front of the head pin. That ought to give us plenty of motivation to bowl strikes."

"That's a really good idea!" Cindy started to smile. "I'll use Dr. Oliver."

"But why?" Heather looked puzzled.

"He's head of the chemistry department. And he made the rule about not allowing students to use calculators on exams. Professor Oliver's the reason I almost flunked my chemistry final."

Diana and Heather watched as Cindy got ready to bowl. There was a fierce expression on her face as she picked up her ball and took her place on the lane. Her steps were deliberate as she went into her delivery and the ball flew from her hand with much more force than usual.

"Wow!" Heather's mouth flew open as Cindy's ball mowed down the pins. "It worked! You're up next, Diana. Who are you going to use?"

"I'm not sure." Diana looked a little embarrassed. Before this bowling tournament had started, she would have used Heather for motivation, but she didn't feel like doing that now.

"How about me?" Heather grinned at her. "I wouldn't blame you."

Diana could feel the blush rising to her face. Had Heather read her mind? "Uh . . . what do you mean?"

"I tried to get Jay away from you. That must have made you mad enough to throw a bowling ball at me."

Should she be honest? Heather was certainly being very candid. Diana sighed, and then she nodded. "That's true. I was really mad at you, before tonight. But you seem a lot different now. I think I'll use Aunt Sharon. She's always trying to convince my mother that I should go to an all-girls college."

"Your Aunt Sharon sounds awful!" Heather nodded. "And I'm glad you don't hate me anymore. I promise I won't try to break up you and Jay again . . . honest."

"Ready, Diana?"

Cindy motioned to her, and Diana walked up to get her ball. She did her best to visualize Aunt Sharon's face as she stood at the end of the lane and concentrated.

"This is for you, Aunt Sharon." Diana whispered the words as she stepped forward and let the ball fly. Then she closed her eyes and listened as the ball struck the pins with a very satisfying clatter.

"That was great, Diana!"

Diana opened her eyes to see that she'd bowled a strike. Then Heather came up and all three girls grinned at each other.

"Hey . . . this targeting really works." Heather watched as Cindy picked up her ball. "Are you going to use Professor Oliver again?"

"No. He's only good for one time. I think I'll use Rita Carpenter. She's the beautician who gave me this beastly hair cut."

Diana and Heather watched as Cindy took her place on the lane. She glared at the pins for a moment, and then she bowled another strike.

"Uh, oh. My turn." Heather looked scared. "Who am I going to use?"

Diana patted Heather on the shoulder. "Use someone who's done something mean to you, someone who's embarrassed you and made you want to cry."

"Okay." Heather took a deep breath and picked up her ball. "I know exactly who I'm going to imagine standing in front of those pins."

Diana and Cindy watched Heather take her place on the end of the lane. Both of them looked a little uncomfortable as they caught a glimpse of Heather's face. She really looked mad enough to kill.

Heather mouthed something under her breath and stepped confidently to the line. Her bowling ball hit the boards with a solid thunk and flew down the lane to knock over every pin.

"You did it, Heather!" Diana rushed up to hug her.

"Good for you." Cindy nodded. "Who did you think about?"

Heather grinned at them. "I took your advice and thought about the person who embarrassed me. And I threw that bowling ball straight at Larry's big mouth!"

"We got prizes for everyone." Hal handed out the packages. "Since we couldn't get trophies, we thought these would do."

Jay grinned as he opened his package. "Oh, great. Just what I wanted. A stuffed something-or-other."

"At least you put my name on mine." Larry looked disgruntled as he ripped open his package.

"But we didn't!" Diana was puzzled. "We didn't have time, unless . . . Hal? You didn't tag them, did you?"

Hal shook his head. "Not me. Heather and I just grabbed seven packages and carried them here."

"Hey! This isn't funny!" Larry stared down at his open box. "There's nothing in here but a packing slip."

"Here. You can have mine." Jay exchanged boxes with Larry. "I'll go out and get another package."

Diana felt her heart begin to thud in her chest as she waited for Jay to unfold the piece of paper. But he didn't. He just stuffed it in his pocket, and headed for the exit.

"Wait for me!" Diana stood up quickly, and hurried to catch up with Jay. She knew he was going to look at the paper in private and she wanted to be there.

The moment they were outside the bowling alley, Diana grabbed Jay's arm. "What does it say?"

"I don't know. And I'm not sure I want to know. I'm hoping it's just a packing slip, but I'm not going to look right now."

Diana nodded, but she shivered slightly as they walked to the Christmas tree. When they were seated on the bench in front of the tree, Jay took the crumpled piece of paper from his pocket and read it.

"Is it from 'Santa Claus Is Comin' To Town?' " Diana knew the answer, without even asking. There were deep worry lines on Jay's forehead. He handed her the note without a word, and Diana read it out loud. It was another line from the Christmas carol, even more ominous than the first two.

"He's making a list and checking it twice; Gonna find out who's naughty and nice." Diana shivered and turned to look at Jay. "Who's doing this? It's scaring me!"

"I know." Jay slipped his arm around her shoulders. "That's why I didn't let Larry read it. I thought maybe if he didn't get the note . . ."

Diana nodded. "Right. But do you think it's just bad luck? Or do you think that . . . ?"

"I don't know." Jay interrupted her quickly, before she could finish her thought. "Let's get a package and go back. I'm going to talk to Larry in private. I'll tell him about the note and warn him to stay close to us, tonight . . . just in case."

Diana nodded, and they started walking back to the bowling alley. A chill had invaded her body when she'd read the note, and she was still shivering slightly. Jay's arm was warm around her shoulders, and it came close to chasing away the chill. But it didn't. Not quite.

Seventeen

Larry grinned as he walked through the deserted mall. He felt almost like a young teenager again, escaping the watchful eyes of his parents. It was nice of Jay and Diana to be so concerned about him, but they were being ridiculously paranoid. Larry wasn't a bit worried about the present with the note inside. There were probably a bunch of presents with lyrics from "Santa Claus Is Comin' To Town" inside. It was someone's idea of a joke, and the culprit had probably left with the group that had driven out before they were snowbound.

There was a noise behind him, and Larry froze in his tracks. It had sounded like stealthy footsteps, and he turned around quickly, peering into the shadows. Of course no one was there. He was the only one awake. Perhaps Jay and Diana's paranoia was contagious. For a second there, he'd been almost scared.

Larry had waited until everyone was asleep, and then he'd left the Crossroads Pub. He was thirsty and he'd decided to go to the bowling alley for a beer. He knew that if he'd poured himself a beer at the pub, he might wake Jay and Diana. The last thing he wanted was to wake up the prophets of doom and disaster!

As Larry passed the mall Christmas tree, he gave an amused chuckle. It was pure coincidence that the other two people who'd opened similar packages had been killed. Take Sue, for instance. She'd been drunk, and she'd wandered outside in the worst winter storm of the decade. It was too bad that she'd been standing in the wrong spot when the wind had blown over that planter, but it had been an accident, and the package she'd opened had absolutely nothing to do with her bad luck.

Dave was another case in point. He'd been careless, and that was what had cost him his life. Everyone knew that it was dangerous to stand in a puddle and fool around with something electrical. They taught you stuff like that in grade school! Sure, Dave's death had been awful, but it had been an accident. And now Jay and Diana were worried because they thought the lyrics in the presents were some sort of omen of impending death.

Larry opened the door to the bowling alley and stepped inside. He didn't bother to flick on the main lights. There was a dim light over the bar and that was good enough for him. He walked around the bar, drew a glass of beer, and chugged it down. There was nothing like beer when you were thirsty. Then he filled his glass again, and sat down at a table with a view of the interior of the mall.

All the stores were decorated for Christmas, but Larry couldn't see the window displays in the dark. There was only one bright window and that was in the huge sporting goods store directly across from him. Larry watched their mechanical Santa for a while. It was really fascinating, and he wondered why he hadn't noticed it earlier.

Santa was sitting in a rocking chair, rocking back and forth as he stared out the window and smiled. Every so often, he would turn his head or touch his beard with his hand. The mechanics were very realistic, and Larry was sure that the sophisticated display must have cost big bucks.

Larry downed his second glass of beer, and got up to pour another. But he didn't sit back down again. He carried his glass out the door and walked over to the sporting goods store for a closer look at the mechanical Santa.

As Larry watched, the Santa stood up and walked to the window. It was really amazing how real he looked. He turned to the left, and then to the right, seeming to search through the darkened mall for customers. And then he faced straight ahead and smiled, directly at Larry.

Larry smiled back. He couldn't help it. The Santa looked so real. Of course, he was getting a buzz from his third glass of beer, and that could have accounted for it.

"Hey, Santa"—Larry chuckled and walked closer—"how about if I tell you what I want for Christmas?"

Santa nodded, and Larry chuckled again. He knew the nod was programmed into Santa's mechanics, but it had come at the perfect time.

"I'd really like a Ferrari." Larry grinned. "Red with white leather upholstery. What do you think, Santa? Can you fit a Ferrari on your sleigh?"

Santa nodded again. And then he did something that absolutely blew Larry's mind. His arm came up and he crooked his finger for Larry to come closer.

"Okay, okay. I'm coming." Larry laughed and stepped closer. "What do you want?"

"Ho, ho, *ho!*"

Larry took a hasty step back as he heard Santa's voice, but then he realized that there was no reason why this Santa couldn't talk. He seemed to be able to do everything else, and the talking feature was probably nothing more than a looped tape fed through a speaker.

"Hey, Santa. Can you say anything else? Ho, ho, ho is pretty boring."

"Ho, ho, *ho!*"

Larry laughed and took another sip of beer. "I guess that's it, huh?"

Santa crooked his finger again, and Larry grinned. He drained his glass of beer, set it down on the floor, and moved up to the glass again. "Okay. I'm here. Now let's get personal. What do you think I should get my dad for Christmas?"

Santa seemed to consider it for a moment, and then he opened his mouth. "Fishing tackle makes a wonderful Christmas gift."

"Wow!" Larry blinked, and then he started to grin. "I get it. They programmed you with ads for the store. But my dad doesn't have time to fish anymore. What else have you got?"

"We have hand-tied flies that will please even the most discriminating fly fisherman."

"No way!" Larry chuckled as he realized that he was talking to a mechanical doll. But there was no one else here, so it really didn't matter. "Sorry, Santa. My dad hasn't done any fly casting in years."

Santa took a step forward and smiled. He was so close, his belly was almost pressing up against the glass, and he stared at Larry as he spoke again. "Our flies are tied by a local expert, a man who fished the river that once ran right through this store, the real winner of the tri-city father-andson fishing contest held on this site, twelve years ago."

Larry didn't stop to wonder how Santa knew all this. He just moved up until he was nose to nose with Santa. "You're wrong, Santa. I was in that contest, and my dad and I won first prize."

"You cheated." Santa's eyes glittered dangerously. "You won because you poured glue all over an old man's tackle box. And you ruined the sport of fly fishing for him."

Larry was so shocked, he was frozen in place. "But . . . but no one knew about that! What's going on here?!"

"I'm going to punish you, Larry." Santa put both palms against the glass. "You've been a bad little boy and you deserve to be punished. Ho . . . ho . . . ho!"

Larry's mouth opened in a soundless scream. But before he could turn and run for his life, Santa pushed against the glass and it shattered, knocking him to the floor. And then Santa was there, standing over him with a stern expression on his face and a long, sharp sliver of glass in his mittened hand.

"No! It was all my father's idea! And I was just a little kid! I never meant to . . ."

But Santa didn't give Larry a chance to finish. His hand slashed down with deadly force. And the shard of razor-sharp glass buried itself deeply in Larry's heart, stilling it forever.

Eighteen

Diana and Jay were sitting in a booth at the Crossroads Bistro, watching the storm outside the windows. The snow had combined with ice crystals to form tiny particles of sleet. The wind drove them against the windows, and they rattled and bounced against the glass. The noise they made reminded Diana of one long drum-roll, building up to something horrible. The tension was unnerving, and it made her want to go back to bed to pull the covers over her head.

Jay had been up early, at six o'clock. When he'd realized that Larry was missing, he'd organized a search party with Hal and Paul. The girls had stayed in the pub, huddled together in a tight group, hoping that they'd walk in any second with Larry in tow. Of course, that hadn't happened. Larry was dead, just like Sue and Dave.

Now it was eight in the morning, but it was still very dark. The blowing snow had completely obscured the sun, and the day was a somber, slate-gray color. Perhaps she wouldn't have panicked if the sun had shone brightly and the skies had been bright blue. But suddenly everything seemed horrendously frightening.

"It wasn't just another accident! You know it wasn't!" Diana's hands were trembling so hard, she could barely hold the cup of coffee that Jay had poured for her.

"Di . . . please." Jay hugged her to him, and stroked her hair. "You've got to calm down. If you get hysterical, everyone else is going to panic. And then we'll have real trouble."

"We've already *got* real trouble! Three of us are dead. Isn't that trouble enough?"

Jay nodded. He looked tired, and Diana almost relented. But she had to convince him that they were in terrible danger.

"Listen to me, Jay. You know that window didn't just pop out of its frame and kill Larry. Somebody moved the safety bar and pushed out the window."

"No, Diana." Jay shook his head. "The safety bar was in place. I checked it."

"Then Larry's murderer put it back! Somebody's trying to kill us, Jay. And he's succeeding!"

Jay opened his mouth to deny it, but he closed it again without speaking. And then he nodded. "You're right. I didn't want to admit it, but you're definitely right. But who's doing it? And why?"

"I don't know who. But I do know he's crazy. And that Christmas carol must've set him off. That's why he writes down the words and wraps them up like presents for his victims."

Jay nodded. "Okay. But who is it? There's only six of us left."

"It's not me, and it's not you. That leaves only four. And it's certainly not Cindy or . . . Heather?" Diana's face turned white. "Heather was really mad at Larry last night. She was so mad she pretended that he was standing in front of the pins when she bowled that last strike."

Jay shook his head. "No. It can't be Heather. She's a total waste when it comes to anything mechanical. There's no way she could have taken off the safety bar and put it back on again."

"Okay." Diana drew a deep sigh of relief. "I'm glad it's not Heather. I'm actually beginning to like her. You don't think . . . it couldn't be Hal, could it?"

"That doesn't make any sense. He's got no motive, and I've gotten to know him pretty well in the past couple of days. He's a really nice guy."

Diana nodded. "That's true. He was really nice to me the

night we found Dave. And he was great when he described my out-fit for the fashion tape. But if it's not Hal, the only one left is . . ."

"Paul." Jay looked very uncomfortable. "It's awful to suspect my sister's boyfriend, but we really don't know him that well. I guess he could be unstable, but . . . it just doesn't make sense. He's got no reason to try to kill us. He didn't even know us until we all got snowbound out here."

"But there's no one else here!" The hair on the back of Diana's neck started to prickle a warning. "Is there?"

Jay caught her meaning, and he frowned. "I don't know. I guess there could be. This is a big mall and there's a million places to hide out. Somebody could have stayed behind when everyone else left."

"Or someone could have walked in, the day the storm started, and just stayed. It's a perfect place to hide if you're avoiding the law, and Greystone Prison is just up the road." Diana shivered again. "Do you think they had an escape?"

"It's possible. There's no way to warn us if they did. We're completely cut off out here."

"Oh, my God, Jay!" Diana's voice was shaking. "We could be locked in here with a psychotic killer!"

Jay laughed and hugged her tightly. "Relax, Diana. They don't keep psychotic killers at Greystone Prison. It's not even a prison anymore. It's a minimum security correctional facility."

"What does that mean?" Diana wasn't reassured.

"They only handle white-collar offenders, and they're not vi-olent. Most of their inmates have passed bad checks, or been convicted of real estate fraud. The guys at Greystone are crimi-nals, but they're not the type to write down lyrics from 'Santa Claus Is Comin' To Town,' and then murder us. Besides, the killer can't be a stranger."

"Why not?" Diana was puzzled.

"He knows our names. He writes them on the tags."

"Oh, my God! You're right!" Diana shivered and moved closer to Jay. Somehow it was even more awful if the killer was someone they knew.

"It'll be okay." Jay gave her another hug and then he stood

up. "Come on, Diana. We'll go round up some weapons. And then we'll find everybody else and pass them out. We've got to fight back!"

Diana nodded and let Jay pull her to her feet. She felt a little better, now that they had a plan of action.

"Don't worry, Diana." Jay smiled down at her. "We'll be safe if we go everywhere together in a group. There's no way any-body's going to attack all six of us at once."

"Are you sure?" Diana's voice was shaking.

"I'm positive. This storm can't last much longer, and the po-lice will be here soon. As long as we stick together and watch our backs, we're going to be just fine."

But as they walked through the mall, Diana's knees continued to shake. She knew Jay would do his best to protect them. But what if Jay's best wasn't enough?

He glanced down at his list and smiled as he crossed out Larry's name. They were beginning to get suspicious, and he knew that he would have to move fast. Not even Santa had the power to make the storm last forever, and everything had to be done before the highway patrol came out to check on them again.

The package was ready, wrapped in a foil paper that she'd be sure to notice. It was her favorite color, deep purple. She'd men-tioned that the first night, when she'd picked out a bright purple satin comforter to put on her bed in the furniture store. The lyrics from "Santa Claus Is Comin' To Town" were inside, the lines he'd especially chosen for her. He'd planned everything very carefully so the others wouldn't see her when she opened her present. If they knew she'd received it, they'd crowd around her in a protective circle. This naughty girl deserved to be pun-ished, and Santa would do it before anyone realized that she was his next victim.

As he stuck a beautiful silver bow on top of the package, he thought back to that awful day when she'd hurt Grandma's feel-ings. She might not remember, but he did.

She'd come to the farm with her high school home economics

class to watch Grandma make strawberry jam. Grandma's strawberry jam had won blue ribbons at the county fair for three years running, and the teacher had asked her to give a demonstration.

Grandma had been very proud that the school wanted her to teach jam making. There were twelve girls in the class and she'd made out labels with their names to put on the jam when it was finished. Each girl would get her own jar to take home and enjoy with her family. Grandma had even spent the money to buy pretty jars, and they hadn't come cheap.

The girls had been very polite as they'd watched Grandma make the jam. And they'd oohed and aahed over the pretty jars with their names on them. When the jam had cooled enough to take home, they had thanked Grandma and left. He could still remember how happy Grandma had been when she'd called to tell him about it.

But the next day, when he'd come out to visit, Grandma hadn't been happy. And when he'd asked her what was wrong, she'd told him that one of the girls had thrown away her jar of jam. She'd tossed it out on the road, as if it had been worth less than nothing. And Grandma knew which girl it had been because her name had been on the jar.

He'd done his best to make Grandma feel better. Perhaps the jam had fallen out of the car accidentally. But Grandma said no, Gramps had seen her toss it out. He hadn't wanted to tell her at first, but she'd wormed it out of him. Imagine throwing away her prize-winning jam! The girl could have given it to someone else if she hadn't liked it, but she'd thrown it out on the side of the road as if it were garbage!

Even though he'd always been allergic to strawberries, he'd eaten Grandma's jam on his toast all that summer. It had given him a horrible rash, but it had been worth it to see her smile. Perhaps Grandma had forgiven the girl for throwing out her jam, but he hadn't. His skin still prickled when he remembered that rash.

He picked up the package and hurried out to the mall. He had to get it in place before anyone noticed. Santa would punish the girl for hurting Grandma's feelings, and there was nothing the others could do to protect her.

Cindy and Paul had wanted her to stay with them, but Heather just felt like being alone. She felt terribly guilty for being so mad at Larry last night. Of course, she knew that imagining Larry in front of the pins hadn't had anything to do with his accident, but she wished she'd picked someone else's image to mow down with her bowling ball.

Perhaps shopping would make her feel better. Heather rode the escalator up to the second level and walked into the most expensive women's clothing store in the mall. Elaine's Boutique was cheap, compared to Le Dome. Le Dome carried only designer originals, and Heather had heard that their prices were astronomical.

Heather flicked on the lights and smiled as five cut-glass chandeliers began to glow softly. There were no racks. The clothing at Le Dome was hung in closets.

When she'd found the closet with her size, Heather opened the door and began to examine the dresses. There were no price tags. If you had to ask, you couldn't afford it. That was the way it worked in exclusive shops.

Heather took a dress from the rack and sighed happily. It was a gorgeous shade of deep royal purple that would look lovely on her. The sleeves and neckline were trimmed with tiny bands of pearls, and she was willing to bet that they weren't synthetic. If the dress looked as stunning on her as she thought it would, she'd make Daddy buy it for her Christmas present.

There were three dressing rooms in the back of the store, and Heather gasped as she entered one. It was a sitting room in miniature. Two wing-back chairs upholstered in a warm, cream-colored velvet were arranged against one wall, with a beautifully carved, rosewood table between them. The three-way mirror was spectacular, with three oval-shaped panes of beveled glass, surrounded by an antique gold frame.

Heather slipped out of her shoes and wiggled her toes in the deep pile carpet. It was also a rich shade of cream, a little darker than the wing chairs. The walls were covered with gorgeous tapestry, and all the lighting was recessed. It was a lovely room that would show off the beautiful clothes to their full advantage.

There was a small closet in the far corner, a free-standing rosewood piece that was carved with the same design as the table. Heather opened the door and saw that there were two satin-covered hangers, waiting to receive her clothes. She slipped off her jeans, and laughed as she hung them up on one of the hangers. It was probably the first and last time these hangers would hold a pair of jeans and a college sweatshirt. And then she slipped on the dress.

As she twirled in front of the mirror, Heather wore a satisfied smile. The dress was perfect for her. She decided to wear it down to the pub, to show the other girls, but her tennis shoes wouldn't do at all. She needed something glamorous, and she'd noticed that Le Dome also carried designer shoes. She'd find the perfect pair and waltz into the pub with a complete outfit.

Heather gave one last glance in the mirror, and opened the door to step out. She was on her way to the designer shoe display, when she spotted a gift-wrapped package on the counter. It was her favorite color, deep purple, and it matched her dress perfectly.

There was a frown on Heather's face as she read the name on the tag. Her name. This present was for her. But no one knew that she'd gone to Le Dome, unless . . .

Heather almost bolted for the door. Sue had received a package with her name on it and now she was dead. And so had Dave. Larry had opened his package last night, and he was dead, too. Heather's hands were shaking as she opened the package. It was empty, except for a folded piece of paper in the bottom. She unfolded it and gasped as she saw the words that were printed inside. *He sees you when you're sleeping; He knows when you're awake.* They were lyrics to "Santa Claus Is Comin' To Town!"

Her hands were trembling so hard, the paper fluttered to the floor. It was like Sue's package. And Dave's. And there had been a piece of paper in Larry's, too, although Jay had taken it away before he could read it. She had to get back to the group! It wasn't safe for her to be alone!

Heather didn't even think about going back to get her tennis shoes. She just bolted for the door. But as she ran out into the mall, she saw something that made her feel much, much better. One of the guys had dressed up as Santa and he was sitting on the bench right in front of Le Dome. She was so relieved, she didn't even stop to wonder why he was dressed in costume. She just hurtled straight into his arms.

"Oh, my God! I'm so glad you're here! I got one of those packages and . . . let's go down to the pub! Quick!"

Santa nodded, and took her arm. He didn't say anything, but that was all right. Heather didn't really want to talk. She just wanted to get back down to the pub and surround herself with other people!

There were tears of fright in Heather's eyes as she huddled close to Santa and they walked quickly away. But then she noticed that they were going in the wrong direction for the escalator. "Wait! The escalator's the other way!"

Heather looked up at him, but Santa just smiled. And then he pointed toward the glass elevator that was only a short distance away.

"Oh, good thinking!" Heather's breath came out in a shuddering sigh. "I forgot they even had an elevator!"

Santa walked her right up to the elevator, and pushed the button. The doors opened and he gave a courtly bow as Heather stepped inside. And then he spoke for the first time, as he reached into the elevator and pressed the button to close the doors. "Too bad you don't like strawberry jam."

Heather stared at him as the doors started to close. What a weird thing to say! But then she realized that Santa wasn't getting into the elevator. "Wait! Aren't you coming with me?!"

Santa was grinning as the doors slid all the way closed. It was a strange grin, and Heather decided not to press the button to open the doors again. She didn't know who was inside the Santa suit. He'd deliberately disguised his voice.

As the elevator started to move, Heather stared down at the lower level. Jay and Diana were just coming out of the sporting goods store. She knocked on the glass and they looked up to wave at her. Thank God! They'd be right there when she got off the elevator. She was safe!

But then something happened that made Heather's face turn chalk white. The elevator shuddered and there was a loud snapping noise. And then she was hurtling down the shaft, too fast to stop at the lower level, too fast to scream. Her last thought, before the elevator crashed into the cement floor of the basement, was of Santa's strange and sadistic grin.

Nineteen

Santa smiled as he peeked over the rail. Diana and Jay had seen Heather fall and they'd called out to Paul and Cindy. The panic on their faces was beautiful to see, and he watched for several moments as they gestured and pointed. But then something happened that made him raise his eyebrows and smile with delight. Paul and Jay were walking the girls back to the pub. And he'd heard them say that they were going down to the basement to take care of Heather. That meant they'd be leaving Diana and Cindy at the pub, alone!

He rubbed his mittened hands together, anticipating what would happen. Jay and Paul would be very busy, wrapping what was left of Heather in blankets, and then carrying her body up the steps to the meat cooler. They were trying to be considerate, going to do the unpleasant task while the girls stayed in the safety of the pub. They didn't realize it, but they had done him a huge favor. They'd given Santa the time he needed to deliver his next set of presents.

The first thing to do was to get out of costume. He dashed into the hardware store and found a pair of jeans and a blue denim shirt. It only took a moment to change out of his costume, and he folded it carefully, putting it behind the counter near the front of the store. He'd already decided that the next set of accidents would take place up here.

The large crescent wrenches were near the back of the store, and he chose the biggest one he could find. Then he headed out to the walkway again. Each section of the rail was held in place with six heavy bolts and he removed them carefully, holding the rail in place. Santa's next victims would fall to their deaths and everyone would assume that the railing had been improperly installed.

He was puffing slightly as he took the stairs down to the security office, and sat down at the desk to wrap the packages. There wasn't much time and he had to hurry. He used pink foil for the girl who had stolen apples from Gramps's orchard, breaking some grafts he'd made on the branches. Gramps had been very angry when he'd seen what she'd done. If she'd asked, he would have given her the apples.

The second package was wrapped in silver foil. It was for the girl who had convinced Grandma to bake all those pies for the charity bake sale. They had been beautiful pies, each one a work of art, but the girl had priced them ridiculously low. Two dollars for one of Grandma's pies was a terrible insult.

As he stuck the bows on top of the packages, he almost had second thoughts. These were small offenses, but they still had to be punished. Perhaps not by death, but Santa didn't really have a choice. The game was drawing to a close and there could be no survivors.

He wrote the names carefully and stuck the tags on the packages. He was almost ready. But first he had to make certain that there would be no interference. He had the master key, and he would lock the guys in the basement. Then Santa would be free to lure the two naughty girls close to the rail, and push them to their deaths.

Diana and Cindy had moved out to a bench near the door to the pub. There was no way they could stay locked up inside, imagining the worst. They were close enough to run for cover if they spotted the killer, but they felt much better now that they could see the whole mall.

Both girls were nervous, and their eyes scanned the length of the mall, checking for any movement. And then Diana gave a little gasp. "Did you see what I just saw?"

"You mean way down there by those offices?"

Diana nodded. "I swear I saw someone. But when I blinked, he was gone."

"I saw him, too." Cindy stood up. "Let's go check it out. Maybe it's Hal."

Diana frowned and shook her head. "We promised the guys we'd wait for them here."

"I know, but we also promised we'd warn Hal if we saw him."

"That's true." Diana began to waver.

"Come on, Diana . . . we'll be safe if we stick together. We've both got canisters of mace."

Diana gave a little laugh. "That's not very comforting. I don't know how to use mace. And by the time I read the instructions, it'll be too late."

"I know how. It's just like perfume. If the killer tries to grab you, all you have to do is point it and spray."

"Okay." Diana took a deep breath and stood up. "You go first and I'll bring up the rear. If I hear something, I'll tap you on the shoulder."

Nothing was moving as they made their way to the other end of the mall. They kept to the center of the walkway, so they'd have plenty of time to whirl around and spray their mace if someone rushed out of one of the stores.

"I think he came out of here." Cindy motioned to a wood-paneled door. "Get ready, Diana . . . I'm going to open it."

Cindy turned the knob and the door slowly opened. It was an office of some kind, with metal filing cabinets and a desk. The room was deserted, but the lights were still on. And there were two packages sitting on top of the desk, one pink and one silver.

"Uh, oh!" Cindy moved forward to read the tags. And when she turned back to Diana there was fear in her eyes. "They're for us!"

Diana's lips tightened into a thin line as she stepped into the office and locked the door behind her. "We'd better open them."

"Let's just get out of here!" Cindy's voice was shaking. "He could come back any minute!"

"The door's locked and we've both got mace. Hurry up, Cindy. We've got to know for sure."

Cindy was the first to get her package open, and she lifted out the note with shaking fingers. "Here . . . you read it. I don't want to!"

"He knows if you've been bad or good." Diana read the words that were written on the paper, and then she unfolded her note. *"So be good for goodness sake."*

They stared at each other with horror on their faces. They didn't have to say what they were thinking. They were next. And the person they'd seen was the killer!

They were moving back down the walkway when Diana heard a noise behind them. She whirled, her finger on the trigger of the mace canister, and gave a relieved sigh as she recognized Hal.

"Hal!" Cindy spotted him at the same time, and she rushed up to hug him. "Thank God it's you! We thought it was the killer!"

Hal looked very puzzled. "What killer? And where is everybody? I just checked the pub, but Jay and Paul weren't there."

"We've got something awful to tell you." Diana's voice was shaking. "The elevator fell, and Heather's dead. Jay and Paul are down in the basement, taking care of . . . you know."

Hal looked dazed, and he shook his head. "That's horrible! But you said . . . a killer? Here?"

"There's somebody else out here at the mall." Cindy took over the explanation. "All those deaths . . . Sue, Dave, Larry. They weren't accidents. And we don't think the elevator fell by accident, either. Somebody's trying to kill us!"

"Are you sure?"

Diana nodded. "We're positive. We caught a glimpse of him a couple of minutes ago. He was coming out of that door down the hall. Cindy and I checked it out and we found presents on the desk. Our names were on the tags and there were notes inside."

"Lyrics to 'Santa Claus Is Comin' To Town?' "

"Exactly!" Cindy nodded. "He's going after us next, and that's why we were so glad to see you!"

Hal squared his shoulders. "Don't worry, girls. I'll take care of you until the guys get back. I'll get a knife, or an axe or something like that. The hardware store's right up there."

"We'll go with you."' Diana grabbed his arm. "We're safer if we stick together."

They walked through the mall, glancing around warily, until they reached the escalator. Cindy was in the lead, and she was about to step on when she heard a loud shout.

"Cindy! We're back!"

Cindy stepped back quickly, away from the escalator, almost bowling Diana and Hal over. "Boy, am I glad to see you! What took you so long?"

"The basement door locked behind us. We had to use the freight elevator to get back up here."

They all stood in a tight little group, glad to be back together again. And then Jay turned to Hal.

"I'm glad the girls found you, Hal. We thought maybe . . ." Jay stopped and swallowed hard. "Did the girls tell you what happened?"

Hal nodded. "We were just going up to the hardware store. I figured I'd need an axe or something, in case he tried to attack us."

"I think we'll be okay if we all stay together." Paul put his arm around Cindy's shoulders and gave her a hug. Then he frowned as he realized that she was trembling. "What happened, Cindy?"

"We saw him! He was down there at the end of the mall."

"Did you recognize him?"

"No." Cindy shook her head. "We just caught a glimpse of him. He was coming out of one of those offices, so we . . . uh . . . we went down there to check it out."

Jay's arm was shaking as he pulled Diana close to his side. "You promised me you'd stay at the pub."

"I know, but we had our mace, and we were getting nervous just sitting there. And at first, we thought it was Hal. You told us to warn him if we saw him."

Hal looked very concerned. "Hey . . . let's not argue. The girls are okay, and that's what matters, isn't it?"

"You're right." Jay nodded, and turned to Diana again. "Sorry. I was just worried about you, that's all. You didn't see him again, did you?"

"No. But we found the office he was using, and there were two presents sitting on top of the desk. They were for us."

"You opened them?"

Jay was hugging her so tightly, Diana could barely breathe, but she was so glad he was here, she didn't care. "We had to know if we were right."

"There were lyrics inside." Hal nodded gravely. "The next two lines from 'Santa Claus Is Comin' To Town,' one in each package."

"I think we'd better get out of here." Jay's voice was hard. "Any suggestions?"

There was an uncomfortable silence while they thought it over. Then Cindy spoke up. "We can't walk. We'll freeze to death before we reach the nearest farmhouse. It's over five miles away."

"We might be able to make it to the truck I left on the highway." Paul frowned slightly. "But there's no guarantee it'll start."

Diana nodded. "I guess we're stuck here. We'll just have to hole up in the . . ."

"What is it, Diana?" Jay looked puzzled as she started to smile.

"The snowmobiles! They're all gassed up and ready to go!"

"Are you sure?" Hal frowned slightly.

"I'm positive. While Cindy and I were waiting for our job interviews, one of the maintenance men came in. The secretary asked if he'd gassed up the snowmobiles and he said he had."

"Diana's right." Cindy nodded. "The secretary told us they

were going to tape a commercial for the mall at the drawing. Two Santas were supposed to escort the winners to their snow-mobiles and drive them right out the front door of the mall."

"That's why they asked us if we could drive a snowmobile!" Jay started to grin. "Come on. Let's go check them out. If you girls are right, we can be out of here in no time flat!"

Twenty

Things were never as easy as they sounded, and they discovered that when they arrived at the snowmobiles. They were on a ramp, and the gas tanks were full, but they were chained down with a heavy padlock.

"No problem." Diana spoke up. "I'll just run up to the hardware store and get a pair of bolt-cutters."

Jay grabbed her arm and pulled her back. "No, Diana. There's no way any of us are going anywhere alone."

"Hey, let's think this out." Hal began to frown. "We're going to need warm parkas, ski masks, gloves, and boots. Somebody's going to have to go to the ski shop for those. And we should have someone stay with the snowmobiles, just in case the killer tries something to sabotage them."

Cindy shrugged. "What could he do? They're chained down."

"He could steal the spark plugs, or loosen the ignition wires. He could even pour water in the gas tanks." Hal looked very serious. "If the killer knows anything about mechanics at all, he could really mess us up."

Jay nodded. "Hal's right. Two of us should stay by the snowmobiles to stand guard. The other three can go for the bolt-cutters, and then they can pick up the survival gear we need."

"It's going to take more time that way." Hal shook his head. "The hardware store's on the upper level, and the ski shop's down here. How about if we split up? Cindy and I can go up to the hardware store, while Jay and Diana get the stuff at the ski shop. Paul can stay here to guard the snowmobiles."

"But then Paul will be alone." Cindy looked worried.

"That's okay." Paul patted his pocket. "I've got a knife, and I can see the whole mall from here. I'll holler if I see anything moving."

"Well . . . okay." Cindy still looked very uncomfortable, and Diana knew she wanted to stay with Paul. But she was going to hurt Hal's feelings if she wasn't careful.

Diana turned to smile at Hal. "I'll go to the hardware store with you. Cindy's never seen a pair of bolt-cutters in her life. She can go with Jay and get the stuff at the ski shop. Is that okay?"

"Sure. That's fine with me."

Hal smiled, but Diana could tell he was disappointed. He'd really wanted to go with Cindy. But why? Was it possible that Cindy, the girl who'd complained that no guy was ever going to ask her out, had attracted two guys at once?

He wasn't happy as he got into his Santa costume. Cindy should have been the one to come to the hardware store. After all, her present had contained the next line of the lyrics. But things didn't always happen according to plan, and Diana had taken Cindy's place. The situation was irritating, but he guessed he couldn't be that choosy. Diana was here, and he'd just have to break with the tradition he'd established and punish her first. When opportunity knocked, it was wise to answer the door immediately. After all, there was very little time left.

He glanced toward the back of the store, and smiled as he saw her, trying keys in the case that contained the bolt-cutters. All the expensive tools were locked in cases, and it would take her some time to find the proper key. It was a pity he couldn't use the rail for her punishment but the others would see and he couldn't take a chance like that. He had to choose another means of punishment, another way to assure her death.

There were plenty of choices. His eyes traveled over the row of chainsaws, but he quickly discarded that idea. Too noisy. The rest of them would come running if he fired up a chainsaw, and then he would be at a disadvantage. He needed something quiet and deadly, some way to dole out her punishment without a sound. And he'd have to be very careful that she didn't see him before he struck. He didn't want to give her time to scream.

A hunting knife could be deadly, but that was also risky. She'd be able to scream if he hit a non-vital spot. That was also true with an axe, or even a sledgehammer. And none of them looked like mall-related accidents. He really hated to abandon his plan to blame the mall for their deaths.

Suddenly, the perfect solution struck him, and he began to smile. He didn't have to kill her now. He could simply immobilize her. The others would come looking for her, and he'd immobilize them, too, one by one. And then he'd drag them all out to the spot where he'd loosened the bolts on the rail, and punish them all together.

Cindy's hands were trembling as she got a big plastic bag from the roll behind the counter. "Here, Jay. You get the parkas."

"What size?"

"Large. That'll work for everybody."

"But won't a large be too big for Diana?" Jay looked puzzled. "She's awfully small. She wears a size seven dress."

Cindy almost laughed out loud. "How do you know that?"

"I asked her. I thought I should know her sizes so I could get her a Christmas present."

Cindy nodded, and stifled a giggle. "What's her ring size?"

"Five and a half." Jay rattled it off, and then he looked embarrassed. "You never know when you might need information like that. Come on, Cindy. Let's hurry."

"Right. You get the parkas and the gloves. I'll go for the boots and ski masks."

Cindy grabbed another bag, and hurried over to the boot section to get five pairs of moon boots. She stuffed them in her bag, and swept a pile of woolen scarves off a counter into the bag. Ski masks were next and she grabbed five of those. "I'm ready. How about you?"

"Let's go!" Jay grabbed a parka and stuffed it under his arm. "Hurry up, Cindy. I'm a little worried about Paul."

"But why?" Cindy was puffing as she pulled the heavy bag across the floor to the door.

"He's the only one who's alone. I want to make sure he's all right."

But Paul was fine, and he shouldered his camera the moment he saw them. Cindy groaned as he taped them running down the walkway toward him, pulling the heavy bags behind them. She probably looked like hell.

"Good job." Paul met her halfway, and took the bag. "You were gone less than ten minutes."

"I wonder what's taking Hal and Diana so long." Cindy began to get worried. "I mean . . . how much time can it take to get a pair of bolt-cutters and a toolbox? Do you think we should check on them?"

Jay nodded. "We'll go up there if they don't show up in the next couple of minutes. Let's spread all this stuff out in piles, so we can get dressed and get out of here."

"Okay. I got the bolt-cutters." Diana lifted the heavy tool from the rack and gave a sigh of relief. "You might know it. It was the last key on the ring. Did you find the right kind of toolbox?"

There was silence from the front of the store, and Diana frowned. "Hal? Are you there?"

Again, there was only silence, and the hair on the back of Diana's neck started to prickle. Was Hal all right?

"Hal! Where are you?!"

Diana's heart beat a rapid tattoo in her chest, and she fought down the urge to panic. Hal could be hurt . . . or dead. And she could be alone in the hardware store with the killer!

There was a sound behind her. An indrawn breath that seemed very loud in the sudden stillness. Diana didn't take time to think. There was a light switch right next to the case, and she reached up to flick it off, plunging the store into darkness. She heard a muffled exclamation as she dropped to her knees, and started to crawl from counter to counter, the bolt-cutters grasped tightly in her hand. The killer was here, and he was after her!

Diana had always been good at playing hide and seek, but this was different. This game wasn't something you played after dark with your friends, popping up from behind a bush to streak toward home before your friend could tag you. This was a deadly contest, and the stakes were much higher. The only way Diana could win was to escape with her life!

It would help if she knew who was stalking her. Perhaps he had a weakness, and she could use it to her advantage. As Diana crawled along in the darkness, carefully feeling in front of her so she wouldn't accidentally knock something over and give away her position, her mind was going through the possibilities. The killer was someone they knew, someone who wanted to make the murders look like accidents. The planter. The two-twenty circuit. The pane of glass that had mysteriously fallen out of its frame. The elevator. The killer was trying to blame the mall for the murders he had committed. But why? What possible grudge could he have against the mall?

Diana stopped moving as another thought occurred to her, a thought so disturbing, she almost gasped out loud. Hal's grandparents had owned this land. She remembered coming out here once, to ask his grandmother to bake pies for a charity bake sale. And that first night, when Hal and Paul had been talking, she'd heard Hal say that he planned to farm someday, on the land he would inherit from his grandparents. But Hal couldn't inherit this land. The mall corporation had bought it. And they'd never sell it back to him . . . unless the mall failed.

No. It was impossible. Diana shoved her knuckle in her mouth, and bit down so hard, she tasted blood. Hal wasn't killing them to try get his inheritance back. Only a crazy person would do something like that. And she didn't really have any proof. It was just her mind, playing tricks on her.

And then Diana remembered something that Hal had said, something that made her know that her suspicions were true. Jay had asked her about the presents they'd found. And Hal had described the contents. He'd told Jay that there were two lines of lyrics inside, one in each package. They'd told Hal about the lyrics, Diana remembered that. But they'd never told him that there were two lines, one in each package!

Hal. Diana's mind spun in horrified circles. Hal was the killer, and she was the only one who knew it. She had to get away from him to warn the others. They trusted Hal, and he would kill them!

Diana began to crawl forward again, taking refuge close to the wall, under the cover of darkness. The door was a dimly lighted rectangle in the distance. It was the best way out of the store, but Hal would be watching and she would be a clear target when she ran out into the light. She had to think of some way to distract him, and get him to turn toward the back of the store. That would give her a chance to dash out the door.

She felt around behind the counter, searching for something that would make a lot of noise. And her fingers encountered a distinctive object, a shape she immediately recognized. Light bulbs!

Her fingers were shaking as she picked one up. It was a large-size light bulb, the kind that fit in hanging lamps and looked like a globe. It would make lots of noise when it shattered at the back of the store. Hal would think that she was back there. He'd turn to look, and she could make her break for freedom.

Diana grabbed two light bulbs and crawled forward as far as she dared, until the door was only a few feet away. Her mind was full of frightening questions. What if the light bulbs didn't shatter? What if Hal saw her when she threw them? Diana shivered and pushed those thoughts firmly out of her mind. Her plan had to succeed. The alternative was too horrible to contemplate. She had to try. It was her only hope.

Her knees were shaking as she stood up and threw the light bulbs toward the back of the store. One exploded with a loud pop, and almost instantaneously, the other one shattered. Diana didn't hang around to hear the tinkling of glass. She just grabbed the bolt-cutters and ran toward the door for her life!

Twenty-one

"It's Diana! Up there!"

Cindy pointed and they watched Diana as she raced down the second floor walkway toward the escalator. She jumped on and kept right on running, taking the steps so fast she almost fell. There was terror on her face and Jay ran to meet her. And when Diana fell into his arms, she was sobbing.

"We've got to get away! Hal's the killer! Hurry!"

Jay didn't ask any questions. He just grabbed the bolt-cutters she still held clenched in her hand, and helped her run toward the snowmobiles. "Cut the chains, Paul! Cindy! You help me throw the clothes in the snowmobiles! We've got to get out of here now!"

Paul took one look at Diana's face and he didn't ask any questions, either. He just cut the chains as fast as he could. They were almost ready to jump in the snowmobiles when Diana looked up at the hardware store and gave a gasp of pure terror. Hal was coming out the door in his Santa suit, and there was a gun in his hand!

"Oh, my God! He's got a gun!"

The words had barely left her mouth, when there was a loud explosion. A bullet whined past the snowmobiles and shattered the plate glass window of the electronics shop. They dove for cover, and huddled behind the snowmobiles as Hal fired another bullet which struck the wall with a solid thunk.

"He's got us pinned down." Cindy's voice was shaking with fear. "What are we going to do?"

Another bullet whined past and struck a bench a few feet away, sending splinters of wood flying. Diana winced and turned to Jay. "Is there some way we can sneak up on him?"

"I don't see how. He's got the perfect spot up there. He'll be able to see us if we move."

"I've got an idea." Paul leaned close. "One of the older cameramen told me he covered a sniper on a roof. The guy was completely nuts, but he had an agenda. He was protesting against the city because they'd condemned his house, and he wanted to be on television. He let the cameraman come right out in the open, and while he was strutting around and posing for the camera, the police climbed up the fire escape and captured him."

Cindy turned to look at Paul in shock. "That's the craziest thing I've ever heard! You're not actually going to try a stupid stunt like that . . . are you?"

"Do you have a better idea?"

"Not exactly . . ." Cindy frowned. "But you can't! It'd be suicide!"

"Maybe not." Paul looked thoughtful. "I just wish I knew if he had an agenda."

Diana nodded. "He does. At least I think he does."

They all listened while Diana quickly told them her theory about the mall-related accidents and Hal's grandparents' land. When she was finished, Paul nodded. "Did he say anything to you at all? It'd really help if I knew how the next accident was supposed to happen."

Diana shook her head. "He didn't say a word. I could be all wrong about the reason why he's doing this."

"Whatever." Paul shrugged. And then he outlined his plan. He would offer to tape Hal, and while Hal was busy posing for the camera, they could hop in the nearest snowmobile and make a break for the entrance.

"But . . . how about you?" Cindy looked very worried. "How are you going to get out?"

"I won't. I'll move around with my camera until I get to some cover. I'm down here and he's up there. I'll make a break for it when you start to move and I'll hide out until you get back with the police."

"It might work." Jay nodded.

"It *will* work. Just wait for my cue. When I tell him to turn a little to the left, count to five. Then hop in that snowmobile and hit the gas!"

Paul leaned close and kissed Cindy. She clung to him tightly, not willing to let him go, but he gently pried her arms loose and pushed her into Jay's arms. Then he turned to Diana and whispered in her ear. "If anything happens to me, make sure the station gets my tapes."

Santa smiled as he watched them huddle behind the snowmobiles. No sense in wasting ammunition. They'd have to make a move eventually, and he had a perfect vantage point. All he had to do was watch and wait. They'd be forced to come out, sooner or later. And when they did, Santa would punish them all.

The Christmas music was playing softly in the background, and Santa sat down on the bench to wait. Christmas was a time of joy, but only for those who deserved it. He thought of the fear on their faces when they'd seen the gun, and he chuckled in pleasure. It was unusual to see Santa with a gun, but drastic times called for drastic measures.

He'd found out about the gun the very first night, when he'd gone through the papers in the security office. Any store owner who had a firearm in his store was required to register it with the chief of security. The owner also had to turn over a key to the locked drawer where the gun was kept.

There were three jewelry stores in the mall, and all of their owners had guns. Santa had the keys for all three drawers, and after Diana had escaped, he'd gone next door to Forever Diamonds, to retrieve the owner's gun. It was a Smith & Wesson, 9 mm, semi-automatic pistol, and he'd found an extra clip in the drawer. He had thirty shots, and even though Santa had learned to shoot with an old army pistol that dated back to Gramps's WWII days, the basic design was the same.

His favorite song started to play on the loudspeakers, and Santa gave a regretful sigh. Too bad he wouldn't have the chance to deliver his last package. It was for the naughty boy who was hiding in back of the snowmobile. He'd been hiding that day, too, up in a tree, chased there by Gramps's bull. He'd climbed over the fence, even though it had been very clearly posted as private property, to fish in the river that ran through the farm.

The bull had been old and ornery, and it hadn't been easy to drive him into another field. Gramps had been forced to ask several neighbors for help. After it was over and the boy had climbed down, the neighbors had told Gramps they didn't think it was wise to keep such a dangerous bull.

Gramps and Grandma had talked it over, and they'd decided the bull had to go. He'd never caused any trouble before, but they hadn't wanted to worry their neighbors. So Gramps had shot the bull, and then he'd had to borrow money from the bank to replace him. None of that would have happened if the boy hadn't climbed through the fence. It had been a naughty thing to do, and that was why Santa had to punish Jay.

There was a shout from below, and Santa stood up to get a better look. Something white was fluttering by one of the snowmobiles. They were waving a white flag, and he began to laugh. What in the world were they doing? This wasn't a war, and Santa didn't take any prisoners.

And then Paul stood up, his camera to his shoulder. He was holding the white flag, and Santa frowned. Paul was the only one who didn't deserve to be punished. But he was with the rest, and that meant he had to share their fate.

"You should be on tape, Hal." Paul walked closer as he looked through the camera. "Don't you think your story deserves to be told?"

Santa raised the gun, but Paul kept right on taping. And then Santa reconsidered. Paul would have to die, but not yet. It would be good to have a record of what had happened. Santa could watch it over and over, and remember how brilliant he'd been.

"I'd like to do an interview with you. You'll do it, won't you, Hal?"

Santa nodded, and lowered the gun. "Don't call me that. I'm not Hal anymore. My name is Santa!"

"Oh, my God!" Cindy's eyes widened as she turned to whisper to them. "He's crazy!"

Jay nodded and gave Diana's hand a little squeeze. "Get ready. When Paul gives us the signal, we're going to get in this snowmobile as fast as we can. I'll drive."

"So will I." Diana squeezed back. "One snowmobile will be too heavy with the three of us. You and Cindy go first. I'll be right behind you."

Jay began to frown. "But, Diana . . ."

"Don't worry. I practically grew up on a snowmobile. When you get to the doors, don't stop to open them. Just crash right through."

Before they could raise any objections, Diana started to crawl around to the second snowmobile. Part of what she'd told Jay was true. She did know how to drive a snowmobile. But the second part had been a lie. She wouldn't be right behind him.

Paul could feel his hands start to shake as Hal finished telling the story about Dave. My God! Hal had killed him for being a kid in a hurry on a date! But he didn't let any of his horror show as he nodded and smiled.

"That was great, Santa. And I understand why Dave had to be punished. Could you move over in front of the toy store? It'll be a better background for the camera. And then I want you to tell us about Larry, and why you had to punish him."

Hal nodded and moved down the walkway, until he was in front of the toy store. "Larry was a very naughty boy! When he was ten years old, he . . ."

"Hold it a second!" Paul fiddled with his camera. "I'm sorry,

Santa. Could you move just a little closer toward me? The shot's not quite right with you back so far."

"Like this?" Santa moved closer to the rail.

"Perfect! Now tell us about Larry. And turn just a little to the left."

"Go!"

Jay whispered the word, and they scrambled into the snow-mobiles. They started their engines at exactly the same instant, and then they were moving, sliding over the slick surface of the floor with a deafening roar.

Diana saw Hal whirl around, confused by the noise. And then she parted company with Jay and Cindy's snowmobile, veering off to drive straight toward Paul.

"Paul! Hop on!"

She shouted the words, hoping he'd hear her over the roar of the engine. And Paul grabbed on and jumped into the passenger's seat as she roared past. But she had to turn around, and that meant that Hal would get another shot at them. Diana gunned the engine and prayed as she turned a tight circle at the end of the mall, to start the return trip.

He was there, close to the rail, holding the gun. All she could do was pray that he'd miss.

"Zig-zag!" Paul shouted the words. And then he turned on the bright light on his camera, hoping to throw off Hal's aim.

There was the sound of a shot and a bullet whizzed past, barely missing their windshield. Diana turned the wheel sharply back and forth, hoping the snowmobile wouldn't tip over as they zig-zagged across the floor.

Hal was aiming again. She could see him out of the corner of her eye, leaning against the rail to steady his hand. It was almost impossible for him to miss at this distance. It was like shooting ducks in a pond.

But then something happened that made Diana almost lose control of the wheel. Hal leaned out, staring directly into their eyes. And the rail gave way! He fell with a horrible scream, narrowly missing them as they sped past.

"Oh, my God! What happened?!" Diana almost turned to look. But the door was right ahead of them and they burst through it and into the snowy world outside, skidding dangerously down the steps that led up to the mall. And then they were barreling down the access road as the wind whipped around them. The snow pelted their faces with its icy kiss as they flew over the snow to the main road, and they skidded to a stop when they saw Jay and Cindy waiting for them.

"Diana! Are you all right?" Jay raced up to the snowmobile, and his mouth dropped open as he saw Paul. "But how did you . . ."

"Oh, my God! Paul! Are you all right?" Cindy was right behind Jay with an armload of parkas and boots.

"I'm fine, thanks to Diana. Let's get into some warm clothes and get out of here!"

"What happened back there?" Jay helped Diana into her parka. "I almost panicked when I got out here and I saw you weren't behind us."

"I just took a little detour." Diana's voice was calm, but she couldn't seem to stop shaking, now that it was over and they were all safe.

"How about Hal? Did he try to shoot you?"

"Oh, yes." Diana nodded. "But Paul told me to zig-zag so we'd be harder to hit. And then Hal leaned against the rail, and it broke, and . . . I don't know, Jay. It happened so fast, I'm not really sure what happened. But Paul's got it all on tape."

Jay put his arm around Diana's shoulders and gave her a little squeeze. Then he turned to Paul. "Can you drive one of these things?"

"Sure. I can't keep up with Diana, but I can get us to the nearest police station."

"Cindy?" Jay turned to his sister. "You ride with Paul. I'm taking Diana with me."

Diana felt numb as Jay led her to the snowmobile and tucked her into the passenger seat. She knew she must be in shock. She was freezing cold, and her body didn't seem to be moving right.

"Here, Diana. Give me your hands." Jay put gloves on her

hands, and pulled up the hood of her parka, tying it snugly under her chin. "Ready?'

Diana nodded again. She seemed incapable of doing anything else. She was shaking so hard, her teeth were rattling.

"I love you, Diana." Jay leaned over to touch her cheek. And then he kissed her, and the most amazing thing happened. Diana felt like someone had wrapped her in a warm fluffy quilt, and she was warm again.

"Better?"

Jay smiled at her. And Diana smiled back. And then he put the snowmobile in gear and they roared off toward town.

Epilogue

It was a warm spring evening and the windows in Jay's apartment were open to let in the breeze. Diana could hear crickets chirping outside the screens as she carried in a tray of appetizers and set them on the table. She still lived with Cindy, but she spent most of her time here. And Paul spent most of his time with Cindy.

"Are we ready?" Jay came into the living room, still toweling his hair. He caught sight of Diana and whistled. "Nice dress!"

"Don't you remember it?"

"I know I've seen it before. But I can't remember where I first . . . Elaine's Boutique! Right?"

Diana nodded. "Paul told them we wore their dresses, and they gave them to us. Cindy's wearing hers, too."

"Are you nervous about seeing Paul's film?" Jay slipped his arm around her shoulders.

"A little. I'm not sure I really want to relive last Christmas. I keep telling myself that it's just a movie, but I still have nightmares when I think about . . . him."

Jay nodded. "And I still have nightmares when I remember looking back, and discovering that you weren't there."

"Is that why you call me on the phone at three in the morning?"

"Sometimes." Jay looked a little sheepish. "But other times, I just want to hear your voice."

Diana stood up on her tiptoes to kiss him, but before she could do more than brush her lips with his, the doorbell rang.

"I'll get it." Jay sighed. "That's got to be my bratty kid sister. She's always had a talent for interrupting me at exactly the wrong time."

"Hi, guys!" Cindy breezed in and tossed Jay a bag of chips. "Where's the dip, Paul?"

"It's in here." Paul lugged in a backpack, and put it on the couch. "Hold on a second. I'll find it."

Diana looked at Cindy in surprise. "You made dip?"

"I sure did." Cindy grinned at her. "I found the recipe in a cookbook. You chop up all these things really fine, and then you mix them with sour cream and mayo."

"Wait a second." Paul pulled out a container of dip and frowned. "This dip is from the grocery store. It says so, right on the label."

Cindy nodded. "I know. But I *did* make some dip. It just tasted so awful, I threw it out."

"Come on . . . it's almost time." Jay glanced at his watch. "Let's grab some snacks and get ready."

They filled their plates with food, and found comfortable places to sit. Then Jay turned on the television, and they all settled down to watch.

Diana held Jay's hand tightly as Paul's documentary came on the screen. He'd changed the title to "Slay Bells," and the station had been promoting it all week. Diana had been anticipating this moment, and she still wasn't sure how she'd react. Would she be terrified, all over again? Would reliving their weekend of horror give her new and even more frightening nightmares?

The story was compelling, and Paul's work was brilliant. Diana realized that at the very beginning. There wasn't a sound out of any of them as they watched the first hour, and then the second. When it was over, they all applauded and talked about the movie for awhile.

After Paul and Cindy had left, Jay pulled Diana down on the couch and draped his arm around her shoulders. "I know you told Paul you loved it. But what did you really think?"

"I thought it was great." Diana smiled up at him. "And I wasn't a bit scared."

"Why not? It was scary, wasn't it?"

Diana snuggled up a little closer, and leaned her head against Jay's chest. "Of course it was scary. It was almost like being there, with one important difference."

"What was that?"

"It was on television. And they never kill off the good guys. They have to keep them alive for the sequel."

WHERE INNOCENCE DIES . . .

Expectant parents Karen and Mike Houston are excited about restoring their old rambling Victorian mansion to its former glory. With its endless maze of rooms, hallways, and hiding places, it's a wonderful place for their nine-year-old daughter Leslie to play and explore. Unfortunately, they didn't listen to the stories about the house's dark history. They didn't believe the rumors about the evil that lived there.

. . . THE NIGHTMARE BEGINS.

It begins with a whisper. A child's voice beckoning from the rose garden. Crying out in the night. It lures little Leslie to a crumbling storm door. Down a flight of broken stairs. It calls to their unborn child. It wants something from each of them. Something in their very hearts and souls. Tonight, the house will reveal its secret. *Tonight, the other child will come out to play . . .*

Please turn the page for an exciting sneak peek of Joanne Fluke's THE OTHER CHILD coming in August 2014!

Prologue

The train was rolling across the Arizona desert when it started, a pain so intense it made her double over in the dusty red velvet seat. Dorthea gasped aloud as the spasm tore through her and several passengers leaned close.

"Just a touch of indigestion." She smiled apologetically. "Really, I'm fine now."

Drawing a deep steadying breath, she folded her hands protectively over her rounded stomach and turned to stare out at the unbroken miles of sand and cactus. The pain would disappear if she just sat quietly and thought pleasant thoughts. She had been on the train for days now and the constant swaying motion was making her ill.

Thank goodness she was almost to California. Dorthea sighed gratefully. The moment she arrived she would get her old job back, and then she would send for Christopher. They could find a home together, she and Christopher and the new baby.

She never should have gone back. Dorthea pressed her forehead against the cool glass of the window and blinked back bitter tears. The people in Cold Spring were hateful. They had called Christopher a bastard. They had ridiculed her when Mother's will was made public. They knew that her mother had never forgiven her and they were glad. The righteous, upstanding citizens of her old hometown were the same cruel gossips they'd been ten years ago.

If only she had gotten there before Mother died! Dorthea was certain that those horrid people in Cold Spring had poisoned her mother's mind against her and she hated them for it. Her dream of being welcomed home to her beautiful house was shattered. Now she was completely alone in the world. Poor Christopher was abandoned back there until she could afford to send him the money for a train ticket.

Dorthea moaned as the pain tore through her again. She braced her body against the lurching of the train and clumsily made her way up the aisle, carefully avoiding the stares of the other passengers. There it started and she slumped to the floor. A pool of blood was gathering beneath her and she pressed her hand tightly against the pain.

Numbness crept up her legs and she was cold, as cold as she'd been in the winter in Cold Spring. Her eyelids fluttered and her lips moved in silent protest. Christopher! He was alone in Cold Spring, in a town full of spiteful, meddling strangers. Dear God, what would they do to Christopher?

"No! She's not dead!" He stood facing them, one small boy against the circle of adults. "It's a lie! You're telling lies about her, just like you did before!"

His voice broke in a sob and he whirled to run out the door of the parsonage. His mother wasn't dead. She couldn't be dead! She had promised to come back for him just as soon as she made some money.

"Lies. Dirty lies." The wind whipped away his words as he raced through the vacant lot and around the corner. The neighbors had told lies before about his mother, lies his grandmother had believed. They were all liars in Cold Spring, just as his mother had said.

There it was in front of him now, huge and solid against the gray sky. Christopher stopped at the gate, panting heavily. Appleton Mansion, the home that should have been his. Their lies had cost him his family, his inheritance, and he'd get even with all of them somehow.

They were shouting his name now, calling for him to come back. Christopher slipped between the posts of the wrought-iron fence and ran into the overgrown yard. They wanted to tell him more lies, to confuse him the way they had confused Grandmother Appleton, but he wouldn't listen. He'd hide until it was dark and then he'd run away to California where his mother was waiting for him.

The small boy gave a sob of relief when he saw an open door-way. It was perfect. He'd hide in his grandmother's root cellar and they'd never find him. Then, when it was dark, he'd run away.

Without a backward glance Christopher hurtled through the opening, seeking the safety of the darkness below. He gave a shrill cry as his foot missed the steeply slanted step and then he was falling, arms flailing helplessly at the air as he pitched forward into the deep, damp blackness.

Wade Comstock stood still, letting the leaves skitter and pile in colored mounds around his feet, smiling as he looked up at the shuttered house. His wife, Verna, had been right, the Apple-ton Mansion had gone dirt cheap. He still couldn't understand how modern people at the turn of the century could take stock in silly ghost stories. He certainly didn't believe for one minute that Amelia Appleton was back from the dead, haunting the Ap-pleton house. But then again, he had been the only one ever to venture a bid on the old place. Amelia's daughter Dorthea had left town right after her mother's will was read, cut off without a dime—and it served her right. Now the estate was his, the first acquisition of the Comstock Realty Company.

His thin lips tightened into a straight line as he thought of Dorthea. The good people of Cold Spring hadn't been fooled one bit by her tears at her mother's funeral. She was after the property, pure and simple. Bringing her bastard son here was bad enough, but you'd think a woman in her condition would have sense enough to stay away. And then she had run off, leaving the boy behind. He could make a bet that Dorthea was never planning to send for Christopher. Women like her didn't want kids in the way.

Wade kicked out at the piles of leaves and walked around his new property. As he turned the corner of the house, the open root cellar caught his eye and he reached in his pocket for the padlock and key he'd found hanging in the tool shed. That old cellar should be locked up before somebody got hurt down there. He'd tell the gardener to leave the bushes in that area and it would be overgrown in no time at all.

For a moment Wade stood and stared at the opening. He supposed he should go down there, but it was already too dark to be able to see his way around. Something about the place made him uneasy. There was no real reason to be afraid, but his heart beat faster and an icy sweat broke out on his forehead as he thought about climbing down into that small dark hole.

The day was turning to night as he hurriedly hefted the weather-beaten door and slammed it shut. The door was warped but it still fit. The hasp was in workable order and with a little effort he lined up the two pieces and secured them with the padlock. Then he jammed the key into his pocket and took a shortcut through the rose garden to the front yard.

Wade didn't notice the key was missing from his pocket until he was out on the sidewalk. He looked back at the overcast sky. There was no point in going back to try to find it in the dark. Actually he could do without the key. No one needed a root cellar anymore. It could stay locked up till kingdom come.

As he stood watching, shadows played over the windows of the stately house and crept up the crushed granite driveway. The air was still now, so humid it almost choked him. He could hear thunder rumbling in the distance. Then there was another noise—a thin hollow cry that set the hair on the back of his arms prickling. He listened intently, bent forward slightly, and balanced on the balls of his feet, but there was only the thunder. It was going to rain again and Wade felt a strange uneasiness. Once more he looked back, drawn to the house . . . as though something had been left unfinished. He had a vague sense of foreboding. The house looked almost menacing.

"Poppycock!" he muttered, and turned away, pulling out his watch. He'd have to hurry to get home in time for supper. Verna liked her meals punctual.

He started to walk, turning back every now and then to glance at the shadow of the house looming between the tall trees. Even though he knew those stories were a whole lot of foolishness, he felt a little spooked himself. The brick mansion did look eerie against the blackening sky.

"*Mama!*" He awoke with a scream on his lips, a half-choked cry of pure terror. It was dark and cold and inky black. Where was he? The air was damp, like a grave. He squeezed his eyes shut tightly and screamed again.

"*Mama!*" He would hear her footsteps coming any minute to wake him from this awful nightmare. She'd turn on the light and hug him and tell him not to be afraid. If he just waited, she'd come. She always came when he had nightmares.

No footsteps, no light, no sound except his own hoarse breathing. Christopher reached out cautiously and felt damp earth around him. This was no dream. Where was he?

There was a big lump on his head and it hurt. He must have fallen . . . yes, that was it.

He let his breath out in a shuddering sigh as he remembered. He was in his Grandmother Appleton's root cellar. He'd fallen down the steps trying to hide from the people who told him lies about his mama. And tonight he was going to run away and find her in California. She'd be so proud of him when he told her he hadn't believed their lies. She'd hug him and kiss him and promise she'd never have to go away again.

Perhaps it was night now. Christopher forced himself to open his eyes. He opened them wide but he couldn't see anything, not even the white shirt he was wearing. It must be night and that meant it was time for him to go.

Christopher sat up with a groan. It was so dark he couldn't see the staircase. He knew he'd have to crawl around and feel for the steps, but it took a real effort to reach out into the blackness. He wasn't usually afraid of the dark. At least he wasn't afraid of the dark when there was a lamppost or a moon or something. This kind of darkness was different. It made his mouth dry and he held his breath as he forced himself to reach out into the inky depths.

There. He gave a grateful sigh as he crawled up the first step of the stairs. He didn't want to lose his balance and fall back down again.

Four . . . five . . . six . . . he was partway up when he heard a stealthy rustling noise from below. Fear pushed him forward in a rush, his knees scraping against the old slivery wood in a scramble to get to the top.

He let out a terrified yell as his head hit something hard. The cover—somebody had closed up the root cellar!

He couldn't think; he was too scared. Blind panic made him scream and pound, beating his fists against the wooden door until his knuckles were swollen and raw. Somehow he had to lift the door.

With a mighty effort Christopher heaved his body upward, straining against the solid piece of wood. The door gave a slight, sickening lurch, creaking and lifting just enough for him to hear the sound of metal grating against metal.

At first the sound lay at the back of his mind like a giant pendulum of horror, surging slowly forward until it reached the active part of his brain. The Cold Spring people had locked him in.

The thought was so terrifying he lost his breath and slumped into a huddled ball on the step. In the darkness he could see flashed of red and bright gold beneath his eyelids. He had to get out somehow! *He had to!*

"*Help!*" the sound tore through his lips and bounced off the earthen walls, giving a hollow, muted echo. He screamed until his voice was a weak whisper but no one came. Then his voice was gone and he could hear it again, the ominous rustling from the depths of the cellar, growing louder with each passing heartbeat.

God, no! This nightmare was really happening! He recognized the scuffling noise now and shivered with terror. Rats. They were sniffing at the air, searching for him, and there was nowhere to hide. They'd find him even here at the top of the stairs and they would come in a rush, darting hurtling balls of fur and needle teeth . . . the pain of flesh being torn from his body . . . the agony of being eaten alive!

He opened his throat in a tortured scream, a shrill hoarse cry that circled the earthen room then faded to a deadly silence. There was a roaring in his ears and terror rose to choke him, squeezing and strangling him with clutching fingers.

"*Mama! Please, Mama!*" he cried again, and then suddenly he was pitching forward, rolling and bumping to the black pit below. He gasped as an old shovel bit deeply into his neck and a warm stickiness gushed out to cover his face. There was a moment of vivid consciousness before death claimed him and in that final moment, one emotion blazed its way through his whole being. Hatred. He hated all of them. They had driven his mother away. They had stolen his inheritance. They had locked him in here and left him to die. He would punish them . . . make them suffer as his mother had suffered . . . as he was suffering.

One

The interior of the truck was dusty and Mike opened the wing window all the way, shifting on the slick plastic-covered seat, Karen had wanted to take an afternoon drive through the country and here they were over fifty miles from Minneapolis, on a bumpy country road. It wasn't Mike's idea of a great way to spend a Sunday. He'd rather be home watching the Expos and the Phillies from the couch in their air-conditioned Lake Street apartment.

Mike glanced uneasily at Karen as he thought about today's game. He had a bundle riding on this one and it was a damn good thing Karen didn't know about it. She'd been curious about his interest in baseball lately but he'd told her he got a kick out of watching the teams knock themselves out for the pennant. The explanation seemed to satisfy her.

Karen was death on two of his pet vices, drinking and gambling, and he'd agreed to reform three years ago when they were married. Way back then he'd made all the required promises. Lay off the booze. No more Saturday-night poker games. No betting on the horses. No quick trips to Vegas. No office pools, even. The idea of a sportsbook hadn't occurred to her yet and he was hoping it wouldn't now. Naturally Mike didn't make a habit of keeping secrets from his wife but in this case he'd chosen the lesser of two evils. He knew Karen would hit the roof if he told her he hadn't gotten that hundred-dollar-a-month bonus after all, that the extra money came from his gambling winnings on the games. It was just lucky that he took care of all the finances. What Karen didn't know wouldn't hurt her.

"Cold Spring, one mile." Leslie was reading the road signs again in her clear high voice. "Oh, look Mike! A church with a white steeple and all those trees. Can't we just drive past before we go home?"

Mike had been up most of the night developing prints for his spread in *Homes* magazine and he wasn't in the mood for extensive sightseeing. He was going to refuse, but then he caught sight of his stepdaughter's pleading face in the rearview mirror. Another little side trip wouldn't kill him. He'd been too busy lately to spend much time at home and these Sunday drives were a family tradition.

"Oh, let's, Mike." Karen's voice was wistful. Mike could tell by her tone that she'd been feeling a little neglected lately, too. Maybe it had been a mistake insisting she quit her job at the interior decorating firm. Mike was old-fashioned sometimes, and he maintained that a mother's place was at home with her children. When he had discovered that Karen was pregnant he'd put his foot down insisting she stay home. Karen had agreed, but still she missed her job. He told himself that she'd be busy enough when the baby was born, but that didn't solve the problem right now.

Mike slowed the truck, looking for a turnoff. A little sightseeing might be fun. Karen and Leslie would certainly enjoy it and his being home to watch the game wouldn't change the outcome any.

"All right, you two win." Mike smiled at his wife and turned left at the arrowed sign. "Just a quick run through town and then we have to get back. I still have to finish the penthouse prints and start work on that feature."

Leslie gave Mike a quick kiss and settled down again in the back seat of their Land-Rover. When she was sitting down on the seat, Mike could barely see the top of her blond head over the stacks of film boxes and camera cases. She was a small child for nine, fair-haired and delicate like the little porcelain shepherdesses his mother used to collect. She was an exquisite child, a classic Scandinavian beauty. Mike was accustomed to being approached by people who wanted to use Leslie as a model. Karen claimed she didn't want Leslie to become self-conscious, but Mike noticed how she enjoyed dressing Leslie in the height of fashion. Much of Karen's salary had gone into designer jeans, Gucci loafers, and Pierre Cardin sweaters for her daughter. Leslie always had the best in clothes and she wore them beautifully, taking meticulous care of her wardrobe. Even in play clothes she always looked every inch a lady.

Karen possessed a different kind of beauty. Hers was the active, tennis-pro look. She had long, dark hair and a lithe, athletic body. People had trouble believing that she and Leslie were mother and daughter. They looked and acted completely different. Leslie preferred to curl up in a fluffy blanket and read, while Karen was relentlessly active. She was a fresh-air-and-exercise fanatic. For the last six years Karen had jogged around Lake Harriet every morning, dragging Leslie with her. That was how they'd met, the three of them.

Mike had been coming home from an all-night party, camera slung over his shoulder, when he spotted them. He was always on the lookout for a photogenic subject and he'd stopped to take a few pictures of the lovely black-haired runner and her towheaded child. It had seemed only natural to ask for Karen's address and a day later he was knocking at her door with some sample prints in one hand and a stuffed toy for Leslie in the other. The three of them had formed an instant bond.

Leslie had been fascinated by the man in her mother's life. She was five then, and fatherless. Karen always said Leslie was the image of her father—a handsome Swedish exchange student with whom Karen had enjoyed a brief affair before he'd gone back to his native country.

They made an unlikely trio, and Mike grinned a little at the thought. He had shaggy brown hair and a lined face. He needed a shave at least twice a day. Karen claimed he could walk out of Saks Fifth Avenue, dressed in the best from the skin out, and still look like an unemployed rock musician. The three of them made a striking contrast in their red Land-Rover with MIKE HOUSTON, PHOTOGRAPHER painted on both doors.

Mike was so busy thinking about the picture they made that he almost missed the house. Karen's voice, breathless in his ear, jogged him back to reality.

"Oh, Mike! Stop, please! Just look at that beautiful old house!"

The house was a classic; built before the turn of the century. It sprawled over half of the large, tree-shaded lot, yellow brick gleaming in the late afternoon sun. There was a veranda that ran the length of the front and around both sides, three stories high with a balcony on the second story. A cupola graced the slanted roof like the decoration on a fancy cake. It struck Mike right away: here was the perfect subject for a special old-fashioned feature in *Homes* magazine.

"That's it, isn't it, Mike?" Leslie's voice was hushed and expectant as if she sensed the creative magic of this moment. "You're going to use this house for a special feature, aren't you?"

It was more a statement than a question and Mike nodded. Leslie had a real eye for a good photograph. "You bet I am!" he responded enthusiastically. "Hand me the Luna-Pro, honey, and push the big black case with the Linhof to the back door. Grab your Leica if you want and let's go. The sun's just right if we hurry."

Karen grinned as her husband and daughter made a hasty exit from the truck, cameras in tow. She'd voiced her objections when Mike gave Leslie the Leica for her ninth birthday. "Such an expensive camera for a nine-year-old?" she'd asked. "She'll probably lose it, Mike. And it's much too complicated for a child her age to operate."

But Mike had been right this time around. Leslie loved her Leica. She slept with it close by the side of her bed, along with her fuzzy stuffed bear and her ballet slippers. And she'd learned how to use it, too, listening attentively when Mike gave her instructions, asking questions that even Karen admitted were advanced for her age. Leslie seemed destined to follow in her stepfather's footsteps. She showed real talent in framing scenes and instinctively knew what made up a good photograph.

Her long hair was heavy and hot on the back of her neck and Karen pulled it up and secured it with a rubber band. She felt a bit queasy but she knew that was natural. It had been a long drive and she remembered getting carsick during the time she'd been carrying Leslie. Just a few more months and she would begin to show. Then she'd have to drag out all her old maternity clothes and see what could be salvaged.

Karen sighed, remembering. Ten years ago she was completely on her own, pregnant and unmarried, struggling to finish school. But once Leslie was born it was better. While it had been exhausting—attending decorating classes in the morning, working all afternoon at the firm, then coming home to care for the baby—it was well worth any trouble. Looking back, she could honestly say that she was happy she hadn't listened to all the well-meaning advice from other women about adoption or abortion. They were a family now, she and Mike and Leslie. She hadn't planned on getting pregnant again so soon after she met Mike, but it would all work out. This time it was going to be different. She wasn't alone. This time she had Mike to help her.

Karen's eyes widened as she slid out of the truck and gazed up at the huge house. It was a decorator's paradise, exactly the sort of house she'd dreamed of tackling when she was a naïve, first-year art student.

She found Leslie around the side of the house, snapping a picture of the exterior. As soon as Leslie spotted her mother she pointed excitedly toward the old greenhouse.

"Oh, Mom! Look at this! You could grow your own flowers in here! Isn't it super?"

"It certainly is!" Karen gave her daughter a quick hug. Leslie's excitement was contagious and Karen's smile widened as she let her eyes wander to take it all in. There was plenty of space for a children's wing on the second floor and somewhere in that vast expanse of rooms was the perfect place for Mike's studio and darkroom. The sign outside said FOR SALE. The thought of owning this house kindled Karen's artistic imagination. They *had* mentioned looking for a house only a week ago and here it was. Of course it would take real backbreaking effort to fix it up, but she felt sure hit could be done. It would be the project she'd been looking for, to keep her occupied the next six months. With a little time, patience, and help from Mike with the heavy stuff, she could turn the mansion into a showplace.

They were peeking in through the glass windows of the greenhouse when they heard voices. Mike was talking to someone in the front yard. They heard his laugh and another, deeper voice. Karen grabbed Leslie's hand and they hurried around the side of the house in time to see Mike talking to a gray-haired man in a sport jacket. There was a white Lincoln parked in the driveway with a magnetic sign reading COMSTOCK REALTY.

Rob Comstock had been driving by on his way home from the office when he saw the Land-Rover parked outside the old Appleton Mansion. He noticed the painted signs on the vehicle's door and began to scheme. Out-of-towners, by the look of it. Making a sharp turn at the corner he drove around to pull up behind the truck, shutting off the motor of his new Continental. He'd just sit here and let them get a nice, long look.

This might be it, he thought to himself as he drew a Camel from the crumpled pack in his shirt pocket. He'd wanted to be rid of this white elephant for years. It had been on the books since his grandfather bought it eighty years ago. Rob leased it out whenever he could but that wasn't often enough to make a profit. Tenants never stayed for more than a couple of months. It was too large, they said, or it was too far from the Cities. Even though the rent was reasonable, they still made their excuses and left. He'd been trying to sell it for the past ten years with no success. Houses like this one had gone out of style in his grandfather's day. It was huge and inconvenient, and keeping it